MW00773124

GRAVE DANGER

DANIELLE GIRARD

ITP
Grave Danger
Previously Titled: Interference
Copyright © 2016, 2019 by Danielle Girard. All rights reserved
under International and Pan-American Copyright Conventions
Third Print Edition: June 2019

Cover and Formatting: Damonza

ISBN-10: 0996308970
ISBN-13: 978-0996308977

By payment of required fees, you have been granted the
nonexclusive, nontransferable right to access and read the text of
this e-book. No part of this text may be reproduced, transmitted,
downloaded, decompiled, reverse engineered, or stored in or
introduced into any information storage and retrieval system,
in any form or by any means, whether electronic or mechanical,
now known or hereinafter invented without the express written
permission of copyright owner.

Please Note

This is a work of fiction. Names, characters, places, and incidents
either are the product of the author's imagination or are used
fictitiously, and any resemblance to actual persons, living or dead,
business establishments, events or locales is entirely coincidental.

The reverse engineering, uploading, and/or distributing of this
e-book via the Internet or via any other means without the
permission of the copyright owner is illegal and punishable by
law. Please purchase only authorized electronic editions, and do
not participate in or encourage electronic piracy of copyrighted
materials. Your support of the author's rights is appreciated.

TOO CLOSE TO HOME

A ROOKIE CLUB SHORT STORY

A ROOKIE CLUB SHORT STORY

TOO CLOSE TO HOME

BESTSELLING AUTHOR OF *EXHUME*

DANIELLE GIRARD

San Francisco Crime Scene Analyst Naomi Muir is doing a job she loves. But something about this case has gotten under her skin.

An unusual partner could help her solve her first case.

But will it also be her last?

YOUR FREE COPY IS WAITING...

Get it here!

Your Free Rookie Club Short Story is Waiting

San Francisco Crime Scene Analyst and aspiring Rookie Club member Naomi Muir is passionate about her work, especially the cases where she works alongside seasoned inspectors, like Jamie Vail. But this latest case has her unnerved. A serial sex offender is growing more aggressive. He attacks in the dirty underbelly of the San Francisco streets... and eerily close to Naomi's inexpensive apartment. Each crime is more violent than the last and also nearer to where Naomi herself lives.

To solve the case, Naomi will have to rely on her own wit and an unexpected new partner as the attacker gets too close to home...

Go to

www.daniellegirard.com/newsletter to claim your copy now!

THE ROOKIE CLUB CAST, IN ORDER OF APPEARANCE:

Mei Ling, Computer Forensics Inspector (also in *Cold Silence*)

Cameron Cruz, Special Ops Team/Sharpshooter (Featured in *Dark Passage*)

Hailey Wyatt, Homicide Inspector (Featured in *One Clean Shot*; also in *Dead Center, Dark Passage, Everything to Lose*)

Hal Harris, Homicide Inspector, partner to Hailey Wyatt (Also in *One Clean Shot*)

Ryaan Berry, Triggerlock Inspector (Also in *One Clean Shot, Dark Passage*)

Sydney Blanchard, Senior Criminalist, Crime Scene Unit

Jamie Vail, Sex Crimes Inspector (Featured in *Dead Center* and Rookie Club Book 5, *Everything to Lose*; also in *Dark Passage, One Clean Shot*)

Roger Sampers, Head Criminalist, Crime Scene Unit (Also in *Dead Center, One Clean Shot*, and *Everything to Lose*)

CHAPTER 1

OYSTER POINT WAS not where one expected to find a police warehouse full of guns. Over the past couple of decades, the area had actually become a rather attractive corporate park. The adjacent marina housed expensive yachts, and a well-developed trail system ran along the water. Natural grasses swayed in the wind. It was all very quaint and peaceful, not at all the way the place had been twenty years earlier when it was basically the cheapest available office space in the area.

J.T. wasn't there to enjoy the view and didn't give a damn about natural grasses. The whole place could have gone up in flames. The only concern was that economic prosperity meant tight security, which translated into extra time to set things up. Eighteen years was a long time to wait for payoff. But maybe the waiting was done. J.T. smoothed the gloves one last time and followed the trail.

Even in the dim predawn light, the phone box was easy to find. Phone companies hired human monkeys, then gave them an impossible-to-screw-up set of instructions. In J.T.'s experience, the monkeys still managed to do things wrong, maybe half the time. Evidenced by the fact that the phone box wasn't even locked.

A pair of wire cutters and the lines would be down. Ten seconds tops, but first, Sam's cell phone jammer had to be working. At this moment, Sam was in the small apartment adjacent to the garage, predictably huddled over his desk. He was likely working on the night's third or fourth Big Gulp of Mountain Dew. The empties would be lined along the desk like fat children at the edge of the playground. Sam was waiting, something he did by playing Minecraft or breaking into small nonprofits and finding ways to occupy himself. Last week, he hacked into a San Jose animal shelter and changed the names of the residents. A six-year-old calico was now called Big Red Pussy, a Goldendoodle who had been named Betsy was now Curly Bitch, and a Rottweiler who had lost an eye in a street fight had been renamed One-Eyed Dick. Sam thought this was hilarious.

Thankfully, Sam was not a field guy. For one, he didn't even have a driver's license, but he was also about as stealthy as farming equipment. No, Sam was hardly even a behind-the-scenes guy. Sam was a train wreck, but Sam could also be managed. Mostly this was accomplished by keeping Sam away from other people, which wasn't difficult because Sam preferred the company of other online nerds, sitting in their own dungeons, drinking their own Big Gulps, and eating some similar diet to Sam's daily feasts of Cheetos and microwave burritos.

Now, to work. The backpack dropped gently on the ground. The cell phone jammer was in a small cardboard box, surrounded in bubble wrap. Sam tended to go overboard on packaging. The device was a silver box not much bigger than a box of Tic Tacs with a black antenna coming out of each end. In the center was a silver switch. In Sam's girlish print, the left side read 'off' and the right side 'on.'

Only gloves touched the box as the switch was flipped from 'off' to 'on.' The call to Sam's number failed, which meant the jammer was working. The clippers made a satisfying snip through the wires and, in under a minute, the first step was done.

At the front of the building, Hank waited in the black van. Hank was a monkey, too, but of a different sort. J.T. might have brought Karl instead, but Karl was smarter, and J.T. didn't want any extra questions. Plus, all interactions with Karl had been electronic. J.T. had never seen his face nor the other way around, and J.T. was hesitant to change that. The fewer people J.T. dealt with in person the better.

J.T. raised a hand, and Hank emerged excitedly from the van and slammed the door closed.

"Watch the noise."

"Sorry, boss," Hank said. He shouldered an oversized duffel that seemed mostly empty.

Monkey. "You have what you need?" J.T. asked.

Hank patted his bag and nodded.

"Okay. It's your turn."

Hank approached the warehouse's back door with its 4-digit entry lock. He, too, wore gloves as he pulled a crowbar from the duffel bag and worked the end of it into the narrow opening between the door and the jam, rocking it up and down until it was wedged in far enough to begin to muscle it. The trim came off first with a loud snap as the thin metal broke away from the front of the building. Hank's hands slipped, and he dropped the crowbar which made a loud clattering sound on the pavement. It rang out like a bullet shot. "Jesus Christ."

"Sorry," Hank muttered again. He removed a long pick-like tool and a rubber mallet from the bag and created a dent in the metal door just above the knob until the latch was fully exposed. With the crowbar, he wrenched it open. Hank was built like a tank. It took all of seven minutes before the door fell open.

They stepped into the warehouse together, and Hank let the door close behind them. Softly. A first. The space smelled of old paper and lemon cleaner. The smell meant someone still cleaned the place, so their footprints would be harder to track. That was good news. The lights were off across the warehouse and the temperature cool, not the kind of place where someone was working, especially not at this hour. Skylights lined the walls almost at the ceiling, which meant someone might notice if they turned on the lights.

J.T. pulled a flashlight out of the small side pocket of the backpack and flipped it on. "You got yours?"

Hank found his flashlight, and the two of them scanned their lights across the inside. The warehouse space was small and lined with shelves where boxes were piled high. Police case files. Overflow. This was not the interesting part. That was in the far corner.

"This way."

Hank followed, finally quiet, as they crossed the warehouse to the last aisle where a cage took up the far corner. J.T. stood back. Hank used his crowbar to open the locked gate in under a minute.

The cage was lined with metal cabinets, some green, some gray, all old-style and flimsy. The first took Hank approximately fifteen seconds to jimmy open. Hank whistled at the contents, the shelves lined with semiauto assault rifles, each tagged with a case number.

"Load those up. And the other cabinets, too," J.T. said. "We don't need all of them. You've got four minutes."

Hank pulled two empty black duffels out of the one that carried his tools and dropped them on the floor. He opened the first and started loading guns.

There was a more important task to be done while Hank stole the weapons. J.T. exited the cage and returned to the main area of the warehouse, using twenty precious seconds to scan the rows before deciding on the placement. The second row seemed the best, most out of the way. Against the wall, certainly, to allow Sam the best signal. J.T. chose a box from the second shelf, two down.

With the box carefully set on the warehouse floor, J.T. loaded the larger of two computers from the backpack into the box. The computer was an inexpensive one—an Acer—purchased at Walmart while dressed in a business suit and leather gloves and scarf for the chilly day. And a wig. With cash. Three months ago. Three others were purchased under similar circumstances in case Sam needed them. A disposable cell phone and an independent battery source were strapped to the computer with Hello Kitty duct tape. Sam's idea of a joke. Sam had bought the tape himself.

None of J.T.'s prints would be on anything. Sam had

been warned. J.T. had gone so far as to bring him a box of extra-large sterile gloves to fit his big, chubby hands. But Sam was sloppy. Hackers, in general, were sloppy creatures, J.T. had learned. Careless criminals, they coveted bragging rights over anonymity. The process over the results. Easily manipulated, too, by the right person. Sam was no different.

The second device was a Raspberry Pi, a computer that was no larger than a deck of playing cards. That needed to be higher. J.T. tested the shelves. The metal shelving was inexpensive. Empty, they would be easy to topple, but the weight of the old case files held them steady. Even spacing made scaling them relatively easy.

J.T. set the small computer, with its own battery pack and cell phone, on the top shelf before climbing up and reaching to the ceiling. The acoustic ceiling tiles were loose; the first one opened up without any trouble. It was almost too easy. Lousy security for police storage.

The bundle weighed maybe 20 ounces, mostly from the weight of the battery. J.T. slid it up into the ceiling so it sat against the building's outside wall and rested on the metal crossbars between acoustic tiles. Checked it twice. The tile slid back down smoothly. It looked just like the others.

Everything was as it had been. J.T. climbed down, retrieved the backpack, and returned to the weapons cage where Hank was loading his last pack. As predicted, Hank had left nothing behind. The guns were superfluous, but Hank was a common thief and common thieves lacked awareness of when enough was enough. Without mention of his excessive exuberance, Hank loaded the remaining handguns into the duffel. Hank didn't ask about the four minutes of absence. Lack of curiosity and brute strength were Hank's best features.

Hank wiped his gloved hands on his pants. "That's all of it, boss."

The two made their way outside and pushed the door closed. Up close, there would be no missing the damage to the door. But, from a distance, it would be hard to see. J.T. flipped the cell phone jammer off before turning to the backpack to retrieve its packaging.

"J.T.?"

J.T. started and spun at the sound of Hank's voice. "Jesus Christ."

There was the sound of metal on metal. The jammer fell between the phone box and the exterior wall of the building. J.T. tried to retrieve it, but it was wedged down out of reach.

Hank backed up. "Sorry, J.T. I wanted to know if you wanted me to wait or go to the van."

J.T. said nothing. The jammer was off, but leaving it was a bad idea. This was supposed to look like a smash and grab. The jammer was too sophisticated for an average burglar. J.T. dropped the pack. "Give me the pick."

Hank rattled through the guns in search of the pick.

J.T. focused on staying calm. Eyes closed. Deep breath in, deep breath out. No breaking necks. Not yet.

"There it is." Hank started to pull the tool free, but it caught up on a gun. Suddenly, a shot fired.

They both ducked as a bullet struck the passenger's side window glass of a utility vehicle parked in back. Glass exploded.

Without hesitating, J.T. grabbed the backpack in one hand and one of the duffels in the other and started for the car. Hank was right behind with the other two duffels.

The jammer was gone. There was no getting it now.

"Shit, boss," Hank said, panting. "I had no idea the guns would be loaded."

"Don't speak."

"Did you think they would be loaded?" Hank went on, nearly whining.

"Do not speak," J.T. repeated, fighting for control. Hank was disposable, but, at that moment, it couldn't happen fast enough for J.T.

Thankfully, Hank went quiet, although he continued to make little sighs and huffs like a high school girl, the need to talk obviously making him crazy. Despite the broken glass, the streets were quiet as they opened the back of the van.

Hank was sheepish as he loaded the bags. J.T. slid in the side door and pointed to the driver's seat. "You drive. I'm going to sit back here and see what we got."

The take couldn't have been less interesting. That was not the reason J.T. chose the back. It was about not being up front with Hank. Especially if something went wrong. Something else.

"We heading home?" he asked.

"Yeah."

Hank pulled away from the curb with a jolt that knocked everything, J.T. included, toward the rear of the van. "Sorry, boss."

J.T. did not respond. It was over. A mile away, the

text came in from Sam. "I can see the networks. Working to get in now."

J.T. knew Sam would ask for the jammer. As much as J.T. would have liked it, Sam would not be distracted by the importance of his task. He'd want his toy back, and he would not take the loss well. J.T. would have to pretend the jammer wasn't lost. Hopefully, Sam could be put off for a day or two while J.T. pretended to "find" it. Better to let him focus on one thing at a time.

The worst was over. Now it was a matter of some cleanup.

The light turned yellow and Hank accelerated hard. Again, everything slid to the back of the van. Then there was the loud honk of a siren turning on and the glow of flashing red and blue lights. A cop.

Fuck.

"Boss?" Hank called in a panic.

"Pull over, Hank. Stay calm." The cop car parked, and Hank twisted his hands over the steering wheel.

"Take your gloves off, Hank. And don't let on that I'm here. I'll tell you when to go."

The plates on the van were stolen. It wouldn't do to have them run. Things were about to get messy, but J.T. was good with improvisation. Hank, on the other hand, was not. The cop car door opened and a single officer started for the van. He had a blond goatee and a wide upper body, the kind of young officer who probably spent a lot of free time at the gym. His left hand hovered on the butt of his gun. A left-handed cop was at a disadvantage. J.T. was surprised he didn't come around the passenger's side. Instead, he approached the driver's side with his gun on the outside. Inside, the Sig Sauer P250, complete with silencer, was now aimed at his head through the van's tinted side window.

When the officer reached the back bumper, Hank started to roll his window down. J.T. released the Sig's safety.

The cop's stride reached the middle of the van. The trigger eased back. One. Glass exploded. Two. Bullets lodged themselves in the cop's head.

Hank screamed.

The officer fell to the pavement. There was a short twitch in his left foot, then nothing. Done and done cleanly.

"Let's go, Hank," J.T. whispered. The police car's camera would pick up everything. J.T. didn't want their voices recorded, but it would be hard to miss Hank's screaming.

"Drive now," J.T. hissed again, but Hank hadn't heard.

J.T. crawled up toward the driver's seat and, resisting the temptation to put a bullet in Hank's head, too, whispered, "Come on. We have to go."

Hank lurched forward, and J.T. held tightly as the van swerved into the street. At the corner, Hank turned right, driving in the opposite direction of home. He was hysterical. He made it around the corner and out of the view of the police car's camera at least.

"Okay, stop here," J.T. said. "I'll drive."

Hank stopped the car in the middle of the road. Obviously, he had never seen anyone shot before. And it was such a clean job, too. He ought to have been impressed.

The two switched places, and Hank sank down against

the wall of the van and pulled his knees to his chest. He made moaning sounds for the remainder of the drive.

"It's okay, Hank."

There were no other incidents. The garage door slid open and soon the van was inside with the door closed behind them. Only with the engine off did Hank pull himself from his fetal position and move toward the door.

Hank had his hand on the van's door handle, the back of his head cleanly exposed when the two bullets entered the back of his skull. The bullets didn't break the glass, so the mess was contained in the van. At least that had gone right.

It would all stay there for a few hours. Right now, the only pressing matters were a shower and a beer. Even at 5:00 a.m., J.T. was ready for a drink.

CHAPTER 2

MEI LING SAT in the back corner of the Special Ops van and studied her computer screen in the strange glow of the van's red interior lights. Around her, officers donned heavy raid gear: thick, black suits and combat boots and helmets with goggles. Mei was working to make herself small in the crowded space. Not that she was large to begin with. The van was maybe twenty feet long and had seemed spacious when they were all seated, but with ten team members, the captain, and equipment everywhere, it felt significantly smaller now.

Mei was working to hack the login on the computer they'd seized from Will Weigman, who the police believed was the meth ring's money guy. If she could break into it before Special Ops got into the building, they could obtain additional search warrants and cast a wider net. Unfortunately, the Special Ops team was gearing up and the brute force password dongle she'd plugged into the computer's USB port was still working on cracking the password. Mei was also waiting for AT&T to respond to their subpoena for the guy's cell phone records. The lab had even gotten the DA's office to issue a subpoena to

Apple to gain access to whatever they could see from his Apple ID. Anything to give them some added insight. But waiting was a lot of what they did.

Computer forensics was never a speedy process, but watching the program from the inside of the Special Ops bus made it seem slower. Even glaciers melted faster than computer forensics these days, what with climate change and all. All around Mei, the Special Ops team was moving. Quickly. Efficiently, in a way the computer team never could. Mei wished she'd opted to do this from the lab, although then she would have had to deal with Aaron Pollack and her new team and that was less than ideal, too.

Cameron Cruz sat down beside Mei and pulled on a thick black jumpsuit. "What do you think of Special Ops?"

"Uh—"

"A little different from the lab?"

Mei motioned to Cameron's suit. "No, no. I've got a suit just like that. I would've worn it, but it's at the cleaners."

"You'd look great in one of these," Cameron told her. "And men love this look." Diego Ramirez laughed and reached down to tie his wife's boot, but Cameron elbowed him away playfully.

Diego laughed. "It's true. We dig it," he said, giving Cameron a quick kiss.

Mei glanced at her computer screen.

"Get a room already!" one of the other guys ribbed the lovebirds. Mei couldn't remember his name.

"Seriously, you guys don't spend enough time together off the job?" another one joked.

Cameron and Diego were the only couple Mei knew who both lived together and worked on the same team at the department.

Diego waved them off. "Hey, we're making up for lost time." Looking back at his wife, though, he couldn't contain his smile and, when Cameron turned her back to pull on her Kevlar vest, she was grinning, too. It was like they were getting ready to go on a scuba diving trip rather than into the center of a known meth ring.

Despite the flirting, Cameron and Diego moved with purpose. No wasted time as they donned equipment—belts, helmets, gloves. Cameron might have been five-eight or nine, but she couldn't have weighed much more than a hundred and thirty pounds, and the equipment she had on had to weigh another thirty-five or forty. In law enforcement for more than ten years, Mei had never donned a bulletproof vest or a gun on the job. She did her mandatory firearms training, but she was way more at home with a mouse than a Glock.

Mei minimized the screen on the decryption program and pulled up the GPS coordinates. The tracking device they'd put on their mole still hadn't moved.

"Anything?" Special Ops Sergeant Lau asked Mei.

She shook her head and glanced at the timer that recorded how long the device had been still. "Hasn't moved in nearly fourteen hours."

The group sobered. The tracking device was his phone. It was possible the small tracking chip had been discovered and left behind. In Mei's experience, when a tracking device was discovered, it was usually dumped. She'd spent plenty of days tracking devices to dumpsters or off bridges and into lakes. It was also conceivable that their inside guy had left his phone. It was normal to see gaps in movement of between seven and ten hours. People slept, after all.

But, with the sensitivity of the tracker and her equipment, Mei could see the movement of the phone off the bedside table, even just a few inches, let alone if it moved across the room. People tended to bring their phones with them from one room to another. This one had not moved a millimeter in fourteen hours. That was not good. Nothing to do now but wait for the team to go in and check it out.

Ramirez led the team through the layout and plan, and Mei watched. Her phone vibrated. Her mother was calling again. She sent the call to voicemail and texted her mother for the third time that morning, *At a scene.* She'd take hell for that later.

Mei heard shouts. The team lined up, moved out. Sergeant Lau went with them and reached inside to close the doors. Mei was alone with her computer. Most days, she ran this kind of program while she was doing a half dozen other things. Computer programs always took twice as long when they were being watched. Mei heard the ding of the dongle. The password was Betsy1082. Quickly, Mei typed it in and, without a breath ran a recursive find command, looking for anything with a modified date in the last week.

Five seconds later, the images began to load. Mei moved through them quickly. The first two were black, most likely accidental. The next image was hard to see, taken from a distance. She double-clicked the thumbnail so the picture filled the screen. At first, the tint of the skin made it look like a costume mask tossed on a pillow. The skin was gray-green where the neck disappeared under the white sheet, the bulk of his torso under the covers. A dead man. Maybe Weigman, but she didn't know what he looked like.

Mei loaded the next image. Somewhere else. Two large green soda bottles sat on a countertop. They looked old, their labels long gone. Each was partially full. Rubber was wrapped around the tops and a single tube ran from one to the other. Beside them was a glass bottle maybe half their size. Its label was turned away from the camera.

Mei quickly scanned the next few images. They seemed to document the place in a full circle. Empty bed through the doorway. A single ratty brown couch in the living room. Kitchen with a '70s style refrigerator in yellow. In the center, a small card table with one chair and the counter lined with the soda bottles. She enlarged the photo. Beside the bottles was a small blue plastic bottle. Though blurry, she could read the words at the top of the glass bottle: ethyl alcohol, USP. Below that, in bright red letters, it read 200 Proof. Ethanol.

In the next image, she saw a label that read H3PO2. Her chemistry wasn't good enough for that one. Instead, she Googled it. It was a substitute for red phosphorus in the production of meth and highly explosive. A meth lab. Mei scanned back through the images to the one with the body. In the background was a window and a single shade.

Mei jumped up from the computer, catching her foot

on the chair that was bolted to the floor. She stumbled across the van and pressed herself against the windows. Stared up at the building as she had been doing when they arrived. The team was walking into a meth lab.

"No. No. No." Mei turned and scanned the tabletop. The radio? Where the hell was it?

She sprinted for the radio on the dash. "Sergeant Lau, do not enter the building. I repeat, do not enter."

The radio was silent.

"Send backup. Sergeant Lau's team is entering a meth lab. Lau, don't go in there!" she called more desperately. She watched out the window, anticipating an explosion.

When there was no answer, Mei opened the bus door and ran down the stairs. "Cameron! Diego!" she screamed down the block. She wasn't exactly sure how they'd entered the building. "Get away from there! Clear the area."

Were they already inside? Even a cell phone call could trigger an explosion. Call 9-1-1. She ran back onto the bus for her cell phone, dialed 9-1-1.

"Dispatch. What is the address of your emergency?"

"This is Officer Mei Ling. I'm with the Special Ops team and we have a potential ethanol leak. It hasn't blown yet, but the team is up there. They don't know it's an active meth production. We need to get through to them and tell them to get away from that building before it blows. We need firefighters and a bomb squad and ambulances."

"Officer, slow down."

Mei glanced at the image on her computer. Two liter-sized soda bottles and ethyl alcohol. Maybe it wouldn't blow. But there had to be enough ethanol in that air to kill Weigman. "Send backup. This place is a meth lab."

There was a loud smack on the side of the bus and Mei jumped. Sergeant Lau's face appeared through the glass. He gave her a tentative smile, which was followed by the comforting thunder of heavy boots on the bus stairs.

"What's all the commotion?" Diego asked.

Mei watched them all flood back onto the bus. All ten of them, plus Lau. Only then did she finally take a full breath of air.

"What did you find?" Lau asked, coming up behind her shoulder.

Mei double-clicked on the image of the meth lab and turned the computer toward the group hovered around her.

"That could be anywhere," one of the guys said.

"Mei, what made you so sure that picture is of this place?" Lau asked.

In the distance, Mei heard the low whine of sirens. She navigated back to the image and zoomed into the window. She pointed to the broken blind that hung asymmetrically in the window. "See that?"

"The shade?" Cameron asked.

Mei nodded. "Look up at the building," she told them. "Farthest window on the right."

The officers moved across the van. It took them a minute to find it. "Holy shit," Diego said. "That place is a meth lab."

Mei sank into her chair. "That's what I've been telling you."

CHAPTER 3

MEI WAS LATE for dinner with her aunt. Again. Ayi, as Mei had called her since she was little, was planning another feast in her celebration of the Chinese Ghost Festival. For two nights in the past week, Ayi had made hugely elaborate meals and served them to empty seats at her dining room table as though their dead relatives were dining with them.

As a child, Mei had loved the Ghost Festival, her favorite of the Chinese celebrations. China's version of Halloween, the Ghost Festival had appealed to Mei's sometimes morbid curiosity about death and the after-life. The Ghost Festival was a time when her mother filled their small apartment with the most delicious smells and, everywhere in Chicago's Chinatown, people burned incense, joss paper, and fake money to worship their ancestors. Traditional Chinese operas were held almost daily in the local parks. For years, Mrs. Luo from the market down the road gave out free rice candies to the children.

Mei leaned back in the cab and tried to gear herself up for the evening. Living with her mother's younger sister when she arrived in San Francisco had been the culmination of a long series of negotiations. Leaving Chicago at all was hard enough. Thirty-three in a few months, Mei was supposed to be having babies, not changing jobs. Her other sisters—one younger, one older—were both already married with children. Chinese parents didn't believe in different lifestyles for different children. No, their daughters should all be married with children. Mei loved her nieces and nephew. Surely, she would have children, too. That was the life she'd always wanted. That had been her plan as recently as a year ago.

Then came a seemingly innocent note on Facebook from Jodi, Mei's closest friend from high school. Jodi whom Mei hadn't seen since college. Jodi whom Mei was sure was living some alternative life in New York or LA or San Francisco. Jodi who, Mei discovered, was an estate attorney in Massachusetts, married to her female partner with two little boys. One boy born to each mom, nine weeks apart, with the same sperm donor. Two-year-old brothers who looked something alike, and Jodi with her partner Carrie. Not her partner. Her wife.

Something shifted for Mei in those months. Questions she thought she'd put to rest resurfaced. Things that Mei used to enjoy—even looked forward to—had lost their appeal. Inside a nine-month period, her entire personality was like a computer that had been restored from a different backup drive. She didn't recognize the feelings that started to emerge. She was restless in a way she'd never been before. She started thinking about moving, looking at job opportunities outside the FBI.

When the position came up with the SFPD, she

applied. When it was offered to her, she accepted. Even before talking to her family. The department recruited her heavily, she told them. A lie. One of a hundred that Mei told herself were just little white lies. Some not so white.

It was all a ruse to buy her time. She was suddenly terrified of the future. That safe, perfectly planned path seemed rife with danger. Coming to San Francisco was supposed to give her room to breathe. She had even imagined having her own apartment. Something tiny. Barely furnished or not at all; she didn't care.

But there would be no apartment. Since her mother's sister lived in San Francisco, Mei had had to compromise. If Ayi didn't mind, she would stay there. Surely her mother's younger sister—an unwed woman in her early sixties—would be less traditional than her parents, not more. Instead, Ayi was obsessed with Chinese culture. Her friends were Chinese; her coworkers at the insurance company where she was a translator for both Mandarin and Cantonese speakers were Chinese.

Since arriving in San Francisco, Mei had heard Ayi speak English only twice: once to a phone solicitor, asking him—with only a trace of the accent Mei always heard in her mother's voice—to put her on the Do Not Call list and once on a call to order more capsules for her fancy Nespresso coffee machine.

Looking at Ayi's tiny feet in the brocade slippers she wore everywhere except to work, Mei considered the possibility that Ayi even bound her own feet.

Mei spent a fair number of evenings at work, but Ayi had specifically requested her presence tonight. Normally, Mei would have taken the J train, but she was supposed to be home at 6:30. It was after 7:00. Plus, the idea of an hour on a noisy bus was not appealing.

Halfway home, her phone buzzed. She pulled it from her pocket and saw a picture text from Hailey Wyatt. Mei double-clicked the picture until it filled the screen. A small metal box with two antennae, it looked like a cell phone jammer.

Mei called Hailey back.

"Are you always working?" Hailey said in lieu of hello.

"Are you?"

"Feels like it."

"Me too." Mei didn't say that, for her, work was better than the alternative. "What's the deal with the jammer?"

"Jammer?" a man in the background asked.

"Mei, I'm here with my partner, Hal. Not sure if you heard about the officer shooting in Oyster Point."

"I did," Mei said. News of an officer shooting spread quickly. "I'm sorry."

"Me too," Hailey agreed. "We found this thing at a break-in at a police storage facility where someone—we think it was our shooter—made off with a lot of weapons."

"You found the jammer there?"

"What the hell is a jammer?" Hal asked. Mei had to smile. So many officers were technophobes and luddites.

"It's a cell phone jammer. It prevents cell phones from being able to make calls." Mei pulled the phone away from her ear and looked at the image. "This one looks homemade."

"We found it behind the phone box on the outside of the building."

"Where the robbery happened?" Mei asked.

"Yeah."

"Well, it's not working now."

"How do you know that?" Hal asked.

"Because Hailey called me on her cell phone. A cell phone jammer jams cell phone calls so they can't reach the satellite."

"That's why they call it a cell phone jammer, Hal," Hailey said with a smile in her voice.

"It was most likely used to block a signal from going to the alarm company," Mei explained. "Most alarms have a primary line that is a landline, but then they also have a cell phone backup. The jammer would prevent that call from getting through to the alarm company."

"There was no alarm at all here." Hailey sounded frustrated.

"Then someone wasted some nice handiwork," Mei said, "but it's likely he didn't know there wasn't an alarm. I wonder why he left it there."

"I don't think that part was on purpose," Hailey told her. "It had fallen back behind the phone box."

"Now that we know what this thing is, can you find anything out from it?" Hal asked her. "Anything that might lead us to our perp?"

"Maybe," said Mei. "There might be some prints on it. If not on the outside, then possibly on the internal components."

"We're leaving the scene now, but I'll get it over to the lab. Maybe you can take a look tomorrow."

"If you get it over to the lab, I'll go look at it tonight."

"What? No hot date?" Hailey teased.

Mei made a sound she hoped sounded like a laugh. "Not by a long shot."

A few minutes later, the cab stopped in front of Ayi's driveway. At least getting to go back into the department later in the evening gave Mei something to look forward to as she headed up the short flight of stairs to her aunt's funky yellow-green house. Ayi had bought the house for $75,000 thirty years ago. Now it was worth about ten times that. Two bedrooms, two baths in the Inner Sunset, it was a great place in a decent location. Rent free.

Mei should have been happy, but instead she dreaded the sight of it. The fog that had shrouded the house that morning still hung like a gray tarp over the neighborhood. It seemed low enough that if she were to climb onto the house's roof, she might be able to emerge above it and see blue sky.

Ayi normally kept the living room lights off, but tonight the room shone brightly as Mei climbed the stairs. Close to the top, she peered through the front window and saw Ayi offering a plate to a man sitting on the couch.

The two looked up and, seeing Mei, the man stood, smiling. Mei pressed herself into the banister for support. The bolt on the door clicked. Mei forced herself to climb the last stair. The door opened, and he rushed to hug her. "Baby, I've missed you so much."

Mei pressed herself to his chest and closed her eyes, hoping that her husband didn't see the dread on her face.

CHAPTER 4

TRIGGERLOCK INSPECTOR RYAAN Berry reached for the cell phone on the bedside table that was quacking like a duck. "Berry," she said and let her head fall back on the pillow. She'd been dreaming of Kevin Durant. She and Kevin. On a warm beach. With cold drinks.

"It's Wyatt."

Ryaan made no effort to open her eyes. Hailey Wyatt was a colleague at the department, a homicide inspector. "Jesus, Hailey. What time is it?"

"Don't ask," Hailey warned her. "There's a backup storage facility near Oyster Point in South San Francisco. You know about it?"

Ryaan sat up slowly and stifled a yawn. "Backup storage for what?"

"That's what I figured. I guess the department rented a warehouse down here to store evidence in some untried cases—nothing biological but there were guns."

Fully awake now, Ryaan swung her feet onto the ground and rested her elbows on her knees. "How many?"

"It's going to take a while to get a firm count."

"Shit. You mean like someone has to go through case

by case?" She wondered if she wouldn't end up being that someone.

"I don't think it's that bad," Hailey told her. "Supposedly, there's a log somewhere."

"Why are you on it?" Hailey was Homicide, so Ryaan thought she knew the answer.

"Officer pulled over a van about a mile from the scene. Guy ran a red. Officer was shot through the van's side window. Hal and I are up."

"Damn, anyone we know?"

"Keith Reynolds. Was only eight months out."

The two were silent a moment. It was hard to lose the rookies. Felt like losing children.

"Text me the address," Ryaan said.

"Thanks, Ryaan. Sorry to wake you up."

Ryaan groaned. "You should be. I was having a hell of a dream."

"Hope he was cute."

Ryaan pictured Durant. "Damn right he was." Ryaan ended the call and rested her head back against the soft suede headboard and told herself not to go back to sleep. She'd been on the force more than ten years, but she never got used to the night calls.

She pulled herself from bed and padded to the bathroom where she splashed water on her face. Her mother was in the hall when she came back out. Ryaan jumped backward. "Mama, you scared the heck out of me."

"Sorry, cub. I'm just not sleeping."

Ryaan looked at her mother's worried face and softened her voice. "I got called to a scene. I'll probably go straight to the station afterward, so I won't be home until tonight."

Her mother touched her face, and Ryaan felt the fine wrinkles on the rough dry pads of her fingertips. "You be careful," she whispered as she did every time Ryaan left the house.

Ryaan arrived at the scene just as the light in the sky was shifting from purple toward red. Sunrise would happen within the hour. Maybe it would even warm up. For now, it was cold, and the wind whipped her thick strands of chemically straightened hair across her eyes and cheeks. It felt like getting slapped by a belt made of ribbon. Her hair wasn't long enough to tie back, so she used one hand as a headband and walked toward the two squad cars and two detective cars that created a poorly formed circle around what must have been the location of the shooting victim. The Crime Scene Unit's van was parked across the street.

Hailey Wyatt's partner, Hal, stood with his back to Ryaan as she approached. He was partially leaned over, his arms crossed and the sweatshirt he wore cut across his back. He didn't even look cold. He and Hailey made an odd couple. She was barely five-three while Hal had to be almost six-four, just a little taller than her own brothers. Hal had the same skin as Antoine, darker than hers and Darryl's. Antoine must have gotten it from their father, though Ryaan barely remembered him.

She had always thought Hal Harris was one of the good ones. Rumor was he had a crazy wife, but they'd been divorced for as long as Ryaan had known him. He was friendly enough to Ryaan but nothing more, and she wasn't about to make the first move. Women did that, she knew, but her mother's Southern culture had seeped into her like a poison that made asking men out on par with putting on pasties and dancing on a pole.

Hailey greeted her as did the two crime scene techs and the patrol officer who was first to respond to the scene.

"Morning, Ryaan," Hal said.

"If you can call it that," she said, with a little smile that probably looked more like a grimace. She was a miserable flirt.

The body was gone, leaving just a blackish stain where the officer had bled out. Judging from the outline and the distance of the spray, he had died quickly. Amazing the things that were considered blessings in their field.

"No casings," Hal said to catch her up. "It was an older model van or truck."

"Reynolds's camera would have images, right?" Ryaan asked.

Hal nodded. "The lab is getting us some stills of the van."

"Any images of the perp?"

"Lab's working on enhancing some of the video," Hailey said. "They might be able to get a partial reflection in the rearview mirror, but—"

"The quality on those cameras isn't great," Ryaan finished.

"Right."

Ryaan crossed her arms and tried not to shiver. "I was hoping maybe the guy got out of the van."

Hal shook his head. "No such luck."

"Two perps," Hailey corrected. "Reynolds was shot through the rear side window of the van."

"So, someone was sitting in back," Hal said.

"You been to the warehouse?" Ryaan asked, looking around for where it might be.

"It's a few blocks from here. I've got to wait until these guys are done," Hailey said, motioning to the crime scene techs. "But you and Hal can head over."

Ryaan nodded. "Great."

"I'll ride with you," Hal said. "We'll see you over there," he told Hailey.

Hal stepped aside and put his hand on Ryaan's lower back as they started toward her car. Inside, Hal rubbed his hands together and blew into them. "Cold out there."

As they drove, Hal sang to the radio. He had a nice baritone voice that filled the car and, while he didn't seem particularly shy about the singing, he also didn't seem to be boasting. She enjoyed it.

They drove about three blocks before she came around a corner and saw two squad cars and another Crime Scene Unit van. Ryaan followed Hal around the side of an office building. The building was sleek with a tall entryway, the glass mirrored and bright blue. The entryway was set back from the street and a sculpture, which looked like a couple of shiny pipes bent around each other, was visible in the foyer of the building. Around it was a fountain lined with overflowing fern plants. "We have a storage facility here?" she asked.

"First I'd heard of it, too."

Ryaan scanned along the front of the building. "There must be a camera here."

"Yep. They've got a few."

Ryaan glanced up at him and saw that he wasn't done. "But?"

"Someone vandalized all three of them two nights ago, along with four others along the street."

"A Friday night. Hard to get someone out over the weekend. Figured they were safe until Monday morning."

Hal nodded. "And they were right. We've got that guy on film. Mask, gloves, black head to toe, clean shoes—like out of the box clean."

"Not your average street kid."

Hal shook his head. "The building's shared by four businesses: an accounting firm, an architecture firm, a pharmaceutical R&D company, and a law firm that deals mostly in estate law. The management company turned the film in to the South San Francisco station. For all the good it'll do."

"Five businesses, right? What about the police warehouse?"

"Technically, it's not the same building." He led her around the corner and pointed to a sad-looking side entrance. "The warehouse is next door. I guess there was a dispute over the property line when the new building went up. The developers thought they'd bought this warehouse, but it turns out they hadn't."

Ryaan looked at the warehouse. It wasn't much of a prize. "The owner didn't want to sell it?"

"Oh, he did. But for a pretty penny more than fair price. Developers told him he could keep it. Then he stopped paying taxes."

"In comes the state," Ryaan guessed.

"Right," Hal agreed. "California waives his back real estate taxes in exchange for a ten-year lease on the biggest space in the building."

Ryaan looked up at Hal. "You got all this in the last two hours?"

"I got all of it in ten minutes from the building's management company. I guess this warehouse has caused a few issues in the past. They were hoping the police presence might help."

"Fat chance." Ryaan stopped and looked across the warehouse's green chipped facade. It was definitely an eyesore. "And there are no cameras here at all?"

"Not a one."

The two entered the warehouse where three crime scene techs were collecting evidence. Small, numbered orange markers were placed across the floor where evidence had been marked for collection.

"Guns were this way." Hal led and Ryaan followed, carefully avoiding the markers.

The room in the corner of the warehouse was, in fact, a cage like one might buy for an aggressive dog. Its ceiling was maybe eight feet high, and the walls were constructed of a solid metal grid, the openings approximately three-inch squares. The cage had been lined on three sides with flimsy metal supply cabinets that reminded Ryaan of the teachers' supply cabinets from elementary school. The doors were flung open, their contents emptied.

Sydney Blanchard appeared at the door. Maybe five-three, Sydney was a triathlete with strong, wide shoulders and solid legs. She always seemed to be moving, even when she was standing still. She shifted now from foot to foot. "Hey."

"Got anything good?" Hal asked.

Sydney shrugged. "Not much. Some footprints in the dust, men's size eight and another size ten and a half so we're looking for two perps. One comes straight in here—" She pointed to the cage. "The other wanders a bit. Spent a little time down the middle row. We're getting a list of the cases stored there, especially in one area with the most disturbances in the dust. Nothing yet."

Hal frowned. "You thinking they were here for something other than the guns?"

Sydney shrugged again. She had shifted to bending one knee at a time, kicking her foot up to bump herself in the backside. It made Ryaan wonder if the same sort of fidgeting would help her take off the ten pounds she'd put on in the last couple of years.

"There's not much of value in this place other than the guns," Sydney said.

"So maybe the guy was just nosing around," Hal suggested.

"There's a good chance."

"What about the guns?" Ryaan asked, wishing she'd made coffee at home. "How many were there?"

"Seventy-two." Sydney opened her notebook and removed a list and handed it to Ryaan. "Here's the complete inventory of what was stored here."

Ryaan scanned the list as Hal read it over her shoulder.

"Some nice guns," Hal commented.

"There's nothing nice about these," Ryaan said, the familiar anger cranking into her jaw. "There are a lot of nasty ones on this list," she added, pointing to the fully automatic weapons that were only useful for all-scale attacks—in wars or nowadays in places like movie theaters and schools.

"Of course," Hal agreed. Ryaan shrugged awkwardly, wishing she'd said nothing.

"How long do you guys need here?" Hal asked Sydney.

"It'll take us another couple hours to process, then we'll be back at the lab and see what we've got," Sydney told him.

Ryaan's phone buzzed on her hip. She pulled it from the holster and looked down at the screen. The message was from Patrick O'Hanlan. Paddy O—or The Leprechaun as he was known to some of the Triggerlock team—was a dark-haired, freckled man with green eyes who looked like a teenager. Ryaan was the only one of her teammates who simply called O'Hanlan by his given name. Most probably thought it was because she was also the only woman on the Triggerlock team. In reality, Ryaan called him Patrick because she didn't want anyone coming up with nicknames for Ryaan or Berry. She'd heard plenty of those in middle school. Ones like Ryaan Scary and Try-on Cherry and those that made even less sense like Fucking Fairy and Fryin' Hairy.

Ryaan read Patrick's message. *Mission and Third. Multiple gunshots reported at the main branch of Pacific Bank.* Just then, the phone rang. "Berry."

Hal's phone buzzed, too.

"Ryaan, it's Patrick. I'm heading downtown."

"Pacific Bank? I saw the call."

"This is about to be a media shitstorm."

"What is it?"

"We've got two dead and six more wounded. Thankfully, it all went down before the bank opened for regular hours. Suspect is a fourteen-year-old kid. Arrested him with a semiautomatic rifle. No parents to contact. Kid supposedly lives with his grandmother up in Bernal Heights, but we can't get Grandma on the phone. I've got a squad car heading over there now."

"Where did the gun come from?" Ryaan asked, glancing toward the empty cabinets in the cage.

"No damn clue. Kid won't talk."

Someone was talking in the background.

"Is that Lomez?" Ryaan asked.

"Yeah. Hang on."

The line was silent a moment before Patrick came back. "He just ran the gun through the database. The serial matches an unsolved from 2009."

"Let me guess. The gun is supposed to be in police custody," Ryaan said.

Hal raised his eyebrows.

"How did you know?" Patrick asked.

Ryaan blew out her breath. "I'll meet you at Bryant in twenty minutes."

With that, she left Hal and Sydney and headed back to her car. Seventy-two guns out there. She needed coffee.

CHAPTER 5

"HELL, NO," DWAYNE said to the text on his phone. Like some guy was going to give him a whole bunch of guns and didn't want nothing up front and 25% on the backside. That kind of deal didn't exist. This J.T. was some sort of cracker if he thought Dwayne would fall for that shit. He texted back.

U a cop. Fuck off.

He'd paid his debt to society and all that shit. No way he was going back. He had Tamara to think about. She had a good gig at the city's engineering office. She was taking classes at a community college. She had moved out of the neighborhood. She had plans, and he had a chance to be part of them… if he didn't screw things up.

He had never known a woman like Tamara. She wasn't boy-crazy. She didn't talk about wanting a ring and babies. She wanted a career. Every day, on the inside, he'd written to her, telling her what he was reading, about the classes he was taking toward his GED. She didn't answer him. Not once. But he kept writing.

"These boxes ain't moving theyselves," Rhonda shouted as she waddled across the warehouse like a gimpy penguin.

Dwayne pocketed the phone and started toward the stack of boxes. "I'm on it now, Rhonda. I was just telling my mama that I'll be bringing home dinner. Maybe some chicken soup," he added. "She sick."

"Yeah, Dwayne. I hear you. I been texting my daddy, too," Rhonda said, her mouth full of food. Something chocolate maybe. Her mouth was always full of food. "Just get your ass back to work."

While Rhonda stood too close, Dwayne loaded boxes until the handcart was full and rolled it to the van in back, unloaded it, then came back for more. He shouldn't have been thinking about that text, but man, would he love to ditch this loser job. He spent a lot of nights driving home imagining the way he'd tell Rhonda off if he could quit. No choice now. Not a lot of people want to hire an ex-con and he didn't have a lot of skills either. Not yet. He would soon. Tamara had him taking a statistics class with her. She'd been proud of him, finishing his GED inside.

He thought that would be the end of him and school, but Tamara wanted a college man so that's what he was going to be. Right now, he had to keep his head down until he had some classes under his belt. All this job required was a driver's license and legs that worked, and a shitload of patience to deal with Rhonda.

Rhonda followed him as he went out the warehouse door on another run. As she walked, her face got all puckered up about the pain in her ankles. She reached the door just as he was putting the last boxes into the back of the van. She was busy licking the remains of her donut or muffin or whatever she'd been stuffing into her face. When she got it all, she wiped her hand on her pants.

She had diabetes which caused swelling and pain in her ankles. The pain didn't keep her up in that office, though. Dwayne sure as hell wished it did.

Dwayne walked by with the handcart. One more load and he could get out of there.

"You do the police station first," Rhonda called after him. "They in some big hurry."

Dwayne nodded.

"Then, you got them three deliveries along Chavez and two others in The Mission and one in Bernal Heights. Do that one last. Come back straightaway, Dwayne. Jerry's working on a bunch more that have to get out today."

Dwayne loaded the handcart one last time and checked his list to make sure he had all the right deliveries. With the boxes all loaded up, he folded the handcart closed and loaded it too before slamming the rear doors closed.

Rhonda was moving toward him again, faster now that she wasn't busy eating. Something creepy about the way she walked. "You hear me, Dwayne?"

"I hear you," Dwayne promised. "I'll be back for the others soon as I get these delivered."

"And no more double-parking. I ain't paying for another ticket. You still owe sixty bucks from that last one."

Dwayne raised a hand at her in a mock salute, climbed into the van, and shut the door. "I heard you, bitch." Damn, Rhonda was annoying. Deliveries had been her deal until the diabetes made her ankles swell up like grapefruits. Now she couldn't deliver. Couldn't pack shit up neither, and she didn't seem smart enough to handle the books. They had that nerdy guy Spencer for that.

Rhonda was just around to drive him crazy was all, but damn if she wasn't good at it.

Dwayne put the key in the ignition and turned to glance out the window for traffic. Rhonda's big face staring through the glass nearly scared the shit right out of him.

He rolled down the window.

"You gonna put that seatbelt on, right, Dwayne? Otherwise, you breaking the law and creating all sorts of liabilities for this company."

"Of course." He reached across and pulled the seatbelt over his chest, giving her a big smile.

"You watch that smart mouth a yours, Dwayne. Your mama might be Jerry's cousin, but he ain't the boss around here."

"I ain't givin' you mouth, Rhonda. I put my seatbelt on just like you said."

Rhonda stood and stared at him, like she was looking for some other thing to start bitchin' about. She was quiet for nearly ten seconds, which was a record.

"Okay if I go now, Rhonda?"

"'Course you should go, fool. I don't know what you waiting for."

Dwayne blew his breath out nice and slow the way they'd taught him in that anger class in prison. "Okay, Rhonda. I'll see you later." Dwayne pulled out of the garage and turned toward the police department. He shouldn't have been thinking about responding to that damn text message, but he was. Selling that gun could raise enough for a down payment on a place for him and Tamara.

CHAPTER 6

MEI WAS GRATEFUL to Ayi. Though Andy had offered to take them to dinner, Ayi had prepared fuqi feipian. Mei was sure her mother had told Ayi it was Andy's favorite. She was grateful not to have to go out. She only knew a handful of places in town and her favorite of them—the Blush Wine Bar—had come to feel like her own private spot. She didn't want to take her husband there. There, she didn't even want to remember she was married. Mei wasn't a huge fan of feipian, which was usually made with beef heart and tongue, but she rarely ate as little as she did tonight. Instead, she moved the food around on her plate and tried to make it look as though she'd eaten.

After dinner, Andy offered to clean up. Ayi went to bed, and Mei joined him in the kitchen. Andy found a bottle of Baijiu, a Chinese liquor similar to vodka, in Ayi's cupboard and poured them each a couple of fingers' worth over ice to drink as they worked. Andy handed her a glass and touched his glass against hers. "To us," he said.

Mei took a long drink and set her glass down.

In good spirits, Andy filled the sink with warm soapy water. She watched him roll up his sleeves, exposing strong, smooth forearms. This was as good a time as any. She would explain her mixed feelings, her confusion. She would ask for his patience and understanding. She went into the dining room and began to clear the dishes, trying to find the courage to start.

"I hope you don't mind the surprise," Andy said as Mei set the stacked dishes beside the sink. "I couldn't wait another three weeks until your trip home."

"Of course not. I'm happy to see you."

Andy reached up with a wet hand and pushed a strand of hair from her face. "You seem tired. Are they working you too hard?"

Mei smiled. "I really like it." Quickly, she went to clear the remaining dishes from the table. Already, her stomach was in knots.

"I'm glad," he said, reaching to take the dishes from her hands. "They're lucky to have you."

"I don't know about that," she said.

Andy lifted her chin and kissed her. "I do."

Ignoring the guilt that seemed to rise from behind her lungs, Mei kissed her husband.

She moved to the dishwasher to load the dinner plates.

Andy grinned at her.

"What?"

He shut off the water. "I was going to wait to tell you."

Mei froze. "Tell me what?"

"I put in for a transfer."

The dish slipped from Mei's fingers and fell onto the linoleum floor, exploding at her feet.

Quickly, she leaned over to pick up the pieces. She held the largest one in her hand, unable to make herself move as her heartbeat thundered at the base of her neck. "A transfer?"

Andy closed the dishwasher and, moving efficiently, began to collect the porcelain shards. "To the local office here."

Mei watched him, unable to answer. He was coming here. Moving here. While she planned to ask him for a break, he was planning to uproot his life to be with her. She stood quickly and started out of the room. "Let me get the broom."

She walked back to her bathroom without stopping and closed the door. Stared at her terrified face in the mirror. *You can't do this to him.*

"Mei?" Andy called from the hallway.

Mei opened the door and found Andy holding a dustpan and broom. "Ah, there it is," she said, taking it from him. "I thought it was in here."

He followed her back to the kitchen and Mei stooped to brush up the shards. "I thought you said a transfer would be taking a step backward for your career," she said, broaching the subject again.

Andy touched her hand.

Mei looked up, trying to seem casual. "I mean, aren't you worried about losing ground?"

"We can't go on like this. It's been a month. I'm going nuts," he said. "Is it that you're afraid you won't want to stay in this job?"

"No. It's not that," she said quickly, still gripping the dustpan and broom like some sort of life raft. "I like it." She stood and dumped the broken pieces into the trashcan.

Andy took the broom and dustpan from her hands and returned them to under the sink. "If you're happy here, then I need to make a change."

"But what if it doesn't work out?" she blurted.

"If it doesn't work out, you'll find another job, or we'll go back to the Bureau in Chicago. They'll take us both back." Andy pulled her closer. "It's not life or death, babe. They're just jobs."

Mei saw the drink on the counter and fought the urge to reach for it as she struggled with a wave of emotion. She might not want to be married to her husband, but she loved him. Andy was her best friend. He was the one she went to when her mother was being especially crazy or when there was an issue at work, when her father had the heart attack scare, when she got the promotion at work, when she'd felt the first pains of appendicitis. Andy was always the first person she wanted to talk to. There was no one to replace him, but the warring emotions she felt, the dreams she'd been having about Jodi or a woman at work or sometimes women she swore she'd never seen before… the things she couldn't say built up between them.

She hated herself for these feelings, for the growing ambivalence she had about her marriage and her husband. He was a kind, honest man. An attractive man. A smart man. A caring man. He was a wonderful husband, would make a wonderful father. Why, then, couldn't Mei be happy just to be married to him?

CHAPTER 7

MEI WAS CALLED in just after 6:00 the next morning. Andy was already up, in the kitchen drinking coffee with Ayi. In a good mood, he had plans to meet with the local office of the FBI and was planning to go look around the city.

He was going to find a place to take Mei to dinner that night. He would leave early the next morning for meetings in LA and be back to Chicago for the weekend for his mother's birthday.

"Maybe I can take you to lunch today?" he said. "I'd love to see where you work."

"I'd love that," Mei lied. "Let me see what happens with this case. I may have to stay close to the station."

On the way to work, she worried about his meeting with the Bureau. Andy's focus was on money laundering and he was well respected within the FBI. He was often loaned to other regional offices to assist in cases. If he pressed for a transfer, Mei imagined the Bureau would grant it rather than risk losing him. She would ask him to wait, to give her another month or two before he made a move. Maybe she'd imply that she wasn't sure about the department or say something about missing Chicago. Or maybe she could just tell him the truth. That would certainly be the right decision. He deserved that.

Sitting at the interview table, Mei tried to push everything else from her mind. Computer Forensics was usually on the back end of investigations, so this was Mei's first interrogation. Ryaan Berry had called her in. She thought Mei might be able to help suss out whether or not this kid, Jacob Monaghan, was lying. So far, he hadn't said a single word, which ruled out lying.

He had, however, told some cops that he lived with his grandmother, which wasn't exactly true. His grandmother had died five days ago. A neighbor had called the police because of the smell, and they'd found her dead in her bed, no signs of foul play. There was no evidence that Jacob had been staying in the apartment since her death. Worse, his grandmother had been his only family. This was all new to Mei. Dealing with anything other than machinery was usually outside her jurisdiction. She'd seen the occasional interview, but usually on hacker cases when she was called in to interpret the tech language. This was her first accused killer.

Mei glanced over at Ryaan Berry, who shook her head. Mei's phone buzzed in her pocket and she pushed the silence button. "Where did the gun come from?" Berry asked again.

The epitome of teenage awkwardness, Jacob looked totally shell-shocked. The glasses he wore were too small for his face, which was red and covered in acne. The whole of him had a sheen of grease—face and hair and hands—that made it seem like he hadn't washed in days. Perhaps he hadn't.

Jacob hadn't informed anyone of his grandmother's death, hadn't been to school. According to the officers who found his grandmother, the smell was impossible to miss, so it was hard to imagine Jacob was still staying in the apartment.

The school's truancy office had called and left messages but hadn't followed up. Until Jacob opened fire on a downtown San Francisco bank seven hours ago, killing two and wounding six others, no one could account for his whereabouts for the past five days.

Mei hadn't met many fourteen-year-old killers, but this one didn't seem especially bright. She'd watched a fair number of interviews from behind glass. Even eye movement often betrayed intelligence. Computer teens were usually highly intelligent, if not always socially adept or even good with commonsense.

Jacob didn't seem bright enough to have built the cell phone jammer that laid on the table in front of him. Also, Jacob made no move to touch the device. He barely looked at it. The computer kids Mei had met loved their handiwork. Even when they were trying to pretend they'd had nothing to do with it, they couldn't manage to keep their hands off.

Jacob had already met with a public defender and had gone through a detailed psych evaluation where he'd been deemed fit to stand trial, a disappointment to his attorney. As a flight risk, the court overturned the request that he be released without bail. Unable to come up with two hundred thousand dollars for bail, he spent the night at juvenile hall. Overcrowding meant he'd been bunked in Solitary, the only free room at the inn. At fourteen, there was a chance Jacob would be tried as an adult for the double homicide. Mei didn't see that Jacob had any good options left.

"Jacob, you're going to have to start talking to us," Ryaan told him.

The kid picked at a bloody hangnail on his left thumb with the opposite hand. He pulled a long thin strip of skin off and let it drop on the table.

Ryaan slammed her palm on the table. "Where did the gun come from?"

The kid jumped slightly. "It's not mine."

Ryaan sat up in her chair. "Whose is it?"

Jacob shrugged.

Ryaan stood from the table, her chair screeching back across the linoleum floor. "Fine, Jacob. When you want to talk, you let me know." Ryaan slapped the two-way mirror and shouted, "Let's get him booked over at juvie."

Mei started to stand when Jacob spoke up. "Juvie?"

"Where do you think you're going?" Ryaan said. "You killed two people."

Jacob looked alarmed. "It wasn't my fault. I didn't know the gun was loaded."

"You walked into a bank, pointing it."

"I barely touched the trigger. I'm not even sure I touched it. It was like it just went off." Jacob scratched his head. "I just needed some money. Not even that much," he added, then looked up, wide-eyed. "Why did they leave a loaded gun?"

Ryaan crossed her arms. "Who?"

Jacob's fingers worked frantically on his bleeding thumb. "If I tell you, what will happen?"

Ryaan leaned back against the two-way mirror in the tiny room. "We'll try to help you, Jacob, but you'd better start talking."

Jacob put his hands under his thighs and sat on them as though to stop himself from picking at his thumb. Mei, for one, was thankful.

"Tell us where you've been since your grandma died."

Jacob glanced at Mei, then back at Ryaan.

"The first night, I stayed at home. Then, I slept in the school gym a few nights."

"But you haven't been going to school."

He shrugged. "It's dry and warm, and I can sleep behind the bleachers. I usually wake up when Mr. Matthews comes in."

"Who is Mr. Matthews?"

"The ninth-grade gym teacher. He's also the coach of the tennis team. He gets in real early."

"Where have you been going during the day?"

"The park usually or one time to the library, but the lady there kind of gave me a dirty look so I left."

Mei stared at the kid. He had just shot eight people, and he was sitting there talking about getting a dirty look from a librarian.

Ryaan moved to the table and leaned across it. "Where did the gun come from?"

"It was in a box by the dumpster."

"What dumpster?"

"The one at school."

"At the high school?"

47

Jacob nodded. "I stop there on the way out of the school."

"Why?"

Jacob stared at his lap. "The school throws out bagels and stuff from the day before."

"Where's the box?"

"I threw it away in the dumpster around the corner from the bank."

Ryaan looked at Mei who nodded and sent a text to the lab to get over to the dumpster and find the box.

"You didn't load the gun?"

Jacob shook his head. "I wouldn't even know how. I've never touched a gun before."

"Do you know what this is?" Mei asked him, pointing to the cell phone jammer.

He seemed startled that she had spoken, like he'd just then noticed that she was in the room.

He glanced at the silver box and shook his head.

"You're sure?" Mei asked.

He nodded.

"You've never seen one of these?" Ryaan asked. She pushed it toward him, but he didn't touch it.

He shook his head again. Mei watched him. She wasn't qualified to judge whether or not he was telling the truth, but it seemed highly unlikely to her that he'd made it.

Just then, the door cracked open and Sydney Blanchard stepped into the room. "Ling, can you come take a look at this? You may want to see it, too, Berry."

Mei rose from the table and stepped into the hallway, Ryaan just behind her. Ryaan closed the door on Jacob.

He was already starting to pick at his thumb again. Sydney handed Mei an iPad. On the screen was an image of a laptop computer. It was a relatively cheap brand, maybe a couple hundred dollars, easy to pick up anywhere. The only thing unusual about it was the two strips of Hello Kitty duct tape that ran across its length and width.

Sydney reached over and swiped the screen to show another image. In this one, Mei saw the top of the laptop. The duct tape held a cell phone and a battery pack in place. "Where did you find this?"

"It was in one of the boxes at the warehouse. A case from '93."

"And it's not from the old case?" Ryaan asked.

Mei shook her head. "No way. This kind of technology didn't exist in 1993."

"Plus, the battery is still running," Sydney added.

"What is it?" Ryaan asked.

"That's why I brought it to Mei," Sydney said.

"It looks like a device for breaking into a network," Mei told them. "Is there case information on a server at the warehouse?"

Sydney shook her head. "We don't have a network there."

Mei paused and looked at the picture again. "We must."

"It's just overflow physical storage," Sydney explained. "All the servers are in this building."

Mei focused on the computer with its cell phone. There was no other reason for a computer like this one, with a cell phone piggybacked and an independent battery source. Someone would be accessing it remotely,

49

trying to break into a network. Unless it wasn't the police network they were after. "Is the warehouse close to another building?"

"Yeah. Directly beside it."

"What's in that building?"

Ryaan glanced at Sydney. "Hal told me yesterday. An accounting office, an architecture firm, a pharmaceutical company, and something else."

"A law office," Sydney answered. "Mostly estate clients." The two women turned to Mei. "Why?"

"Because this computer might have been trying to access the network of one of those businesses."

"Someone can do that from a computer?"

Mei nodded. "It's not as hard as you'd think. Companies are really good about protecting themselves from people coming in through their websites, but they often leave their wireless networks way too vulnerable. Where was the computer found?"

"In an old case file."

"Close to the warehouse's exterior wall?"

"Right beside it."

Mei nodded. "Someone is trying to break into one of the businesses. We need to talk to their IT guys."

"But what about the kid?" Ryaan asked. She waved toward the room where Jacob Monaghan was probably making his thumbs bleed more. "You think he made this thing?"

"No way," Mei said without hesitation. "He wouldn't even touch the jammer. He's not capable of something like this." She pointed to the image. "We're dealing with someone who knew how to build an independent battery pack and could jailbreak this phone. Not to mention the kind of programming that has to be working on the computer."

"Well, that kid got one of the guns, so he's related somehow," Ryaan said. "And what about the rest of them?"

Mei shrugged. "Maybe stealing the guns was a distraction and this—" she pointed to the computer "—was what they were really after."

"A distraction," Ryaan repeated. "Shit. They stole seventy-two guns. That's a hell of a distraction."

"What were they really after?" Sydney asked Mei. "Will you be able to tell from the computer?"

"Not likely. A pro would have a software program to scrub the entire contents of the computer once they were into the network."

"You think they already got in?"

"The break-in happened Sunday night. Now it's Tuesday. It's possible."

Ryaan rubbed her face. "Well, I hope you can figure out who's behind this because I need to find out where the rest of those guns are."

Ryaan's cell phone rang. "Berry." She was quiet a moment, then she lowered the phone and put it on speaker. "Wyatt, go ahead. We're here."

"A homeless man just opened fire at a busload of commuters pulling into the terminal building. He was carrying two guns. No fatalities, but we've got nine injured."

Mei glanced at her watch. It was already after 10:00. "Where's the computer now?" Mei asked.

"It was en route to the lab," Sydney said. "It might even be there now."

Mei started down the hallway. "Let's go."

"Call me as soon as you find anything," Ryaan called after them. "I've got sixty-nine more guns to find."

Mei moved quickly down the hall, Sydney beside her. Seventy-two guns stolen. One at a high school, two in a bus terminal. Computer criminals were rarely violent, but it seemed impossible to imagine that there were two separate groups at work, one who had stolen those guns at the same time that the other was trying to hack into the network of—what? An accountant's office? A pharmaceutical company? No way. Too much coincidence.

Mei was betting that they were dealing with a computer criminal who was both highly technical but also had an affinity for violence. That was a new combination for her. Criminals tended to focus and specialize. In her experience, a multi-departmental investigation usually involved a fugitive or perhaps drugs. A couple years back, Mei worked a white-collar crime where the perp had killed his wife and her sister but never anything like this.

Mei reached the elevator and punched the down button. The phone in her pocket buzzed as the doors opened. She drew it out and saw Andy's name. She hesitated a moment, then sent the call to voicemail and slid the phone back into her pocket.

Sydney was typing on her phone as the two women stepped into the empty elevator. "I swear I don't know how these kids are going to survive college if they can't take a list and manage to come home with groceries."

"Your kids?" Mei asked. She was antsy and not a fan of the department's elevators, which were ancient and creaky and frustratingly slow, especially compared to the ones at the FBI.

"I've got twins starting at San Francisco State," Sydney said, pocketing her own phone.

Above the elevator doors, the red light bled from 2 to 1 as the box descended with a series of groaning noises. "An empty nest," Mei said.

"Hardly," Sydney said, laughing. "We've got a two-and-a half-year-old."

Mei shifted on her feet in the small space, hoping they wouldn't have to stop on the department's main floor. No such luck. The elevator lurched to a halt on 1 and the bell rang. She was about to say something inane about having college-age kids and a toddler when the doors began to stutter open. From the lobby, Mei heard the unmistakable rat-a-tat of the rapid gunfire of an automatic weapon.

CHAPTER 8

AFTER A SHOWER, a beer, and three hours of sleep, J.T. was on the move again. From the age of thirteen, sleep and J.T. had pretty much parted ways. A mother who drank too much and men of all sorts coming and going required a level of alertness that didn't mesh well with sleep. The best nights were the ones when J.T.'s mother drank and passed out before dinner. Or the times when J.T. took a blanket and hid in the low cupboards of the garage, but that only worked when the weather was warm.

Alert enough on a few hours of rest, J.T. continued with the plan. The first step had been to transfer the guns into the new white van. The black van was officially out of commission. It likely would have been anyway as it had been the plan to dispose of both Hank and eventually Sam before the fire, but Hank had gone a little sooner than expected. Sam had been sleeping when J.T. returned, which was odd as Sam was usually a night owl, but it made things easier too. It meant Sam hadn't heard the gunshot that killed Hank. Even with a silencer, a gunshot was loud. It also meant Sam wasn't around to ask a lot of questions while J.T. moved things around. The black van into the far garage, the one Sam couldn't access. No use letting Sam get wind of Hank's death. He was only a kid after all. It also meant there was no opportunity to ask Sam about progress, but since he was asleep, there likely hadn't been much. Another delay. Nothing to get upset about.

Plans were meant to be changed. This, J.T. always counted on. Like stepfather number three: Martin Lockston in his fancy suit with his graying temples and his supposedly great job. No more than an abusive drunk with a couple of diplomas. Things changed, and people either adjusted or they got trapped as victims. J.T.'s mother was the kind to get trapped, but J.T. was not.

Some of the guns still had a bit of Hank's blood on them, but not enough to bother cleaning off. Most of the blood ended up on the gloves J.T. had worn to package them. The gloves were just something else to be added to the fire pile.

The white van was utility style and new with solid rear door panels, like the kind small companies used for deliveries. On the outside of the van was a magnet with the FedEx logo, ordered eight months before off a cheap sign place online, delivered to a PO Box that hadn't been active since. It certainly wouldn't fool the FedEx office, but it would be enough for most. That and the dorky navy outfit J.T. wore, which J.T. had stolen from a FedEx facility nearly a year prior.

The rear of the van was filled with special FedEx tubes, meant for thick rolls of architectural plans but large enough to hold many of the guns. The huge MKs and such had to go in a different style box, but J.T. had these as well. It was all about planning. And clean up. These were things J.T. excelled at.

The first three deliveries were done by 4:00 a.m. Then three more before 6:00 a.m. It had taken a while before Jacob appeared at the school dumpster. Jacob was an unexpected addition. J.T. had even planted the seed for Jacob, telling him that the school dumpster was a good spot to find yesterday's leftovers.

J.T. had been that kid in high school, anything to avoid going home to Martin and his faux snakeskin belt. Originally, it seemed like a good idea to put those seventy-two guns in seventy-two needy hands, but that was more effort than it was worth. Not to mention more risk. Seven was enough to make the point.

The others could get out there without so much effort, and J.T. had just the person in mind to unload them.

CHAPTER 9

FROM SOMEWHERE ABOVE came the raining ting sound of shattering glass. Sydney Blanchard went down first, sliding into Mei's legs as she dove for cover. Mei dropped, too, and pressed herself against the cold elevator wall. Another burst of bullets, high frequency, tinny like an automatic weapon. Then the heavy sound of return fire. Beyond the elevator, two men in suits ran toward the courtrooms while a female patrol officer, gun drawn, went toward the main door. Another shot rang out, and a woman screamed close by. Mei looked to Sydney, but the sound wasn't from her.

"Help," came a soft voice. Mei dropped to her knees and darted her head out the elevator doors. A woman knelt outside the elevator. Vaguely familiar, she might have worked in the department.

Another shot rang out over their heads. Mei flinched before reaching her hand out. "Come on."

The woman looked up, dazed.

"Come on," Mei repeated more emphatically. Her pulse was like waves filling her ears.

Her face was pale and attractive, her expression

tightened up in pain. Mei waved her hand in a rolling motion. "Get on. Hurry." The woman crawled into the elevator. As soon as she was close enough, Mei pulled her toward the door.

"Sophie," Sydney said, reaching out to help. "Are you okay?"

The woman didn't answer but clasped her hands around Mei's as Mei and Sydney pulled her inside.

As soon as she was over the threshold inside, Mei stood tall on her knees and jabbed at the door close button.

Another shot rang out. The woman flinched against her. Mei put an arm around her, the two of them sharing the tight corner. They watched the doors close. *Don't let him come in. Whoever he is, don't let him come in.* When the doors finally shut, the three women remained as they were, silent. Still pressed to Mei, the woman shivered as the elevator lurched to the basement. When the doors opened, no one moved until they were reassured by the long quiet of the basement hallway.

Sydney was the first to get to her feet. "Let's get out of here."

Mei helped the stranger to her feet. Sydney took hold of her arm and gasped. "Sophie, you're shot."

Sophie blinked slowly as though she didn't recognize her own name.

Mei felt her start to fall and reached around to hold her. Sydney took her other side, and together they carried her into the hall. Their offices were down another hallway, so instead of moving her farther, they lowered her to the floor against one of the basement's yellow walls.

Her breathing was shallow. Her white blouse was

stained red on her left side from the bottom of her ribs down. There was a hole in the back.

"Mark is here, too," Sydney said.

"I'm sure he's okay," Mei said, sure of nothing of the sort. She pulled her phone out and dialed 9-1-1. "This is Officer Ling. We're in the basement of 950 Bryant, just outside the lab. We have a—" She glanced at the woman's attire, unsure if she was a detective or an attorney or what? "A woman's been shot. She's bleeding."

"I need to try to reach him."

Mei nodded.

Sydney seemed to be unsure of what to do next.

"Call him," Mei said, holding her hand over her own phone.

"We have ambulances en route," the dispatcher said.

Mei watched as Sydney dialed. A moment passed while she said nothing. Then she lowered the phone, hit another button, and lifted it to her ear again.

"Are there any casualties upstairs?" Mei asked Dispatch.

"I'm not sure yet, but officers are still searching for the shooter."

"He got away?" Mei said. How the hell did a shooter get away from a building full of cops? And what kind of crazy person took aim on a police department?

"Don't hang up," Dispatch said. "I'll be right back with the status of that ambulance."

Sydney looked up and shook her head, a look of panic on her face. "I can't reach Mark."

"I'm sure he's fine."

"This is when he goes to lunch. He might've been on the street outside or coming back."

Sophie was paler. "Help me get her onto her back," said Mei as she shrugged out of her jacket and balled it up on the ground. With Sydney's help, they lowered Sophie onto the makeshift pillow.

Sydney hit Send again.

"Sophie," Mei said. Sophie looked up at her and Mei noticed that straight-on she looked a bit like Jodi with her hazel eyes and blondish hair. The same small, perky, Anglo-Saxon nose that always made Mei jealous. Her fuller lips. "Can you hear me?"

Sophie nodded. Her eyes fluttered closed.

"Stay awake with me, okay?" Mei took her hand. "Squeeze my hand if you understand."

Mei felt the squeeze.

Sydney shook her head again.

"Go find him," Mei told her.

She seemed to be holding her breath. Sydney's husband, Mark, was an accountant in the finance office, not a police officer. The wives of officers expected this kind of risk, this fear, but not the wives of the administrative officers. What place could be safer than inside these walls? What kind of idiot would open fire in the lobby of the police department? And how had he gotten through the metal detectors?

For a moment, Sydney didn't move.

"Go," Mei commanded. "The ambulance is on its way."

Sydney looked from Mei to Sophie then back again.

"Go," Mei said again. "Text me when you find him."

Sydney blinked, and her eyes met Mei's. With a brief nod, she turned and ran for the stairwell.

"Officer," came the dispatcher.

"Yes. I'm here."

"Your ambulance is en route. ETA is four minutes."

"Okay, we're in the basement."

"They know. Hold the line."

Sophie's eyes closed again. Mei touched the side of her shirt, but the blood stain hadn't grown much. "You're doing great."

Sophie squeezed Mei's hand again.

Mei studied her face. "Where do I know you from?"

Sophie tried a smile, but it stalled on her lips.

"You work in the department, don't you?"

Sophie squeezed. Mei wasn't sure it was appropriate to ask a lot of questions, but maybe it would keep her distracted until the paramedics arrived.

"Finance?"

Two squeezes. "That's a no, then?"

One squeeze.

"Police officer?"

Two squeezes.

"Detective."

Another two.

Mei made unsuccessful guesses until she heard the drumming of feet on the stairwell. The metal fire door sailed open and slapped against the wall. Two paramedics set a gurney down and pulled it to full height, then jogged it down the corridor.

They were both tall, thin men. One was white-blond that had to be real because he had the kind of skin that got sunburned in minutes and never tanned. It was now a deep, uncomfortable shade of red. He'd obviously been somewhere other than the city to get that burned. "We've got this," he announced, waving a hand as though to clear her from the area.

Mei hesitated.

The other man was dark-haired with a kind of hooked nose and a thin, small mouth that seemed almost circular. "A little space, please," he added.

Mei stood and pried her hand from Sophie's.

They huddled over her. Checking pulse ox, heart rate, things Mei had seen done a million times on cop shows. This was the first time she'd seen it in person. Before she could ask how Sophie was, they'd lifted her on the gurney. "Clear to come up?" the hooked nose one asked into the radio.

"All clear," came the response.

The other paramedic pressed the button to call the elevator. It came faster than it had the last time, and Mei was caught off guard as the doors started to close again before she could join them.

"Wait. I'll come with you," Mei said, reaching.

"Are you family?" small pursed lips asked from under the hooked nose.

"No."

The sunburned one shook his head, making little white lines in the burn as he moved. "Sorry, then. Can't take you. You can call the hospital and see how she's doing."

"Where are you going?"

"General," Sunburn said just as the doors met with a little thump.

Mei turned back to retrieve her jacket and her phone.

"Officer Ling?" The dispatcher's voice sounded a little urgent.

"Yes, I'm here."

"The paramedics are there?"

"They just left with her."

"Good. You need anything else?"

Mei shook her head then realized she hadn't spoken. "No. Thanks."

The dispatcher hung up without another word. Mei reached down for her jacket and shook it out before pulling it slowly over her shoulders. Just then, her phone buzzed with a text from Sydney. *He's fine. Was at lunch without his phone. Sophie?*

Ignoring an incoming call from her mother, Mei texted Sydney that Sophie was on her way to the hospital. The message went out with a little whoosh as she looked up and down the corridor. She needed to go look at the computer from the police warehouse, but she couldn't get herself to move in that direction. Her heart was still racing. She needed to call Andy. He'd know about this soon if he didn't already.

What she really needed was a walk.

Mei headed for the stairwell and climbed the stairs slowly, steadily moving in the direction of out. As a kid, she'd often walked as a way of clearing her head. Her parents owned a small two-bedroom apartment above her father's accounting office in Chicago's Chinatown. As Mei made her way home from school, the streets had always been filled with women carrying pink plastic bags. Every shop used the same plastic sacks, so a woman might have white cotton underwear in one bag and a dead fish in another. It made every woman seem interchangeable and, to Mei, boring. Her sisters were always anxious to go straight home where, most days, their mother would be watching one of the long-running Chinese dramas on television.

In particular, Mei's mother had been crazy about the Kangxi Dynasty series, never missing an episode, which meant Mei's older sister, Man Yee, and her younger sister, Lai, got to watch, too. The house only had one television, and it sat in the room that was both the living room and family room. With no walls between it and the kitchen, there was no way to keep the girls from watching without sending them to their bedroom.

None of it interested Mei. Instead, she preferred to walk the fifteen minutes it took her, even on short legs, to get from their house off 24th to any place outside Chinatown. By the time she was in high school at Lake View, Mei was spending as many afternoons as possible at school to avoid going home. It was at the library where she first met Jodi, seated on the floor in the aisles of YA fiction just minutes before it was due to close, neither of them wanting to go home.

All those years, Mei had assumed that it was the tradition that she wanted away from. She blamed the Chinese heritage and its rigid rules. She wanted to be an American—a real American—like Jodi and girls who looked like her with their wide-set eyes and their blond hair. While Man Yee and Lai wanted nothing to do with school sports or clubs, Mei used activities as an excuse to be away from home and from Chinatown as often as possible. Mei's parents encouraged her to participate in school activities, always nudging her away from sports toward math club or the school's finance committee. Acting the part of the dutiful daughter, Mei joined those groups or others, though she rarely attended their meetings.

Instead, Jodi and Mei took the train and headed in one direction or another after school. They saw movies or hung out at a little run-down diner a mile or so from school. On days when both of Jodi's parents were working late and her older brother was sure to be out, they went to her house. Only once had Mei brought Jodi home. For months, Jodi had been begging to meet Mei's mother and sisters. One spring afternoon, after getting caught in a rainstorm, the two girls had taken the bus to Chinatown.

Mei realized her error in judgment before they were in the door. Jodi's hair had a bright bleached streak down one side. Her left ear was pierced three times; the jean shorts she wore barely covered her backside while her tank top rode up around her middle, exposing a wide stripe of white midsection. Her mother's dislike was both obvious and instant.

After twenty minutes of her mother's stony silence, Jodi left. The following day, Mei's father had announced his disappointment in her choice of friends. Jodi's name was never mentioned out loud and her father offered no explanation for what it was about her friend that had offended them, but Mei knew. She had been naive to think her mother could see beyond Jodi's clothes or, worse, her race.

For weeks, Mei's father made sure Mei was too busy to see Jodi or anyone else. Mei came to his office straight after school and did her work at the small table in his office or—when he was with clients—on the floor in the room he used for file storage. When she finished early, he put her to work filing or copying or cleaning out the little refrigerator where he stored his lunch of her mother's leftovers.

Some weeks later, her father finally loosened the reins. Perhaps he assumed that Jodi was just a passing phase; maybe she had even promised him that they were no longer friends. She didn't remember exactly. What she did remember was that Jodi was the only friend she ever brought home until Andy. She brought him home only because she knew her parents would approve. Early in their relationship, Mei thought about how much her parents would like him. Had her parents' approval subconsciously weighed into her decision to marry him? The only person they had ever approved of. How, then, would they react if she told them that she no longer wanted to be married to him?

No, they would never understand that. Mei paused only long enough to send a text to Andy.

Am OK. Needed here. Will call when I can.

She pocketed the phone and left through the back of the building to avoid the lobby scene. On the front sidewalk, half a dozen patrol officers interviewed bystanders. Paramedics were checking reflexes on the last of the victims who were seated on the department's front steps. No wounds evident, so likely they were suffering from shock.

That was surely what Mei felt, too. One stopped Mei on her way out, but Mei assured him she was nowhere near the action. Others appeared to be waiting, perhaps for family or friends to arrive and take them home. She knew there would be a press release and changes to security measures, a whole backlash from the event. At the FBI, she could have predicted what it would be. First, Davidson, the Special Agent in Charge of their field office, would give a talk and start with a brash statement about those few citizens who made this perfect country imperfect. Then, he would outline, ad nauseam, the ways in which processes were already in motion so that this kind of travesty could never happen again.

Davidson would use the term "travesty" at least three times, as it was his favorite word. That and "reckless"—the reckless disregard with which these perpetrators had... blah blah blah. But today, Mei had no idea how things would go. She knew the chief of police by sight but had never heard her speak and had no idea what kind of promises she might make, what kind of threats she would launch at those who took aim at her department.

As Mei breathed in the cool San Francisco air, she wished she could walk the familiar streets of Chicago. Even the pungent smells of Chinatown would have offered the reassurance of normalcy. Accustomed to spending a good deal of time alone, Mei felt lonely in this strange city. Not that she would admit that to Andy. Or to anyone. How could she? Meeting new friends meant opening herself up, letting people in on who she was and what she wanted. How could she do that when she didn't even know?

Short on time, Mei made a loop around the area across from the department and returned ten minutes later. She wanted to walk farther, but it would have to wait. For now, she needed to find out whatever she could about the computer they'd found in the warehouse. Whoever left it was likely the same person who'd stolen seventy-plus guns and was now spreading them out across the city.

As she stepped back up the stairs of the department, her phone rang. "Nah ho ma, A Mā," Mei said, greeting her mother.

Mei was surprised to hear her father's voice. "Someone fired a gun in your department?" he asked.

"I wasn't there, A Bàh," she lied.

"But there was a shooting in your building?"

"Yes."

There was a pause as her father explained this all to her mother. "You are all right?"

"I'm fine, A Bàh."

Her father exhaled, a long slow breath. "You didn't call to let us know."

She felt selfish. "I'm sorry. I've been dealing with the scene," she lied.

The response was one of those small noises that Mei thought meant he didn't believe her. "Andy is there?" he asked.

"Yes. He came in last night."

"Good. You should be together."

Mei said nothing.

"And we are very relieved that you are all right," he added.

Mei thought of her father's parables, the incessant one-liners highlighting best practices. The one she remembered hearing the most as a child was: respect for one's parents is the highest duty of civil life. "Thanks, A Bàh. I should get back."

Other than his parables, her father was a quiet man,

but he made a sound that was as familiar to her as words. While her mother seemed always to use as many words as possible to express herself, her father needed only that one sound. Mei understood it perfectly. It meant he was unhappy with her life decisions. Again.

CHAPTER 10

DWAYNE PARKED ON 7th Avenue, around the corner from the station, and checked the street signs a second time to be sure he was parking legally before heading to the back of the truck. This was his least favorite stop. What were the odds that the company he worked for would be the one to provide personalized letterhead, envelopes, and business cards to the entire San Francisco Police Department? It wasn't a slow business, either. There was no end to the people the department was bringing in. Budget cuts should have slowed things down, but Dwayne was still delivering here at least twice a week without fail.

He'd never been arrested in San Francisco, but he had spent time in prison. After that, every police station made his skin crawl and his stomach roll. He'd been in the wrong place at the wrong time. That was what it was, but it didn't make any difference in the end. And he wasn't arguing either. He'd been in the passenger's seat when someone had fired on the car. The guys in the back had a couple AKs and shot back. Dwayne wasn't telling them to stop. Someone fired on you, you fired back. That was how things worked.

Thankfully, they hadn't shot anyone, but a little girl had been playing and her ball rolled into the street. The driver didn't even see her, ran the car right over her. Dwayne served twenty-two months of a six-year term. He'd used the time to get smart, but that fact didn't make police stations any less terrifying. Getting text messages from some guy trying to get him to bite on some bullshit story and a truckload of guns didn't help. The last text was, *Maybe you'll change your mind.* Hell, no.

Dwayne loaded his handcart and locked the back of the truck. The cart Rhonda sent him with always wanted to pull to the right, so Dwayne walked on the left side to fight it into going straight. The sidewalk in front of the station on Bryant was busy and Dwayne stopped several times to let a group of two or three cops walk past. They nodded at him, but it wasn't always clear that it was in gratitude.

Some of them seemed to be saying, "Yeah, you'd better get the hell out of my way." Black, white, Asian, Latino, they all looked at him funny. Like they knew. He saw the guys in prison with tats across their knuckles. What kind of dumbass branded his hands to announce he'd been inside? And despite his regular, unmarked hands, it seemed like they still knew he'd done time.

He rolled the cart up the ramp and into the lobby. There were a few people waiting in line for the metal detector. An older guy backed out of the arches and reached into his pocket, pulling out a handful of change and keys before going through again.

Dwayne looked at his list of deliveries. One on the first floor, two on the second, and the last one was in the basement. Crime Scene Unit, but not like the guys on TV. No one was running around down there breaking open cases from what he could see. It took less than ten minutes to do his deliveries and he was happy to be on his way out again. Not to mention, there was no way Rhonda could bitch about him being slow. Not that Rhonda was the reason he moved so fast in there.

As he came back past the metal detectors, he saw the line had grown. A nice-looking woman waved her badge and crossed through the second metal detector, the one reserved for department employees. As she raised her hand, Dwayne could see the creamy curve of her breasts through the gaps in her button-down. He stared until she glanced over at him. She smiled. "Morning."

"Morning," he responded, following her with his eyes as she walked out of view.

"Move along," the guard yelled over to him, and Dwayne shook his head as he pulled the cart out the main doors of the department. "Enjoying the view ain't a crime," he muttered under his breath.

He led the empty cart straight down the stairs instead of taking the ramp. As he reached the bottom stair, his phone vibrated in his pocket. He pulled it out and read the text message.

Enjoy. More where this came from.

"What the hell?" He looked around and put the phone back in his pocket. Screw that. How the hell did this guy get his number? Or maybe this was Rhonda. He could see her trying something like this, just to trip him up. Except Rhonda didn't seem smart enough.

He was just putting his phone back into his pocket when he heard the low thunder of gunfire. He dropped the cart and rolled into the line of bushes that ran along the side of the department. His handcart clattered to the ground beside him, just missing his phone. People screamed. There was more gunfire. Cops ran past him with their weapons drawn. Dwayne didn't move for several minutes. He started to see people walk by, looking over their shoulder, and he got up, too, wanting to be as far from there as possible. The gunfire had come from inside, someone said. Someone was inside the police department, firing a gun.

Dwayne brushed himself off as he hurried toward the van. He tried not to run, but found it was too hard to walk. By the time he got to the van, he was short-winded and sweating. Instead of opening the back, he loaded the handcart behind his seat and pulled himself into the truck. He started the engine and switched the A/C on high, then pulled away from the curb. He made a left turn on Harrison, away from the department and only after he'd driven a couple blocks did he finally start to relax.

His phone rang. Rhonda. He debated answering it, but decided he'd better.

"Hey, Rhonda."

"Dwayne? Where are you?"

"Heading to Cesar Chavez," he told her, wondering why she was still on his back.

"We got the news on. They showing a video from

someone's phone about people shooting at the police department. You okay?"

Dwayne swallowed, pressing down the panic that was still rattling around his chest. "Yeah. I'm fine. I left there awhile back."

"You're lucky," Rhonda said, then to someone else, "No. He's all right. He's already done at the station."

Dwayne told her he'd see her soon. As soon as he hung up, he pulled over to the curb and put the truck in park. He wiped both palms across his sweaty face and dried them on his pant legs. It was only then that he noticed the oversized white FedEx tube propped behind the passenger's seat. They never used FedEx boxes for deliveries, and that box hadn't been there when he left the warehouse. Dwayne opened the truck's door and started to get out. A car blared its horn and swerved into the oncoming lane to avoid hitting him. Dwayne felt sick to his stomach as he rounded the front of the truck to the passenger's side and glanced through the glass.

"Screw me," he whispered and pulled the door open. On the side of the box, someone had written one word in black marker: Kalashnikov. Another name for an AK-47.

He opened the FedEx box and found himself staring down the barrel of an AK-47. He looked around to make sure he was alone and slid the gun out. It was a beauty all right. Last time he saw one of these, it sold for almost two grand. It took him more than two months to make that now, not counting taxes.

He slid the gun back into the box and climbed back into the truck. Revving the engine, he already knew he was going to screw up. He continued on Harrison to the onramp for 101 South. At the Potrero Street exit, he should have turned left toward Cesar Chavez. Instead, he went right up Potrero to 24th and drove west to South Van Ness. Queen Pin was only a few miles off his route to Cesar Chavez.

It wouldn't be hard to convince Tina to watch his package, for a price. And her kid could run through it for any tracking shit. If nothing came of it in a week or so, he'd find it a nice home, pocket a little extra cash. No harm done. Just this once.

He lifted his phone to dial Tina when he saw another text message.

Believe me now? Tommy wants to go home with you too.

Dwayne wondered what a Tommy gun would fetch.

"You a stupid asshole, Dwayne," he said to himself. "A stupid, stupid asshole." Maybe just these two. He started to turn into the Queen's lot. Tina was standing outside the side door, smoking a cigarette and talking on her phone. She was wearing neon green tights and leopard print shoes. It reminded him of the time she'd visited him inside.

When he asked her why she was dressed like a glow-stick, she told him that neon was all the rage. On the outside. Not something he could've known, since he wasn't on the outside. Hadn't been on the outside in almost two years. He didn't care about neon, but he wasn't going back in there. No way.

Without stopping, Dwayne made a U-turn and headed back to the police department. He used the sleeve of his shirt to wipe his prints off the box and continued driving until he was in the same parking space he'd been in when the gun had appeared.

He parallel parked and put the van in park. Without shutting off the engine, he reached across the gearshift and opened the passenger's side door. He gave the white box a kick and let it tumble out onto the street. Aside from a woman getting into her car about a half block down, the side street was quiet. Let someone else fool with getting arrested. He spun the truck around and headed toward Cesar Chavez, speeding to make up time. He was at least twenty minutes behind now and Rhonda was going to have his ass, but he wasn't going back inside. And that was something.

CHAPTER 11

MEI ENTERED THE building twenty minutes later, feeling worse. The aftershocks of fear had settled in, creating waves of something that felt like sickness. She'd been shot at. Sophie had been shot. She might have died. Beyond that, the call with her father had upset her. She was angry at the way he spoke to her, at his comment that it was a good thing Andy was here. Like she needed a keeper. She hated herself for allowing him to make her feel like she was a disappointment.

Worse yet, she was plagued by the reality that she *was* a disappointment to her parents. Maybe they didn't know it yet, but they would. There was no avoiding it. If she was going to live the life she wanted, her parents would find out. What would it be like with them after? Whatever happened, she'd have to find a way to accept—and make peace with—her decision and its consequences.

Back at the department, Mei went to the bathroom to wash her hands and face. The woman in the mirror was a stranger. Her eyes were dull with a hint of panic. Her black slacks were dusty from sitting on the floor of the elevator, and she had some sort of grease streak across her right sleeve. The lab had a shower space and lockers, but Mei had yet to bring a change of clothes. Instead, she crossed to the bathroom and scrubbed her hands, splashed cold water on her neck, which always grew red and speckled after a fight with her parents. Then she rolled up her shirtsleeves, dusted the dirt off her slacks, and marched into her office. No voicemails. There were a few administrative emails to respond to, but they could wait.

Down the hall, she entered the lab's main office where a young man was seated in one of the hardbacked orange chairs that, together with a handful of years-old magazines, made up their waiting area. No one else was around.

"Someone helping you?" Mei asked.

"Got a delivery." He stood up and slid a white box out from under the seat. He held it under his left arm and handed Mei a clipboard. "Sign on fourteen."

He checked her signature carefully before handing over the package. The package was addressed to Alice, the office secretary, so Mei left it on her desk and headed on into the computer lab. A central console took up the far corner of the space. Beside it was a flat screen large enough to fill Ayi's living room where they could project images from anywhere on the network.

Aaron Pollack was in his regular spot in front of the corner console, hunched over a Dell computer that had been seized as part of a killer-for-hire case. He didn't look up. Aaron had been on that computer for three days now, and Mei was starting to wonder what was taking so long. Questioning Aaron wasn't easy. He had been the second in charge in the computer lab since computer crime officially got its own division almost ten years earlier. When David

Tilley retired, Aaron had assumed the head job would be his. As had several other members of the team. Mei wasn't privy to all the reasons Aaron hadn't gotten the job, but some were obvious. While Aaron was a computer genius, his inability to communicate made working with him a challenge. Not to mention that he wrote emails without the use of any punctuation or capitalization, which made it seem like corresponding with a seven-year-old. Still, his GQ-esque looks and affinity for nice clothes made Aaron a sort of poster boy for the computer lab. Their sergeant, Grace Lanier, seemed particularly fond of him, and Mei's attempts to discuss her issues with Lanier had received a frosty response. Luckily, Aaron was very well suited to and very adept at his specialty, so Mei had little reason to manage him too closely.

At the moment, Mei was giving Aaron an especially wide berth as he adjusted to her presence. She'd all but stopped asking what he was working on, as any question, no matter how casual, seemed to make him feel like she was spying on him. This had come out after he'd called in sick three days in a row the month before, and one of the other lab techs, Amy Warner, had explained to Mei that all her questions were making his psoriasis act up.

"That and he's still taking the demotion kind of hard," Amy Warner told Mei, her eyes barely making it as high as Mei's knees, which was a feat considering that Amy was a few inches taller than Mei.

"Demotion?" Mei had asked.

"Well," Amy said, shrugging until it looked like her head might fit all the way down between her shoulders.

Mei wasn't surprised that Aaron was taking it hard,

but the team's support of him was harder for her to grasp. He was misanthropic to a fault and unpleasant even to those who considered him a friend. Despite that, the team was very protective of him. Mei had learned quickly that she had no ally in the lab when it came to the subject of Aaron or his myriad of quirks. Not that Mei wasn't used to that. Quirks were prevalent all across law enforcement, but they seemed particularly rampant in computer forensics.

"Morning, Aaron," she called out as she passed.

Aaron didn't look up but made a noise that, before Aaron, she would have called a grunt. Now, she recognized it as acknowledgement. She ought to get her dad and Aaron together sometime.

Her other two lab techs, Blake and Teddy, stood at the far table dressed in white coats and purple gloves. Between them was a computer that Mei assumed had come from the police storage facility. A small orange feather duster and a plastic container of matching orange powder sat on the table. As she approached, Mei could see the fine layer of fluorescent powder on the computer. Off to one side were the cell phone and battery pack that had been attached to the computer in the image Sydney had shown her. Both were covered in the same fine powder.

She picked up the camera and flipped through the images Teddy had taken. Images of the computer with the cell phone and battery bundled, from every angle. Nothing else. If there had been fingerprints, Teddy would have documented them.

Mei watched the light scan across the computer. Nothing lit up. They would begin with the computer's exterior then take it apart. She couldn't help but feel impatient. "No luck?"

"Nada," Blake said.

"Nope."

Holding only the edges, Blake turned the computer over, and Teddy scanned the bottom and each edge with his battle light. Blake then opened the computer to reveal the screen and keyboard. He dusted while Teddy waited with the light.

When they had searched the surface of the computer, Blake released the disk drive and they printed that. Nothing. Blake set the computer back down.

"You try a blue light?" Mei asked.

Teddy shook his head. "Not yet."

The blue light was used to check for biologicals like semen or urine. A computer wasn't necessarily a likely spot for either, but she'd seen stranger things. Teddy unscrewed the tip of his battle light and replaced the orange light with a blue one. The two men put on orange goggles. Mei used the third pair and watched as Teddy shined the blue light across each surface. Computer, cell phone, battery. Nothing.

Mei took a glove from the box on the table and pulled it onto her right hand. Tucking her left hand behind her as a matter of habit, she lifted the battery pack and turned it over with her right hand.

"Cool, right?" Blake said. He pointed to a spot of welding at one end with the working end of a very long, thin slot screwdriver.

"Homemade?" Mei said.

"Definitely," Blake agreed. "And well done."

"Guy knew what he was doing," Teddy added. "It's still got juice."

"LiPo," Blake said with awe.

"Right?" Teddy agreed.

She figured they were referring to the fact that the battery was lithium powered. Both Teddy and Blake had engineering degrees. She knew from his file that Teddy had spent some time in his late teens as a Black Hat, getting his start hacking into his school to change his grades. He went on to teach himself to hack into a few of his favorite online video games and give himself extra credits rather than buying them. Caught when the hacking escalated to adding his own credit card account to the automatic bill pay of the company where he had spent a summer internship, Teddy was a find for law enforcement because he still had some fingers in the Black Hat world.

Blake wasn't nearly as well versed in the hacking universe, but he had a mechanical engineering degree from Cal Poly, which made him very talented with the hardware. They were twenty-three and twenty-four, respectively, but, to Mei, they seemed much younger. Considering she was only thirty-two, the gap shouldn't have felt as large as it did.

The three took off their goggles, and Blake set the computer back down. "So, we have nothing," Mei said.

Teddy shook his head. "No."

"We'll take apart the battery pack and the jammer to see if there are any latents inside," Blake said. "I don't expect anything inside the computer or the cell phone since they don't appear altered, but we'll check."

"Any chance we can track the computer?"

"We can probably find out where it was purchased. Maybe we'll get lucky and find the buyer, but it's a cheap brand. Whoever sold it probably sells a lot of them," Blake said. "Couple hundred bucks."

"If that," Teddy pitched in.

"Totes," Blake agreed, using a vernacular Mei had just learned, short for "totally."

"The battery pack is homemade," Blake continued, "so we might get something there, but there are no unusual pieces."

"Right," Teddy agreed. "Everything here could've come from RadioShack."

"Or Walmart," Blake added.

"Exactly."

Mei wondered if there was any sense in separating the two of them to eliminate the echo. "How about registration on the computer?"

The two shook their heads in unison. "Nada," Teddy said.

"Nothing," Blake agreed.

"The phone?"

"Prepaid," Blake told her.

Before Teddy could agree, Mei cut in. "Let's try to find out where it was bought and get records on where it's been used. Any other numbers outgoing or incoming."

"I'll work on it now," Blake said.

"Then see if you can find out where the computer came from."

Blake nodded.

"Teddy, can you start it up and see if there's any trace of the programming?"

"Waste of time," Aaron announced from across the room.

"Right. It'll probably be wiped clean, but maybe we'll get lucky," Mei said.

"Not probably," Aaron said. "Definitely a waste of time." He hadn't turned away from the screen, his shoulders still hunched over the keyboard.

"Why so sure, Aaron?" Mei asked, trying not to sound frustrated. Maybe it was FBI versus police or maybe San Francisco versus Chicago, but she felt like she was in middle school around this group.

"Aaron, man, she's talking to you," Blake said.

Aaron spun around in his chair, wearing a smile. Aaron was not the stereotypical computer nerd. He was five-ten and well built. Most women probably thought he was good-looking. He wore his hair the way the guys did in GQ magazine at the moment—not that she read GQ other than in the grocery store line. It was cut close on the sides, longer up front, with a dab of gel to create a little lift right above his forehead. He dressed nicely, surprisingly metro, in button-downs that were pinstriped on the outside and had checks or paisley under the cuffs. She'd heard from a woman in the ballistics lab that he was quite the chick magnet, too. According to gossip, he was currently dating someone from the "San Francisco social scene," whatever that meant.

Despite that, Mei couldn't separate the sound of his voice from the spine-crawling reaction she had to the pompous nerds who were her peers as a computer science major at Northwestern. Amazing what links the brain made without conscious input.

Lover of the pregnant pause, Aaron waited until Mei asked again, "Why are you so sure?"

Aaron rose from his chair and pulled his white lab coat off a hook that hung over the edge of his cube. The professor coming to lecture. "Generic everything," he began.

"You mean the computer."

"An Acer, to be exact," Aaron said. "The most popular brand sold at Walmart, Kmart, and Target, among other retailers."

Mei hadn't had a chance to look at the brand name yet. "And the phone is a prepaid," she added.

"But not new," Aaron said, as though correcting her. "Probably picked up at a pawn shop, and I'd be willing to bet it hasn't been scrubbed. But whatever is on it isn't from this guy."

Mei looked over at the worn flip phone. It was true. It didn't look new. It would be near impossible to track a phone bought at a pawn shop.

Aaron straightened his shirtsleeves from under his jacket and crossed the room to her. "Not just that. I looked at the jammer. There's no personalization at all."

"There has to be something we can get from it."

Aaron crossed his arms and shook his head. "No," he said with utter certainty. "I'm afraid not."

"Someone wrote 'on' and 'off' on it. That's something."

Aaron shrugged. "Perhaps. If you find a way to match the handwriting."

Mei looked over to see Blake and Teddy nodding in agreement. "You could be right, Aaron," she said carefully. "This guy probably thinks he has us."

As suspected, Aaron frowned at her use of the plural. He certainly didn't want to be included in the group that was "had."

"Maybe he's smarter than we are," she went on.

Aaron's mouth fell open just slightly as though he'd just developed a bad taste.

Mei had to resist the urge to continue. Aaron wasn't dumb and baiting him with the idea that this was a puzzle he couldn't solve might land her straight on her face. Instead, she did what the FBI had trained her to do. Play to his ego. "What do you think is our best chance?"

Aaron seemed to relax. "I'd start with the battery pack. It's a three cell and the cells are held together with double-stick tape. It's hard to work with sticky tape wearing gloves. If we're lucky, there might be a print there."

"Good idea, Aaron."

Aaron nodded and turned back to his desk.

"I suggest checking the cell tabs, too," Mei told Blake. "Likely, there was some sort of hot glue used to insulate them. We might find something there."

"Good idea. I didn't think of the insulate," Blake said.

"Also, as I recall, there is an optimal temperature for LiPo batteries. If our guy used any type of heat sink or fan to keep it cool, there's a greater chance of being able to identify where that came from. Hard to build one of those yourself."

Mei glanced over to see Aaron watching her intently. As soon as she caught his eye, though, he turned back to his computer. Mei heard her phone's ringtone, a quacking duck.

"It's over here, I believe," Aaron said, motioning to

the empty workspace behind his desk. Mei crossed the room. The iPhone was bulky. Mei often set it down when her hands were full. She was going to have to get one of those goofy holsters for it before she lost it. Last week, it had ended up in the administrative office because she'd left it on the coffee cart. The screen showed a text from Ryaan Berry.

Meeting in TL conference room. You avail?

Mei responded. *TL?*

Triggerlock.

On my way.

Mei told Teddy and Blake that she was heading into a meeting and asked them to leave the components disassembled so she could see them when she came back. "Text me if you find anything."

On her way out the door, she ran into Amy Warner coming in with a carrier full of Starbucks coffees. "Oh," she said, her eyes on the floor.

"Hi, Amy. I'm going upstairs for a meeting."

Amy nodded dumbly, and Mei glanced at the coffees on her way out the door. Four of them. One for everyone but her. Eventually, she told herself. Eventually.

CHAPTER 12

J.T. HAD FOLLOWED the kid from the police station down Van Ness, then in reverse again. At first, it looked like maybe the kid had figured out he was being followed. Seeing Dwayne push the gun back out onto the street was surprising. People were usually more predictable than that. Still, it didn't change the plan. J.T. merely gathered the returned gun and dropped it, along with the rest of them, at a place where they were sure to be appreciated.

San Francisco was losing its edge in gang violence. Oakland was so much cheaper, after all. But there were still a few choice areas left. One of J.T.'s favorites was near the corner of Eddy and Mason in the Tenderloin. If Dwayne didn't appreciate the gift, certainly the kids there would. J.T. considered taking the load over without help. How fun to be like Santa delivering a bag of toys to all the kiddies.

It was only caution that prevented it. With the abundance of cell phone videos, the risk of being filmed was too great, even to enjoy the thrill on those young faces when the delivery was made. J.T. arranged to pay Karl six hundred in cash to drop them off late that night.

J.T. loaded the guns into a 1988 brown Ford Fiesta bought with cash in Arizona by Hank. J.T. had suggested that Hank register the car in his name and Hank, not the brightest or sharpest student, had agreed readily. He had liked the idea of owning all the cars, which J.T. offered as additional payment when the jobs were done. J.T. had registered the vans in his name for the same reason. Forfeited now, of course. But that wasn't J.T.'s fault. Hank had that coming.

Karl was to park the car, pop the trunk, and walk away. The vehicle's VIN had been removed, the plates were stolen. The keys and cash were under the driver's seat. It had taken J.T. the better part of an hour to load the guns and park the car in General Hospital's parking garage.

Guy's expecting a full delivery, J.T. had told Karl via text.

I never steal from the hand that feeds, Karl texted back.

J.T. was certain that wasn't true but left it at that. Likely, this would be the last interaction with Karl.

J.T. dropped the burner phone in a trashcan before catching the bus back to the apartment.

Dwayne, Karl, Hank, and Sam were cogs in the plan. The only one left to deal with was Sam and surely he would be done by now.

CHAPTER 13

RYAAN AND PATRICK were set up in the Trigger-lock conference room, which smelled of scrambled eggs and cheap breakfast sausage patties from that morning's captains meeting. Spots of half-dried orange juice made finding a clean spot on the table a challenge. Already one of Ryaan's forearms had stuck to the faux wood veneer.

Ryaan opened her file and pulled out the list of guns that had been stored in the facility at Oyster Point. Ten seconds later, Hailey Wyatt came through the door. Hal followed behind her, looking like he was not having an easy time keeping up. The sight of him rushing in behind a woman who was at least a foot shorter made Ryaan smile for the first time in hours.

Hal seemed to know what she was thinking. "She's faster than you'd think."

Hailey glanced between them without a word. "Six more shootings," she said out loud, although they already knew the count.

Ryaan nodded. She'd heard about the one downstairs. In the damn police department.

Mei pushed through the door in a rush. "Sorry I'm late."

Ryaan watched as she crossed the room and found an empty chair. She looked less pressed than usual. Mei glanced in her lap before adjusting her shoulders back and raising her head.

"Any word on injuries from this morning?" Patrick asked.

"Four wounded, no fatalities," Hal said.

"You see it, Mei?" Ryaan asked.

"No. But I was close. Sydney Blanchard and I were in the elevator. Doors opened on the main floor and we could hear it. We helped a victim onto the elevator. Sophie something. Sydney knew her."

"Sophie Turner," Hailey said. "She works in Administrative. Is she hurt?"

"Not sure. I stayed with her until the paramedics came."

Hailey nodded. "I'll find out how she's doing."

"Thanks," Mei said.

Patrick turned a page in his notebook. "We've identified the shooter from footage taken outside the station."

"How did that guy get away?" Mei asked.

Hal sighed. "Crazy, isn't it? The station is the last place we were ready to defend. Guy just slipped through the cracks and was gone."

"There's going to be some hell to pay," Patrick added.

A moment passed while Ryaan considered whose neck was on the chopping block for letting the shooter escape. Likely, they were all thinking the same thing. It wasn't theirs, she knew that much.

"Guy's name is Justin Sawicki," Patrick started again. "He's twenty-three. Applied to the department in '11, '12, and again this past March. He failed the test the first two times. This time, he passed the test but was turned down after a psych assessment."

"Any idea why?" Hailey asked.

"The recruiting officer I talked to was vague. All he told me was that Sawicki did three tours in Afghanistan."

No one had anything to add. Three tours might explain a failed psych exam.

"Watch the table," Ryaan warned Hailey before she set her notepad on the desk.

"What happened in here?"

"Captains meeting," Ryaan explained.

Hal grabbed a stack of paper towels from the end of the table and handed them to Hailey who laid them out like a tablecloth before setting the file down again.

"Okay, in order, we have Jacob Monaghan, fourteen, a sophomore at Lowell High School," said Hal, sticking a picture of Monaghan on the whiteboard. Kid didn't even look fourteen.

Ryaan thought of the pictures in her mother's living room. Of Antoine in his Christmas suit a month before he was killed, only thirteen when he was hit by a spray of bullets as regular in their New Orleans neighborhood as the spray from sprinklers was in others. Of Darryl with a basketball tucked under one arm, his gangly dark legs jettisoning out of a pair of frayed shorts. His hair was as big as the ball, his grin bright except for the space between his two front teeth. Her mother swore the picture was taken the day he was killed. The metal picture frame was blackened on the side where her mother had clung to it, grieving.

"Monaghan lost his grandmother about a week ago," Hal said. "No parents in the picture."

"How did the grandmother die?" Mei asked.

"Heart attack. In bed."

No one said anything for a moment.

"After Monaghan, we have Albert Jackson. Jackson is sixty-seven. Homeless, Vietnam vet, arrested a half-dozen times for indecent exposure—" Hal turned to Hailey. "You got a picture of him?"

She handed it over. Hal clicked his tongue. "I'll be damned. That's the guy from McDonald's."

Patrick looked up. "What?"

"You don't recognize him?" Hal asked.

The others shook their heads.

Hal laughed and scratched the top of his bald head. "He hangs out near that McDonald's down the block. He seems to have trouble keeping his pants up." No one said anything. "Guess you all don't eat at McDonald's." He looked around the table. "The guy seemed harmless."

There was a brief silence before Hailey spoke again. "So, Jackson had two weapons but only discharged one. Fired nine rounds at the bus depot. Didn't hit a single person."

"Nine rounds isn't much," Ryaan said. "How many were in his weapon?"

"Both magazines were fully loaded," Patrick said.

"AKs?"

He nodded.

"So, Jackson had sixty rounds. Why not shoot them?" Ryaan asked.

Hal checked the paperwork. "Witnesses say he fired the nine shots slowly and then set the guns down and started to walk away."

"And why is he all the way over at Sansome if he lives down here? And why only fire nine bullets out of sixty?" Hailey repeated.

No one answered.

Hailey made a note and looked up. "After Jackson, we have Sawicki?"

Patrick nodded. "Another vet."

"Can we connect him to Jackson? Maybe through some vet program?" Mei asked, her head down as she worked on her tablet with a stylus. She held it up so the others could see the bubble diagram. In each circle was a victim's name, and she was drawing dotted lines between them. Between Sawicki and Jackson was the word "vet."

Ryaan made a note. "I'll look into it."

"Sawicki had two weapons and fired from both. Twenty-seven rounds."

Hailey looked down. "Last on our list is Martha Witter, thirty-four."

Hal tacked up a picture of a woman smiling. Under one arm was a little boy, maybe seven, holding a basketball. "Her kid died two weeks ago," Hal told them.

"Of a toothache," Hailey added.

"A toothache?" Patrick said. "How the hell do you die from a toothache?"

"No insurance," Hailey said. "Kid had an untreated infection in a molar. Bacteria spread to his brain."

"And the mom didn't shoot the dentist?" Patrick said, then caught himself.

"No," Hal said soberly. "She shot herself. Left behind her husband who has been out of work since '09 and two other kids."

The room went still. Sometimes the heartaches were brutal.

Ryaan looked over Mei's diagram where she'd drawn a fourth bubble with Witter's name. "This list doesn't even make sense," said Ryaan.

"Unless this is all Sawicki's design," Mei offered.

"How so?" Patrick asked.

"Well, you've got a guy who didn't make it into the department. He's got a beef. What better way to get retribution than to throw a bunch of guns out on the street and create a mess for us to clean up?"

"But why be a shooter himself?" Hailey asked. "Why not just keep the guns going?"

"The psych assessment suggests he's not alltogether there," Patrick agreed. "Maybe it doesn't have to be logical."

"How many shots have been fired so far?" Mei asked.

"They're estimating forty-eight rounds fired in all," Ryaan said.

"Why do you ask?" Patrick said.

Mei nodded to the list Ryaan had. "I was wondering where the ammo came from. There's none listed in the warehouse inventory, is there?"

Ryaan shook her head. "Nope. Perp had to have bought it. We'll get the manufacturer information from the lab and see if we can track down where it was purchased."

Patrick made a note. "I'll go through Sawicki's credit

cards, track his whereabouts in the last few days, see if I can find something there."

"By some miracle, we've only had three fatalities," said Hal.

"It's possible that one of the AKs Jackson had was jammed. He never fired it. Ballistics is testing it," Patrick pointed out.

"Were the other guns fully loaded?" Ryaan asked.

Patrick nodded. "All but one."

"Which one?" Ryaan asked.

"Witter's," Patrick said.

"I'm thinking she got rid of the extra bullets," Hailey said. "In case one of the kids found the gun with the body."

No one argued. The logic made sense. The only mother in the room, Hailey would know better than any of them.

"It's not that many rounds fired if you figure six guns had thirty rounds each," Mei said.

"Well, Witter only shot herself," Hal said.

"The numbers are encouraging until you realize we've only found six of the seventy-plus weapons," Ryaan said. At that rate, they might easily have another twenty-five bodies. The thought made her sick. Triggerlock tended to attract officers who loved guns. That was not Ryaan.

"Anything useful on the computers?" Hailey asked Mei.

Mei's head came up. "Not yet. There are a few possibilities to track down some peripherals. No prints though." She glanced at her watch. "They should have some results on the programming by now, if there's anything left to find."

"Let's keep in touch, then."

Ryaan stood and gathered her papers as Patrick and Hal left the room talking. Mei had closed the cover to her tablet, but she remained seated.

"You okay?" Ryaan asked her.

"It's been a long day."

Hailey pushed in her chair. "This your first shooting?"

Mei nodded.

"Sophie Turner is fine," Hailey told her. "Her wound wasn't even from a bullet."

"It wasn't?"

Hailey shook her head. "A piece of debris, probably loosened by a bullet. She was lucky. Didn't even need stitches. Just a couple suture bandages. She'll be at work tomorrow."

"Good," Mei said.

"It gets easier," Hailey told her.

"Or else you learn to let it out, so it doesn't weigh you down," Ryaan added, thinking hers was the more truthful answer.

"Rookie Club dinner next week," Hailey told Mei. "You have to come."

"Maybe by then we'll have this thing cracked," Mei responded.

"I would definitely drink to that," Ryaan said.

"Me too," Hailey agreed.

The three women walked from the room in silence. It was a hell of a long shot to think they could solve this thing in a week, but some things were better left unsaid.

CHAPTER 14

MEI WENT DIRECTLY from Triggerlock to a meeting with Finance on the third and fourth quarter budgets and another with the captain of forensics, Lance Finlay, to discuss how to allocate the increasingly limited resources for her computer forensics group. When she finally surfaced from the meetings, she had forty-two emails waiting in her inbox. Mei decided they could wait until morning.

In the lab, Blake was still running test programs on the warehouse computer. It was nearly 6:00 and everybody else had left. "How's it going?"

He stood tall and rolled his neck. "I've been working on this thing all afternoon. I'll have to pull the battery apart tomorrow to start looking for prints."

"Maybe Amy can help you," Mei suggested.

"I think she's working on something for Aaron," Blake said without looking up. Of her team, Amy was the one Mei thought least qualified, and she always seemed to be working on something else. Often for Aaron.

"How much longer on this?" she asked.

Blake glanced up at the screen. "Says eighty-three minutes."

"Let's lock it up and go home. We'll check it in the morning."

One of the department's new toys was a walk-in, fire-proof safe with a whole bank of electrical outlets. Because so much of computer forensics required tedious processing, it was useful to be able to continue that process even when they weren't there. The "docking safe," as the team called it, enabled them to make forward motion without the risk of interrupting the chain of custody.

While Blake stored the computer, Mei looked over the pieces of the LiPo battery that had powered the computer and cell phone. At the sight of the heat sink, she felt a surge of satisfaction. "You find out where the heat sink came from?"

"Teddy's working on it. It's a deepcool mc3002 gx. He's requested a search for matching models for sale. We should hear back tomorrow. We should have some results on the glue then, too."

"Good. Thanks for your help today, Blake."

Blake nodded and began to pack up while Mei took out a glove and turned the pieces over, looking at the cells and the casing. The soldering was home done, and they might be able to learn something from the markings. The tape was still adhered to the individual batteries. They hadn't gotten around to dusting it for prints yet. Mei could do it herself, but she was tired tonight, unmotivated in a way that felt distinctly unusual for her. Plus, she was supposed to meet Andy and Ayi.

Blake was still getting everything put away for the night and, when he came to retrieve the battery pack, Mei moved her attention to the jammer. It, too, had been pulled into pieces, but more thoroughly than the battery pack. The aluminum box was open, the antennae off one side along with the nine-volt battery. The UHF connectors had been detached. What remained was the small mini-circuit, no bigger than a thumb drive and a fourth as thick. Mei used a penlight to shine in and look at the components.

The surface was free of dusting powder. Too small and uneven to capture a print. There appeared to be a drop of something inside. Maybe a glue of some sort, maybe not. She pulled a cotton swab out of one of the station's drawers and broke off the protective plastic top. Carefully, she swabbed the spot and returned the cotton swab into the cap, clicking the plastic down to seal it. She wrote the case number on the outside to drop it off at the lab on her way out.

"What'd you find?" Blake asked, returning from the safe.

"Not sure. Some sort of liquid inside."

"Maybe we'll get lucky and it'll be blood," Blake said, smiling.

"Not sure we'll get that lucky."

Blake gestured to the jammer. "You done? I can get it put away."

Mei looked down at it. Not quite ready to let go. The text message from Andy said he was meeting her at the restaurant at 6:30. If she left in the next five minutes, she would be on time. As much as she dreaded it, she had to go. There would be time tomorrow, she told herself. She pulled off the purple gloves and tossed them. "Thanks, Blake."

The two left the lab together; Mei crossed to Chem to leave her sample while Blake headed to the elevator. Sydney Blanchard was gone. Only a tech Mei didn't know was in the lab to log in the evidence. With a sigh, Mei left.

She walked down the quiet hallway and opened the door to the stairs, colliding with someone coming through the door from the opposite side.

"Oh, my God," Mei said, pulling the door open. "I'm so sorry."

On the other side was Sophie Turner. She held her nose.

"Are you okay?"

Sophie removed her hand and looked at it as though expecting blood. "Fine. You scared me. You must be in some hurry to get out of here." In her free hand, she held a bundle of Gerber daisies in bright colors.

"How do you feel?" Mei asked.

"Fine. It wasn't even a bullet," she said. "Doctors think it was something that came loose with a bullet."

"No stitches?"

Sophie raised her shirt. "Nope. Not even stitches."

Mei saw three thin strips of white bandages running across her side. She also noticed that Sophie wasn't wearing the same clothes.

"You changed?"

"I went home from the hospital and showered."

"Then you came back to work?"

Sophie smiled awkwardly. "Actually, I was just going to put these on your desk?"

Now it was Mei's turn to feel awkward. "My desk?"

"As a thank you. For today."

Mei felt the heat rise up her neck. "Wow. Thank you."

"It's nothing. I appreciate you staying with me. Offering to come in the ambulance and everything."

"They wouldn't let me."

Sophie nodded. "I know. But still." She handed Mei the flowers.

"Thank you. They're so bright."

"You heading out?" Sophie asked.

Mei nodded. The two women walked up the stairs together. There was nothing weird about a female coworker bringing her flowers after the ordeal earlier. That was what Mei was telling herself. Maybe it was a little strange that Sophie had come back to the station after being shot. But maybe she lived close by. She couldn't have known that Mei would still be here. Don't read so much into it, Mei scolded herself.

"You have plans tonight?" Sophie asked. Mei got the sense it was more than a casual question. "I'm having dinner with my... aunt." Mei stopped, unable to say the word "husband." No one in the department, or even in San Francisco, knew she was married.

Sophie didn't seem to notice the hesitation. "Maybe I could buy you dinner sometime."

Mei smiled, heat flushing her cheeks.

"As a thank you, I mean," Sophie added.

"Of course," Mei said. "I'd really like that."

"How about sushi? Thursday night?"

Andy would be in LA by Wednesday. Mei had no plans for Thursday night. "That sounds great," Mei said, both embarrassed and a little giddy. When was the last time someone asked her out? It wasn't a date. Just a thank you. But still…

"Great. Meet you after work? Say 6:00? I'll take you to Akiko. It's this great little place. I think it seats like ten people, but I know the owner's daughter. They make the most beautiful sushi."

"It's a date," Mei said. "I mean—"

Sophie touched her arm. "A date."

Before Mei could say anything else, Sophie headed down the hall toward the stairwell. Mei looked at the flowers and ducked back in the lab, setting them on her desk. It seemed smarter than bringing them to dinner with Andy.

Mei walked slowly toward the bus stop. It was warm with a breeze off the water, the most pleasant weather she'd experienced yet. Or maybe it wasn't the weather. Maybe it was the idea of a night out. No, not just a night out; she was having that tonight with Andy and Ayi.

The plans with Sophie were different. This was what she had come to San Francisco for: to explore the feelings she'd been hiding—even from herself—since she started dating Andy. Since before then. She didn't even know if she was attracted to Sophie, but the erratic fluttering in her stomach told her that there was something there.

CHAPTER 15

SAM WAS SLOW, much slower than he'd originally promised. All that would have been okay if he hadn't started asking about Hank. Unbeknownst to J.T., the two had originally made some plan to roll around in the money they made off the guns like a couple of apes. Sam had his ten thousand—in denominations of tens, fives, and ones just as he had requested—but he wanted to share the moment with Hank. Hank wasn't answering his cell phone.

"Hank was a little paranoid," J.T. had told Sam, not entirely untruthfully, when Sam would not let up about why Hank wasn't answering his phone. J.T. had already dumped it, otherwise a few text messages to Sam would have eliminated all this chatter. This was likely why Sam was taking longer. He might have been a genius with a computer, but he lacked the power of concentration above a first-grade level.

The first server was easy, according to Sam. Security would be looser at an architectural firm than at a pharmaceutical one. A few sets of stolen schematics filed on a drive somewhere and done. The doubt was established, and the police could spin on that.

This last part was the real deal, the goal. All the rest of it was just a game to keep the police occupied. It should have all been done by now. It seemed Sam hadn't expected this to be so tough, which planted a seed of doubt that Sam was the right person for the job. Lots of deep breathing over the past two days and now J.T. was ready to relax.

"I'm into the server. One of their IT idiots put a script, running as root, in the DMZ, and didn't sanitize their inputs. I just did a buffer overflow and gave myself root access," Sam explained, like he was lecturing a four-year-old. "I already installed a virus that corrupts the data when they make a backup or a copy."

"Sam, no need to explain. You and I both know it's too complicated for me."

Sam snorted his laugh. He loved it when J.T. reminded him of how smart he was.

"Just tell me when you're done."

"Right. Right. I could explain it to you, but it would take some serious time."

"We don't have that kind of time." It was true. J.T. understood only about two percent of what Sam said, but it was more than a little grating when Sam acted as though his little assignment made up the mastermind of the entire operation. "Now, I'm in the database server. They aren't even tracking logins. Vastly undersecured," Sam said scornfully, despite the fact that undersecured wasn't a word.

J.T. said nothing.

The snort again. "Okay, now I'm stopping the database replication and dropping the tables."

"Remember who you're talking to, Sam."

"Right. Maybe after. When Hank gets back, then I can explain it. Hank wants to understand it too, so I can explain it to you both at the same time."

"That would be great, Sam."

"I'm writing a script to check for any other copies." Sam couldn't help himself. He probably talked to himself on the shitter. Everything about being around Sam made it difficult not to just stand up and snap his neck. The way he acted as though everyone else was a total moron, but then proceeded to speak in a language that was reserved for the small percentage of people who spent one hundred hours or more every week playing online video games; his snort of a laugh; his thick jowl; the endless Big Gulp sodas; the dark fur that spilled out of the neck of his black T-shirt. And over his ears and the front of his shirt too. It was tempting to lean him back in his little swivel chair and take a straight razor to all that hair.

Plus, the smell. Whatever collection of trans fats and red dye number three that went into his body was leaching out into the air like poison. The small space made matters worse. There were no windows in the workspace, only a small desktop fan that had been working overtime for weeks.

"Okay, I'm there." His fat fingers clacked on the keys. "Running the script." A moment of silence passed. "Done."

"Done?"

"Should take about an hour and you'll have the results you want." Sam grinned, and J.T. gripped his shoulder.

Okay, J.T. thought. Maybe Sam deserved some credit. After all, he was very good. He'd spent his teen years ignored by his parents. His mother worked for Cisco, his father for Oracle, so while he lacked access to their attention, he never lacked access to computers. While most kids rebelled by taking out their dad's car and buying beer, Sam hacked into his parents' companies and sent emails with top-secret patent information and signatures like "We're out of milk" or "I want tacos for dinner."

Mostly, his parents did little to discourage him, other than making it very clear that he'd better not get caught. After all, if a thirteen-year-old kid could get into these networks, he was, first, brilliant and, second, saving the companies billions of dollars in potential losses at the hands of other hackers.

At the same time, what Sam's parents didn't know was that he was actually selling some of Cisco's and Oracle's less crucial systems information to competitors in order to amass a savings account that would reach several million before the end of high school. He rarely attended school. The truancy officers became such a nuisance that his mother finally enrolled him in an online homeschooling program which, rather than completing, Sam simply hacked into and gave himself perfect scores.

At thirty, Sam was estranged from his parents, wanted for questioning by at least six government agencies, and the best hacker money could buy. After tonight, Sam would also be history.

"Did you save me a Tommy gun?"

"Of course," J.T. told him. "Did you load the magazine?"

"I loaded three. Just like you showed me." Sam continued typing, then, like a child realizing he hadn't gotten what he wanted, stopped. "When will I get the gun?"

"I'll bring it up as soon as this is done."

The best way to ignore Sam was to practice breathing. A goofy-looking activity, to be sure, but it worked. Better on a comfortable mat or pillow, but even on the hard linoleum floor it worked. In for two, out for two. Silently. Normally, the ohm sound was especially helpful, but Sam needed to concentrate. The sooner Sam was done, the sooner his endless commentary ended.

Wearing earbuds made it look like there was music. Theoretically, this should have made Sam talk less, although it wasn't clear that it did. It did make his voice a little quieter, which was a pleasant adjustment. Not quite enough noise reduction to block out Sam's endless garble but that was not an option.

"An hour, then?" J.T. confirmed before turning to hole up in a corner and pretend to be busy with something. Anything to get a little distance from Sam, even if seven feet was the farthest possible.

Sam glanced at his watch. "Fifty-seven minutes."

J.T. glanced at the clock on Sam's monitor and had a thought. "I've got a good way to kill an hour."

Sam looked up.

"How about I let you try out one of those guns?"

Sam's mouth dropped open. "Really?"

"Really."

Sam jumped up. His thighs hit the table, sending him

back into his chair before he spun it around and launched himself out of it. Like a kid in a candy store.

"You have your magazines?"

He pulled the loaded clips from under a pile of trash and papers and handed one to J.T. "That's okay," J.T. said without touching it. "It looks perfect. You hang on to it."

J.T. grabbed the list and nodded toward the computer. "That thing can run on its own?"

"Oh, yeah," Sam assured J.T. "I don't need to do anything."

"Let's go then."

It looked like the kid was going to hug J.T. as they started out to the van. "Thank you, man," Sam said, gripping the magazine in his right fist like a trophy. "This is so cool. So, so cool."

CHAPTER 16

ANDY LEFT WEDNESDAY morning for a meeting in LA. Mei drove him to the airport in Ayi's car while he fielded calls on a case that had come up in Fort Worth, Texas. Their goodbye had been quick and anticlimactic. He was between phone calls, and they were going to see each other in less than three weeks when she went back to Chicago. For the two days he was there, Mei tried to tell him how she was feeling. Every pause in their conversation, she gathered her courage and, every time, she failed to find a way to start.

Then, on the way out of the restaurant the night before, a gay couple passed them on the street. The two women were holding hands. They stopped just down the street and kissed. Andy stared at them while Mei averted her eyes. She didn't want to see the look on his face. Maybe it was simple curiosity. Didn't all men supposedly love to watch women kiss? But what if it wasn't that?

She and Andy didn't have any gay friends. He didn't know about Jodi. Andy was open-minded and generous, but how would he possibly deal with the news that his wife wanted to be with a woman? He would feel betrayed.

The news would be devastating. How could it not be? Surely, it would make him question his life. His manhood. How could she possibly convince him that he was the most wonderful man she'd ever known? But it was just not enough.

Like hers, Andy's family was traditional. How would they react? What if they argued that gays could be "straightened out"? What would she do if they tried to convince her to try therapy or some crazy religion? Would Andy have to defend her against them? She couldn't bear to think about the impact this would have. Mei went to work, heavy with guilt. There were moments when she considered staying. How bad could a life with Andy be? And then came the sickening pit.

On the way out of the lab, Mei rewrapped the flowers from Sophie to take home. She'd considered leaving them at the lab, but she'd already deflected a couple of unwanted questions from Blake and Teddy. If Ayi asked, Mei would just say she'd bought them. On the way home, Mei stopped by Blush Wine Bar. She wasn't ready to talk to Ayi yet. Mei had gone to Blush hoping to catch Julie, but there was no sign of the architect. Though they were friendly, they were hardly friends. Maybe it was that Julie was Chinese that made it so easy to talk to her that one night. Whatever the reason, Mei could have used a friend right now, especially one without ties to the department.

Seated, Mei reached down to her bag instinctively but hesitated to pull out the computer. Once she did that, it would be tough to stop herself. She was here for one drink, then she had to go home to Ayi. That meant no computer. Instead, when the waitress brought her the glass of red wine, Mei leaned back against the smooth vanilla-colored clay wall and watched the other diners.

Several tables were occupied by older couples, one Mei had seen a few times before. They ate slowly, leaning in to talk and sharing bites across the table. The woman had a long, gray braid and the man a goatee in the same shade. They wore solid button-downs and khakis, and practical shoes, and moved with great patience and precision. The woman cut her meat in a slow, carving motion then returned the knife to the proper side of the plate, lifted her fork, prongs curved to the ceiling, and brought the small piece casually to her lips. Every bite. While she chewed, she looked up at her husband and smiled. He reached over to touch her hand, pausing a moment.

To some, they might have looked conventional, maybe even boring. But Mei envied them. She imagined they were the kind of people who had saved for retirement from their first paychecks. Either of them might be an accountant or a teacher. They had been married forty-plus years, had grown children, maybe even grandchildren. Loneliness washed over Mei. She wanted that kind of partnership. She wanted to raise children with someone, grow old with someone.

There had been a time in her relationship with Jodi where she'd convinced herself that her life would never be like Lai's or Man Yee's. There would be no children, no marriage and family. Jodi hadn't wanted children. Even the idea of marriage was unappealing to her. Mei had assimilated Jodi's views because she loved her. In truth, Mei didn't think it was possible to have both—to be in a long-term committed relationship, an enduring partnership, and have children if you were gay.

When Jodi left Chicago, Mei fell naturally back into mainstream life. She focused on school, then on getting into the academy. Her position at the FBI required total commitment. An alternative lifestyle would have posed a threat to her position. Or that was what she told herself. She avoided places where she and Jodi had gone and, in doing so, blocked herself off from meeting someone else. When she met Andy, it felt right. She genuinely loved him. She thought she could be happy with him and have the things she wanted. She could be married and have children and, best, she could be accepted. Wasn't that the perfect life?

With every passing day, Mei recognized that acceptance came at a very steep price, one she no longer felt willing to pay.

Watching the plates pass by, Mei finished her glass of wine. Butternut lasagna, a bowl of thick tomato-based soup, a salmon-topped salad. It all looked delicious. Her stomach grumbled. She debated ordering a salad, but it was already getting late.

She hailed a cab and, in an unusual spurt of luck, one stopped right in front of the bar. Mei immediately recognized the Asian woman who got out. "Julie!"

Julie turned and pushed the long hair away from her face. She wore a gray pantsuit and red heels. "Mei! Are you just getting here?"

Mei shook her head. "Leaving, actually." She caught the eye of the cab driver who waved her in impatiently.

"Shoot," Julie said. "Beautiful flowers. From an admirer?"

Mei blushed. "Just a friend."

"I'm going to send you my cousin's number. The realtor. For when you do decide to look for a place. I meant to do it today, but time got away from me."

"That would be great," Mei told her. Over drinks one evening, Mei had confessed to Julie that she'd love to find her own place. It was the only thing Mei had confessed, though she had been tempted to share more.

Julie waved. "Talk to you later."

Mei got in the cab and gave the driver Ayi's address. Before the cab had driven fifteen feet, her phone rang. "Ayi told me Andy is thinking of changing jobs," her mother said in lieu of a greeting.

"Hi, A Mā. Wow, news travels fast."

"So it's true? You're staying out in California?" The last word came out like something distasteful.

"A Mā, I don't know yet. Andy just met with the office here. We haven't made any decisions."

Her mother was quiet.

"What's wrong?" Mei asked.

"Nothing," her mother said quickly.

There was something her mother wasn't saying. "A Mā?"

"I just assumed you would be home when you started your family. Like your sisters."

"I don't know when I'm going to start a family." Mei took a quick breath and whispered, "A Mā, I'm not even sure I want to be married anymore." Maybe the courage came from the wine or from watching the couple in the bar, but the words just came out.

"What do you mean?" her mother whispered. "Did you two have a fight?"

The driver watched her in the rearview mirror. Mei gave him a hard stare until he looked away. "Nothing. Andy is great. He's smart and kind. I just—"

"Is there another... someone else?" her mother interrupted.

"No," Mei said. "Nothing like that."

"Did you tell Andy you felt this way?"

"No, A Mā. I haven't told anyone but you."

"Good, good." Her mother was still whispering. "Listen. All couples go through this, Mei. I remember it myself. Maybe even more for us women than the men. It is very normal. Do not make a decision in haste. Remember nature does not hurry, yet everything is accomplished."

Mei closed her eyes and thought about her mother's proverb. Wasn't nature the thing she was listening to?

"You are tired, Mei Ling," she went on. "They are working you too hard. Are you still at work?"

"No," Mei said. "I'm almost at the house now."

"Good. Get some rest and give it time. This will be better."

"Okay," Mei told her mother, unsure what else to say.

"Also, don't speak to your a bàh about this. He will not understand, and it will upset him."

"I won't." As Mei ended the call with her mother, she thought about her father. If hearing she wasn't happy in her marriage would upset him, she didn't want to consider how he would feel about the truth.

At Ayi's, Mei set her bag down and tucked the flowers on the floor behind the bag, out of view. She could hear Ayi in the kitchen, but rather than go in, Mei used the small half-bath to wash up first. "Néih hóu ma?" Mei asked Ayi. How are you?

Ayi searched her face carefully. "How are *you*?"

"Why do you say that?" Mei asked, confident she was walking into a trap.

"You are tired."

Mei frowned at her aunt's choice of words. The same words her mother had used. "You talked to my mom."

"Of course. She is my sister," she added, as though that explained it. Mei tried to remember the last time she had spoken to Man Yee or Lai.

"Come. Dinner is nearly ready." Ayi waved her hand and turned back to her mapo tofu, which smelled amazing. Tofu with ground beef and green onion and a special Chinese pepper powder, mapo tofu was one of Mei's favorite dishes.

Mei set the dining table and joined Ayi in the kitchen. "That smells amazing."

Ayi added pepper and tasted it, making a little sound of approval. Mei wondered if her mother had told Ayi what Mei had said about Andy. Could the two of them have had that conversation in the ten minutes after Mei hung up with her mother? Mei doubted it, but maybe she didn't know how close her mother and Ayi were. If Ayi knew, maybe Mei could talk to her. After all, Ayi had never married.

"Ready," Ayi announced. "You bring the rice."

Mei carried the covered pot of steamed rice to the

table. She pulled her chair out to sit as Ayi came into the room with enough mapo tofu to feed six.

As Ayi placed the ornate porcelain platter on the table, the huge expanse of the front plate glass window exploded.

CHAPTER 17

MEI DOVE FOR her aunt, hitting her just above the knees. The two of them went down. Mapo tofu was strewn across the carpet. A car engine revved on the street. Ayi screamed as another spray of bullets struck the wall above the table. The bullets ripped a line of holes in Ayi's gongbi print.

"Don't move," Mei commanded. The old woman looked like a small child as she pressed her face to the rug, gripping her fingers into the tight weave.

Mei's purse with her cell phone, the couch, even the flowers from Sophie were covered in shattered glass. She lifted Ayi's coffee table book on the Ming Dynasty and turned it upside down on the carpet. She put her hands on the book and pushed it through the broken glass, upended her purse, and grabbed her phone.

Mei pointed to the kitchen. "Go. Hurry!"

One of Ayi's brocade shoes had fallen off and, from the back, she was as small as a frightened child. Mei followed close behind, prepared to cover her aunt if the gunfire started up again. When they reached the kitchen, Ayi moved to the far corner and curled into a ball against the oven door. Mei sat beside her, closer to the door, and dialed 9-1-1.

"This is Officer Mei Ling. I want to report gunfire at my home."

Ayi began chattering in Mandarin, which Mei didn't speak, as Mei gave Dispatch the details and her address. Mei moved to retrieve the home phone off the kitchen counter and handed it to Ayi. "Do you know Hui's number?"

Her aunt took the phone and stared at it blankly.

"Call Hui," Mei pressed.

Ayi's small, bony fingers trembled as she pushed the buttons and handed the phone to Mei. Hui was a widow, with two grown boys, who lived three doors down. About Ayi's age, the two traveled together and had a standing date for shopping Saturday mornings. Hui answered on the second ring, speaking English, because Hui's native language was Mandarin. Mei explained what had happened.

"I'm coming now," Hui said, and Mei thought she might have hung up.

"No. Wait," Mei said quickly. "Wait until you see police cars. We don't know if he's still down there." A beat passed. "Hui?"

"I'll wait," the woman said softly. Mei hung up the phone and put her arm around her tiny, trembling aunt. "It will be okay, Ayi. The police are coming." She rocked the old woman slowly until the police arrived at her door.

When Mei let them in, Hui was right behind them. Mei pointed to the kitchen. A moment later, Ayi began to cry. The officers cleared the house, then worked to check the yard and canvass the neighborhood.

After sometime, Hui lured Ayi into the dining room, sat her on a chair far from the broken glass, and hovered over her like a Chinese bulldog. "She shouldn't be here. She can stay with me," Hui said more than once.

"The police will need to ask her what she saw," Mei said. "Then, Ayi, you should stay with Hui for a few days."

The two of them looked at Mei as though surprised Mei was in agreement that Ayi should move out.

"Yes," Hui said quickly. "Of course. She will stay with me."

After a brief hesitation, Ayi nodded as well.

"I'll make tea," Hui said and moved quickly into the kitchen. Ayi continued to cry softly, staring down into her hands. Mei tried to sit beside her but was too restless. "I'm so sorry, Ayi," she said and stood to check on the police's progress.

The patrol officers roped off the front of the house and the street before coming inside for statements. They were both young men, one Hispanic, one Korean, polite, to the point. Neither was familiar, not surprising, considering there were over two thousand officers in the San Francisco Police Department. They addressed Mei as Inspector Ling, so someone had told them who she was. Still, even the deference couldn't be confused with control. They could address her with whatever platitudes were deemed appropriate; she was the victim here.

The two men went through the same rundown Mei had heard on the TV shows she always thought were so unrealistic. They were sorry to have to do this. They knew this was a difficult time, but it was important that they try to obtain as much information as possible while the incident was still fresh. Any little thing might be helpful. Hui returned with tea for Ayi and sat beside her, urging her to drink, before asking Mei if she wanted anything. Mei declined. She should have been starving, but even the thought of Ayi's mapo tofu turned her stomach.

"Is there anyone who would want to harm you?" Officer Alvidrez asked.

Mei watched Ayi and Hui both turn to her. She realized the officers were both looking at her as well. "Nothing obvious," she responded. "I'm not working any high-profile cases or due to testify."

"I'm sure the inspector assigned to the case will want to circle back with you."

Mei nodded.

Officer Kil turned to Ayi. "And I assume no one would want to harm you?"

Hui frowned. "Of course not. She's just an old lady."

"Not that old," Ayi said, the crying halted.

The officers continued through the list. Ayi and Mei answered, while Hui pestered Ayi to drink her tea and occasionally asked how much longer this would take. When the police were done with Ayi, Hui helped her pack a bag, and one of the patrol officers escorted them down the block.

Mei was relieved to see them go. She had never witnessed either of her parents cry. They had both lost their parents and her father had buried his sister, but Mei had never witnessed a tear. The sound of Ayi's crying was deeply disturbing, as was the certainty that the gunshots were not meant for Ayi. Somehow, this was Mei's doing. She was the target.

Shortly after Ayi left, Sydney Blanchard arrived along with three techs. She looked like she always did. Freckled, without makeup, wearing a navy SFPD windbreaker over her uniform. Mei was short, but Sydney was smaller. Maybe five-three with narrow hips and shoulders but solidly built. Only the small lines around her eyes and mouth and a sprinkling of gray hair almost invisible in her reddish mane suggested Sydney wasn't a teenager.

"You okay?"

Mei sighed without responding.

"Sorry. Dumb question."

Mei said nothing.

"Any ideas?"

"None," Mei said.

"Ryaan's on her way."

"Sorry to get everyone up," Mei said.

Sydney laughed. "We were up at my house. The baby has an ear infection."

Mei glanced at the clock on Ayi's wall.

Sydney picked up her evidence case. "We'll get to work. Where did the slugs hit the wall?"

Mei pointed to where the bullets had torn through Ayi's gongbi of the mountain covered in snow.

"Ah. Bummer. How about where you were standing when the shots went off?"

Mei walked to the area where the mapo tofu covered the floor. She'd been closer to the front door. "Maybe here."

Sydney looked back at the street. Mei followed her

gaze. She could only see a thin section of the street and the far sidewalk. Had the gunman had her in his sights? Or was this more of a warning shot?

Sydney knelt down and put an orange marker at Mei's feet just as the front door opened. Ryaan stepped in. Unlike Sydney, Ryaan looked like she'd been asleep. As she crossed the room, Mei's guard began to slip.

"You okay?" Ryaan asked, taking hold of her arm.

Mei let out a little shake of her head.

"You see anything?"

"Nothing."

"He left the gun," Ryaan said.

"Left it?" Mei edged toward the window and looked down to where numbered orange stands marked evidence. The gun was marked with the number one. A patrol officer stood guard over it while a photographer documented its position.

Ryaan nodded.

"Is that unusual?"

Ryaan shrugged. "Happens sometimes if it's dirty, if the police can trace it to a recent homicide."

"What about ballistics?" asked Mei.

"We don't have any ballistics out for one like that in this county," Ryaan said. "Sydney's tech just checked. We'll expand the search beyond San Francisco and see what we find." Ryaan paused a beat and said, "It might be one from Oyster Point."

Mei crossed her arms. "Why do you say that?"

"I've got one like it on my list. I have to check the serial numbers."

"If it's from Oyster Point, then this was not a random attack," Mei said.

Ryaan held her gaze. "It seems unlikely."

Mei looked over at the line of bullets along the wall, glad Ayi hadn't heard that.

"We'll get someone over here to board up that window. Someone will be posted here tonight, too," Ryaan added.

Mei looked at the front window. She hadn't even thought about that. She imagined trying to sleep.

"Not for you," Ryaan said as though reading her mind. "You're coming home with me."

Mei looked at Ryaan, saw the resolve in her face. She wasn't going to argue. She didn't love staying in Ayi's house most nights, but she hated the idea tonight.

CHAPTER 18

DWAYNE WAS NOT sleeping well. Not since the incident with the gun. He never should have touched it. He was smarter than that. He wanted out of the old life. Dwayne had the day off, so he and Tamara had gone over to City College and walked around. Tamara had seen a couple people she knew, including one real book smart-looking guy who had given Dwayne a look like he was on the way out. Dwayne knew better than to talk to Tamara about it. She hated when he was jealous. She wasn't something to be owned or fought over. He'd learned that.

Just the fact that she would consider moving in together was monumental. She had gotten him the application forms for the college, helped him fill them out, and now he was a student. The two of them spent date nights studying in one of the libraries on campus, drinking coffees. Dwayne felt out of place in his low-rider jeans and T-shirt. While he pretended to study statistics, he took note of what other guys were wearing. Jeans like his but not so low and shirts with collars. People in his neighborhood would have made fun of them, calling them whitewash. These people weren't whitewash. They were well-dressed black folks and Dwayne thought they looked all right. He wondered what Tamara would say if he showed up in a collared shirt.

Dwayne looked up from his book and rubbed his eyes like he'd been focused on the problems in front of him. Math was always his best subject, but he was struggling tonight.

Tamara stretched her arms above her head. "I'm hungry."

"Let's go get something to eat," he said.

"Finish your practice test first," she said, pointing back to his book.

"Sure, baby." Dwayne pulled the book toward him and read the word problem again. *A fair, six-sided die is tossed. What is the probability the first 3 occurs on the fourth roll?* Dwayne couldn't see how this would ever be something he'd need to know. He wasn't going to Vegas. Still, he could do this. He wrote down, "Fourth roll = 3." Okay, so what about those first three. Six sides on a die. He could get anything but a 3, so that was 5 other numbers out of 6. So, $5/6 \times 5/6 \times 5/6$ for the first 3 rolls, and the 3 on the last roll was a one in 6 chance. He wrote out the problem: $5/6 \times 5/6 \times 5/6 \times 1/6$.

He felt her eyes on him. A few years ago, he would have gotten in a girl's face about staring at a guy doing math. Even now, he felt the heat in his neck. But Tamara was looking out for him, so he glanced up and smiled instead.

"Sorry. I like watching you work," Tamara told him.

"You make me nervous," he admitted, surprising himself.

"I'll read."

She looked down at her book. Something thick by a Russian author. Nothing he would ever read. He entered the equation into his calculator and came up with probability of .09645. He looked back at the book. *Round to three decimals.* He looked down at the answer choices and found .096, circled C, and moved on to the next question. It took another ten minutes to finish and he was pretty sure he'd gotten them right. He closed the book.

Tamara looked up, startled.

"You ready to eat?"

She smiled and stood from the table, leaning over to kiss him. "Starving."

Dwayne laughed.

Tamara packed up her bookbag and slung it over her shoulder.

"Why don't you let me carry that?" Dwayne said, and she was grinning as she handed it over.

"Why thank you, sir."

As they walked across the campus, Tamara linked her arm in his. They passed a few more people Tamara knew, but the guys didn't give Dwayne anything more than a nod of respect. It was clear to them that Tamara was with him. He felt good. He made a mistake with the gun, but he made it right. He was moving on. Tomorrow, he would meet with his PO, and he had nothing but good things to report.

CHAPTER 19

RYAAN'S MOTHER WAS up when Mei and Ryaan arrived. The house was single-story, built in the '50s. Ryaan told Mei that the house was in an area of Palo Alto called Crescent Park, one of the few areas that hadn't been leveled and rebuilt with dot-com money. Ryaan's mother helped settle Mei into a yellow guestroom with toile wallpaper and gingham sheets. She laid out towels and a blanket in case Mei was cold. All yellow. Convinced that Mei had everything she needed, Ryaan's mother excused herself.

Mei and Ryaan settled into the living room. On the sideboard was a picture of Ryaan as a little girl. She had been mostly legs; her hair formed a halo around her face and the dust was highlighted against her dark skin. Another of Ryaan with two boys. All three shared their mother's high, strong cheekbones. "Bourbon?" Ryaan asked.

"A short one would be great."

Ryaan poured two bourbons, neat, and handed one to Mei before settling into the chair across from her. The two were quiet. "It's a nice house," Mei said for conversation.

"It's an old woman's house," Ryaan joked. "That's what I get for living with my mother."

"I'm not one to talk," Mei responded.

"I used to think a lot about moving," Ryaan admitted. "To be closer to the city at least. But then I realized living this far away is probably the one thing that stops me from working more than I do."

"I'm sure your mom is happy to have you."

Ryaan nodded. "It's just the two of us."

Mei wondered if Ryaan's father had passed away, if it was recent. Here was the chance for Mei to tell Ryaan about Andy, about how she came to live with Ayi. She might even confess her real reasons for leaving Chicago.

For several minutes, the two women drank their bourbon in silence. Only the sounds of Ryaan's mother in the kitchen filled the room. Mei tried to find a way to open up, but she could only think about the exploding glass, see the fragile form of her aunt as she knocked her to the ground.

"How many guns went missing?"

Ryaan nodded. "I keep coming back to that too. Seventy-two."

"But six of them were involved in the shootings so far, right? So, we're down to sixty-six?"

Ryaan watched Mei. "Sixty-five now."

"You really think that gun was from the warehouse?"

"Sydney confirmed the serial number is from the warehouse list."

Mei set her drink down. "How could someone have linked me to the investigation? Teddy signed in the jammer, and I'm pretty sure Amy signed in the computer. There's not even any paperwork with my name on it."

Ryaan shook her head slowly. "I've been thinking about it too."

"Where is Jacob Monaghan?" Mei asked.

"In the detention center, why?"

"He's the only other person I've had contact with."

"But I never even introduced you."

It was true. If someone was going to be targeted, Ryaan was a more obvious choice. Ryaan's phone buzzed on the table. She lifted it up and stood. "I need to take this. You okay?"

Mei nodded. "I think I'm going to head to bed."

Ryaan answered the call, and Mei heard a series of short, muffled responses that made her think Ryaan was discussing the shooting at Ayi's. She tried to put it out of her mind. She needed rest but there was one call to make first. Settled into the bedroom, she called Andy and was grateful when he didn't answer. Even his voice on the recording made her feel sad and scared. How many times had she heard that voice? How many times had she turned to him for comfort? Soon, she would lose that, too.

She cleared her throat and left him a message about what had happened. "They think it was probably random," she lied. "Don't worry about me. I'm fine, I promise." She hung up before the tears came.

Andy called back almost immediately. "I'm coming straight up from LA. I can be there by midnight."

"No," Mei said. "I'm down in Palo Alto, staying with a friend tonight. I'm fine."

Andy hesitated. "What friend?"

"Ryaan Berry."

"Ryaan?" he repeated.

"Yes. She's an inspector in the Triggerlock group."

"Mei, you've been shot at. You're in danger. At least let me call in the local office."

"Absolutely not. No."

"Mei, it's reckless not to contact them. I can't go back to Chicago knowing you're in danger."

"You have to," she insisted.

"I have to take care of my wife."

"No, Andy. I can take care of myself. You have to go home," Mei said.

A beat passed. "Mei, what is wrong with you?"

She took a breath. "Please. Just go home to Chicago. Don't come here. I need to be alone right now."

Andy's voice dropped to a whisper. "Mei, what is this about? What's going on?"

"I'm focusing on a case."

"I thought you said the shooting was random."

Mei said nothing.

"This isn't just a case, Mei. This is a case where you're the target."

"Maybe. But it's my case and I'm not working alone. We've got a good team."

"Why wouldn't you want me there?"

Mei hesitated. "I need space, Andy. To figure things out."

"Figure things out? What things? Talk to me! I'm your husband," he shouted. A momentary pause followed, then he said, "There's someone else."

"No."

"This Ryaan…"

"Andy, I told you. There isn't anyone else."

Andy said nothing.

Startled at the silence, Mei pressed on. "She's my colleague. I'm staying here with her and her mom tonight because Ayi's front window is blown out. That's all."

Still, Andy was silent. Only his deep breaths confirmed he was still there.

"I'll call you tomorrow. Okay?"

Nothing.

"I'm sorry, Andy."

After a moment, there was a dull void on the line. Andy had ended the call.

Though Mei was grateful to be staying at Ryaan's, she didn't sleep. Instead, she rose before 5:00, took a quick shower, and called a cab to the BART station, then rode the train to the city.

Linda James, captain of the precinct that included Ayi's house, called to confirm that there had been no further incidents during the night. Officers were still stationed outside her home and also in front of Hui's. According to Linda, Ayi had come home about an hour before, and there was already a glass repair van at the house.

"We'll keep someone out there tonight, too, and I've got a couple extra cars in the neighborhood," Linda assured her.

Mei thanked her. The momentum of action made it easier to shrug off her worries. It was all part of the job. She was a cop. Maybe not the kind of cop who was usually targeted, but a cop all the same. Somewhere just below the surface, Mei knew this logic was wrong. This was not status quo for a police officer. They didn't get shot at in their homes—certainly not computer forensics officers. Andy was right about that.

As right as he was, Mei hoped their argument would give her a little space. She knew her parents would be calling soon to remind her that this was not normal, demand that she acknowledge the danger, answer to it. Amazingly, she had yet to hear from them. Perhaps Ayi had been distracted—too frightened—to tell them what had happened. It wouldn't last.

For now, Mei would keep her head down and work. She arrived at the lab just before 7:00 a.m. and was grateful to find it empty.

Her first move was to check on the status of the chemical tests being run on the liquid she'd found inside the cell phone jammer. She sat behind her computer and stared at the screen as it booted. Logged in, she launched the case tracking system and scanned for results. The file indicated it was complete, but no results were listed. She picked up the phone and dialed the chem lab. At least she shouldn't have to wait for the results. With the department's workload, the lab was staffed twenty-four seven. "Gordon," came the response.

"This is Mei Ling in the tech lab," she said. "Looks like you've got some results for one of our cases, but they're not in the system yet."

"I can get 'em. Case number?"

Mei read the case number.

"Mountain Dew," Gordon said after a brief delay.

"Excuse me?"

"The liquid sample was Mountain Dew."

Mei thanked him and hung up. Soda. Not the break she'd been hoping for. She found the case number for the shooting at her house and tried to open it. A gray box popped up on the screen. "You are not an authorized user on case QF17643294AL."

Mei sat forward in her chair and broke the dead flowers off the orchid plant her sister had sent as congratulations on her new job. Mountain Dew. Americans drank millions of gallons of the stuff. That was not going to help her narrow her search. Frustrated, she crossed to the small room that housed a refrigerator, a coffeemaker, and a printer. She filled the glass with water from a dispenser, drank half, and poured the remainder into her orchid. Don't overwater it, her sister was always saying.

She left the drowning orchid and the glass and went to the safe to retrieve the computer and peripherals they'd found. Surely, there was something someone had missed. At an empty station, she pulled on gloves and removed them from their storage box. She set the computer aside and studied the cell phone jammer pieces. Blake's notes were beside it. She checked off the components he listed as she went. Generic aluminum box, UHF connectors. Blake had tracked the connectors to a Motorola brand phone. Last built in 2003. Too old to track. It used a clock oscillator, but there were no markings to indicate what it had come from. No lead there either.

A decent soldering job, probably someone used to building this sort of thing. Mei removed the nine-volt battery and unwrapped the yellow foam plastic insulate in which it was encased. Using neon orange powder, she coated it, then blew off the excess. Holding the ends lightly, she turned the battery over on the desk and shined the orange light on each surface. Nothing.

Removing her gloves, Mei logged in to the main

computer. No notes in the file. She searched cell phone jammers. Forty-six results came up. She clicked through the files one at a time to search the images. If their suspect had built another cell phone jammer, it would likely look similar to this one. In a half-hour search through the images, nothing remotely similar came up. She expanded the search to the entire State of California and got three hundred and ninety-three hits. Too many to search. She'd get Amy to work on it.

Mei went back to the table and snapped on a new pair of gloves. She stifled a yawn, wishing for apple juice, her equivalent of morning coffee or tea. Nothing like that in this office. She rolled her neck and focused on the home-made battery pack.

Just then, the lab door opened and Blake came in.

"Morning," Mei said.

"Morning. You're here early."

Mei nodded.

"Glad you've got that out," Blake said, crossing straight to her and setting his bag on the floor. "Did you see my notes on the heat sink?"

"No."

Blake reached into the box of gloves marked XL and pulled two out. Using one to cover his fingers, he pulled out the LiPo battery back and carefully lifted the top off. He pointed to the heat sink.

"You traced it?"

"It's an Acer, same as the computer."

Mei stared down at it. "You think the perp bought more than one computer and used them for parts?"

Blake smiled. "I do. They're the identical version and,

according to the manufacturer, the two were made within weeks of each other."

"So, we need to search for purchases of multiple computers."

Blake dropped the gloves on the table and crossed to the main computer terminal. "Already done."

Mei waited for Blake to mention the shooting, but he didn't say anything. Teddy and Blake were easy to work around. They were friendly and outgoing, but they rarely asked questions about non-work-related subjects and never probed into her personal life. Something she was particularly appreciative of today.

He checked his open inquiries. The Acer one showed no response. "I'll follow up with them today."

"What parameters did you enter?"

"At least two sold at once, within the state, in the past sixty days."

Mei nodded. It was possible that the computers were bought outside the state, but buying two computers for three hundred-dollars each couldn't be very unusual. Getting back thousands and thousands of matches wouldn't be useful. Better to make some assumptions on where and when they were purchased.

"Anything else we can check on?" asked Mei.

Blake shook his head and pulled on his gloves. "The cells are generic. I sent a sample of the soldering material to the lab."

Mei pulled a magnifying glass from a drawer. She put a little pressure on the soldered connection. "It looks heavy duty."

"Probably automotive," Blake said.

Mei moved the glass over the pieces and across the black electrical tape that held the individual battery cells together. "Let's see if there are any prints on this black tape."

Blake handed Mei a pair of tweezers and held the cells steady as she unwrapped the tape. The first piece wound around the cells twice. The second piece only went around the sides, across the top, and partway down the sides and had been cut jaggedly as though with a boxcutter or a knife.

"Why doesn't this piece go all the way around?" she asked as she lay the tape, sticky side up, on the table.

"Maybe he ran out."

There were no cardboard fibers on the tape. "Doesn't look like the end of the roll."

Mei held the tape down while Blake dusted the center for prints. Halfway down the length of the piece, the beautiful curve of a print appeared.

Blake whistled.

"Let's get some images."

Mei used an orange light on the tape to illuminate the dusting powder on the print while Blake took photographs. Then, carefully, Blake lifted the print.

"I'll get this run now."

Blake carried the tape with the print to the main console and set it on a sheet of glass to be scanned. Mei carefully flipped the tape over, dusted the other side, and brought the magnifying glass close. A shape emerged.

Blake returned a moment later and looked over her shoulder. "What is it?"

"There's a '2' written here."

"Like number two?"

"Yeah." Mei studied the shorter piece of tape. "Let's dust this one, too."

Blake dusted orange powder on the sticky side, and Mei shined her light along the length of it. Once, twice, a third time.

"Nothing," Blake said.

Mei flipped it over and they did the same thing on the smooth side. Again, nothing.

"No number on this one."

Blake lifted the camera and took pictures of the number.

"Put that on the overhead along with the words that were written on the jammer."

A minute later, Blake and Mei were staring up at the screen on the wall. On the left side, was the small, printed '2.' Opposite it were the words 'on' and 'off' that had been written on the cell phone jammer.

"Looks like the same handwriting."

Mei nodded. "Let's send it to the lab for their opinion." She looked back at the battery cells that were now loose on the table. The vertical pieces of tape ran full circle around the cells, but the horizontal pieces only went edge to edge. It was as though there had been a bigger batch of cells taped together before someone cut them apart. A number one to go with the number two? "Why would he need two LiPo batteries?"

Blake looked up. "What?"

"It's like he had more cells, all taped together. Then cut them apart to make two separate batteries rather than one big one. Why?"

Blake nodded. "So, he cut the cells apart, left half the black tape on these and the other half on the other stack, then wrapped these with a fresh piece of tape."

"Is it possible there were two battery packs?"

Blake shrugged. "Sure, it's possible."

Mei pulled her gloves off to call Sydney Blanchard.

"What are you thinking?" Blake asked as the phone started ringing on Sydney's desk.

"I'm thinking maybe there's another one we missed."

CHAPTER 20

RYAAN ARRIVED AT the police impound lot with a full cup of coffee. In the twenty-minute drive from home, she hadn't had a chance to take more than a couple of sips. It had been one phone call after another. Ballistics had a partial print off a slug pulled out of Mei Ling's aunt's wall that they were running through the police database. Patrick had news about a car that was dropped in the Tenderloin with a trunk full of guns. It was called in by a schoolteacher who lived on the block.

According to Patrick, the teacher had watched a few kids walk off with guns before the police arrived. Kids she knew, probably, but she said she had no names. She also couldn't say exactly how many guns she'd seen walk off before the police had arrived.

"Too many," was all she'd said. When Patrick pressed, she'd added, "Even one is too many."

Ryaan parked her car on the curb in front of the impound lot, half in the red, and got out, taking her coffee with her. It was mostly cold now, but that wouldn't stop her from drinking it.

She walked across the gravel lot and entered through

the open door of the police garage. At a glance, it might have been a Jiffy Lube. Three bays stretched across the space. Each bay had a pit big enough for a forensic team and a hydraulic pump strong enough to lift a midsize commercial truck. From the high ceiling, fluorescent lights gave off a hard, yellow light. In a far corner, one of the bulbs flickered as though having a seizure. Two of the bays were empty. The third held a small sedan, centered over the pit. The pit appeared empty. Made sense. The techs would be focused on the car's exterior and the trunk where the guns had been.

Standing off to one side, Roger Sampers directed the team. Ryaan recognized his light complexion, even from the side. Roger had been hairless from birth due to some condition whose name Ryaan couldn't remember. He rarely referred to his condition but was vigilant about avoiding the sun. She'd heard he was married with a couple of kids, lived somewhere out in the East Bay.

He wore a white lab coat which he seemed to favor whether a crime scene was inside or out. Roger also had a white raincoat, straight at the bottom like a blazer, that she'd seen on occasion as well. It, like his lab coats, was embroidered with his name.

Standing in the impound lot, Roger wore a white baseball cap backward as though protecting his neck from burning despite the fact that they were inside and the sun had yet to rise above the horizon. He glanced up as she approached, his eyes covered in blue-lensed sunglasses. The combination made him look like an aging hip-hop star.

Today, Roger had four other techs working with him.

Ryaan knew two of them from scenes like this over the years. She said hello to Bill and Stacy as she walked to get a better look at the car, which had been painted brown with something other than auto paint, giving it a flat finish. In several places along the front wheel well and back bumper, the brown was stripped and a similarly dull white paint applied.

"Morning," Roger said, and Ryaan took a long gulp of her lukewarm coffee before responding.

"What've we got?"

"1988 Ford Focus. Originally white but it's been repainted." Roger motioned to the dull finish. "Inexpensively. Front quarter panel appears to be from a newer model, but we won't know for sure until we pull it apart."

Ryaan took another drink and set her mug on the cement floor to pull out her notebook. "How about the weapons?"

Roger introduced his two younger staffers, an attractive young black woman named Naomi and a slightly older, but still very young, blond man named Chase. The two were huddled close together over the pile of weapons.

Chase said something indiscernible, and Naomi laughed, covering her mouth with the back of a gloved hand. She reached out and punched his shoulder, playfully. Dear God, they were flirting over a pile of weapons in the middle of the night.

Ryaan abandoned her mug and crossed the lot. Chase and Naomi had the guns laid out on a tarp and were tagging them. "How many?"

"Forty-seven," Chase said, the flirty smile disappearing. "They were all in the trunk."

"But the back was open, and the teacher who called it in said she watched kids take some of them. No idea how many," Naomi added, looking equally sobered by Ryaan's appearance.

Chase nodded. "We're creating a list of them now. Then we'll get them to Ballistics."

"Was there ammo?"

Naomi nodded. "So far, all of them have been fully loaded." Ryaan scanned the guns. She'd have to cross reference the list with the inventory from the storage facility, but even at a glance, Ryaan knew there were still some big AKs missing.

If the car had been left on Mason Street near Eddy, at midnight, with the trunk open and the guns in full view, it wouldn't have taken more than fifteen or twenty minutes for them to disappear. They were lucky that they had as many as they did. She wondered if it was luck and wrote herself a note to check on the call they'd gotten from the teacher.

When she walked back to the car, Ryaan saw that someone had kicked over her coffee. She lifted the mug and turned it sideways, the last dribbles spilling onto the cement ground.

"Sorry, Berry," Roger said, noticing her. "I think Bill did that when he was photographing the car."

Bill raised a hand in apology and continued documenting the car.

Ryaan set the empty mug out of reach and stifled a yawn. "Is there anything on the car to tell us where it came from?"

"No plates and the VIN's been destroyed. Nothing

in the glove. Plenty of prints, though. And some hairs…
if we find something to match them to."

Ryaan walked up to where the VIN plate had been
removed. She glanced into the car. It was clean. Not
cleaned up. There was still plenty of dirt on the floormats,
and the seats were stained and torn. But there were no
papers, no receipts, no documents. Nothing to provide
a paper trail.

She glanced at a divot the size of a dime in the windshield, just above the driver's side wiper. "This from
a bullet?"

Roger shook his head and approached. "Pebble, I'd
guess. Suggests some freeway driving, probably outside
the area. I've got a sister up in Wyoming. Her cars always
have those kinds of cracks in the glass."

Ryaan tried to picture Roger's sister but quickly gave
up. She moved to one side to get a better look at the glass.
There was a small square smudge on the passenger's side
of the windshield. "What was here?"

Roger leaned in. "Some sort of decal. Nice catch.
Naomi, come dust this."

Naomi brought over a black, hard-sided case and
knelt beside it. As she opened it, the top drawer lifted
up and displayed two lower shelves. Naomi pulled out a
blue fingerprint brush and matching powder and applied
them to the spot on the windshield while Ryaan wished
she had coffee.

Naomi blew off the excess and bent in for a closer
look. "I think we can make out something."

Bill took a series of shots with his wide-angle lens

camera and brought the image up on the screen. "Here. What does that say?"

"Expires 08/08," said Naomi. "Looks like a parking pass."

Ryaan pulled on gloves and took a roll of adhesive—almost like wide packing tape—from the evidence box. She laid a long strip across the fingerprint powder, ran the edge of her hand over the tape, and pulled it off. Ryaan stuck the tape on the clear sheet Roger had put on the top of the evidence box. She slipped the sheet into a clear page protector and held it up to the light.

Roger stood over her shoulder. "Ancala."

"Country Club," she added.

"Where is that?" Roger asked.

A moment later Chase looked up from his phone. "Scottsdale, Arizona."

"Excellent, Berry," Roger told her. "Especially considering you didn't get to finish your coffee."

"If I'm lucky, maybe I'll get another cup before I have to really start thinking." Ryaan glared over at a sheepish Bill. "I'll follow up with the golf club," she said to Roger.

"We'll run the prints and see if we get any other trace. I've already got a call into Ballistics to let them know the guns are coming."

On the far side of the car, Naomi and Chase were, once again, huddled over the guns. Naomi wrote on the tags and handed them to Chase to label the guns.

Roger glanced over. "Remember being that young?"

"Never."

"I don't believe that for a second," Roger said and turned his attention back to the car.

"Thanks, Roger. I'm going to get some coffee."

"I'd say that's a good idea."

"I am choosing not to take that as an insult."

Roger laughed. "Your choice, Berry."

*

Ryaan parked in her spot behind the department and crossed through the lobby toward Bryant Street. Today, she was treating herself to Starbucks. The habit was too expensive for every day. But, after last night, she'd earned it. She was just coming out the front doors when Hal Harris called her name. "I'm glad I caught you."

"I was just going to get some coffee," she told him, picturing Naomi's smile and trying to look at least somewhat friendly.

"I've got Albert Jackson upstairs. We held him overnight, so he's lucid, which is rare, according to the patrol guys who usually deal with him."

Ryaan looked across at the mermaid on the Starbucks sign across the street, then back at Hal. "Fine, I'm coming."

"I'll buy you a coffee after, I promise," Hal said, steering her back inside.

"I'm holding you to that."

Hal chuckled. "No doubt you will."

"How did you guys get Jackson?" she asked, bringing the subject back to the comfortable territory of work.

"They did a psych eval last night." Hal reached around Ryaan and opened the door for her.

"And?"

"They say he's competent to stand trial."

Flashing her badge, Ryaan walked past the metal detectors, followed by Hal, and headed for the stairs. "You don't buy it?"

Hal took the stairs in twos, his long legs making it look easy, while Ryaan tried to keep pace. "Wait till you see him."

They passed through the homicide waiting room and down the hall to the interrogation room. Hailey stood in the closet-sized viewing room, watching Jackson through the two- way mirror. Albert Jackson sat with his hands folded on the table in front of him. He was dirty and unshaven, but he held his back straight with a degree of pride that was both unusual and admirable. He wore a flannel shirt, torn at one shoulder, and a gray T-shirt of some kind underneath it. His lips moved like he was chewing something or maybe talking to someone, but otherwise he looked lucid.

Hailey turned to them. "Morning."

Ryaan nodded. "Hi."

Hailey nodded to Jackson. "You ready to meet him?"

Ryaan glanced back at Hal, who was watching her. "Something you two want to tell me first?"

"No," Hailey said. "You should see it for yourself."

Ryaan frowned.

"She was on her way to get coffee," Hal told Hailey as though explaining the frown.

"Got it. I tried to reach Patrick," Hailey offered.

"It's okay," Ryaan said. "I'm ready."

Hailey went first. She opened the interview room door and watched Albert Jackson jolt in his seat. He turned his head in the general direction of the door.

"Hello, Mr. Jackson," Hailey said.

"Oh, yes, you back, then. I sure could use something to drink, ma'am. Did you bring an old man something to drink?"

Ryaan stared at the swollen masses of Albert Jackson's eye sockets. The whites of his eyes were only visible in the inside corners and, rather than white, they were a bright scarlet red. Whitish stains trailed along each side of his nose from the stream of infected discharge, and the lids were so swollen that they essentially held his eyes closed.

"He's blind?" she said.

Jackson's face shifted toward her. "Who's there? I thought you were the inspector. You're not the inspector. Who are you?"

Ryaan glanced at Hailey, then back to Jackson. "I'm an inspector, too, Mr. Jackson," she said. "My name is Ryaan Berry. I'm with the Triggerlock group, and we're trying to find out where the gun you fired came from."

"What gun? Who's got a gun?"

Ryaan looked over at Hailey who shrugged. "Seriously?"

Hal shook his head.

"I don't know nothing about a gun, but I really could use a drink. Can one of you ladies find it in your heart to get an old man a drink?"

"Mr. Jackson, I'll get you a drink," Ryaan told him, pulling up a chair and sitting across from him. "I just have a couple of questions first."

"Sure. 'Course. Anything you need, Inspector."

From closeup, his eyes looked even worse. There was a layer of yellowish crust that sealed them closed. The left one appeared to have a laceration on it as well. Maybe from a fingernail, but she couldn't see his hands. "How long have your eyes been infected?" she asked him.

"Oh, I don't know," Jackson said, reaching a hand up to touch his face. Ryaan looked at the gnarled shape of his hands and turned to Hal and Hailey. Hailey shook her head. "They been like this a little bit, I guess."

"Since earlier today? Or yesterday?"

Jackson wiped across one eye with a knobby knuckle. "Oh, no. Month, maybe two. I got something in one and I guess I rubbed it wrong then it went to the other eye."

Ryaan watched him put one hand down on the other. They were both misshapen. "How have you been taking care of yourself?"

"Same as always, I guess," Jackson told her.

"Where are you living?"

Jackson hitched the thumb on his gnarled hand over one shoulder as though pointing. "Oh, I got me a place down near 9th."

"You sleeping on the streets?"

Jackson shrugged. "Sometimes. Or I got some other places I go."

"Where do you eat?"

"Here and there."

Ryaan stood from the table.

Jackson seemed to follow her movement with his head. He licked his lips. "I sure would love that drink now."

"Sure, Mr. Jackson. I'll be right back."

In the hallway, Ryaan shook her head at Hal and Hailey. "There's no way he shot up a bus."

"He did," Hal said. "Witnesses ID'd him."

"He can't see," Ryaan argued. "And did you see his hands? How did he get there? How did he hold the gun?"

"Two guns," Hal interrupted.

"Right. It's amazing he didn't kill anyone. He's totally blind." She looked back toward the interview room. "What does he say about it?"

Hailey shook her head. "Doesn't remember anything. Totally blacked out."

"You believe him."

"I wouldn't if we hadn't found roofies in his system," Hailey said.

Ryaan leaned into the wall. "What? Someone roofied a homeless man and set him up to shoot up the bus station?"

Hal nodded. "It's a bitch, ain't it?"

"I'll say," Ryaan agreed. "We need to find out where he's been the past week and get a list of everyone who was a witness at the bus station. Maybe there's someone who will jump out."

"I've already got patrol checking on Jackson's whereabouts," Hal said. "They're going down to his regular sleeping spot and checking a few of the shelters he frequents. I'll get a list of people who were in the terminal, but it'll be a long list and it won't be inclusive. It was 9:15 on a Wednesday morning. There are hundreds of people coming off those buses."

"Was he up on the platform? Maybe we can pinpoint a specific bus."

Hal shook his head. "He was standing at the top of the stairs, where you enter the terminal. Gun was aimed at the ceiling, which is how he missed everyone. There was some ricochet, but no one was hurt."

"Damn," Ryaan said. "I'm going to get the old guy a Coke. Then I'm going to get some coffee and try to get my head around this mess."

"I'll get someone to take Jackson and go with you," Hal said.

Ryaan fed the vending machine a dollar seventy-five, highway robbery for a soda, and pressed the button. The plastic bottle landed in the tray with a thwack. She missed the days of soda in cans. Maybe she was getting old.

Jackson took the bottle awkwardly from her, holding it between his two hands. Ryaan stared at his hands. Arthritis had made them permanently hooked. He pressed the palm of his hand onto the top and struggled to twist it. Ryaan reached over and did it for him. "Thank you," he told her. "These hands aren't what they used to be."

Jackson took a drink. "That tastes nice, Inspector."

"No problem."

"Don't suppose you have a little something to go in, help loosen the joints."

"Sorry, Mr. Jackson, I don't."

"Doesn't hurt to ask."

Ryaan turned from the room as two patrol officers returned for Jackson. "Make sure he doesn't spill his soda, okay?"

One of the patrol officers gave her a strange look. The other one nodded. "Sure thing, Inspector."

Ryaan stepped out of the room to where Hal was waiting and exhaled. "I need that coffee."

"Let's go."

Hal took one step down the hall when Ryaan's cell phone buzzed on her hip. She pulled it off and recognized Patrick's number. "Berry."

"Sampers called. They matched a print in the car. Steering wheel and rearview mirror were wiped clean, but our guy adjusted the seat and left a nice clean index and thumb."

"Who is it?"

"Name's Karl Penn. I've got his address. Want to go over there with me?"

"I'm at Bryant. Where are you?"

"I'll pick you up out front in five," Patrick said.

"Five minutes from now?" she asked.

Ryaan looked up at Hal who smiled and shook his head.

Patrick didn't even answer her. He'd already hung up.

"Guess that coffee's going to have to wait," Hal said.

Ryaan started for the stairs. Maybe she'd have time to grab a cup of departmental slop on her way out.

CHAPTER 21

J.T. HAD LEFT without finishing business last night. Sam had thrown a wrench in the plan. Again. Something or other wasn't done or he wasn't sure if it had been done right. He needed more time. "I'll have it done by morning," Sam said, more snippy than usual.

It didn't help that J.T. was sick of Sam. The patience that had enabled Sam to live these extra days had worn thin. Plus, it felt like maybe Sam was manipulating J.T. Something about the more recent series of delays and Sam's refusal to show J.T. exactly what was going on. "You won't understand it anyway," Sam had said of this last one.

Words that should have gotten Sam killed within minutes. Either way, J.T. had decided it would be today. The gun incident last night had only further reinforced the need to end Sam. Letting him shoot that gun was a mistake. At the time, it seemed it would all be over within an hour afterward, but giving Sam the night to work also meant he had the night to get online and start talking. And J.T. knew he would.

In fact, J.T. was so confident of the geek's impending online blathering that Sam's alias was being tracked and reported into J.T.'s email. Something, ironically, Sam had set up himself for J.T. to track Hank and Karl. Once those were established, it didn't take rocket science to collect Sam's account name and alter the program for Sam.

Sam had been especially petulant on the ride home from Mei Ling's residence. He had wanted to keep the gun and J.T. forbade it. All that time and energy explaining why keeping a dirty weapon was a risk. "We've got tons of them," J.T. had assured Sam, although Sam would never shoot again.

Sam had, in turn, whined that it was his first shot, like bagging a first deer or some such thing. J.T. had been anxious to leave and was not entirely anxious to return. But things were already coming loose, and there was no room for error. J.T. arrived forty-five minutes before the time they'd agreed on and parked around the far side of the garage rather than in front.

Rounding the side of the building, J.T. heard rustling sounds from the garage. J.T. halted and pressed an ear to the wall. Someone was definitely in the garage. But how? J.T. had armed it and no one else had the code. J.T. crossed to the front of the garage. *Damn it, Sam.* The keypad on the front was pulled loose from the building's facade and was hanging from the wires. J.T. got close and saw that a small screwdriver was wedged between two pieces. J.T. had underestimated Sam. That was more infuriating than anything.

J.T. stared at the door. It was closed. Opening it would be too obvious, so J.T. went past the garage door toward the apartment. The door to the house was ajar. It was Sam in the garage. No unwanted guests. At least that was good news. To be sure, J.T. crept up the stairs and checked the office. Sam wasn't there. No, it had to be Sam in the garage.

Back downstairs, J.T. used the key to open the first garage bay where the white truck was parked. It looked the same as it had. Sam had been after the guns. He would find Hank if he hadn't already. J.T. closed the door to the apartment and crossed the garage to the far door, taking a moment to listen. Even with the door closed, the smell made it hard to swallow. This place should have been destroyed two days ago. Instead, Hank's body was likely deep into putrefaction, his intestines distended, his skin green. What the hell was Sam doing in there, and why was he so quiet?

"Oh, God," Sam screamed. "Holy shit. Oh, shit. Oh. Oh."

He'd found Hank. J.T. unlocked the door and started the process of breathing without smelling. Six months in the morgue had been plenty of time to learn how to handle the smell. The trick was using only your mouth and not thinking about what little particles were floating in the air. J.T. did not get sick. At least now Sam would come out. But the door didn't open. The only sound from inside was Sam's wailing. At least it would be easy to find him.

Cracking the door, J.T. listened. Something clattered and Sam grunted as though he'd fallen over. J.T. froze, listening. Sam was on the far side of the van. J.T. crept through the opening and slowly inched the door closed until it latched. Drew the gun then crept to the back of the van. Surely Sam would come around the front side toward the garage door.

Suddenly, Sam went quiet. The windows of the van were dark and, while the inside was visible, J.T. couldn't see through the far side. Where was Sam? J.T. halted against the van. The slightest sound of breath. J.T. pivoted as Sam was swinging.

The tire iron screamed through the air.

J.T. leapt out of its path. The tire iron hit the gun. J.T. hit the side of the van hard and felt a painful crack. J.T.'s wrist screamed in pain as the gun flew across the room.

"What the hell did you do to Hank?" Sam shouted, the words spraying from his mouth.

"I didn't do that," J.T. said. "I swear. It was a cop. He shot through the window." Hands held high, innocently, J.T. backed up slowly. "I swear."

Sam's eyes narrowed. "Why didn't you tell me?"

"You were busy and focused. I knew you'd be upset. You kept asking about him. I was going to tell you. I just didn't know how." J.T. made a prayer sign. "I swear. I was just scared to tell you."

Sam hesitated.

J.T.'s gaze slid to where the gun had gone.

"You're lying," Sam shouted, raising the tire iron again.

J.T. jumped back to the far wall, but the van was pressed too close to pass.

"You killed him, and you came here to kill me."

J.T. dropped to the ground and slid under the front of the van. Pain pulsing in one wrist, J.T. moved in an awkward army crawl to the other side. Sam was too big to follow, but J.T. knew he'd come around the other way. J.T.

was trapped in the back corner of the garage. No weapon, no exit. Control the panic. There had to be something to use. There wasn't time to load a gun. On the floor beside the van was a spare tire, the compressor... Shit.

"I'm calling the police," Sam announced.

J.T. resisted the desire to scream. A weapon could be anything. *Ignore the pain in your wrist and get creative.* On the workbench was an orange plastic case with a set of snow chains.

J.T. spotted Sam on the far side of the van, maybe eight feet away, searching for J.T.'s gun. The tire iron was still in his hand, but it was lowered to his side as he searched. J.T. pulled one set of the chains out of the bag and, using the good arm, heaved it onto the roof of the van with a clatter. When Sam looked back, J.T. ducked down behind the van and watched Sam through the tinted glass. Sam continued his frantic search for the gun.

He was counting on that gun. Moving quickly, J.T. climbed on top of the van as quietly as possible and lifted the chain by one end. The pain in J.T.'s wrist was nauseating, but it wasn't enough to save Sam. J.T. grimaced at the pain and swung the chain once. Then, letting out a long, deep shout, J.T. hurled all fifteen pounds of it at Sam. It was heavier than J.T. had anticipated and, for a moment, it seemed like it wouldn't reach Sam. Most of the chain fell short but the tail end snapped across Sam's side, shredding his shirt. Sam dropped to his knees, the tire iron clanking to the floor.

J.T. ran across the top of the van and dropped to the cement floor, reaching Sam before his head came up. J.T. took the end of the chain and looped it around Sam's neck, pulling a short length of chain taut against his flesh. Pain surged in the wrist, but J.T. bit hard on the inside of a cheek and kept the chain held taut. Sam struggled, clawing at J.T.'s leg, but J.T. used a foot on Sam's back to press him down and the chain to pull him back.

J.T. began to count out loud. Sam tried to get up on one foot, but J.T. used the chain like reins to pull Sam off balance and continued counting. Slowly. Sam turned his attention to the chain, clawing at his own neck to loosen it. "Thirteen. Fourteen." Giving up on the chain, Sam tried to get his hands to the floor, to give himself purchase to stand, but J.T. was pushing down too hard. Sam was too weak.

"This is why people need to stay in shape, Sam. Twenty-nine. Thirty." Sam started to arch his back to throw J.T. off balance, but that, too, failed. "Too much Mountain Dew, Sam. Not enough time on the playground with the other boys. Forty-six."

At fifty-four, Sam's weight deadened, making it harder to hold up his neck. J.T.'s wrist throbbed an angry drumbeat. J.T. slowly let Sam sink to the floor, keeping the chain taut. Once Sam was facedown on the floor, J.T. simply sat on his back, shifting both ends of the chain into the uninjured hand. Finished the count. By eighty, Sam was motionless. By one hundred, he had wet himself.

J.T. gave it to one hundred and ten for good measure, then let go of the chain long enough to check Sam's pulse in his neck. That took more time than it should have because of the considerable layers of skin hiding the carotid. But eventually, J.T. was satisfied that there was no pulse left to find and let the chain fall slack onto the floor.

It took longer to find the gun, which had fallen into one of the boxes of Sam's extra computer equipment. J.T. had been about to give up on it. But it had the silencer. Pity to lose that one. Slowly, the calm set in as J.T. went to work.

Using the red gas container, J.T. soaked the bedsheets from the upstairs bed and put them directly under Sam's computer equipment, then soaked a rag and stuffed it down into the gas compartment of the black van, whistling a little along the way. J.T. left the door open between the two garages and between the apartment and the garage. Good ventilation was key to a strong fire. J.T. had seen that somewhere. When all that was done, J.T. went upstairs and built a pile of crumpled newspapers on top of the old electric stovetop. Checking again to make sure there was a clear burn path, J.T. turned all four burners on and exited the building for the last time.

Only in the safety of the car, several blocks from the burning building, did J.T. pull up the sleeve and look at the wrist. The angry purple welt said broken, or fractured at least. That was not in the plan either. J.T. took some deep breaths and drove calmly toward home. A beer and some aspirin, and this day would be officially over.

The farther J.T. got from the apartment, the stronger the rage grew. Sam had almost won. If he had found that gun, J.T. would be dead. "He almost killed you, that fucker," J.T. seethed. There was no way to breathe through all that fury.

CHAPTER 22

MEI INVITED AMY to come along to Oyster Point, thinking a girls' outing might break the ice between them. During the car ride, Mei asked Amy what sort of projects she liked working on, what her interests were in moving up in the department.

"Aaron usually has me handle data searches and more admin-type stuff," Amy said, the most words Mei had heard from her yet.

"You enjoy that?"

Amy shrugged and turned her attention to her phone. "I'm easy. Whatever he wants."

Mei wondered if Amy heard the way her words had come out, but she didn't seem to notice. When Mei said nothing else, Amy turned on the radio and began to flip through one annoying pop song after another. When she found one she liked, she began to text. Mei thought she saw the name James or Jones on Amy's screen.

"Any word from the lab?" Mei asked.

Amy didn't answer. Mei wasn't sure she'd heard the question. Finally, Amy said, "Yeah. The soldering material on the battery was automotive, whatever that means."

"Means it's easy to get and there's no good way to track it," Mei said, trying to keep her patience. "What else?"

"Blake says they just finished running the print from the electrical tape through the database of known offenders. No match." Amy ran her finger down the screen. "And Blake's got fifty-seven hits on multiple computer purchases. He's getting a list of names."

"Fifty-seven," Mei repeated.

"He started with a search of California and got three hundred matches, so he limited it to a forty-mile radius around San Francisco in the last ninety days," said Amy.

"Okay. And he ended up with fifty-seven? That's not too bad."

"That's fifty-seven at Walmart alone. He's still running seven other retailers."

Mei tried to imagine how they'd pick their hacker out of that list without a name. "Just Walmart," Mei repeated.

"Just Walmarts within forty miles and ninety days," Amy confirmed, her voice flat.

Discouraging news. "Anything else from the cell phone jammer or the computer?"

"No," Amy said, her thumbs working in overdrive.

"The glue?" Mei asked.

"Generic super glue."

"Ask Blake to cross reference the purchase of super glue with the computers, and also the cell phone jammers in the database with the purchase of computers. Maybe we'll get lucky and be able to narrow this thing down somehow."

"Yep," Amy said without looking up.

A subpoena had gone to AT&T, the phone's carrier, for records on the phone's history. In the meantime, the only lead left to pursue was the possibility of a second LiPo battery which might mean a second device. Or it might mean nothing.

Both Mei and Ryaan had made attempts to get in touch with the businesses that shared a wall with the police storage facility. Mei had left several messages for Brad Archer, the managing partner at Archer Decker Architecture. Brad's father, Colin, who was the original Archer, had passed away a few years before and Decker was now retired. So far, Mei hadn't been able to reach Brad. Teddy ran a series of web searches to gain more insight into the architects but there was nothing to suggest they'd experienced a breach.

The accounting firm had told Ryaan that their system had experienced no breaches, while the law firm's IT group reported that they were still analyzing their logs and had nothing to report as of yet. Mei had offered her team's help. It was standard practice to bring a computer forensics team into the office in a case like this, but getting inside wasn't easy. Certainly, the estate law firm wasn't giving the police access to any of their logs without a warrant. With no way to definitively link the patrol officer's murder or the gun thefts to these breaches, obtaining a warrant was unlikely. There had been no word from the pharmaceutical company at all.

Not surprisingly, no company was interested in filing a complaint and making a breach public unless it was absolutely necessary. Without proof that something had been stolen, the police didn't even know who to put pressure on. Yet another way that police work felt so different from the FBI. Federal jurisdiction moved things along. People heard

"FBI" and they moved aside. Mei couldn't remember a case where there had been so many obstacles.

Mei made one last call to Brad Archer's phone. His secretary, Hannah, answered. Mei recognized the voice immediately. She'd spoken to Hannah before. Young.

"Hannah, this is Inspector Mei Ling with the San Francisco Police Department. We spoke earlier. I was trying to reach Brad Archer."

"Oh, right," Hannah said slowly. "Just one moment."

A hundred moments passed before there was a click and a very different voice came on. "This is Kyle Ramsey. I'm head of IT. Mr. Archer said you had a couple of questions."

For the first time in fifteen minutes, Amy looked up from her screen.

"Yes. Mr. Ramsey. Thank you. This is Mei Ling with the SFPD's Computer Forensics Unit. We have reason to believe that your system may have been compromised. We discovered a device that appeared to be trying to access local Wi-Fi networks. Archer is one of a few businesses within range of the device."

"Thank you, Officer. We are aware of the breach."

Amy looked over at Mei. "Can you tell me what was accessed, Mr. Ramsey?" asked Mei. "The information may help us locate the individual who hacked into the system. That same person is wanted for questioning in a murder that happened several blocks from your offices."

"We've reviewed the logs, and we show that four files were accessed on Tuesday between 3:20 a.m. and 3:55 a.m."

"Can you tell me what the files were?"

"All design schematics."

Maybe the guns were a distraction meant to throw

the police off the track from what the thief really wanted. "What kind of schematics?"

"Retail stores. Retail spaces are about sixty percent of our business. The first file accessed was for the Gap store on the corner of Market and Powell Street across from the San Francisco City Centre. We did that one in '87, nothing recent."

Mei glanced at Amy, who shrugged. A Gap? That didn't make sense. "How about the others?"

"The second was for an Apple mini retail store at the Stanford Shopping Center, opened in 2004."

"And the other two?"

"Both are businesses that are no longer open. One was a jewelry store at Sutter and Grant and the last was a candy shop, also in the Stanford Shopping Center."

"When were those stores opened?"

"The jewelry store in '98 and the candy shop in '01."

"Can you think of any reason why someone would access these particular files?"

"No. And our files are saved by job number, which means that if someone wanted these specific schematics, they'd have to know the job number to get the correct file."

"Is there a master list of job numbers?"

"Yes, but that file wasn't accessed in the breach."

Mei was stumped. "If retail is sixty percent of your business, what else do you do?"

"The other part is mostly residences, but we've also done hotels, several banks, restaurants, including MG-252 which is Michael Mina's newest restaurant."

Amy's brows rose.

"Back up."

"To Mina's restaurant. MG-252?"

"No. Not the restaurant. Banks. You mentioned banks."

"Right," Ramsey said. "We've done four in South San Francisco and Colma in the past year. One was actually just completed."

Mei was puzzled. "And you're completely confident that those schematics haven't been accessed?"

"We're very confident."

Mei noticed he didn't say he was certain.

"Have you had problems with any employees?" The question came from Amy and, when Mei glanced over, Amy continued, "Is it possible that a disgruntled employee breached the system as some sort of statement about the company?" The tone in Amy's voice suggested she knew something about Archer and Decker, but Mei was almost certain she didn't. Almost.

When Ramsey didn't answer right away, Mei said, "Let me introduce my colleague, Amy Warner."

"I was just thinking about the company's attrition," said Ramsey after a pause. "I've only been here a year and a half. A few people have left to pursue other opportunities, but no one has been fired or anything. I can't think of anyone who would break into our system."

"No one passed up for promotion?" Mei asked, picking up Amy's line.

Ramsey was quiet again. "Well, we did have one IT guy who left after I was hired."

Mei got off the freeway in South San Francisco and turned toward Oyster Point.

"What was his name?"

"Martin Ziino. Z-I-I-N-O."

Amy nodded that she had it.

Mei came back to the files that were accessed. "Can you think of any reason why someone would be interested in these four buildings specifically?"

"Not off the top of my head. The jewelry store was completely destroyed in a fire."

Mei tried to think about how schematics of a burned down jewelry store would be useful, but nothing came to mind. There had to be some connection between the four places. "The job numbers aren't consecutive, are they?"

"The job numbers begin with the year so these four were fairly far apart on the server," Ramsey explained.

"How about the architects involved? Who headed up each project?" Mei asked as she turned onto Grand and passed Archer and Decker on her way to the police warehouse.

"Let me look that up." A minute passed.

Mei pulled to the curb and threw her police pass on the dash.

"Okay, it was Rebecca Harding on the Apple; Michael Edwards on the Gap; Jabe Thompson was the lead architect on the two others. All three of them are still at Archer."

"What can you tell us about Mr. Thompson?"

"Jabe? He's a great guy and very talented."

"Anyone who might have an issue with Mr. Thompson personally or with his work?"

"No. Absolutely not. His clients are very pleased, and Mr. Thompson and his partner have been together for years. They have two daughters. I can't imagine anyone having an issue with Jabe."

"How about the others? Harding and Edwards?"

"The same. There have been no complaints about any of our architects."

"One last question for you, Mr. Ramsey. Does it seem odd that the hacker left a trace?"

"What do you mean?"

Mei wondered how savvy he was. A lot of the so-called experts had very little experience with actual IT security. "Well, why tell you which files were accessed? Why leave a trail?"

Mr. Ramsey had no answer for that.

"Have you considered that other files may have been accessed and no trail left?" Mei pressed.

"We've performed a very thorough investigation."

Mei thanked him and said she'd be in touch. She ended the call and turned to Amy. "What do you think?"

"I texted Teddy to look into Martin Ziino," Amy said.

"Thanks."

"You think Ziino did it?"

Mei shook her head and put the car in park. "He's been gone eighteen months. I can't imagine a guy going to this effort after that long."

Amy nodded.

The two got out of the car and crossed the street toward the warehouse. There was a patrol officer posted out front. Mei showed her badge. "Officer Blanchard is inside," he told her.

"Sydney?" Mei called from the doorway.

"I'm in the last row," Sydney called back. Mei and Amy made their way across the floor and found Sydney on a ladder. Wearing purple latex gloves in what looked like a child's size, she held a small yellow device similar to a stud finder.

"What does that do?" Amy asked.

Sydney looked down.

"This is Amy Warner from my department. Amy, this is Sydney Blanchard. She's a head criminalist in CSI."

Amy nodded, then pointed to the yellow device.

Sydney glanced at her, and Mei smiled. She imagined Sydney was thinking the same thing she was. That Amy was a bit like an insolent teenager. Everything out of her mouth seemed sullen and slightly rude.

"It's a scanner," Sydney said, starting down the ladder.

"What does it detect?"

Sydney reached the bottom of the ladder and turned to Amy. "I was just about to tell you."

Amy just blinked and waited.

"It detects low levels of electricity like the ones that might come from the computer we found."

"Any luck?" Mei asked.

"No. There were three of us here, and we've gone through the place twice. We got another call, so I sent the others there and I've been trying to go through one last time."

"No hits at all?" Mei asked, looking around.

"Oh, no. We had one. Was a box on the next row down, second shelf."

"What was it?"

"Old transistor radio."

"How long has it been on?"

"Case file is four years old. The radio looks completely dead, but for some reason, it's letting off some current."

Mei frowned.

"I know what you're thinking," Sydney interrupted. "But we pulled it apart. It's just a radio."

"What now?" Amy asked.

"Not sure," Sydney said as they walked back down the aisle. Mei gazed across the boxes, scanned case numbers and names for anything that might give her an idea. "Walk me back through what you found the first time," Mei said. "What evidence was here and where did you find it?"

Sydney took Mei to the middle row of files and pointed out where the box had been that held the first computer. "The first one was here."

Mei looked around. "Any other evidence here besides the computer?"

"Footprints down this row. Men's size nine. Sneaker tread. Nikes we think, but we're waiting on the lab."

"No prints?"

"No. Someone leaned against the file cabinet here," Sydney said and pointed to the metal support beam between the shelves. "And we found a small bit of dirt that was consistent with the soil outside."

"Where was that?"

"On the shelf beside the box," Sydney said. She pointed out a spot on the metal shelf. "About here. We figure it was probably carried in on whatever he used to bring in the computer."

Mei nodded. "So, he set his bag on the shelf and opened it up, pulled out the computer, then opened the box and set it in?"

Sydney frowned and stared down at the ground.

"What?"

"I just realized that the soil seems weird now."

"How do you mean?" Mei asked.

"We found soil on the shelf but no other soil deposits on the floor. If he'd set the bag down outside and picked up dirt, you'd expect him to have dirt on his shoes, too."

"Maybe he cleaned up?" Mei asked.

Sydney shook her head. "We'd be able to tell where he'd wiped or even vacuumed. No, there was evidence of footprints all around this area, tread disturbance in the dust on the floor…"

"Is it possible that the surface on the bottom of his backpack picked it up?" Mei suggested. "Like Velcro or something?"

Sydney moved down along the shelf and pretended to hold a pack over her shoulder. "We have to assume it was heavy. That's why he set it down there." Sydney looked around. "But heavy with what? It might have had a weapon, but the only thing we know he was carrying was the computer and that didn't weigh more than a few pounds."

"Maybe he raided the gun cabinet first," Mei suggested.

"But then he would have had more than one bag. We would have seen the imprints of those bags in the dust pattern."

Amy sighed.

Mei and Sydney turned to look at her. Ignoring them, Amy picked up her foot and set it on the edge of the shelf and loosened the buckle on her bulky Mary Jane shoe like all this standing around was uncomfortable.

"This is a crime scene," Sydney snapped.

Amy looked up as though she had no idea what she'd done.

"Your shoe," Mei told her.

Amy lifted it up and set it slowly back on the ground without a word.

"You want to go check in with the lab," Mei told her, handing over the car keys. "See if they have any results on Martin Ziino."

Amy shrugged. "Sure."

Sydney and Mei listened to her make her way slowly across the warehouse floor. Then the sound of the door opening and closing. "Seriously?" Sydney said to Mei.

"I keep telling myself she's just young."

"She's not that young. I've got a toddler who's smarter than that about a crime scene and eighteen-year-old twins with twice the work ethic."

Mei laughed. "It's an interesting team." Mei noticed something where Amy had been. "Look." A small pile of soil now sat on the edge of the shelf. "It must have come off Amy's shoe just now."

"Huh," Sydney said.

Mei looked up. "Which means the soil you found before might have come off his shoe."

Sydney followed Mei's gaze and the two women looked at the acoustic tiles in the ceiling. "So maybe it came from…"

Mei nodded. "When he climbed up the shelving."

Sydney pulled the stepstool to the spot where the original soil had been and climbed to the top step.

"You're going to need a taller ladder."

"Or I could just climb up the shelves." Sydney pulled

her shoes off and handed them down to Mei. Then she shook the shelving. When it didn't move, she pushed herself off the stool and scaled the top shelf. Sydney was short enough that the ceiling was still well above her head. "Can you reach up there?" Mei asked.

"I think so. Get me the flashlight out of the bottom of the evidence kit."

Mei found the heavy-duty flashlight and passed it up.

Sydney set it up on one of the boxes and turned it on, then stood on her toes and pushed the acoustic tile up and off to one side. Standing back, she shined the light up into the ceiling. "I can't see. You're going to have to pass the stepstool up here."

"Are you sure that's a good idea?"

Sydney frowned and waved for the stool. "Of course, I'm not sure, but do it anyway, would you?"

Mei closed the stepstool and passed it up over her head until Sydney could reach it. Sydney rearranged the boxes to make room for the stepstool. The shelves made little rattling noises, and Mei held on for good measure, although if they came down there would be absolutely nothing she could do.

A few minutes later, Sydney was standing on the stepstool with her head in the ceiling.

"See anything?"

Sydney looked around then called down. "I found something." Her head disappeared into the ceiling along with her right arm and when she came out, she was holding something. "Do you know what this is?" she asked as she climbed down the stepstool. She held the smallest PC available on the commercial market. On the top of it was a cell phone, strapped on with Hello Kitty duct tape.

Mei smiled. "That is called a Raspberry Pi, and I'll bet it's powered by the second LiPo battery." Mei pulled a glove over her fingertips and took the computer from Sydney.

"Let's hope this thing has some answers," Mei said, placing the device in an evidence bag.

"That part's your job," Sydney said, patting Mei on the back as she reached the floor again.

Just then, Mei's phone buzzed. The text said, *Looking forward to Akiko. What time works?*

Mei had completely forgotten about dinner with Sophie.

"Everything okay?"

"I forgot I made dinner plans," Mei said.

"You go on. I'll get this entered into evidence. It'll be waiting for you in the morning."

Mei held onto the computer, but Sydney was firm. "Go, go. You deserve to have some fun."

Mei felt herself blush, but she let go of the evidence bag.

"I hope he's cute," Sydney teased as Mei hurried out of the warehouse.

She texted Sophie. *6?*

The reply came before she had reached the car. *Perfect.*

CHAPTER 23

MEI STOPPED BY the lab after her last meeting of the day. Amy's desk looked shut down for the night. She had sent Mei a text to tell her that nothing came of Martin Ziino. He was gainfully employed and was still friends with some of the people at Archer Decker, so he didn't seem like a good suspect. Another dead end.

Teddy was gone on a different case, and she'd sent Blake down to Oyster Point to try to meet with the IT departments of the other three businesses. So far, he'd been shut out of the law office and the pharmaceutical company. In the meantime, the Raspberry Pi sat untouched. Aaron was packing up his bag and, from what she could see, doing his best to ignore her. Mei put the machine in lockup then returned to her desk.

"Didn't get to that today," Aaron said without looking up.

She might have asked what he had done, but she wasn't in the mood for a pissing match. "Sure," she said.

Aaron did look up then as though testing her sincerity. She gave him a smile and sat down at her computer to take a last look at emails. Between the caseload and the incident at Ayi's, she was quickly falling behind on paperwork. Aaron fumbled with his computer, catching it just before it hit the ground. He winced and drew his right arm to his chest.

"Nice catch," she said. "You drop it on your finger?"

"No," he said, lifting his bag with his left arm. He moved quickly then, across the lab, without looking back. "Night," he said as he pulled the door open. Then he was gone.

Mei shook her head. If he wasn't such an ass to her, she might have felt a little bad for him. She glanced at the clock on her computer. It was already almost 6:00. There wasn't time to deal with the emails; instead, she scanned through the list in search of something about last night's shooting. They'd found a print. Ryaan had texted her earlier, but she'd heard nothing else. Surely if they had a print, they could find a suspect.

Mei wanted to call Ayi and tell her that they'd found the shooter, that everything was safe again. There was nothing about it in her inbox. Mei texted Ryaan to see if she had any news. An answer came back almost immediately. *No match in the database.*

Mei stared at the words. A fingerprint but no match. Just like on the electrical tape. She hadn't thought much about that print. No print in the system meant someone without a driver's license. A kid, maybe. But Jacob Monaghan was in the database now, so it wasn't his.

What kid would be after her specifically? Or after Ayi? No, it had to be about Mei, but why would someone be after her? Let alone a kid. She was new to San

Francisco. She only knew maybe a dozen people and most of them worked in that very building.

Mei crossed to Aaron's desk. Clean except for a couple of Post-it notes. She tested the top drawer of his desk. Locked. What did she possibly think he was capable of?

Dragging herself back to her own desk, she shut down her computer. There was no way someone in this office had shot at her. They may not have been thrilled that she was in charge now, but gunfire? That was a huge stretch.

On her way up the stairs, Mei dialed Ayi's cell phone. It was still ringing when Mei emerged from the department doors. She had no idea what kind of car Sophie drove or exactly where they were meeting. It wasn't easy to stop in front of the department these days. Bryant Street was busy on a normal day, and the curb in front of the department was designated no parking. That was before Sawicki. Now, the entire block and the street across from the department were cordoned off. Two patrol officers monitored traffic fourteen hours a day. Who knew how long it would last.

To Mei, this was another police peculiarity. At the FBI, they'd have been back to business as usual within forty-eight hours. Perhaps not internally, but certainly on the exterior. For the FBI, appearance was reality. Saving the face of the department was always the priority.

On Mei's second try, Ayi's voicemail picked up. Mei disconnected. No word from Andy all day. She thought about dropping him a message, but what would she say? She'd asked for space. He was giving it to her. She was putting her phone into her pocket when she heard a quick double honk. Sophie pulled up in a light blue Camry. The window was down, and Sophie leaned across. "I'm glad I found you. I was afraid you wouldn't be here, and I'd have to find a place to park out here. What a nightmare."

Mei opened the passenger's door and slid into the car as one of the patrol officers started toward them.

"Just leaving, Deirdre," Sophie called out to the tall blonde.

Deirdre's expression shifted into a smile, and she waved to Sophie.

"Isn't she gorgeous?" Sophie said.

Mei looked at Deirdre's cropped hair and big eyes. "She is," Mei agreed, feeling awkward.

Sophie headed down Bryant toward 7th. "You excited?"

Mei looked over at her. "For tonight?"

"Yes, for tonight," Sophie said, laughing.

"I am looking forward to it. Definitely."

"Long day?"

Mei felt herself yawn and covered her mouth. "It really was. I'm still working that Oyster Point case."

"I thought that was a Triggerlock case."

"It is, but there is also a computer component."

Sophie looked over. "Computer component?"

Just then Mei's phone rang. Ayi. "Sorry, I have to take this. It's my aunt."

"Don't worry," Sophie said, touching her leg. "Answer it, definitely."

Mei glanced at the place where Sophie's hand had been. "Ayi."

"Sorry. I missed the other calls. My phone was in the other room," she said in Cantonese.

"You're not at home, are you?" Mei responded in

English. She felt awkward speaking Cantonese in front of Sophie. As if it weren't awkward enough to be on the phone with Ayi.

"No. I'm with Hui," Ayi continued in Cantonese, ignoring Mei's English.

"Okay. I got a call that the window has been replaced and they're keeping an officer on the street again tonight."

"I'm just going to stay with Hui tonight," Ayi told her.

"I'll be home relatively early if you want me to call you. Then you can come home," Mei suggested.

"I'm already settled in," Ayi said.

A girls' sleepover, for geriatrics. "Okay, have fun. I'll see you in the morning."

"Probably tomorrow night," Ayi said.

"Okay. I'll plan on coming home from work early so I'm there when you get home."

As Ayi said good night, Mei heard Hui in the background. Ayi had hung up the phone without waiting for Mei's response. Mei stared at her phone, half expecting Ayi to call back. Her parents were always accidentally hanging up on her from their cell phones. But the phone remained silent.

"Everything okay?" Sophie asked.

As casually as possible, Mei explained about the gunfire from the night before.

"Where do you live?" Sophie asked.

"I'm staying with my aunt right now," Mei said, feeling her cheeks warm at admitting that she didn't have her own place. In her mind, it led immediately to Andy and she wasn't sure she wanted to talk about him. "Her house is at 22nd and Irving, a couple blocks from the park."

"Wow, that's surprising. It's a nice neighborhood, isn't it?"

"It is," Mei agreed, without dispelling the idea that the shooting had been random. She didn't want to think about it. She shifted the conversation to Sophie and asked about her family.

"I have three half-brothers, all younger," said Sophie.

"Did you get along with them?" Mei asked.

"Mostly I babysat them. They're six, nine, and eleven years younger."

"Oh, fun."

"A blast," Sophie said and rolled her eyes. "I decided early that kids weren't for me."

"I don't think I'm decided," Mei said. "Although my parents would love it."

"Do they pressure you for kids?"

"Sometimes," Mei admitted.

"I think my mom gave up on grandkids from me when I came out of the closet."

Mei sucked in a small breath and held herself still an extra moment.

Sophie didn't seem to notice.

"A girlfriend of mine from high school is married to her partner," Mei said. "They've got two little boys—each of them inseminated by the same donor." Only then did Mei realize how much she'd been wanting to tell Jodi's story out loud.

"Oh, yeah. There are a million ways to do it now."

"But not with my parents," Mei added. "They're traditional. Very Chinese."

Sophie nodded. "I understand."

Mei glanced out the window and felt the phone vibrate in her lap. The name on the screen was A Mā. "Ugh."

"Your aunt?"

"My mother."

Sophie laughed. "Better answer it. I swear mothers know when you ignore them."

"Hi," Mei said. "Everything is fine, A Mā. Ayi is with Hui and I stayed with a friend last night." Mei felt Sophie's gaze on her momentarily.

"You could have been killed."

Mei wished her mother were speaking Cantonese.

"We're fine. There is a police officer at the house tonight."

"What about tomorrow night? Or the next one? Andy called your father today, Mei. He said you wouldn't let him come, that you asked him not to."

"I did," Mei admitted.

"What is going on, Mei?"

"Can I call you tomorrow morning before work?" Mei asked.

"Mei, you can't just put your husband on hold," her mother said.

Sophie pulled to the curb and shut the engine off. Mei looked up to see the sign in the window. Akiko Sushi.

"Talk to you later, A Mā. Love you," she added for good measure then hung up.

Sophie turned in her seat. "Your mother is loud."

Mei grew hot.

"Sorry. I didn't mean to pry. I just heard the word 'husband.'"

Mei turned back to Sophie. "I am married. He's in Chicago. I'm here."

"Now I'm the one who's embarrassed," Sophie said. "After the shooting… when we were in the hall, I thought you were gay."

Mei turned back to the street. "Guess I'm still figuring things out."

"Come on," Sophie said. "They serve some amazing sakes in here, and it seems like you could use one."

"Could I ever," Mei agreed.

CHAPTER 24

FOR THE SECOND night in a row, Ryaan got out of bed to go to a crime scene. First, Mei's house and now a fire in Bernal Heights where they had found guns from the Oyster Point warehouse burglary. Patrick wasn't answering his phone, otherwise Ryaan would have been able to sleep through this one. It was definitely Patrick's turn, although they'd already had one goose chase today. They'd spent the morning and half of the afternoon trying to find Karl Penn, the man whose prints were found inside the Ford Focus abandoned in the Tenderloin with a trunk load of stolen guns. The address on file for Penn led them to the home of a ninety-four-year-old Asian woman who had never heard of Karl Penn.

When they asked her about her mail, she admitted that she hardly ever got it. Her daughter came on Saturday mornings and usually brought in the whole week's worth. Ryaan got the daughter's number to give her a heads-up about the mail fraud, but as far as the woman knew nothing had gone missing. It was possible that Karl was just using her address to avoid the run-in that Patrick and Ryaan had planned for him. Which meant he probably lived close enough to visit the woman's mailbox—one of the few in the neighborhood that wasn't either a lockbox or a slot through the front door—but not too close to be recognized. Either way, it left Patrick and Ryaan with nothing on Karl. Patrick said he'd start on known associates tomorrow.

Maybe that's why he wasn't answering tonight. That and the fact that they weren't technically on call. Patrick was highly adept at getting out of these "off call" nights by not answering his phone. Ryaan hated to admit that the reality meant Patrick was smarter. "Not on call" equaled no phone. That was his rule. If there was a natural disaster, he'd turn on his phone.

Ryaan's phone was always on. She might have ignored it, but it wasn't like she had anything else to do. Aside from sleep, that is. And she was going to need some of that pretty soon. Without so much as a glance in a mirror, Ryaan left a note for her mother and drove up to Bernal Heights. They'd found some of her guns on the scene. That was what had motivated her out of bed. Her guns. She had taken to thinking of the city's guns that way. Stolen ones. They were hers to find and return to their owners, like children taken from parents. The guns were in danger. Danger of being put into the wrong hands and used to kill. She suspected there was something wrong with thinking about them that way. A department shrink could tell her what it was, but she didn't want to know, not really. In the same way, the shrink might be able to explain why she was both obsessed with guns and repulsed by them.

A man she'd liked had taken her out on a first date to a firing range where they could shoot high-powered rifles and an assortment of guns with high-capacity magazines. It was a first and a last date. Any man who would take her to a gun range was not someone she wanted to see again. Ever. And yet, how could he have known? Guns were everywhere in her life and she rarely shared her mixed emotions around them. Almost no one knew about her brothers.

Out of bed, Ryaan wished that she'd gone to bed earlier. Instead, after dinner, Ryaan had spent a couple of hours on the case. First, listening to the emergency call from the woman, Erica Wilkins, over in the Tenderloin who had called in the Focus full of guns. Then, she read the transcript of the interview Patrol had done with her, trying to glean some hidden jewel. There was nothing. From every angle, Erica Wilkins was what she said she was—a retired schoolteacher who saw something suspicious and called it in. Mrs. Wilkins kept a pair of binoculars by her bedside table. She said she'd been in bed when she heard an unfamiliar car. Before his death, Wilkins's husband had been a mechanic for forty years and she had grown quite adept at hearing the small differences in motor sounds. When she heard the unfamiliar car, she used her binoculars to look out her window.

Beyond that, it was the police's fault that it had taken them almost twenty-five minutes to respond. They were lucky that the guns weren't discovered sooner. According to Mrs. Wilkins, the car had sat quietly, undisturbed for almost fifteen minutes after her phone call before a couple of boys had come up the street and seen the trunk popped, the guns in full view.

Wilkins hadn't seen faces, she'd said, although Ryaan

knew that wasn't true. Erica Wilkins undoubtedly knew exactly which kids had taken guns from that car, but if she hadn't told the police in the interview, it was unlikely she would offer names now. The only other lead they had on the Ford Focus was the old sticker from the golf club. When Ryaan had called them earlier, the country club had confirmed that the sticker was indeed a parking pass issued from their club, but they couldn't tell her who it had been issued to. Another dead end.

Ryaan followed her phone's GPS to the street where the fire had been. As soon as she turned the corner, the building location was obvious. The fire engine was gone, but two fire trucks remained parked on the street alongside a patrol car, a detective's car, a CSU van, and two civilian cars she didn't recognize. No surprise visit from Patrick. Not that she expected one.

There were a few residents standing on their porches or on the sidewalk in front of their homes, but Ryaan guessed most had already gone back to bed. Ryaan looked up at the building. The front door was located on the left side, which appeared to be two stories while the rest of the building was single-level, occupied by a double garage with two separate doors. It looked relatively undamaged considering there had been a fire, which was evident only in the broken glass of the upstairs window and in the splintered remains of the front door where the firemen had entered. Ryaan had no desire to go in, but with nothing left to do, she passed under the crime scene tape and showed her badge to the patrol officer guarding the perimeter.

He gave her a strange look but pointed to the door. "Crime scene team is inside."

Ryaan looked up at the building. "The structure is stable?"

The officer gave her a half nod. "There's a city engineer inside who says it is."

Ryaan headed for the door and heard voices coming from upstairs. "Hello," she shouted up.

There were feet on the stairs before Hal Harris appeared around the corner. "Hi there."

"Hi," she responded, feeling awkward. "I didn't realize you'd be here."

"Fire came with a double homicide," Hal said like he was ordering french fries with his meal.

Ryaan hated dead bodies. "Is Hailey here, too?"

Hal smiled at her. "Nope. She's with the family. How about Patrick?"

"Same, I'm sure."

"It's just us single folks, then," Hal said, smiling.

Unable to come up with a witty response, Ryaan nodded and hoped she didn't look scary.

Hal reached for her face. Ryaan jumped back but Hal laughed. "You've got some white stuff," he explained, running his fingers across her cheek. "Soap, maybe."

It was only then that Ryaan remembered the cream the dermatologist had prescribed for her eczema. She covered her face with both hands. "Oh, God. I forgot all about it."

Hal laughed. "It looks like we got you out of bed."

Ryaan rubbed at her cheeks for several seconds before Hal reached over and pulled her hand away. "You got most of it," he told her. "Come on." With that, Hal turned and started back up the stairs. With a couple last swipes across her face, Ryaan followed.

The city engineer stood at the top of the stairs with one of the firemen. They were tall white men, average-looking, and about her age. Behind them, Ryaan saw a series of small orange markers indicating potential evidence. She was glad to know the crime scene team was already there. The place was a mess. Between the fire and whatever was used to put it out, things were wet and scattered across the room. The smell of burnt plastic and chemicals was almost overwhelming.

Ryaan noticed the small refrigerator and a microwave with a melted door. On the other side of the room was a flat modern desk like an architect's drafting table that might have been from IKEA. It was covered with computers, mostly in pieces. Ryaan rubbed her hand over the back of her nose and nodded hello. "We okay to be in here?"

"Yep," the fireman said. "Come on in."

The engineer shook his head. "There's actually surprisingly little damage."

"The arsonist started with a lot of accelerant," the fireman explained, "but with no windows, the fire pretty much choked itself off."

"Not an experienced arsonist," the engineer speculated.

"Definitely not," the fireman agreed.

"The fire was almost certainly a cover-up for the murders and maybe to burn some evidence," the engineer said. Ryaan watched him and wondered how many crime scenes he'd been to. It seemed like a lot of speculation for a city engineer.

"Well, thank you, gentlemen," Ryaan told them and

joined Hal, who was standing with Naomi from Roger Sampers's team. Ryaan took some comfort in the fact that even Naomi looked a little less fresh tonight.

"Looks like someone was living here," she said to Hal.

"Definitely," Hal agreed. "And doing something with computers. We've found two so far. Plus, a soldering iron, a glue gun, lots of small tools."

Ryaan looked over the contents on the desk, then pointed to a pink mound of melted plastic. "What is that?"

"I think we decided it was Hello Kitty duct tape," Hal told her.

Ryaan felt a little sick. "Any other evidence of kids?"

"None," Hal assured her. "And both bodies were adult males. That same tape was found on the two computers. No kids."

She exhaled. At least there was that. She glanced around. "Where are the bodies?"

"Coroner took them out about an hour ago," Naomi said.

"When did the fire happen?"

Naomi looked at her watch. "According to the firemen, they got a call around 6:15, 6:30. It will be on their log, but that left with the engine."

Ryaan glanced at her watch. It was almost midnight. "You've been here since then?"

Naomi shook her head. "No, we got here about 10:00. They had to clear the smoke and make sure there weren't any hot spots."

Ryaan couldn't imagine what it was like before. "What do we know so far?"

Naomi caught Ryaan up. The first man had been shot

and not recently. His body was well into decomp. "Coroner's guy guessed he'd been dead a week," Hal added.

"The second man was killed early today, strangled," Naomi finished.

"We found the van that was involved in the robbery," Hal said. "We confirmed it was the same one used in the cop shooting."

"Is one of the bodies our cop killer?" Ryaan asked.

Naomi deferred to Hal who said, "Maybe. We've got an ID on one. He's the hacker, we think, but we don't know who the other one is. No ID, and the fire did some damage to the bodies. Not so much the fire," he corrected himself. "More the heat."

Ryaan put up her hands. "That's okay. You don't have to tell me any more about the bodies. What about the guns?"

"There are a few here. Plus some ammo," Naomi explained. "I'll get them to the lab to run prints."

Ryaan thought about the guns. "We're still short."

"Safe to assume they walked out of that Ford when it was parked in the Tenderloin?" Hal asked.

"That would be my bet," Ryaan said. "Where are the guns that were found?"

"Down in the garage."

Ryaan pulled out her notebook. "I'll get the description before I go," she said. Then she'd know exactly which guns were still AWOL. At last count, they were missing four of the big ones. She hoped they'd be here.

"I'll come with you," Hal said, then turned to Naomi. "You okay up here?"

"Sure," she said.

"Cool," Hal said, then turned to Ryaan. "Let's go." As they headed toward the stairs, Hal called back to Naomi. "Text me if you find anything interesting."

Two other crime scene techs were at work in the garage. The smell there was worse. It wasn't the smoke but the smell of flesh, rotting and burnt. Someone had opened the garage door several feet to allow fresh air to get in. It also made it colder. Ryaan zipped up her jacket and tried not to think about how tired she was.

"Breathe through your mouth," Hal said.

Ryaan nodded.

Hal stepped in front of her. "Darren, you know Ryaan Berry from Triggerlock?"

The man who looked up had nice eyes. He nodded hello. "I'd shake, but—" He held up gloved hands.

"No worries," Ryaan said. "Nice to meet you."

"Where are the guns you guys found?" Hal asked.

"Michael's got them on the far side of the van."

Ryaan followed Hal around the van. There, Michael was photographing the inside of the van. Ryaan turned away.

"Damn," Hal said, covering his nose.

"You're telling me," Michael said. He stepped out of the van and pulled the booties off his shoes. "Darren, did you call us a tow for this thing?" Michael shouted.

"Should've been here already," Darren called back. "I'll call again."

"You want to see the guns?" Michael asked, returning his camera to the bag.

"If it's not too much trouble," Ryaan said. Exhaustion was making her nauseated. She'd take a look, snap a couple photos, and head home. She really had to curb her compulsion to respond to every call, no matter what the hour. What she really needed was a life.

Michael led her to a black satchel and knelt to unzip it. She followed, trying to shake the hold of exhaustion. What was it about being tired that made her doubt everything? She was thirty-four. She knew better than to let herself get this way.

"Here's what we've got," he said.

It was the curved clip of an AK. That quickly, she felt alert again. She wanted all seventy-two guns off the streets, but mostly she wanted these big ones back. "You have an extra pair of gloves?"

Michael pulled two gloves from his jacket pocket and handed them to her.

Ryaan opened the satchel until she could clearly see the three guns. "Two AKs and a 10mm Glock with a high-capacity mag."

"Good news?" Hal asked.

Ryaan stood and thought back to the running list she was keeping of the stolen guns. "We're down to eighteen missing guns. About ten of those have high-capacity magazines, but only two assault weapons are still missing."

"That's something," Hal said.

Ryaan nodded. "Definitely."

"Lab's got this case on priority. We'll get these printed first thing tomorrow," Michael told her.

"Thanks," Ryaan said and struggled to suppress a yawn. She pulled off the gloves and tucked them in her pocket to throw away later. "I'll follow up with the lab in the morning."

Hal followed her to the door, then reached around to open it for her. Ryaan stepped into the cold night air. As tired as she was, she hesitated to leave.

"Guess it's kind of late to grab a drink," Hal said.

Ryaan laughed. It came out a loud, sharp bark, the side effect of being half-asleep and trying to flirt. It was only then that she realized he was serious. "Oh," she said.

Hal watched her.

"Sorry," she told him, leaning into the cool exterior. "I'm too tired to be charming."

"I think you're doing okay," he said.

"I'd love to have a drink," she told him.

Hal smiled. "Really?"

"Really. But not tonight."

"No," he agreed. "Not tonight."

"Maybe this weekend?" he asked, then added quickly, "Give you one night to catch up on your rest first."

"Perfect," she told him.

Hal grinned. Ryaan waved good night and started to her car without another word. She made it past the officer on duty and all the way to her car without looking back at Hal. He'd asked her out. Only after rounding the car and unlocking it with her key fob did she look up. The door was closed. He was gone. He had asked her out, though. Unless she woke up this moment, that part hadn't been a dream.

CHAPTER 25

MEI WOKE FRIDAY morning to her alarm with the fleeting thought that she'd set it incorrectly. It had to be Saturday. She read the word Friday across the phone screen. Rolled over and laid her arm across her face. Ugh. Outside, an electric bus passed with a static crackling. Behind that was the wheezing rattle of old cart wheels on the sidewalk and a long, angry horn on the next block.

It was definitely not Saturday. Saturday sounded like the father and son playing basketball against the garage door two houses down, the group of women who power walked and complained about husbands and children in loud, shrill voices, and kids riding bikes with their phones blasting Rihanna, Gaga, and Macklemore.

She had never once called in sick in Chicago. She and Andy used to joke about playing hooky. That other newlyweds were off to Mexico or Hawaii while they were spending Saturdays at work. Now she was in a new city with a new job, and she was desperate to roll over and go back to sleep. To have a day without thinking about work.

Weeks had been long at the FBI. She was used to the erratic hours and the cases that chased her through nights and weekends. What she wasn't used to—doubted she'd ever be used to—was how close to home this case had hit. Literally. Mei reached for her phone and loaded her emails, hoping for an update about the shooting. Surely someone would let her know if they'd found out who did it. When they had him behind bars, then she'd feel rested. The idea that they'd found a print on that gun but couldn't match it to anyone was not reassuring.

Ayi had slept at Hui's again last night. Mei had received a quick text from Ayi halfway through dinner with Sophie. *At Hui's tonight.* Ayi was stubborn and strong and someone Mei had always regarded as unflappable. Since the shooting, that image of her aunt had shattered as completely as the front window.

The evening with Sophie was sort of a disaster too. Mei had said too much in the car, making the subject of her sexuality too much at the forefront of the evening. Even when Sophie took the clue to stop talking about it, the subject remained in the air. While Sophie was cute and engaging, she seemed to be trying too hard. Mei couldn't relax. Not that it was Sophie's fault.

With everything going on, Mei should have canceled. She needed to keep her head down until this case was over, but who knew how long that would be, and Mei needed to get out of her own head too. Maybe the real issue was that Sophie wasn't her type. Mei was shy, introverted by nature, and she tended to attract people more like her. Sophie was anything but. She had the kind of ease with people that Mei once aspired to and now felt the desire to avoid.

Meeting Sophie right after the shooting had made her

seem like someone more like Mei, but in hindsight, Mei realized it was not Sophie herself who was vulnerable and awkward. It was the circumstances that had removed her cloak of confidence. Last night, Mei had seen a different Sophie. Where Mei found herself conversing in a near-whisper to avoid catching the attention of other diners, Sophie engaged them. Mei ordered strictly by guessing at what might be good from the menu. Sophie asked the waitress for a list of her favorite dishes and requested that the California rolls come rice on the outside rather than the house standard of seaweed out. "It keeps the seaweed from getting too dry," she explained to the waitress.

Mei had felt slightly embarrassed at what felt like a lack of decorum, but it wasn't that Sophie was rude. Not at all. It was that Mei judged everyone through the same, strict perspective as her conservative, traditional parents. To them, Americans were a loud, overly demanding and disrespectful bunch.

It felt deeply ironic that Mei had grown up to be a police officer, a gay or at least bisexual woman, and still retained some of her parents' traditional bigotry.

When Sophie dropped her back at the station after dinner, Mei had the distinct feeling that they were on different pages about how the evening had gone. Mei gave Sophie a chaste kiss on the cheek, thankful again that she'd insisted on splitting the check, and hoped it wouldn't be awkward at work. If she had to, Mei would use the shooting at Ayi's as an excuse to stick close to home.

That Mei needed to focus on Ayi was hardly an excuse. What little time she'd been at the house the last two days, she'd spent making sure that the house looked as clean and undisturbed as possible. Other than the art, it was now exactly as it had been before the shooting. Before work that morning, she took Ayi's gongbi to a place in Chinatown that handled art restoration. From the look the man gave her, he seemed to think that Mei had shot the piece herself. "What you expect me to do with this? I'm not miracle man," he'd said in awkward English.

"I know. I'm very upset as it is my aunt's picture," Mei replied in her most formal Cantonese. "Is there anything you can do?" She offered no explanation of what had happened. He was clearly traditional Chinese, which meant that telling him she was a police officer was not going to win her any favors. In fact, it might be preferable that he'd thought she'd shot it herself. Maybe she should tell him her husband was a police officer.

The man's expression softened. "I can't promise, but I will try." He pulled a card out of the plastic business card dispenser on the counter and handed it to her. "You call me end of next week."

She thanked him and left in a slightly better mood. She was determined to spend the weekend at home with Ayi. Ayi needed to come home and the longer she put it off, the harder it would be. Plus, Hui had to be growing tired of the company. The effort wasn't entirely unselfish either. Mei certainly couldn't move out of Ayi's house or even tell her parents about a break from Andy until Ayi was comfortable there again.

Mei pulled Ayi's car into the entrance to the police parking lot and slid her card in the machine. The card returned. The barrier lifted. Friday. It definitely was Friday.

Her phone vibrated. *Thanks for a great night. Hope*

the family drama doesn't rear its ugly head today. Will keep you posted on weekend plans.

At the end of the night, Sophie had suggested getting a group to go out over the weekend. Mei had been careful not to agree, but she also hadn't said no either. She was intrigued by the idea. She could decide later.

Mei sat down at her desk in the lab and booted up her computer. The room was quiet but for the whir of the case fans and coolers of the computer. The mechanical platters buzzed softly as the tiny magnetic head leapt around to access her hard drive, the platters spinning at upwards of 10,000 times per minute. She loved the sounds of the machinery, could diagnose a sick computer just by the sounds. She used to wear headphones plugged into her computer without music simply to hear the computer speak to her. Data was tangible, secure, predictable. You didn't need to listen to its tone or watch its body language to know if it was telling the truth. Data was always honest.

As head of the department, Mei no longer felt comfortable wearing headphones in the lab. It felt like she was telling people not to bother her. Which, of course, was exactly what she wished they would do.

Amazingly, Mei was able to work through all of her emails and run downstairs to buy an apple juice before anyone arrived. She arrived back at her desk to a voicemail from Amy saying she had a family emergency and wouldn't be in. Mei was just settling back in at her desk when the lab door slammed open against the far wall. Blake struggled through the door, arms loaded with equipment.

Mei stood. "Let me help you."

"I'm okay," Blake said, breathless. "Someone parked

in my spot. I had to walk two blocks." He set down a large, handled briefcase that contained everything they needed for collecting evidence and took his own computer bag and a department computer bag to his desk before coming back for the evidence kit.

"How did it go yesterday?"

Blake shook his head. "Not great." He motioned to the outer office. "Mind if I get a cup of coffee first?"

"Sure. No problem."

While she waited, Mei heard the annoying ding of a new email. From Aaron. The subject line read "Late."

Running late. Be there by ten. AP

Mei stared at the words. It should have been a relief that she wouldn't have to deal with Aaron this morning. There was something going on with him. Not only was he unhelpful, he was deceitful. He'd clearly hurt himself yesterday. Why hide it? And what else was he hiding?

Blake came back with a cup that said "#1 Dad" and sat down. She remembered the first time she'd seen it and asked about his kids. "I don't have kids," he'd said, motioning to his weathered appearance like that should have been evidence enough to deduce his parental status. The mug, it turned out, was a relic from some earlier employee of the team. At this point, no one could even remember who the "#1 Dad" had been.

Blake sat in the chair and brought the mug to his mouth. He took a long drink.

"Rough morning," she said.

Blake shook his head. "Totally."

"You want to talk about yesterday or do you need some time?" she asked.

"No, I'm fine." Blake set the mug on the edge of her desk. "They weren't exactly cooperative. The law firm denied any access at all. They didn't let me anywhere near their logs. I know it's bullshit—excuse the French—because all the junior guys were acting like they'd been handed their asses on platters. Excuse the—"

"French," Mei interjected. "Don't worry about it." She slid open her top drawer and reached in for her tablet to take notes.

"One of the younger guys stood in the corner, staring at his shoes," Blake went on. "The other two junior guys just took notes like they'd never heard the kind of bullshit this guy was spewing."

Only half listening, Mei pulled the drawer open farther. She shuffled through all her papers. "My tablet isn't here." She tried to move casually, but panic was setting in. She'd locked her desk. She was sure of it.

"Did you take it home?" Blake asked.

"No." Her heart raced. She opened her side drawers even though she never put it there. She always left it in the center drawer. It was the best locking drawer. Something her first boss at the FBI had told her; he'd always been full of idiosyncratic facts. The others could be opened a few millimeters and picked or pried, he'd explained. The center drawer was much harder because it closed under the lip of the desk.

"Maybe you left it somewhere else?"

Her tablet held all her crime scene reports, all the photos, and documented evidence. All of it was backed up, of course, but losing the tablet was like losing the case file. She opened her computer bag and searched it. Nothing.

"Maybe you locked it in the safe storage," Blake suggested.

That was ridiculous. She would never have done that. "Do you mind checking?" she asked.

Blake rose from the chair. She just wanted him out of her space. It wasn't the missing case information. She wished it was only that. Worse. It was much worse. She'd been tracking her team's hours, keeping a file on case progress and activities to document which of them were working—i.e., Teddy and Blake—and which were not—i.e., Aaron and Amy. The period for annual review was nearly up, and Sergeant Lanier had made suggestions for salary adjustments that felt completely out of line with the performance she'd seen. That file, including all the documentation of Aaron's absences, his stubborn denial of the projects she assigned him, and his secret refusal to divulge what he was working on and for whom. It was all on there. Not to mention a journal of her feelings, her most honest reactions to seeing the pictures of Jodi and her wife, and a hundred other things that were deeply personal.

Teddy stood at her desk. She hadn't even heard him enter the lab. He held something small in his hand and for a fleeting moment, she thought it was her tablet. Then she recognized the Raspberry Pi. "You want me to start on this?" he asked.

Mei nodded, forced herself to say please.

Blake returned a moment later. "It's not there."

Teddy looked at Blake. "What's not where?"

"She can't find her tablet."

"I have it," Teddy said. "I found it on my desk when I got back from the Lindley scene last night. I didn't even notice it until I was packing up to go home."

Teddy took the tablet from one of his drawers and brought it to her.

"Thanks," she said, trying to sound casual. "Had me worried for a second."

"You must have left it there before you left."

Mei took the tablet back and thanked Teddy. Blake sat back down and Mei stood. "I have to run one quick thing up to HR," she lied. "Can we talk about yesterday when I'm back? Say fifteen minutes."

Blake shrugged without standing. "Sure."

"Maybe see what you and Teddy can find out about that Raspberry Pi."

Mei took the tablet and, remembering her excuse about HR, grabbed a random folder from the files in her drawer and held them both to her chest as she walked out of the lab. She didn't go to the women's bathroom on her floor but instead walked up three flights to the third floor and went into the farthest stall.

Someone flushed and washed her hands. Mei waited until she was positive she was alone before entering her password and opening up her tablet. She did not believe for one second that she had left her tablet out. She knew she'd locked it in her desk last night.

Data security was as ingrained in her as brushing her teeth before bed. Maybe even more ingrained.

Mei entered her passcode into her tablet and went to Dropbox. She opened the app and clicked "show change log" on the dropdown menu and waited while the log populated, scanned the times. Nothing last night. Which meant… nothing.

The files were unchanged, but that didn't mean they hadn't been accessed. Teddy had found the tablet on his desk. She had been by his desk before leaving last night. Her favorite professor in college always adhered to Occam's razor, which said that among competing hypotheses, the one with the fewest assumptions should be chosen. In this case, the simplest possible explanation—that she herself had left it there and Teddy had found it and put it into his desk—would be the correct one. Mei changed her login code to something less obvious than her Chicago street address and hoped Occam was right.

CHAPTER 26

ROGER SAMPERS'S TEAM brought in three boxes of computer equipment from the warehouse. It had all been fingerprinted on site. Sampers himself arrived a few moments later.

"There is only one set of prints that came up." Roger handed her a copy of a print card. "Sam Gibson. His prints weren't on file because he doesn't have a driver's license." Roger paused before saying, "These are the same prints on the electrical tape and on the gun found at your home."

Mei felt like she was breathing through a straw. The man who tried to kill her?

Roger nodded. "You know him?"

"I don't think so. What do *you* know about him?" Mei asked.

"Surprisingly little. We're working on obtaining records from his schools, but so far we only know that his parents are both very powerful in Silicon Valley. Gibson is an only child and one of the youngest hackers to shut down a major website—"

Mei made notes on her tablet.

"He chose Cisco," Roger continued. "That's the company where his mother worked, if that tells you anything about the family dynamics."

"How did he shut it down?" Mei asked.

Teddy walked to her desk. "I remember him. Greeneggs."

"Green eggs?" Mei repeated.

"That's his screen name," Teddy explained. "He shut down Cisco's site for six or seven hours with a denial of service attack."

"I remember," Blake added. "He was like twelve."

"You need anything else from me?" Roger asked.

Mei shook her head and looked down where she'd written only two words. "Gun. Gibson." She didn't know Gibson. She certainly had never had interactions with him at the Bureau. She couldn't imagine that he knew her well enough to choose her as a target. That meant someone else had made her the victim.

Roger left and Mei closed her tablet, returning her focus to the case. The answers had to be there. "The first step is to confirm his identity and link him to the Raspberry Pi since the first computer was completely clean," she said. "Then, we need to track down any known associates."

Blake looked at Teddy, who shook his head. "It's a pretty loner occupation. Not a lot of hackers sitting together in rooms. At least not outside the movies."

"He's working with someone," Mei said.

Blake nodded. "At the very least someone who was driving during the shooting at your place."

Mei said nothing.

"I'll try to track the username through some forums or IRCs," Teddy said.

Mei hadn't heard anyone refer to inter-relay chat in ages. "People still use IRC?"

"You'd be surprised," Teddy said.

"I'm on DALnet all the time," Blake added.

"I use Quakenet pretty regularly, too," Teddy added sheepishly.

Mei laughed, shaking off the uncomfortable thoughts about Gibson. "And I thought I was old school."

Mei's phone rang. "Ling."

"It's Sydney... Blanchard."

"Hi, Sydney."

"So, we finally got some news on the cell phones piggybacked on those computers."

Mei tried to unlock her tablet with the wrong password twice before she remembered she'd changed it to Jodi's birthday. "What've you got?"

"It's not much," she admitted. "Both phones are disposable, of course. The first one, which ends 9008, was piggybacked to the Acer computer we found first. That one was never used for voice, only data, and only from a single location."

"The apartment that burned down last night."

"Exactly."

Mei sighed. "The other one?"

"The second phone, which ends 7651, was almost exclusively used for data, except for a period of about fourteen hours on a Monday at the end of July. That day, it made seven calls."

"To—"

"Four of them were to another disposable phone. We've requested records for that one too… which we'll have sometime next week."

"Next week?" Mei repeated.

"I know. It's ridiculous," Sydney agreed. "The good news is that the last three calls were to a traceable line. It belongs to a Cecilia Criado. Goes by Cici. No record."

Mei typed. "We have an address for Cici?"

"We do. I just texted it over to Patrick."

"Great. I'll follow up with him. Anything else I should know about?"

"Not at the moment, but I'll keep you posted the second I hear."

"Appreciate it." Mei stared at the name. She emailed Ryaan to ask if she wanted company on the follow-up. Then, she went back to searching the underweb for references to Sam Gibson aka Greeneggs. She was also running any searches that might link Amy or Aaron to Gibson. Aaron had shown up at 11:00 and spent most of the day either huddled over a computer taken in an embezzlement case or out at a series of meetings about which he offered no details. Mei considered following him if it weren't so obvious. Everything about him made her suspicious, but it was nothing more than a paranoid delusion until she found evidence to take to Sergeant Lanier or Captain Finlay.

Teddy and Blake had drifted back to their workspaces and were talking animatedly as they worked. They already knew that whoever had configured the Raspberry Pi had set it up to self-destruct. The first computer had been set up the same way. Teddy searched for any bits of code that had survived with the hope that the hacker left his digital fingerprints. He'd also put out some feelers to his Black Hat friends to see if he could identify the components and confirm that Sam Gibson was the hacker that way. Blake, meanwhile, was breaking down the physical components with the same goal.

They made zero progress the rest of the day, but Mei had the sense that they were slowly homing in on their suspect. The best news of the day had come from her friend, Julie, from the wine bar. Julie's cousin, Sabrina, agreed to meet for a quick drink after work to give her some tips on finding an apartment. Julie was going to try to join them, too. Maybe apartment hunting would take Mei's mind off the strong sense that someone she worked with wanted her dead.

CHAPTER 27

SATURDAY MORNING, RYAAN slept late. For the first time in longer than she could remember, she had turned her phone off. In fact, she had turned it off when she'd gotten home Friday night and settled into the couch to watch X-Factor with her mother over dinner. After that, one of her mother's sleeping pills.

It worked. When she rolled over to look at the clock beside the bed, it was almost 10:00 in the morning. Her mother was already out with her church group and Ryaan spent the morning in her pajamas, drinking coffee and reading four weeks of newspapers that she kept telling her mother not to throw out. She should have done something useful like go grocery shopping, take a run, or even do laundry, but instead she spent the day being one hundred percent lazy. When she finally turned her phone on, it was almost 5:00 in the afternoon.

Within forty-five seconds, she'd gotten eleven text messages. One from Patrick saying he had Karl Penn's cell phone number and had issued a subpoena for the records. The next one was from Sydney Blanchard to confirm The Rookie Club dinner for next Wednesday, which set off a flurry of responses. Hailey had to make sure she had kid coverage. Cindy Wang would make it. Jamie Vail and Linda James would not. Then there was a message from Hal. "Want to grab dinner?"

Ryaan looked at the time stamp from 4:48 tonight. She hated that she couldn't tell the time the text message had been sent. Yesterday? Or today? She scrolled back through the messages about the dinner, but none said anything that placed the time.

What the hell. *Just turned on my phone after twenty-four hours.* She paused, trying to think of something clever. She stared at the ceiling. She was not clever. She was not coy. She was the kind of woman who went out without realizing she had eczema cream on her face. But, he had asked her to dinner. That was a vote in her favor. *Pity*, came the quick response in her head. *Ridiculous*, she shouted back. *Catching up on some much-needed beauty sleep.* Did she assume the message was for last night? For tonight? Did she want to go out to dinner tonight? Was it pathetic to just want to curl into bed with a book on a Saturday night? Of course, a little pathetic, but she already knew she was a little pathetic. She usually embraced that part of herself. She stared at the screen and finally wrote, *Would love to grab dinner soon.* Let him figure out when. If he asked for tonight, she could easily say she'd made other plans.

The response came within three minutes. *Basketball game tonight (at the old folks' home). Maybe tomorrow?*

Ryaan smiled. *Perfect. Talk tomorrow. Good luck tonight.*

Thanks. Just trying not to break anything.

Ryaan smiled. A date. A real date, and she still got to stay home on Saturday night. By 7:00, her mother had been home and gone back out to play pinochle with a group of widowed ladies as she did almost every Saturday. Ryaan made herself tomato soup and a grilled cheese sandwich and curled up on the couch to read a Nelson DeMille novel that had been out for over a decade. She hadn't even finished her dinner when her cell phone started ringing from the bedroom.

It was the idea that it might have been Hal that got her off the couch. By the time Patrick's name showed on the screen, she was resigned to answering. "Berry."

"I found Penn. Got his phone records, and there were a bunch of calls to a landline. We got a hit on the address of a Cecilia Criado. Neighbors say Karl's been staying with Cici. I thought I might drop in for a visit."

Ryaan groaned. "Tonight?"

"Patrol did a drive-by. Looks like he's home. Come on, Berry. Gotta strike when the iron's hot. Plus, when was the last time we did a stakeout?"

"Well, I went to a burned down building two nights ago while you were asleep."

Patrick laughed. "Hey, I hear you. I can handle it. Just wanted to keep my partner in the loop."

Ryaan sighed loudly. "Text me the address. I'll meet you there."

"Thatta girl."

Ryaan got dressed in warm, dark-colored clothes. She put on her bulletproof vest and a black windbreaker and ran the A/C in the car to keep from sweating. It was only sixty-four degrees out, but the vest always made her overheat. From her mother's house, Bayview was a straight shot up the freeway, which would likely be quiet this time on a Saturday. Or relatively quiet anyway. Ryaan plugged the address into her phone and followed the directions.

Ryaan called Patrick when she was a few blocks away. "I'm close. Where are you?"

"Come down Thomas. We're parked in front of the Jehovah's Witnesses Church." Ryaan heard one of the patrol officers make a crack. Patrick laughed.

She hung up and followed Ingalls past Van Dyke and Underwood until she reached Thomas Avenue. The patrol car was parked closest. Patrick's Blazer was farther down the block. Ryaan stopped beside the men and rolled her window down.

"We're ready to move," Patrick announced. "Right, guys?"

The patrol officers nodded.

"When was the last time you had eyes on him?"

Patrick touched his phone. "Got it covered from an apartment on the next street down. Captain Marshall had access to a snitch in the area who owed him a favor."

Marshall was the captain of Homicide. This was the first she'd heard about his snitch, but every department negotiated with lesser criminals to hold on to the more serious ones, and the chits the department gained from the offenders who got off were a valuable commodity.

"I'm surprised Marshall doesn't have his people down here," Ryaan said.

"Oh, he does. O'Shea and Kong are sitting on their guy until we find Karl."

"Should we head over?" she asked.

"Yes, ma'am," one of the patrol officers said.

"Let's go," added the other with a little pump of his fist. Rookie.

Patrick opened the door and got into Ryaan's car. As he directed, he called in to confirm their move. "You got backup?" Patrick asked whomever was on the line. Someone responded and Patrick said, "You'd better, asshole." Not even a hint of a smile.

When he ended the call, Ryaan looked over. "Everything okay?"

"Just a precaution," he told her, pointing at their turn.

"I didn't say anything."

"You didn't need to," he said. "You have a lousy poker face."

Ryaan drove around the corner and onto a street that looked like it was in the midst of being rebuilt. Large metal plates scarred the road like Band-Aids. The plates were sometimes used in areas where utility crews were working on gas lines and water mains. In many parts of the city, though, the metal plates were laid down to cover potholes that had become too large to leave and for which the city had neither the budget nor the interest to fix. As she made her way down the barely lit street in Bayview, she counted seven in a stretch of about fifty feet. Her car moaned as it rocked over the bumps the edges of the plates created.

Kindly, Patrick didn't mention the sorry state of her shocks. She'd already heard it from him a half dozen times. It was a city car, after all. It wasn't like she had to pay for the repairs. It just meant that she had to give up access to the vehicle for the five or seven or nine days it would take them to repair it. With no extra vehicles, a loaner was out of the question and Ryaan didn't have another vehicle. She'd get the shocks fixed when she took her next week-long vacation—next year, if she was lucky.

Patrick pointed to a green stucco building with a large white wrought iron gate in front. "Cici lives in the top unit, facing the back." Patrick waved her farther down the block and pointed to a long stretch of empty sidewalk. Veering around a couple of caution road signs which covered smaller potholes—ones only large enough for full-size men rather than full-size trucks—Ryaan parked along a warehouse-like building with a metal corrugated facade.

She shut off the car, tucked the key into her jacket pocket, and zipped up. She shifted the holster under her arm to try to minimize the way it cut into her shoulder along the edge of her vest. It was easier to wear the getup when she was on her feet rather than sitting.

Patrick adjusted his earpiece. Ryaan took hers from the center console and wedged it into her left ear, tucking the plastic tubing around the back of her ear before clipping the microphone to the collar of her jacket.

"You hear me?" Patrick asked.

"Like you're sitting beside me," she told him.

Patrick frowned. "Through the radio?"

Ryaan smiled. "And through the radio."

Patrick cracked the door and got out first. Ryaan could tell he was nervous. He lost his sense of humor. He moved faster. Some people faked it better than Patrick. Ryaan appreciated the tells. These calls made her nervous, too, so knowing her partner wasn't about to go in without some hesitation was comforting.

Ryaan walked over to where Patrick stood with two uniforms.

"Berry, this is Officers Chad Desantis and Len Garrison. Garrison was in the same class as my nephew, Mitch."

Garrison nodded. "Mitch's a good guy."

Patrick slapped him on the back. "Glad you think so."

"We ready to move?" Desantis asked, rubbing his hands together like a teenager going into a fight. Since she'd first seen him, Chad had been bouncing on his feet, fidgeting. Ryaan glanced at Patrick, and he gave a little nod like he already knew it was an issue. Everything about young Desantis made her think he could be a real liability.

Ryaan studied the green apartment building. "You're sure he's there?"

"I don't need to be. O'Shea's watching him," Patrick reminded her.

Despite her doubts, this was happening. She had opted in. Now she was here, and there was nothing to do but move forward. "What's the plan?" she asked, forcing herself to engage.

"You and Garrison cover the street," Patrick told her. "Desantis and I will go around the back." He glanced down the street. "O'Shea and Kong are watching, and they'll join us as soon as we've got Karl."

Desantis started to move when Ryaan took hold of his uniform sleeve. "Hold on, cowboy."

Desantis pulled himself free and crossed his arms to show her he wasn't taking any shit.

"What's his best exit?" Ryaan asked still blocking his path.

Patrick nodded. "Good question. Easiest egress is down the back stairs. I will cover that exit. Desantis will be positioned to cover the balcony. That door is the only other way out, and it's a twenty-foot drop."

Ryaan smiled. "Sounds foolproof."

"It is," Desantis snapped.

"Bullshit," Patrick snapped. "Don't be cocky, kid. Nothing's foolproof. You'd be smart to listen to Inspector Berry's questions and take some fucking notes."

"Yes, sir," Desantis said, turning his gaze to his shoes.

"We all clear?" Patrick asked, touching his earpiece.

"We're set," Ryaan assured him with a hand to her own.

Patrick set off with Desantis on his tail.

Ryaan scanned the long wrought iron fence. There was only one gate, on the far left. "I'll cover the gate," Ryaan said. "You keep an eye on the street for unwanted company or a runner."

Garrison nodded. "Yes, ma'am."

Ryaan walked diagonally across the street, keeping clear of the apartment windows as she made her way to the gate. The fence itself was sturdy and thick, a lot of iron and expensive for this area of town. Someone either had a lot of extra metal and some serious welding experience or they were looking to keep people out. The gate, too, was solid with a fancy keyed lock that she expected to be locked. When she pulled on it, though, the gate swung open. Ryaan looked back at Garrison and pointed to the inside of the gate. Then she pointed to herself and into the gate again. *I'm going in.*

Garrison nodded, and Ryaan drew her weapon as she stepped over the white base of the gate. With her left hand, she swept the beam of her penlight across the side yard of the apartment where between ten and fifteen cars were parked. Looked like a junkyard. She switched off the beam and touched her earpiece. "Status."

There was nothing for a moment, then came the crackle that made her jump. "Ringing the bell."

"Roger," she said back, which made Patrick groan.

Ryaan waited for sounds from the apartment. They always assumed the suspect would run, but maybe Karl Penn would come willingly. A lot of them did. More than you ever saw on the TV shows. Ryaan heard a television in someone's home and cars on the streets. There were no human voices. She waited for the sounds from her earpiece, feeling her legs grow stiff in the cooling air. A light went on at the far side of the building and Ryaan moved slowly toward it, straining for the sounds of something happening.

She reached the edge of the pack of cars and stood by an old Buick. Her first car had been a Buick. A 1984 Skylark that had belonged to her mother's sisters. It had fewer than fifteen thousand miles on it when Ryaan got it in 1994. Someone had painted this one a deep metallic purple. A single dingy red die hung from the rearview mirror, the broken string of the other one dangling beside it, limp and frayed. She moved closer and saw what had once been a bobblehead on the dash. What remained was the bottom half of a dog's body with a bare spring emerging from its neck. It made her think of Taco Bell.

She took a couple more steps into the thick of the cars and reached for her flashlight when Patrick spoke. "We got him."

Then a woman screamed, "No. You can't take him. He didn't do nothing."

"Step back, ma'am," Patrick said.

Garrison ran into the yard, stopping with Ryaan.

"I think the girlfriend is upset," Ryaan said, starting for the back of the building. Ryaan walked. Garrison ran. "You need some backup?" she asked Patrick in the radio.

"No," came the terse reply.

"Get off him," the woman screamed. This time Ryaan had the benefit of Patrick's radio, leaving her feeling deaf in her right ear.

Ryaan paused, waiting to see if her assistance was needed. A couple of minutes later, Officer Chad Desantis strutted around the corner, pushing a handcuffed suspect in front of him. Ryaan assumed it was Karl Penn, who tripped as Desantis pushed. Patrick was a few feet behind.

"Where's the girlfriend?"

"Garrison's calming her down. Her sister's coming over."

"What's with all the screaming?"

Patrick gave a wry smile. Relaxed. "Guess she's going to miss him."

Ryaan shook her head, holstered her gun. "Well, we got what we came for."

"Didn't even put up a fight," Desantis bragged as

though the mere sight of the young officer had driven Karl Penn to surrender.

"Right," Penn said. "I didn't fight, so why these handcuffs so tight? They're cutting into my wrists, man."

Desantis ignored Penn, but Patrick told him to wait up. "Keys," Patrick said when Desantis hesitated. The young cop gave Patrick the handcuff keys and Patrick undid Penn's cuffs, redid them in front, and loosened the wrist bracelets. Desantis looked disappointed, but he was smart enough to keep his mouth shut.

Voices called out from the street and the white metal gate swung open. Ryaan froze until O'Shea and Kong clamored through the gate, making the noise of a group twice as large. There was back slapping and fist bumping. She remained in the shadows. Beside the cars, she could go unnoticed until it died down. She was never going to feel like one of the guys. No use starting now.

Desantis took Karl Penn back out to the street, and Ryaan felt her phone buzz in her pocket.

"Berry," Patrick shouted. "You coming?"

"On my way." She pulled her phone out of her pocket and saw a text from Mei Ling. She sensed movement. Glanced back and saw a shadow duck between the cars. Ryaan crouched down and drew her weapon. Slowly, she scanned the vehicles, which seemed darker after looking at the bright phone screen.

"Berry," Patrick called out.

Ryaan looked back among the cars. There was probably a family of cats living out there. Slowly, she stood again. She glanced away long enough to holster her weapon when he came at her. She dodged away from the cars. Not fast enough. His arm wrapped around her neck, tightened. Young and fast, he moved like someone used to being in the dark. Light-haired in a dark jacket and cap.

She had hesitated, hadn't anticipated a fight. She knew better. They'd caught their suspect. The man who had hold of her was much more frightening. She could just barely make out the shape of an automatic in his hand, but she smelled it. "Don't move," he hissed. She guessed he was in his early twenties. The shape of his wool cap, the speed with which he moved made her think military.

"You make a move for your gun and I'll shoot." His gun was close. She could smell the wet metal. The same scent covered her hands after playing on the bars in elementary school. Every recess in third and fourth and fifth grade, she spent learning to perfect some new maneuver and, in the process, she'd learned to love that metallic smell. The smell of something all her own, the feel of the bars in-between her hands or under the backs of her knees. A safe place, she worked the bars until her hands were permanently the shade of rust and the soft pads under her fingers were the hard gray of old women's feet.

"Where the hell is she?" O'Shea asked.

Ryaan was dizzy at the thought that they'd leave.

More talking. Someone asking if she'd walked past. Then, Kong's voice, words she couldn't hear.

The beam of a flashlight illuminated his eyes. Light brown, hazel. Flecks of yellow and tired. Very tired. "Who are you?" she whispered.

She felt the men moving in. Sensed it in the tightening of his shoulders, the narrowing of his gaze.

"Back off or she dies," he shouted. His spittle sprayed her cheeks. His breath was sour, like he had gone too long without eating, the smell of stomach acids. She closed her eyes, fought against nausea and panic.

He yanked her to him and shifted the barrel of the gun to the base of her skull. With the metal jammed against her, he removed her gun out of her holster and, for a moment, he seemed to fumble with his jacket. She focused on what she could control, what she knew. Her gun was in his left pocket. "Turn around very slowly and keep your hands where I can see them."

Ryaan did as he said.

Patrick whispered in her ear. "Who the fuck is that?"

She shook her head.

"Don't hurt her," Patrick yelled. "Just tell us what you want."

The gunman gestured with his free hand and she waited for the barrel to break contact with her skull. "Bring him back. The man you just arrested."

"Go get Penn," Patrick shouted. Desantis went running.

"Is Karl Penn your friend?" Patrick shouted. "Is that it? You want us to let him go?"

"Karl Penn," the man behind her whispered. "Penn." The name seemed to mean nothing to him.

She gave a quick shake to her head, wondering if Patrick could even see it, if he would possibly understand what she was saying.

The gate creaked open. Penn stepped back into the yard, pushed by Desantis.

"What the fuck?" Penn shouted.

"Now, let him walk forward on his own," the man shouted.

Desantis pushed Penn forward, but Penn shouted. "No fucking way," he said, backing up against Desantis who struggled to hold him forward. "I'm not going near that guy."

Kong spoke to Penn. "You don't know him?"

"Crazy white man with a gun? Hell, no, I don't know him."

Patrick was ignoring Penn, but Ryaan had heard him and Kong, and she knew the man behind her had, too. They were too loud.

"If we send Karl Penn over there, how do we know you'll let the officer go?"

"You don't."

There was more rustling.

Ryaan wanted to sit. A tremor had started in her legs, like the one she got from doing wall sits for too long back in the day when she'd spent more time in the gym. "I can help you if you tell me what you need," she said.

"I need that guy."

"Okay," Ryaan said. "Does he have something you need?"

"Yeah."

"Can one of the officers get it from him?"

Ryaan started to edge her face toward him. It was harder to shoot someone who was facing you. Make a personal connection. Engage him. "Seems like you're having a rough time—"

His jaw was held tight, the muscles like gears on either side of his face that he worked while he stood there.

Keeping her right hand still, Ryaan slowly moved her left hand toward the radio button clipped to the collar of her jacket. "You want to tell me your name?"

He looked at her, his gaze hard and angry. "Why should I?"

She pushed the button and hoped Patrick hadn't pulled his piece out. "Because maybe I can help you."

The gun was steady as he glanced up to check on the men. "I don't need your help. I should just fucking shoot all of you."

Patrick's breath was audible in her ear. Her own caught in her throat.

He was controlling the situation well. Too well.

Ryaan kept silent.

He jammed the gun hard against her neck, and Ryaan let out an inadvertent yelp. "What the fuck do I need you for?"

Patrick separated from the group, cupping his hand over his mouth like he was blowing on them to keep warm. "Keep talking, Berry," Patrick whispered. "Just talk, nice and soft."

Ryaan took a shaky breath. "The way I see it, if you shoot me then those guys over there are going to shoot you, and you'll never get to Karl Penn."

The man wiped the back of his hand across his forehead. For part of a second, the gun wasn't pointed at her head.

"Good girl," Patrick urged.

"That's what you want, right? To talk to Karl Penn?"

The jaw gears were working again.

"My name's Ryaan. Ryaan Berry."

He glanced at her, then back over her head. His jagged Adam's apple moved down his throat as though it might slice straight through his youthful skin.

"Justin Sawicki."

"Sawicki," Ryaan repeated. The name was familiar, but she couldn't place it.

Then Patrick's voice said, "Sawicki is the guy who shot up the department."

In that moment, Karl Penn's girlfriend came around the corner of the apartment building and saw Sawicki with the gun to Ryaan's head. She let out a scream that Ryaan could feel in her toes.

CHAPTER 28

MEI MET UP with Julie and her cousin, Sabrina, at the wine bar Friday night. Though they'd only had time for one glass, Mei really enjoyed Sabrina. She looked like Julie but was easily three or four inches taller and less fine-boned than Julie. Not so stereotypically Asian in appearance. Mei knew that Julie's mom and Sabrina's mom were sisters but wondered if Sabrina's father might be Caucasian. When she asked, Julie made a crack that Sabrina's father was a Chinese giant.

"He's from Shandong," Sabrina explained. "I guess they're known for being tall."

As they left, Sabrina invited Mei to go look at apartments the next morning. Mei was tempted. The timing certainly wasn't right to move out of Ayi's, but she would like to see what was available. And she really enjoyed Sabrina's company.

When Sabrina went to the bathroom, Julie leaned into Mei and whispered, "I knew you two would get along. You are exactly her type."

Mei couldn't bring herself to ask Julie why she thought she was gay, but she had to admit the comment was pleasing. She was drawn to Sabrina, too. In the end, Mei accepted the invitation to look at apartments.

Saturday morning, Sabrina picked her up at Ayi's and the two visited four different apartments. Any of them would have been fine. The idea of living alone was so appealing, Mei would have agreed to live inside a windowless box. The first two places they saw weren't much better than that, but the third place felt absolutely perfect. A studio in Bernal Heights, the apartment was on the top floor in a building with no elevator. That might have been a drawback for most people, but it was a perk for Mei.

She appreciated the building's old charm and its quiet halls. She liked the ancient, miniature refrigerator and the oven that fit perfectly between the door and the sink and could not have measured wider than twenty inches. The appliances worked. She and Sabrina had spent almost half an hour in the tiny kitchen, debating if it would be possible to have two people in there at once and, if so, where each would stand. Sabrina had suggested that one could sit on top of the refrigerator if there were a stepstool available, but then she'd realized there was literally no place to store a stepstool. The more they made fun of it, the more Mei fell for its Lilliputian charm.

Located on Bronte Street, which Sabrina and Mei agreed was both stupidly cheesy and also kind of charming, the apartment was only a few blocks from the 101 freeway, but the distant humming of eighteen-wheelers and the occasional blaring of a horn were nothing compared to the noise that had leaked into the Chicago apartment where Mei had grown up. There, Mei told Sabrina, the downstairs neighbors had kept a rooster for all the years of her youth.

Sabrina even thought Mei had a decent shot of getting the place and was contacting the rental agent.

"You can always change your mind," Sabrina told her. "We might as well try for it."

On the car ride home, Mei felt lighter than she had in weeks. When Sabrina asked about Mei's plans for Saturday night, she surprised even herself by inviting Sabrina to join the group Sophie was putting together to go to a club called Blue.

"Fun," Sabrina said quickly.

Mei actually laughed.

"I haven't been to a club in years," Sabrina said.

Mei turned in her seat. "I've never been to a club in my entire life."

Sabrina looked shocked. "You're kidding."

Mei made an "O" with her fingers.

"God, now we have to go," Sabrina said.

They arrived at Ayi's a few minutes later and Sabrina wrote her cell phone on the back of a business card. "Text me and I'll meet you guys there."

Mei took the card and thanked Sabrina. She cracked the door and turned back. "God, what am I going to wear?"

Sabrina laughed. "You can never go wrong with the LBD."

Mei shook her head. "LBD?"

"Little black dress."

Mei jogged up the stairs to Ayi's front door, feeling good. A lead on a perfect apartment, a fun night out where she could be who she was. Maybe things were turning around. Just the idea of two whole days off in front of her was appealing. She wanted to visit the gym she'd joined and been to twice and maybe sit down with the *New York Times*. Not the electronic version but the real one. All three pounds of downed forest on a quiet, corner table with hours to waste and hot apple cider that burned her tongue. That would be her entire plan for tomorrow.

Ayi arrived home a little past 5:00, her arms lined with small pink grocery sacks and dim sum leftovers for Mei. Shrimp dumplings. Food Mei had loved as a child. Ayi was in a good mood, putting away her food and chattering about the market and who she'd seen. None were people Mei knew, but she listened patiently and helped unwrap fresh bok choy and white radishes, tung ho, and shui qua, all things Mei had grown up eating but never cooked herself.

Hui had gone to visit her son, so Ayi was back sleeping at home. Mei didn't pry but Ayi seemed comfortable. Mei offered to stay home with her on her first night back, but Ayi insisted she go out. In fact, her aunt seemed pleased that Mei had plans and oddly not inquisitive about where or with whom. Since the shooting, in fact, Ayi seemed distant but also oddly mellowed. Mei had spent only a short time debating her lack of an LBD before deciding on jeans and a button-down silk blouse in deep purple. She was not, nor had she ever been, a dress girl.

Sophie and two friends picked Mei up at 7:30. They stopped for a drink at the wine bar where Sabrina met them before heading over to the club. Mei was thankful for the glass of wine before the club. When they arrived at Blue, the beat of the music was so loud it seemed to vibrate her organs. Without the mild buzz of the wine, Mei was sure she'd have turned around to go home.

Sabrina took her arm. "You ready for this?"

Mei shook her head. "No."

Sophie led, followed by Jordan and Kendra and finally Mei and Sabrina. Sabrina bought a round of shots—something sweet and lemon—and then Mei bought beers. The group spent much of the next two hours on the dance floor. The music was something called electronica, heavily techno, that made Mei feel like she was at her first rave.

"Can I buy you a drink?"

Mei turned to the woman beside her, an attractive redhead, and raised her beer bottle. "All set."

The redhead nodded and signaled for the bartender's attention. That was the third offer for a drink she'd had. Purple really was her color.

From her perch at the bar, Mei saw Sophie dancing with her friends, Kendra and Jordan, and Sabrina talking to a woman she knew from the real estate world. Mei was happy to lean against the bar and take it all in. She was so often in the position of guessing the sexual orientation of the women around her. Over the years, she had developed a fairly adept "gay-dar," as it was often called, but she was still wrong on occasion.

It was no wonder that women came to a club like Blue. Here, there was no question that they weren't interested in being hit on by men. At least not tonight. Here, they were understood. Perhaps not fully, but at least in some very essential way. It wasn't Mei's scene. She was not a dancer and she rarely had more than a couple of glasses of wine, but she was glad she'd come.

Sophie appeared at her side and set her empty beer bottle on the bar before shrugging out of the thin blouse she wore over a white camisole. "It's so hot," she shouted over the music.

Mei nodded, setting her bottle beside Sophie's.

Sophie pulled a twenty out of her pocket. "I have to go to the bathroom. If the bartender comes over, will you order me another one?"

Mei pushed the money aside. "Sure. I got it."

Sophie pressed the bill into Mei's hand and closed her fist on it. The bass grew loud, and Sophie covered her ears for a moment.

Mei cringed.

"Get one for you, too," Sophie shouted, then turned for the bathroom.

Mei waved down the bartender and pointed to the empties in front of her in lieu of making an order that would have been impossible to hear.

The bartender returned with the beers, and Mei paid, setting Sophie's change under her bottle. Sophie returned quickly. "It was a miracle. No line."

"The only women's bathroom with enough stalls."

Sophie laughed and, for a few minutes, the two watched the crowd. Soon, Jordan joined them, then Sabrina returned.

"Who was that?" Sophie asked Sabrina.

"A realtor. We did a deal together a while ago. Her client was this total nut with like seventeen cats. She was just telling me the story of finding this woman a place to live."

"No worries. Do you want a drink?"

Sabrina nodded. "I'll get something."

Mei turned away from the bar to look at the crowd of women. She hadn't thought she would fit in, but the truth was, none of them did. Every end of the spectrum was represented. Women in jeans and steel-toed boots and women in miniskirts so short they might have been long tank tops. Many were dancing but others were standing around the edges, wallflowers even in a gay bar. Mei glanced at the ones who stood alone. That took guts. Along the back wall was one such girl, trying to make herself invisible. Her straight brown hair hung over her face, which was buried in her iPhone. Mei felt like she'd seen her before. A blonde approached her, trying to make conversation. Mei watched them. The shy woman shaking her head, begging off the attention of the blonde. And then she looked up. Mei recognized the face. She was stunned. Why would she be in a gay bar?

Mei took a step back to the bar and lost her footing. The floor was no longer level. In a single step, it had dropped six inches. Or maybe her leg had buckled. She pitched forward and caught herself against an empty table.

The redhead from earlier was back again. She touched Mei's arm, but the touch felt distant as though it was water pushing against her rather than a person. "Are you okay?"

Mei nodded. "Thanks." The word felt like a large bite of something sweet and sticky. Her tongue was too big; it filled her mouth and made her want to gag.

When she looked up, the woman was gone. Keeping hold of the table, Mei turned back to the bar. Faces were fuzzy and out of focus. She had to close one eye to find Sophie and Sabrina, who were leaning across the bar, trying to get the bartender's attention. The distance was farther now. Something was wrong. The smart thing to do was to stay still. Wait. She pressed the back of her hand to her face. She was hot. It was loud and hot.

She remembered the leftover shrimp Ayi had brought home. She felt the firm texture of their pink bodies between her teeth, tasted the warm flavor. It had been so good then, but now it rose against the back of her mouth. She gasped and swallowed. She was going to be sick. She set her full beer on the table and aimed her gaze at the bathroom. She had been sick from alcohol only twice before. The last time was over a decade before. The memory of it made her shudder.

She searched for Sabrina or Sophie in the crowd, but faces were smeared as though she were spinning too quickly in a circle. Or they were. She touched the comforting bulge of her cell phone in her back pocket and headed for the bathroom. She would text them from there. Tell them she was sick. Or not. Maybe it would pass. She took slow, shallow breaths. *Don't be sick. Don't be sick.* Jodi had laughed when Mei got sick the first time. On peach schnapps and gin. A terrible combination. She had never recovered a taste for gin, and the smell of peaches still gave her a twinge of nausea. The lights on the dance floor were hot and blinding, the bodies pushing against each other as she tried to move through them. Her feet were unsure. She swayed into a woman who turned and put her hands on Mei's hips. She didn't stop walking, felt the hands slip off, one trailing down her right thigh. A woman stood outside the bathroom door, something in her hands. A phone. She was staring at a phone.

Mei stepped toward the black bathroom door.

The woman lowered the phone, said something. Mei shook her head. She took the knob and tried to twist it. Locked.

"It's occupied," the woman repeated in the slow, enunciated speech of someone talking to a foreigner. Mei stopped and pressed her hand to the wall. With her eyes closed, the room stopped moving momentarily. She hung her head down and tried to breathe through her nose. She felt the cool breeze of air and opened her eyes again. An exit. She just needed some fresh air; air would help. She started down the dark corridor, pressing both hands against the wall for support. As she reached the door, she felt an arm on hers. "I'm sick," she whispered.

There was no response. Mei turned her head to look, but suddenly she was falling forward. Her arms cartwheeled out in front of her. Where was the ground? And then her face smacked against the ground. Or maybe it wasn't the ground. She fingered a hard, flat surface with ridges. Something hit her again, vibrating like metal on metal. It rang loud in her ears and made her stomach roil. Still blind, she reached for her face just as her stomach let loose its contents. She vomited into her own hands. Behind her was a sharp sound like a cough or a laugh. Short and cruel. Another blow. This time her entire body struck the hard ground. The last sensation she felt was gravel tearing at the skin of her palms and a burning sensation on the right side of her face. She closed her eyes and surrendered to the blackness.

CHAPTER 29

THEY REMAINED AT a standoff. Ryaan knew the police would be putting people in place around them. She wanted to picture Cameron Cruz on a rooftop, cradling her rifle under her arm. Ryaan had seen Cameron in action, watched her crouched with her gun, waiting for an hour or more until the time was right for a kill shot. Cameron could be still much longer than most. She didn't get impatient and she wouldn't take an unnecessary risk in hopes of gaining information from Sawicki. When Cameron pulled the trigger, she shot to kill. Ryaan forced herself to believe Cameron was there, somewhere close by, getting ready to shoot.

Likely, there were multiple officers moving in from behind. Although Ryaan hadn't heard anything specific, she had been trying to make enough sound to cover any noises the police might make as they moved in. For close to an hour, she had been doing that. How long did it take to get someone close enough to take a shot? She thought of the dozens of times she'd been at a takedown when something had gone wrong. Either they couldn't get in touch with the right people or there were multiple calls out. People were occupied elsewhere.

After all, it was Saturday night. How many other crises were going on at that same moment? Was she a priority? Over a drug dealer, probably, but what if someone had kidnapped a room full of children? They would come first. She would want them to come first. A theater holdup like the one in Colorado. How many officers would something like that pull away from her? She struggled to be still, to remain standing.

A cold sweat burned in her eyes. The radio had gone silent. She'd heard the warning, the slow beep in her ear. Low battery. She'd had this problem before on stakeouts. The rechargeable batteries in the old radios no longer held their charge. She could have planned better, but they so rarely used the radios for longer than thirty or forty minutes. Equipment failure. Budget cuts.

Would the report on her shooting include that detail? Would someone high up in the department determine that she was partially culpable? It was so much easier for them if she were to blame. Especially if she died.

The concept of her death was becoming more imminent. Sawicki seemed to realize he was trapped and was growing impatient. He had stopped asking for Karl Penn and started to talk to himself. Or, rather, he was responding to himself with short bursts. "That wasn't supposed to happen."

"She never called back." And most recently, "Why set me up like that and just leave me?"

She had tried to reason with him. "Let me go and we can get you the help you need. I can help you." She made dozens of platitudes, but Sawicki didn't respond to a single word. The only time he reacted to her at all was when she moved and then only to tell her he would shoot her if she wasn't still.

Her muscles burned. Not just the quads that ached when she ran through the park or her calves when she did the stairs or her upper back when she made it to the gym to lift. Every muscle was on fire. The small ones in the back of her neck and her jaw, the big ones in her glutes and across her back. Her abdomen ached. Adrenaline tightened the musculoskeletal system, but that was an hour ago. Her muscles were tired, weak. Adrenaline didn't last.

"I have to sit," she whispered.

"Do it and I'll shoot you in the head."

Sawicki didn't seem to struggle. His body was tense, aware, alert. He seemed not to have fatigued at all. She worried her phone would ring and he might shoot her accidentally. Her mother would be home from pinochle and it wouldn't be long before Ryaan's absence caused her to panic. The end of summer was a hard time for Ryaan's mother. In three weeks, it would be the twenty-first anniversary of Antoine's death. Eleven weeks later, the sixteenth for Darryl. Her mother would invite Deacon Carson to the house often in those weeks. The two would sit in the living room with the furniture that had been brought from their tiny home in New Orleans, set in exactly the same arrangement, with her mother's chair facing the front door though the living room was now on the opposite side of the house.

That room was frozen in time but had simultaneously

deteriorated like the furniture that filled it. The weathered floral pattern, the cotton shiny and flat from years of wear. The white had yellowed, and the arms were covered with small lace doilies in the spots where years of worrying fingers had frayed the fabric.

Ryaan rarely stopped in the living room. As kids, they had never been allowed in there. It was the adult room. When her aunts came to visit, her mother entertained them in the living room. But mostly, the person Ryaan remembered in that room was Deacon Warren from the small Baptist church they attended. Warren sat with her mom with each of her brother's deaths and on the anniversaries of their deaths and their birthdays and holidays for years afterward. After a while, it seemed like he was always there.

His presence in that room had stayed with the furniture. The old yellowed couch, the scratched, faded coffee table, even the tattered rug flattened in spots where the same pieces of furniture had sat for too many years—they all felt like death to her. That room had always been about her brothers.

Sometimes, after a sting, Ryaan stood on the periphery of the room and peered in. She could see Deacon Warren with his shiny bald head and his dark goatee, still looking like a young man, sitting with her mother who looked like a woman twice her age. Her mother would talk about how good they were, her brothers. Maybe they were, maybe not. They'd made mischief and lied the way kids did. In most neighborhoods, boys would knock down cans with slingshots or BB guns, play baseball, ride bikes, steal a piece of gum, maybe break a window.

In her neighborhood, there were no bikes, no grass for baseball. In her neighborhood, kids played with sticks and dirt, and watched the older ones buy things they never dreamed of owning. When the chance came for the younger to make money too, very few could walk away. Her brothers had been no different. Maybe she was no different either. Maybe her mother was meant to bury all her children.

Sawicki shifted his hold on her. Ryaan decided it was time. She squeezed her eyes closed and thought about Cameron. *Someone have my back.* There was no way to broadcast her intention to the police officers in front of her, so she could only hope that they were paying attention. She closed her eyes and thought of Deacon Warren and Deacon Carson, the men in her mother's life. She thought of Hal. Her mother would have liked him. She pictured them meeting at her funeral, Hal in her mother's living room.

With that, Ryaan drew a deep breath and let the muscles in her legs collapse. She sank free of Sawicki's grasp. "No," he shouted. His grip tightened on her shoulder. There was gunfire. A single shot. Heat flooded through her core and out into her extremities. Her ears rang, then she could hear nothing at all. Feel nothing. Not even numbness or the sensation of the ground. After, a tiny electrical hum began in her limbs. Not pain but awareness.

She waited for the pain for several seconds. When she opened her eyes, Patrick and O'Shea and Kong hovered over a body. It must have been hers. They were shaking their heads and smiling. Why were they smiling?

Patrick rolled the body onto its back. Blood ran

down the face. A white man's face. Justin Sawicki. Patrick handed his gun to Kong and turned to her. Then he was talking to her, touching her face and she felt it, felt his freezing hands on her face. He wrapped them behind her head and tried to lift her.

She didn't help him. She didn't move at all. Sensation returned to her back and hips and slowly spread upward to her face and down into her fingers. The ground was cool beneath her, comforting, but also solid, fixed. She ached. Resting her body against it was like being a baby, bundled by a parent, and Ryaan was perfectly content not to move at all.

CHAPTER 30

MEI WOKE WITH something heavy pinning down her head. Like a rock. Or a car. She pressed her hands toward it, but she couldn't find the weight. Instead, she touched a wiry knot in the back of her hair. Her fingers got tangled in the web. When she pulled them free, she took out a few pieces of hair. The pain in her head was unbearable. She needed to get up. She tried to press herself free, but her arms collapsed under her weight. She moaned.

A voice was low in her ear. Someone speaking Cantonese. She heard her mother. More voices, a ringtone. People hovered above her, watching her struggle with the weight.

"Mh'hóu gáau ngóh." Leave me alone.

"She's waking up." Something was wrong. Ayi was speaking English.

Mei forced her eyes open, saw the lavender of her bedsheets. Home. When she rolled over, it was as though a giant ship attached to her brain had capsized and gone under water as she turned. She put both hands on her head and held tight.

"Don't worry, Ms. Chiu. A nasty headache is a pretty common side effect."

Mei opened her eyes to the familiar voice. "Hailey?"

"Yep. I'm right here."

Without moving her head, Mei scanned the room. Her bedroom. Her jeans on the floor of her bedroom. She fingered the collar of her blouse. She was still dressed. Why was she dressed?

"Can you sit up?" Ayi asked.

Mei opened her eyes. "I don't think so."

"I've put Advil and water here on the table," Ayi told her, speaking in Cantonese again. "I am going to call your mother before she gets on a plane. Then, I'll make Hui's migraine tea to help your head." Mei looked around, eyes narrowed against the bright light. Hadn't she heard her mother's voice?

A woman Mei didn't know closed the door behind Ayi and stepped closer. Beside her stood Sophie, who raised a hand in greeting. Mei gave her what she could manage of a smile. Was she hurt? She touched her head, half expecting a bandage of some sort. Why were they all there?

She had so many questions, but her brain hurt. It was all she could do to close her eyes against the searing pain. "What happened?"

"Rohypnol," Hailey said. "Roofies."

Roofies. "I was drugged?"

"You were," Hailey confirmed.

"Is that why my head hurts so much?"

"More than likely," said the other woman.

"We want to talk to you about that night," Hailey explained.

"What night?"

"Saturday."

Mei motioned to Sophie. "She was there. We went to the wine bar. Then out dancing."

"We talked to Sophie and the other women Saturday night," Hailey explained. "We just need to hear what you remember."

"Do you remember someone buying you a drink?" the other woman asked.

Mei looked at her then back to Hailey. "What I remember?" She pushed herself slowly up in bed. Like moving a boulder uphill. "What happened?"

"Mei, do you know Jamie Vail?" Hailey asked.

"No." Hailey had just said the woman's name and already Mei couldn't remember it. "Drugged?"

"With roofies," the woman said.

"Jamie's an inspector in—"

The two women glanced at each other.

"Jamie has a lot of experience with roofies," Hailey said.

Mei reached for the water and Advil. Hailey shook out three of the orange pills, more than Mei would normally have taken. She swallowed all three with water.

At a glacial pace, she sank against the headboard. *Jamie has a lot of experience with roofies.* "You're talking about rape." Mei spoke above the thundering of her heart.

"I work in sex crimes, yes," Jamie said.

Silence hung in the room for several seconds before

Sophie moved closer. "I should get out of here so they can talk to you."

Mei licked her dry lips. "Okay."

"I just wanted to check on you." Sophie came to the bed and patted Mei's leg. "Sabrina called a couple of times. She had appointments this morning, but she wanted to make sure you were okay. I'll come by after work."

"Thank you," Mei breathed. It felt like so much effort. "You don't need to."

"I want to," Sophie said. "Text me if you want me to bring food or anything."

With that, Sophie left. The latch on the door was a thousand decibels. Ayi's voice from the other room, ten thousand. Hailey pulled the chair across the carpet, which sounded like a chainsaw running.

Mei glanced at Hailey and Jamie. They had to know that Sophie and Mei had been at a gay club last night, but her expression belied nothing and, for that, Mei was thankful. "My aunt doesn't know where I was last night."

"The club, you mean?" Jamie confirmed.

Mei nodded.

"She doesn't need to know it was a gay club if that's what you mean."

"It is," Mei said. "For now, she doesn't know."

"Understood." No judgment. The shame Mei felt wasn't from Hailey or Jamie, but it was distinct all the same. She was at a gay bar before she'd told her husband she was gay. There was shame in that. She'd been drugged by a stranger in a bar. Maybe some would say there was no shame in that, but Mei felt it. Shame in being unaware, in being vulnerable. Weak.

Mei tried to collect her thoughts. Last night. They'd been at the club last night, but Sophie said something about work. The silence stretched out as Mei struggled to put it together. "She was going to work?"

Hailey sat in the chair and leaned toward Mei. The motion felt morose like she was delivering the news of a death. "It's Monday."

Monday. Mei tried to sit up again.

"Don't," Jamie warned. "You'll make it worse. At least, wait until the Advil kicks in." She came around the bed and handed Mei the glass of water. "Try to get this down."

Mei drank two long mouthfuls of water. Her phone lay on the bedside table. She lifted it up. The screen was filled with missed notifications. At the top, it said 10:14, then just below that, Monday. "We went out Saturday. I slept through Sunday?"

"Mostly," Hailey said. "You woke a few times, but never fully."

Mei stared at Hailey. "You were here?"

She nodded. "Part of the afternoon. Ryaan, too. And Jamie."

She was mortified. They'd been there, watching her sleep. No. Watching her passed out. "I should be at work," Mei said without any conviction. She was going nowhere. "I'm sorry."

"Don't be sorry," Jamie said. "This isn't your fault. Someone drugged you. I'm just glad you had friends with you."

Tears stung behind her eyelids.

"Mei, listen to Jamie," Hailey said. "She's absolutely

right. I made the hospital take blood on Saturday night for a tox screen. Sophie and Sabrina said there was no way you were that sick on alcohol. You'd had what—a glass of wine, one shot, and maybe two beers in five hours."

Mei nodded. "I guess. I can't quite remember—"

"When the tox screen showed the Rohypnol," Jamie told her, "Hailey called me."

"You okay to talk for a few?" Hailey asked.

"I got sick," Mei said. "I need to shower first."

Hailey looked at Jamie who stared at Mei. "It's actually a good thing you didn't shower," Jamie told her.

"Then you obviously can't smell me." Mei felt the joke stick in the back of her throat.

Jamie smiled again. "I can. But if you had showered, we'd have lost any physical evidence that might lead us to our suspect."

Jamie was from Sex Crimes. Mei tried to feel some part of her body other than the steady drumming in her skull. Her stomach was clenched and empty. Her throat sore. Her tongue rough. Her backside was numb from being in bed. But… no. She shook her head. "I wasn't raped."

Hailey nodded.

"I'd know if I'd been raped," Mei said more emphatically.

"Probably," Jamie agreed. "Your clothes were intact and there was no outward sign of an attack, but if there is a chance, I want to collect a rape kit.

"Plus, if you came into contact with whoever drugged you, there may be transfer. Rape is unlikely but transfer isn't." Jamie reached down and opened an evidence kit Mei hadn't noticed before. She pulled out a pair of purple gloves and handed them to Hailey, then put on a pair herself. "I'd still like to scrape under your nails and through your hair. Those and your clothes are our best bets for transfer."

Mei sat frozen.

"Then you can shower," Hailey told her.

Embarrassment burned hot in her cheeks. She'd been passed out in her bed for thirty-six hours while her colleagues and friends had been in and out of her bedroom, watching her, smelling her vomit. Not to mention that she'd been sleeping in the same clothes, in her own vomit, for a day and a half. Maybe it was good news that she hadn't showered, but Mei wished desperately that she had. Then, at the very least, she could pretend to herself that she'd retained some small bastion of self-respect.

As though sensing her hesitation, Jamie and Hailey worked in silence. Between them, Jamie set out plain white butcher block paper across Mei's lap then pulled out two paper bags, a metal tool for scraping under her fingernails, and a pair of clippers. While Jamie labeled the pages and sacks, Hailey lifted Mei's right hand and set it on top of the paper. Working from the pinky finger in, Hailey scraped under Mei's fingernails then lifted a set of nail clippers. "You mind if I take clippings?"

Mei shook her head. With every inhale, the vomit smell grew stronger and she could hardly sit still, waiting for them to be done. She wanted to be alone. When they were finished, Mei watched them pack up the samples. Jamie pulled out a large paper bag and handed it to Mei. "I'd like to take your clothes with me, too."

When Mei didn't reach for it, Jamie set it on the bed. "Why don't we go get some lunch and we'll come back in about an hour?"

"Good idea," Hailey agreed. "You up for a burger?"

Mei was starving. "Sure. Thanks."

"There's a great place down on Judah," Jamie said. "We'll pick something up and be back soon."

Jamie turned for the door, taking her evidence kit with her. Hailey stayed back. "It's been a busy weekend. Take a shower and we'll catch you up when we get back."

"Okay."

Hailey nodded and started for the door. It was only after she'd closed it behind her that Mei thought to say, "Thanks." She realized she'd forgotten because she didn't feel the least bit thankful.

CHAPTER 31

J.T. POCKETED THE two casings and stood over Karl Penn's motionless body, listening to the predawn sounds. The radiator hissed and spit in the other room. A garbage truck was grumbling down a street a few blocks away. Other than that, the apartment was blissfully silent. So few people appreciated 4:00 a.m. the way J.T. did. And on a Monday no less.

J.T. would have liked to handle Penn over the weekend but the police had held him until Sunday morning. Too many people coming in and out on Sundays—sleeping late or going off to church, shopping. Better to wait until Monday. And now it was done.

J.T. watched the pool of blood around Penn's head expand. A slow, viscous sea of red. There was something soothing about the sight of blood. It was time to go, so J.T. took three steps away from the body and unscrewed the silencer from the end of the Sig Sauer. A great little gun, J.T. would have liked to keep it. Unfortunately, there were plans for this one. Tucking the gun in one pocket and the silencer in the other, J.T. paused on the threshold of Karl's apartment to scan the room. Clean. Pulled up the hood. Used a gloved hand to open the door. Outside, J.T. walked slowly down the stairs, blowing on cold hands as though just out for an early morning walk or a jog. To a passerby, J.T. was nondescript. Under a hood, not necessarily black or white. Not short, not tall. Medium. Average. Forgettable.

J.T. walked three blocks to the car and got in and started the engine, pulling away quickly but without rushing. Another item checked off the list. One more stop, and then it would be a matter of planning the next series of moves.

Before the planning, J.T. had to clean house. A good business practice in general, there was also something extremely cathartic about starting new. Out with the old, in with the new. Hank. Sam. Justin. J.T. paused a moment. J.T. had not anticipated that Justin would play more than a tiny part. After all, Justin's role was to shoot up the police department. Who would have wagered that he'd get out of there alive, let alone actually get away? That feat earned Justin some additional attention.

He would have been useful a little longer, but you can never tell when some people are going to crack. Yes, shooting up the department and escaping was impressive, but going after Karl Penn on his own just because J.T. wouldn't let him in on all of it? That was not impressive. After all, this was about J.T., not Sawicki.

That J.T. had shared more of the plan, let Sawicki in on the delivery of the weapons to the young masses, had been an error in judgment. No, J.T. could be honest. It was ego. A flash of weakness when the temptation to share one moment of glory outweighed the risk. Sawicki had made you want to talk. The quiet ones were like that.

J.T. had known it was an error. After the fire, J.T. severed contact with Sawicki. Knowing it would require cleanup eventually, J.T. had assumed Sawicki would lie low a while longer. With every police officer in the Greater Bay Area looking for him. But no. Instead, Sawicki had immediately taken it upon himself to find J.T. through Karl Penn.

It would have been very troubling if the police had gotten a chance to talk to Sawicki. That Sawicki had gone and gotten himself killed eliminated a step for J.T.

Lesson learned, though. No more wasting time. J.T. liked to think judging character was a personal strength, but after Sawicki, there would be a little less faith in that skill. Which put one more person on the list.

J.T. pulled up behind the battered Camry. The street was dark, although the glow of dawn was beginning to cast its blue shadow over the street. J.T. rounded the driver's side of the Camry and tested the door. Locked. J.T. had expected that. The car had been locked behind the office building when J.T. had practiced breaking into it.

With the exact same motions, J.T. pulled out the long, flat rod and slid it smoothly through the small slit at the top of the window. With three motions, J.T. maneuvered the rod until the lock released. Slid the hook back up the left coat sleeve, then pulled out the gun. This, J.T. tucked well under the driver's seat. The silencer, though, J.T. hid in the elastic pocket behind the driver's seat, leaving only an inch of it visible.

The owner of the car likely wouldn't notice it. To the

untrained eye, it might have been a random piece of pipe or a metal cylinder. Easily overlooked.

The police would know what it was, and that was what J.T. was counting on. Pulling away, J.T. thought about assembling a new team. Or better yet, maybe it was time to fly solo for a while. After all, there wasn't much left to do before they could collect their rewards and leave town.

CHAPTER 32

DWAYNE WAS ACTUALLY getting the hang of his statistics class. The first days were like being in a foreign country. The teacher talking about stuff like probability, Bayes Rule, and correlation versus causation. A few of the students were nodding their heads like they understood perfectly, but Dwayne hadn't been in a math class in four years and he hadn't been paying attention then. He'd gotten his GED online and that had required some math, but nothing like this.

The instructor gave little quizzes at the end of each two-hour lecture and, in those first classes, Dwayne thought he might just fail before the second week was over. He'd been ready to quit. If Tamara hadn't been sitting next to him in that class, he'd have stood up and walked out. He certainly wouldn't have come back. Nothing more frustrating than having some old white man talk about something like it was easy when you couldn't understand a word of it. And that was exactly how he felt. Every once in a while, the guy would ask for questions and Dwayne would wait for some sucker in the class to ask the question Dwayne would ask if it wouldn't be embarrassing as shit. He would ask, *What the fuck are you talking about?* No one asked that question. Even the questions people asked made no sense to Dwayne.

He was only taking two classes: statistics and an American history class, and he was doing okay in history. It was just reading and memorizing so far. But that statistics class was something else. He was afraid he'd have to drop it. If he dropped that one, then he'd only be in one class and that seemed lame, which meant he had to quit it all. He was up one night at home, trying to figure out how he was going to tell Tamara that he wasn't cut out for school. He was on the school's website, looking for information on how to quit and get his money back, when he read something about a site for tutoring. Not tutoring, really, but a webpage where you could watch videos of a guy walking through problems. Dwayne followed the link and typed in "Introduction to Statistics." The screen was a sort of blackboard where the guy worked out the solutions and all you heard was his voice, which was something between a cheesy narrator from one of those kids' shows like *Blue's Clues* and the dorky Indian kid who taught his stats recitation class.

Dwayne could picture the guy with his pants riding up all high and his pocket protector and some shit, but he had to admit that the guy made sense. Unlike his TA, this guy explained it well. Dwayne watched some of the videos five and six times. Spent most of the night watching, same way he used to stay up watching YouTube videos of stupid skateboard tricks or nasty bike crashes. That guy on the Khan Academy website got through to Dwayne. By the time that night was over, he had started to get it.

In class, when Professor Revis went on about the relationships between data like it was some magical thing, Dwayne could kind of feel it. His quiz scores started getting better and, when it came to making predictions with the numbers, he was getting to be pretty good. Simpson's Paradox made sense. He even helped another kid understand it. People always talked about things just clicking in school, but Dwayne had never had that happen before. Now it was. It was clicking. Clicking. Clicking. He had Tamara to thank. This whole school thing had been a ruse to get her to go out with him. But now he knew he wanted to stay.

It wasn't going to be easy, though. It was hard to lay low in his neighborhood and harder to do anything as big as start college—even community college—without someone talking about it. Where he grew up, people believed in sticking close to your roots. Some of the morons in his neighborhood would say that his going to college was disrespectful. They would believe it, too. That it meant he was getting ahead of himself, trying to act like he was better. He knew they'd think that way because he'd been one of them once. When he was in high school, he thought there was no getting out. Not just that it couldn't be done, but why would you want out? It wasn't like there was a ton of violence where he grew up, not like some places. They mostly worked no-end jobs, but they had family all around, kids they'd known since they were in diapers. What was so bad about that?

There was a kid named Charlie Ware who left the neighborhood for community college when Dwayne was a sophomore. Some of Charlie's old friends harassed him about school, going so far as to steal his books and slash his tires so that he couldn't get to campus. Bunch of dickheads, those kids. Dwayne had personally slashed two of those tires himself. He wondered where Charlie Ware was now.

What he needed to do was move out of the hood. He'd been trying to convince Tamara to move in with him, but she said it was too soon. And why should she? She had a decent place that she shared with a couple of other girls who were in school and working like she was. Dwayne needed something like that.

He thought about the guys he was supposed to hang with this weekend. Trevyn who was living at home and working at the Costco tire place and Ethan who was out of the army and looking for work. Dwayne had known these guys all his life, but they weren't going to understand why he was going to college. His phone vibrated on the table. The screen said Kevin. Another person he couldn't live with. Two years younger than Dwayne, Kevin grew up in the apartment next door. Already had a baby. She had to be almost two now. Dwayne waited for the phone to stop ringing before returning to his stats homework.

Maybe he could post something on campus, find a roommate or two. Guys like that Khan Academy guy with the smooth voice who could explain stuff. Smart guys. A week ago, he was driving a gun across town ready to sell it for cash. Now, he was trying to figure out how to stay in college. Whatever happened, he had to hang on to Tamara. That girl was legit. One hundred percent legit.

CHAPTER 33

MEI DIDN'T WANT Hailey and Jamie coming back to Ayi's. There, she was a victim. Before getting in the shower, Mei texted Hailey and told her she'd meet her downtown in ninety minutes. At the station, it would feel like work. At least that was what Mei told herself. She was desperate to transition this whole thing toward work.

She showered quickly, ate two bowls of Ayi's vegetable fried rice with peas, eggs, and scallions and then, at Ayi's insistence, drank a cup of Hui's migraine tea. The tea might have helped her head, but it did nothing for her stomach. Since Ayi had taken the day off work, she sent Mei to the station in her car. At midday, the traffic was light and the trip quick. Along the way, Mei thought about Saturday night.

The memories appeared first in a random collage of images and faces. The faces were all in parts and pieces— a full or thin mouth, a large or small nose, blue eyes, gray ones, hair or height, a bright orange blouse, a blue silk scarf. The disjointed feel of the memories may have been partly due to the lighting. The club was lit by the combination of a large spinning disco ball and flashing lights, along with tiny floodlights whose beams swung, seemingly randomly, across the room. A person's face was lit in patches and never for more than a few seconds.

But some of her memory must have been affected by the Rohypnol. Even women she had spoken with before she felt the effects of the drug were no longer clear in her mind. Or maybe they were there but she just couldn't loosen them. A redhead, tall with wavy hair and bright pink lipstick that made her hair look like the wrong color. A blonde who tucked her hair behind her ear when she spoke and another who looked at the ground rather than at Mei, making her difficult to hear. A tall woman in a low-cut tank top whose height made Mei feel like she was speaking directly into her bra.

Then, there were groups of women Mei could recall as a collective unit but not as individuals. Goth-looking women with cropped, dark hair who wore chains and boots. The women Jordan and Kendra had spoken to, people they knew from somewhere else, wearing short dresses and high platform heels or skinny jeans and boots. The three bartenders in black T-shirts and jeans. One with a tattoo of a tree that extended the length of her arm, the leaves a bright, clear green and pink-red cherry blossoms. The bartender had told Sophie her name, but Mei couldn't remember it now. Mei couldn't recall the other two bartenders at all. They had been farther down the bar, she told herself.

But it was more than that. Mei had given herself Saturday as a reprieve from the stress of work. Conscious of her alcohol intake, Mei had also largely ignored her surroundings. She was with friends, in a place that was exclusively women or almost exclusively. She should have been safe.

When she could come up with no new faces, Mei tried to work through the night chronologically, beginning with the wine bar. The five of them—Sophie, Sabrina, Jordan, Kendra, and Mei—had sat in a back corner. It was Saturday, so the place was busy. Mei had been focused on her group, so she hadn't noticed the other patrons. Was it possible that someone had been following her the entire night? She'd have to ask the other women if they'd seen any of the same people at the club as the bar.

Mei arrived at the department and dropped the paper sack with her clothes—minus her bra and underwear which she'd refused to bring—at the lab on her way in. Arriving at the conference room, Mei was unprepared for the number of people in the meeting. She'd anticipated seeing Hailey and Jamie, but Sophie and Ryaan Berry were there too. It wasn't the women who made her take pause at the door but the presence of her own captain, Lance Finlay. He and a huge man, Mei thought was Hailey Wyatt's partner in Homicide, sat opposite one another at the far end of the table, making the room seem small and crowded. Next to Captain Finlay was Mei's sergeant, Grace Lanier. Mei set her water bottle in the seat farthest from Finlay, pulled out the chair, and sank slowly into it.

"Glad to see you in the office, Inspector," Captain Finlay said. They had only spoken a few times. His expression looked now as it always had, but Mei couldn't help but wonder if he saw her differently now. As a victim. As a gay woman. There were plenty of stories of how personal traumas had ruined police careers.

"Thank you," Mei told him, holding his gaze. She was impressed that he didn't look away. Maybe Lance Finlay was one of the good ones. Then, when the attention became too much, Mei opened her tablet and unlocked the screen, navigating to her notes file.

"Captain Finlay wanted to join us," Jamie told her. "He's going to leverage multiple departments to help us find this guy."

Mei took hold of her water bottle and looked around the table at the faces aimed at hers. The acid at the base of her stomach rose in a wave to coat her insides, making her hot and nauseated. She reached to take off her jacket, but she wasn't wearing one. The way they looked at her, she knew. "You've made a connection," she said out loud. "One that involves me."

There was shifting in the room that reminded her of the way bugs scuttled out from under an overturned rock.

Berry nodded. "We've connected the drugging at the club to the shootings."

"The shootings," Mei repeated and looked down at her notes. "Jacob Monaghan and Justin Sawicki, Albert Jackson? The woman with the child, the one with the tooth infection?"

Around the room, people nodded and watched Mei as though waiting for her to figure out the next part as well. She was stumped. How could those be related to her?

"We matched the Rohypnol chemistry in your blood to the drug given to Albert Jackson," Hailey told her. "The two samples are identical."

"We also matched the print on the gun that was used to shoot out your front window to the one on the electrical tape and on the computer equipment," Ryaan added.

Mei started to look down at her notes, but she didn't need them. "So, the man who shot at me was Sam Gibson, the hacker on our Oyster Point case?"

"One and the same," Ryaan said. "You don't know him from anything else?"

"Maybe another case back in Chicago?" Sergeant Lanier prompted. "One of his first Internet names was—"

"Greeneggs," Mei interrupted. "I know." She shook her head. "I've never heard of him. So why would he want to shoot at my house? And why would the shooter want to roofie me?"

"That's what we were hoping you could help us with," Hailey's partner said from his spot at the end of the table.

"You know my partner, Hal," Hailey said.

Mei didn't respond. She was thinking of Sam Gibson. A hacker. She tried to remember the hackers she'd known in Chicago. The FBI had plenty of white hat guys who helped them and some gray hats. "Where is Gibson now? I'd like to speak with him."

Again, the room was caught up in a series of exchanged looks. Sophie tried to give her a reassuring smile, but even that looked flat with pity.

"Gibson's dead," Mei guessed.

"Yes," Ryaan said. "He was killed sometime Friday evening. Then the building was lit on fire. We think as an attempt to destroy the evidence, and maybe hide the identities of the victims, though thankfully it wasn't successful."

There was more shifting in seats, and Sophie gave Mei a little smile of encouragement.

"So, if Gibson died on Friday, he couldn't have roof-ied me on Saturday," Mei said.

"Right," Hailey agreed. "We believe he had a partner."

Mei snapped her tablet closed. "Someone needs to tell me what we know."

"We think…" Ryaan started. "You were…" Hal said at the same time. They both stopped talking. "You go," Hal told her. "No, you," Ryaan said in a back and forth as each tried to get the other to take the lead.

"Someone go. Please," Mei said, feeling desperate.

Jamie Vail spoke up. "At some point after you were drugged Saturday night, Sophie—" Jamie motioned to Sophie, "—and your friend Sabrina realized you had left. We think the lapse was pretty short. Sophie and Sabrina both thought it can't have been more than about fifteen or twenty minutes."

Sophie nodded in agreement as Jamie went on. "They both recall being at the bar, ordering drinks. You were there with them and then one of them noticed you weren't. They didn't see you on the floor and assumed you were in the bathroom. A little time passed and they went to look for you. Sophie came out of the club—via an alleyway—and saw you getting into a white van."

"A white van?"

More glances all around.

"I don't remember any van," Mei said before anyone could ask.

Mei focused on Jamie as though she were the only person in the room. "The van took off when Sophie came out. Thankfully, whoever was driving hadn't managed to get you inside. Sophie also got the plate number."

"And?"

"Sophie checked records and found the van was registered to a man named Hank DeRegalo."

Mei shook her head. "I don't know——"

Jamie nodded. "Hank was the other man we found in the warehouse fire alongside Sam Gibson. But unlike Gibson, DeRegalo had been dead awhile—maybe as long as a week."

Mei's head was pounding again. She forced herself to open her water bottle and take a few deep drinks. "What else do we know?" she asked, not sure she wanted the answer. What she wanted even less was to be the only one in the room who didn't know something.

"Hal and I have been working another angle," Hailey said. "Some of the people who received guns—Sawicki, Jackson, Monaghan, and Witter—were all active in the same church. We have a call into the church administrator to see if we can link these people to a specific group within the church, a meeting of some sort and narrow down who else they might have interacted with."

It appeared that the church connection was news to most people in the room. There were a series of hushed comments around the table. Sophie and Sergeant Lanier were exchanging a look, and Mei saw Sophie mouth the word "church" in surprise.

"We also made an arrest on Saturday night of a man named Karl Penn," Hal said with a sideways glance at Ryaan Berry. Berry kept her head down as Hal continued. "We believe Penn was the man who delivered the car of weapons to the Tenderloin last Wednesday night. Unfortunately, we haven't been able to link him to Gibson or DeRegalo yet."

"So, Penn drugged me?"

"No," Jamie said. "Penn was in police custody Saturday night. He was released early Sunday morning, but he was definitely in custody when you were drugged."

Mei waited. When no one spoke, she did the math herself. "So, the guy who shot up my house and the guy who owned the car that was driven when someone tried to kidnap me from an all-women bar are both dead and died before someone put Rohypnol in my drink. And the guy who might be their associate was in police custody when I was drugged. So, we have no viable suspects for the drugging."

"That sums up what we know so far," Jamie admitted.

Mei was seized by the desire to laugh. Looking at the faces around the room killed the humor. Why didn't they have a way to connect this? Why hadn't any of these leads led them to someone they could arrest? "What now?" she asked finally.

"Let's walk through what you remember about that night," Jamie said. "You up for that?"

No. Mei nodded.

"Why don't you just start with the last thing you remember. Then back up maybe a half-hour and tell us what happened."

Mei frowned, thinking. She remembered tripping and grabbing hold of a table. A woman with red hair. She felt sick. From there, the room sort of folded into itself and disappeared as though the memory fell off into a vacuum.

"We got to the bar around 9:00," Sophie interjected.

Mei pulled herself back. "Sabrina bought lemon drops and I bought a round."

"We had beers," Sophie confirmed.

"Draft or bottled?" Jamie asked.

"Bottled."

Mei nodded. She remembered holding a bottle. Something light and foreign, something she never drank. Who had chosen those beers?

"We were on the dance floor for a long time," Mei continued.

"And you felt okay then?" Hailey asked.

"Yes. Fine."

"Do you remember talking to anyone?"

"There was a redhead. Tall, freckles, kind of fresh looking but older than us. Maybe early forties."

"Pink lipstick. I remember her," Sophie agreed.

"Who bought the next round?" Jamie asked.

Mei looked at Sophie. "You did."

"Right," Sophie agreed. "But you ordered them, remember? I gave you cash when I went to the bathroom."

"That's right," Mei said. "I ordered them."

"Who passed you the beers, Mei?" Hal asked.

Mei shook her head.

"The bartender put them on the bar," Sophie answered. "I think we each just took one."

"Is that how you remember it, Mei?"

"I'm not sure," Mei answered.

"And the bottle was cold?" Jamie asked.

Mei thought back. "Yes."

"Why?" Sophie asked.

"Sometimes people will drug a full drink and leave it on the bar, waiting for someone to pick it up," Jamie explained. "Oftentimes the drink is sort of warm when the drinker gets it."

"No," Mei said. "It was cold."

Jamie took notes. "Let's go back to the redhead."

Mei felt herself blush. In front of this entire room, they were going to have a conversation about who she had flirted with in a bar. A gay bar. As a married woman. She had never talked about her personal life at work. Not even as a newlywed with Andy. That part of their lives was always carefully separated from their jobs. Now this room was going to talk about the first night in a decade that Mei had gone out and her first ever visit to a club.

"Did you set your drink down to talk to her?" Jamie asked.

Mei thought back to that night. The redhead was holding a clear drink that Mei had assumed was gin or vodka. They had been standing at one of the high tables just a few feet from the bar. Mei had been looking back at Sabrina and Sophie who were trying to get the bartender's attention. But why? They already had drinks. Or maybe that was later. Had she spoken to that woman twice?

"Mei?" Jamie prompted.

"I don't know. The whole night—at least the part after dancing—is a jumble. It's like I was drunk the whole time, but I don't even think I finished the second beer."

"I don't think so, either," Sophie confirmed. "We were trying to get the bartender's attention to close the tab when we noticed you were gone. The place was getting really crowded, and we'd decided to leave. At that point, we'd probably had those second drinks for fifteen minutes."

"Does that ring true to you, too?" Jamie asked.

Mei rubbed her face. "I don't know. I couldn't tell you if it was ten minutes or an hour."

"Okay. I think we've tortured you enough," Jamie announced. "I've only got one more question."

Mei sank into her chair and nodded.

"Have you noticed anything out of the ordinary? At work, at home, on the commute? It could be anything. Something as obvious as an unfamiliar car or person, maybe a new person at a place you've been going a long time. Your dry cleaner, the grocery store."

Mei pictured the surly smoker who took her bundles of laundry across the counter, the vague smell of menthol emanating from her yellowed fingertips. An unhappy woman, yes, but a killer? It had been an unusual week in general. "I can't think of anything specific."

Jamie nodded. "It could be strange activity on a credit card or spam email," Jamie continued. "Evidence that someone broke into your car? Anything even a little bit unusual, I'd like to know about it."

"Okay."

With that, Jamie stood and effectively ended the meeting. "We'll work on known associates for DeRegalo and Gibson to see if we can come up with a list of suspects who were actually alive and not in jail on Saturday night."

Mei was thinking about the few places she went, trying to remember if there was a new waiter at the wine bar. Maybe once, someone subbing. Mei didn't think she'd even spoken to him. The name Gibson pierced through her thoughts. Sam Gibson, the hacker. But she didn't know him.

The room began to clear. Lanier rose with Finlay. Ryaan and Jamie left. Mei remained seated. Anxious for everyone else to leave the room, she wanted to sit in silence and think. When was the last time she'd had real silence? Hal and Hailey filed past. Hailey gave Mei's shoulder a reassuring squeeze. The conference room door opened and people exited. Mei was thankful that they didn't stop. Even Sophie, who Mei knew was anxious to speak to her, just walked by with a quick, "We'll talk later."

Mei didn't see who closed the door, but soon, she was alone. Despite the industrial grade surfaces, the far wall was pocked with dents and scrapes. The majority hit close to hip height, right at the level of belts loaded with flashlights and guns. What she'd always assumed was white paint was actually a faint yellow. The tint made the halogen lights seem harsher. Was that even possible? Her phone vibrated and she pulled it from her pocket. Her mother. Again. That was eight or ten missed calls. Three from Andy. He had heard. Maybe from her mother or more likely from his colleagues in the San Francisco office. A call to tell him that his wife was drugged in a gay bar. Something he didn't know. Because Mei hadn't called him. He wouldn't believe it. Surely not Mei.

She didn't even recognize herself in the scenario. She saw her tablet in front of her with its navy cover. She'd chosen a navy cover. She wore gray dress slacks and black shoes. She didn't own a pair of shoes that wasn't black except her sneakers. She didn't even own a red top. Or a pink one either. Not a single one. She did not go to clubs. She did not get shot at or drugged. She was Mei Ling. Straight A student. Quiet. Thoughtful. Smart. Married. Conservative. She'd never lived on her own, never made out in a public place, never even had a speeding ticket. What the hell was happening? Where had she lost control?

No. She straightened up in the chair. She was in control. She would take this as she did everything—cautiously, systematically. She would do exactly as Jamie said. She would go through her life and document the changes. She would analyze and observe. The answer was there. Even if no one else could solve this thing, she could. And she would start now.

With no one to interrupt her, Mei opened her tablet and scrolled across the pages for her notes. The ugly fluorescent light caught the screen and lit up the smudges. Mei pulled her hand away quickly. The tablet. Someone had gotten hold of her tablet. It hadn't been in her desk. Someone had moved it. Or she had left it on Teddy's desk, but she didn't believe that.

She never left it out. Lifting from the bottom edge, Mei tilted the screen to get a better look at the fingerprints on the screen. Most were likely hers. She moved the screen left and right. There were tons of prints. Probably all hers, but maybe not. Mei tucked the tablet into the crook of her arm and left the conference room. Several people from the lab were in the corridor talking. Mei said hello, pretending to be relaxed, and hurried toward the main lab.

"Is Sydney Blanchard in?" she asked the receptionist.

"I'm here," Sydney called from the tiny room that

housed a coffeemaker, a small fridge, and a copier that worked only about thirty percent of the time. Sydney was in the process of trying to clean out a paper jam when Mei found her. Sydney pulled out a scrap of paper and added it to a pile she had formed on the countertop beside an ashtray filled with mismatched paperclips. "What's up?" Sydney asked, reaching back into the machine.

"I have a favor to ask."

Sydney looked at Mei then back at her hand, realizing she'd come up empty. "What sort of favor?"

"I'm not sure how much you've heard—"

"Enough," Sydney told her. "Tell me what I can do."

Mei exhaled. "Fingerprint this tablet and run the results through the database."

"Whose is it?"

"Mine."

Sydney took a piece of copy paper and set it down on the counter. "Lay it on this."

Mei did.

"I'll call you as soon as it's done."

"Thanks, Sydney."

"Don't. Whatever you need, just ask, okay?"

Mei nodded and left the room. She glanced at the receptionist who seemed distracted by something else. One less person to hear about her private life today. Maybe the receptionist had already heard. This thing was going to be public. She had to let go of that. Mei glanced at her watch. It was nearly 3:00. A couple more hours and she could return to the lab without an audience, sort through email and case files in peace. But she would have to face her colleagues soon enough.

She was supposed to be in charge there. What sort of example would it be to run? Disappearing still sounded like the best option, so Mei settled for delaying the torture a little longer. Taking the stairs, she went up to the little coffee cart and ordered four lattes. Two caffeinated, two decaf, three regular milk, one skinny. She had no idea how the techs took their coffee. For herself, she chose an apple juice. Her phone showed Andy's missed calls. He'd left two voicemails. The station was not the place to have that conversation. Buying herself a couple of hours, she sent Andy a text message. *I know you have all sorts of questions. I'll call as soon as I get home.* The message sent with a little buzz. Coffees and her apple juice loaded in a cardboard carrier, Mei started back down to the lab.

Her head was starting to ache again, and Mei wondered how long it would come and go. The research she'd done on Rohypnol said the drug was completely out of her system in twenty-four hours. That was why Hailey had insisted on taking blood on Saturday night. If they had waited until Mei woke up on Monday, the drug would have been gone. So maybe it wasn't the Rohypnol giving her the headache. She hoped the juice would help. At the lab, she balanced the juice in the center of the coffees and reached for the door. She got it open partway and used her foot to hold it. Across the room, Blake was at his desk. He said something Mei couldn't hear, and Amy walked toward him. Something about the angle of her face…

Mei halted. A memory of Saturday night flashed in her mind.

Blake noticed her in the doorway. "You need help, boss?"

269

Mei said nothing as Blake crossed to her. He took the carrier. "They're for everyone," Mei told him.

Teddy's voice came from behind. "Awesome."

"Thanks, Mei." Blake took a coffee without bothering to see what it was. When Blake walked back to his desk, Mei caught Amy looking at her. And she knew. She wasn't wrong. It was Amy she'd seen in the club Saturday night.

CHAPTER 34

AMY HAD BEEN in that crowd Saturday night. Was that even possible? Amy wasn't gay. Amy had a boyfriend, or she'd had a boyfriend until recently or had just gotten a new one. She was sure she'd heard Amy talking about a guy.

Mei forced herself to look away from Amy. "I brought enough for everyone," she said, pointing to the coffees. "I didn't know what you guys wanted, so some are decaf and nonfat."

"Thanks, Mei." Teddy came up and spun them around until he found one that was regular milk. "Hate that skim stuff," he said. Then, as though remembering who he was talking to, he dropped his head toward her and said, "You doing okay?"

Mei nodded. "Thanks."

Aaron came over and inspected the two remaining coffees and chose a low-fat with caffeine. "Thanks, boss," he said, drawing the word out, then chuckling as though the idea of someone being in charge of him was nothing short of hysterical.

Amy did not come over.

"Amy?"

Amy looked up from her desk.

"There's one for you." Mei carried the last coffee to Amy's desk. She felt her pulse quicken as she got close. There was no way Amy was the one who had shot out her window or drugged her. Amy didn't fit any violent criminal profile. Young, clueless Amy? Plus, why would she want to hurt Mei? Certainly, she might not have been thrilled to have Mei as a boss, but that kind of violence was a very extreme solution. "There's a low-fat left," Mei told her.

Amy forced a smile. "I don't need it."

Mei stopped at her desk. "No. Please…"

Amy's hand trembled ever so slightly. "Um. Okay. Unless you want it."

Mei handed it to her. "All yours." She glanced around to see that Aaron and Blake and Teddy were otherwise occupied.

Amy sat frozen. If there had been any doubt about Amy's presence Saturday night, it was gone now. Mei stood tall, cornering Amy at her desk. "Did you have fun at Blue on Saturday?"

"What?" The tension in Amy's shoulders hitched higher, the trembling worsened.

"The club. Blue. I saw you there."

Amy glanced around the room, landing her gaze on Aaron. Mei followed it, but he was hunched over his laptop, his back to them.

"You want to go somewhere else to talk?"

Amy shook her head. "I don't know what you're talking about. I have a boyfriend."

"So, you do know what Blue is."

Amy said nothing.

"Why were you there?"

"I wasn't. You're wrong."

"We both know I'm not," Mei responded, feeling the tension cranking down in her jaw.

"I thought someone slipped you a drug or something. You probably imagined you saw me." Amy sat up straighter. "Which makes me really uncomfortable."

Mei grabbed hold of the arm of Amy's chair. "Do you know something about how I was drugged?"

Amy spun her chair and bolted, knocking against the desk and spilling her coffee. "God, no. Leave me alone."

Mei stepped away to avoid the coffee that poured off the desk.

Her face crimson, Amy righted the coffee and stormed out the door.

When Amy was gone, Mei felt the room staring at her. "I'd have thought she'd have been done with that search by now," Mei announced. "I guess not."

Blake and Teddy exchanged looks. The two turned back to their work, but Mei felt the heat of Aaron's gaze as she retrieved paper towels from her drawer and laid them across the puddle of spilled coffee.

She considered going to Sergeant Lanier or even Captain Finlay. Certainly, they needed to know. She wasn't just remembering something from a drug-induced state. And if she was, then Amy was right to be uncomfortable because the idea that Mei might have dreamt Amy's presence made her more than a little uneasy, too.

Hailey would listen as would Ryaan Berry. But Jamie

Vail seemed like she knew the most about this kind of thing. Mei sent Jamie a text from her computer. *I remembered something from Saturday.*

Waiting for a response, Mei glanced across the room. Aaron had moved into Amy's chair and was cleaning her desk with wet towels. Was he involved somehow, too? And if so, how did they know Mei was going to the club? Mei thought about the tablet. She was surprised she hadn't heard from Sydney about the fingerprinting.

She had to know more before she decided what to do. Mei launched the human resources application. Since Amy was her employee, Mei had access to her personnel records. Mei worked with an eye on the room. If everyone was at their desks, no one could see her screen. Mei had guessed that Amy was young, but she hadn't guessed twenty-three. This was her first job after graduating from Cal State Poly. There was a scanned copy of her application with some handwritten notes on her interview. Conducted by Aaron. Amy had been working for the department for sixteen months. She'd gotten a small raise last summer. Nothing especially large or small enough to be considered punitive. Average. There was absolutely nothing remarkable about Amy Warner's record.

Want to share it? came Jamie's response.

Mei typed. *I'm almost positive that one of my direct reports was at the club.*

You talk to him/her that night? Jamie replied.

Her. No.

But you're sure.

Mei nodded to herself. *Pretty sure.*

You confront her?

Yes. Denies.

There was a moment's pause then Jamie wrote. *We can work with that. Could she have followed you?*

Mei thought about the wine bar. Amy would have had to be there or on that street somewhere. But Mei had come in Sophie's car and left in Sabrina's. *Maybe,* she wrote back. *But would have been tricky.*

Any other reason she might have been at the club? Jamie wrote.

She's straight. Has a boyfriend.

So no.

Right, Mei agreed. *Also, I think someone might have accessed my tablet. I gave it to Sydney to run prints. I might be going crazy but one of my guys supposedly found it lying out on Wednesday night. I never leave it out.*

How much detail do you keep in it? Schedule and stuff?

Mei thought about it. *A lot.*

Was the club on there? Jamie asked.

Don't think so. Hang on. Mei launched her calendar program and scanned the weekend. The calendars from her phone, her tablet, and her computer were all synced, so if something had been on her tablet, it would be here, too. Mei was shocked to see an appointment for 6:00 p.m. Saturday. "Sophie pick up for Blue." Why would she have put that in her calendar? She hadn't even decided that she was going until Saturday after meeting with Sabrina. It was a matter of habit, she realized.

She scrolled back through the last week and studied the colored blocks of time. Everything was on there: her meetings, dropping off Ayi's gongbi print, ideal workout times, marked as tentative, because she rarely made them, a reminder to pick up the gongbi print this morning, which she'd missed.

If someone had access to her calendar, they would have known where she was supposed to be ninety percent of the time. She scrolled back to last week and stopped on Wednesday. The evening hours of her calendar were empty. Thursday, she had "Dinner with S." at 6:00 p.m. Similarly, Tuesday night's calendar showed "Ayi" at 6:30. Wednesday, there was nothing. She had stopped at the wine bar on the way home, but she hadn't put that in her calendar. Was that why someone had chosen Wednesday night to shoot up Ayi's front window? Had they assumed, from the absence of a date on her calendar, that Mei would be home?

Just then, Jamie pinged. *Anything?*

Everything.

Just called Blue. Bartenders show up at 4:00. Meet in the lobby at 4:30?

Mei glanced at her watch. It was already almost 4:00. *Yes. Thanks, J.*

Anytime.

Mei thought again about her sergeant and Captain Finlay. Like Amy said, she was drugged. Maybe she did hallucinate Amy. She didn't believe that. Something was definitely going on, but what was Captain Finlay going to do about it? She needed something more. She thought about her tablet and called down to the main lab.

"I'm so sorry," Sydney answered. "We had a homicide come in with a carload—literally—of potential evidence and got buried."

"I can check back later—"

"No. I just printed it. Only your prints on the screen. A few smudges that could be someone else, but they aren't clean enough to match."

"Did you print the cover?"

"Yes. Yours and Edward Berger's. A few of them. He's in your department, right?"

"Teddy, yes. That makes sense. He found it." Mei tried to hide her disappointment. "I appreciate the help. Good luck with the homicide."

"Oh, God. Thanks. Hope to make it to dinner on Wednesday."

Rookie Club Dinner, Mei remembered. "Me too," she lied. She hadn't even thought about it. "Thanks, Sydney."

"Sure thing."

Mei hung up her phone. She'd locked up her tablet. She never left it out. Never. In Chicago, colleagues teased her relentlessly about how fanatical she was. How suspicious. Yet she didn't remember putting the club date on her calendar. Very possibly, the stress was getting to her. The evidence certainly pointed in that direction.

Mei shrugged off the self-doubt, pulled herself tall. No. She knew herself. She walked to the lab to retrieve her tablet. Thanked the receptionist who gave it to her. She held it a little tighter on the way back to her office. Something was wrong. Someone had taken her tablet. She was sure of it. At her desk, she slid her tablet carefully into her bag to take home.

She would find out what they were looking for. And who was behind it.

CHAPTER 35

LYING ON THE ground that night, Ryaan swore she'd felt the bullet puncture her brain. Felt the heat and absence of pain. Felt herself lifted off the earth. Looked down on her own corpse. Since that moment, she felt removed from her life. It was as though some part of her was still above, watching the rest of her go through the motions. She felt like some part of her was dead.

Ryaan hadn't told her mother a thing about Saturday night. It was all over the news that a police officer had been held hostage by a gunman, but the officer remained unnamed. The department had put a temporary restraining order on news station helicopters, and the streets had been blocked off for several blocks. Ryaan had remained anonymous. This probably wouldn't last. The news teams would be tireless about finding out who the officer was. It would have been smart to tell her mother before then, but Ryaan was banking on her mother's adeptness at ignoring the news. Her mother watched old movies and the occasional sitcom. She watched National Geographic until they started to talk about natural disasters. There was a good chance her mother would never know. More than that, Ryaan didn't want to relive it, let alone through her mother's fear.

Patrick was already at his desk when she arrived. She could tell he'd been there for a while. His coffee cup was empty, and he was drumming his fingers the way he did when he was puzzling a problem. It was only 8:00.

"Morning."

Patrick spun in his chair. "Hey."

"Why so early?"

"New lead."

Ryaan set her bag down on her desk.

"We got a print off one of the guns in the warehouse fire. New guy by the name of Dwayne Henderson."

Ryaan remained standing. She was ready to go pick up Henderson. "Priors?"

"Twenty-two months on a weapons charge."

"He lives down on Larkin. Patrol went over there about a half-hour ago. If he's there, they'll bring him in."

"Why don't we go?"

"Because I'm also waiting to hear back on the history of those two cell phones so we can triangulate our main guy."

"Is Henderson our main guy?"

"No way," Patrick said. "He's too small time. There has to be someone else."

"Maybe he's graduating."

Patrick waved to the breakroom. "Get some coffee, Berry."

She didn't want to wait around, but she knew Patrick was right. It made sense to have Patrol pick up Henderson. Plus, she still had the report on Saturday night to finish writing. That was why she wanted to leave. She'd been avoiding it. There was no way to write up being taken over from behind by an armed gunman that didn't make her look incompetent.

Yes, they had already apprehended their target. No, they had no reason to believe Sawicki would be at Penn's residence. Yes, he'd clearly been lying in wait for some time, and the environment was not an easy one to survey with all the old cars. But Ryaan would have seen him coming, if she'd been paying attention. If she hadn't been lazy and half-asleep from being up late two nights in a row. If she hadn't been checking text messages or thinking about a date with Hal Harris and whatever else she had been doing.

Now, Sawicki was dead. Their best lead gone. Cameron Cruz had saved her life. Ryaan had yet to call her. When a cop saves your life, it was customary to go out and celebrate, buy a round of drinks, hoist him (or her) up on your shoulders, prance around one of the police bars like you'd won the lottery. No one had asked Ryaan if she wanted a drink Saturday night. She'd been checked over by an EMT, and Patrick had driven her home where her mother was waiting. Ryaan made up a story about a little fender bender and retreated to her bedroom where she laid and stared at the ceiling for half the night. Frozen. She'd tried to explain it to Patrick.

"You got a nasty bump on the head, Berry." That was his answer. And what else could it be? She was alive. She hadn't been shot. She hadn't seen her body. The body she'd been looking over at—not down on—was Justin Sawicki's. She knew that and yet she still couldn't shake the feeling that something more had happened in those moments.

"Drink this."

She looked up and saw Patrick, standing with a cup of coffee. She took it and turned to her desk, sat in her chair, and booted up her computer to show that she was fine. Everything was normal. She put away the lunch she'd brought and replenished her store of Diet Cokes in the bottom drawer, folded her bag and placed it on top. She was just opening her email when the phone on Patrick's desk rang.

She stopped and watched.

"O'Hanlan."

A moment passed and Patrick turned to her. He gave her a smile and a thumbs-up. Ryaan stood from her chair. "Perfect," Patrick said. "Bring him to Booking and we'll meet you there in twenty."

Twenty minutes. Ryaan sat again. Patrick hung up. "We got him. Patrol picked him up coming out of his house. Said he was going to school." Patrick laughed and shook his head. That wasn't even close to the best story they'd heard.

Ryaan could have spent the time going through emails or starting her report or any of a dozen other ways, but she couldn't sit still. "I'll meet you at the jail in twenty," she said, pulling her jacket off the back of her chair.

"Where are you going?"

"Stop by the lab. See how Mei's doing."

"The roofies, right. I heard." Patrick turned back to his desk.

"I'll meet you over there."

Patrick nodded. "Got it."

She wasn't going to see Mei. She was going to the jail to wait because she wanted to see this Dwayne Henderson the moment he walked in the door, and she didn't want company. She wanted someone she could beat the shit out of for putting a weapon in Justin Sawicki's hands and almost getting her killed, and she hoped to God that Dwayne Henderson was that guy.

Ryaan wasted her time walking circles in front of the jail, crossing over the star-shaped badges set into the tiles, and staring up at the shiny brass sheriff's star above the door. Twenty-five minutes passed and still no Henderson. It was Patrick who came out the front door of the jail.

"How'd you get in there?" Ryaan asked.

"Back door. Same way Henderson came in."

"Henderson?"

Patrick aimed his thumb over his shoulder. "We've got him set up in interview three."

Ryaan halted. "He's here."

Patrick nodded. "I had them bring him in through the back."

"Why?"

Patrick raised an eyebrow. "Because you and I have been partners a long time, Berry, and I know when you're hot under the collar."

"Hot under the collar? This guy almost got me killed!" Ryaan barked.

Patrick nodded. "So, I was right to bring him in the back."

Ryaan stalked past him toward the interview room.

Patrick chuckled, which only made her angrier. But

he knew that too. He followed close behind her until they were at the door. Before she could open it, he reached around her and took hold of the knob. "We going to do good cop/bad cop? Because I'm usually the bad one."

"I'll calm down," Ryaan said.

"Probably should do that out here."

"I'll behave."

"He may not be what you expect."

"I just want to see his face, Patrick."

"As you wish." And with that, Patrick opened the door and let it swing wide.

A young man—maybe nineteen or twenty—sat up straight in the chair on the far side of the interview table. He wore a yellow collared polo shirt tucked into his jeans. With a belt and tennis shoes. The laces were tied. She could tell from his face that he'd been crying. She glanced around the room. This was her mastermind?

"Dwayne, this is my partner, Inspector Berry."

Dwayne stood up as Ryaan crossed to him. "Where are you going?" she snapped.

"Nowhere. Was just going to say it's nice to meet you, Inspector," Dwayne said and sat quickly back down.

Ryaan looked back at Patrick, who shrugged. Patrick dropped a folder on the table and sat down. Ryaan was too amped to sit. Instead, she stood, hovering as Patrick flipped open the manila folder. On top was a picture of Sam Gibson, their hacker. They were still tracking down Gibson's parents who were somewhere in Italy or Spain. The picture was at least five years and fifty pounds outdated.

Dwayne was already shaking his head before Patrick asked the question.

"Do you know this man?"

"No. I've never seen him before."

"Well, he looks like this now," Patrick said, flipping to an image of Gibson from the neck up, lying on the autopsy table. They had tilted his head a little to the right to hide the damage the fire had done to the side of his face. Most of it, anyway.

"Oh, God." Henderson pushed the picture away. "No. I don't know him. I've never seen him before."

"How about this guy?"

Dwayne didn't look. "Is it another dead guy?"

"You tell me."

Dwayne steeled himself and glanced down at the picture of Hank DeRegalo. This one had come from his Facebook page because by the time they found him, his body was way too bloated to be recognizable. "No. I don't know him either. Who are these guys?"

"One more." Patrick showed him Karl Penn.

"No. Never seen him."

Patrick sat back in his chair and crossed his arms.

"I don't even know why I'm here," Dwayne said.

Patrick tipped his chair back and balanced it on two legs. This was one of Patrick's signature moves. Ryaan was still waiting for the day when he fell back on his ass. Statistically speaking, that day had to be coming. "Are you in possession of a firearm?" Patrick asked him, coming down to the floor again.

"A what?"

"A gun, Dwayne. Do you own any guns?"

Dwayne shook his head even harder now. "No. No, sir. I don't have any guns." He kept shaking his head even after he was done talking.

Patrick pulled Dwayne's arrest report out from behind the pictures and turned it so Dwayne could see it. "Six-year-old girl was killed. Bunch of kids in a car full of weapons. You served twenty-two months for owning an illegal weapon."

"That's what they charged me with, but none of those guns were mine."

"Sure," Ryaan said.

Dwayne shook his head. "Whatever. I finished serving my time. I'm working now. I'm in school. That's why I don't own any guns. I'm done with that stuff."

"Done?" Ryaan said and Dwayne looked at her.

"Yes, ma'am. Done."

"Then how do you explain that your fingerprints are on an AK-47 that we found at a warehouse along with two dead bodies?"

Dwayne shook his head. "I don't know. It must be old. From before or something."

Ryaan yanked the empty chair away from the table and took its place, standing over Dwayne. "Bullshit," she charged.

Dwayne looked to Patrick for help.

"I'm afraid she's right, Dwayne," Patrick told him. "Those guns were stolen from a police facility ten days ago. Before that, they'd been printed, and we have the records of whose prints were on them before. Your prints don't show up in those records."

Dwayne sat on his hands and closed his eyes.

Ryaan slammed her hand on the table. "Tell us how your prints got on that gun, Dwayne. Right now, you're looking like our best suspect in the murder case."

"Okay, okay," Dwayne said hurriedly. "I just—shit." He rubbed his face with both hands. "You're not going to believe the truth." He shook his head. "Man, this is so messed up."

"Try us," Patrick said.

Ryaan pulled up a chair and sat, waiting. It took Dwayne Henderson twenty minutes to tell them a cock and bull story about getting a bunch of text messages offering him free guns. Which he declined. Even after saying no, he told them he found a gun in a FedEx box in his delivery truck after making a stop at the police department. Dwayne, having turned over a new leaf and all, left the gun, in the box, on the street beside where he had been parked.

When he was done, Ryaan stared at him. He was right. She didn't believe a word of it. There was so much wrong with his story, she didn't even know where to start. "How did this gun fairy get into your delivery van? Don't you lock it?"

"I do," he agreed, thinking. "I usually do. I don't know. Maybe I forgot."

"You forgot," Ryaan repeated.

"You're driving around with a lot of expensive stuff, aren't you?" Patrick added.

Dwayne nodded.

"And you might have forgotten to lock the door?" Patrick went on.

He nodded again.

"But no one took anything out of your car. Instead they left you a gun," Patrick offered.

"I know. I know it sounds nuts."

"You left the gun there? On the curb?" Ryaan said.

"I swear."

"And what time was this?"

"I don't know. About 10:00, I guess."

"In the morning."

"Yeah. Yes."

"No one saw you?"

"I don't know."

"Well, we never got a report of it. Patrick?"

Patrick shook his head. "Nope. So, you're saying that you put down a big box, within a block of the police department where it might have been a bomb or anything else—" Patrick walked back through Dwayne's story. "And even stranger, whoever put this box in your delivery van must have come back for it, right? Because it was used to kill these people who we believe were involved in the original burglary."

Dwayne nodded then paused to rub his face again.

"If you left the box on the curb, how did your fingerprints get on the gun?"

Dwayne licked his lips. "I might've touched it first."

"Touched it," Patrick repeated.

"Yeah."

Patrick glanced at Ryaan before saying to Dwayne, "That's the story you want us to believe?"

"More or less."

"More or less?" Patrick repeated.

"I left out one thing."

"Maybe you'd better share that, too," Patrick suggested.

"Well, I didn't leave it there at first. When I saw what it was, I thought about taking it to someone I know." He looked at Ryaan, then at Patrick, and rolled his hand. "To sell, you know. The money would have been helpful with school and all."

"But you changed your mind?" Patrick asked, and Dwayne must have caught the sarcasm in his voice.

Dwayne laid his hands flat on the table and spread out his fingers as though to press off. "I told you that it was hard to believe."

"You should have used the word 'impossible,'" Patrick said. The sarcasm was replaced by something much more like anger.

"I guess maybe I need a lawyer."

"Do you still have these text messages?" Ryaan asked, trying to steer away from the talk of lawyers.

"No. I deleted them." Dwayne remembered something. "But I took a screen shot of one of them."

"Can we take a look at that?" Patrick asked softly, again working to avoid the subject of a defense attorney.

"Sure. Yeah." Dwayne pulled out his iPhone and, after a minute of searching, he placed it on the table in front of them.

Got to unload 70+. No cash needed. Split profits 75/25, 75 2u. Killer deal.

"How did you know he was referring to guns?"

Dwayne picked up the phone and scrolled through his photos. "I thought maybe I had a picture of the first messages. He sent a couple short ones about getting back into the business. Something about my record."

"Maybe someone from your time inside?"

Dwayne shook his head. "I'm no monkey mouth, man. I laid low. I spent every minute I could in the library, and I didn't talk about my past."

"But that doesn't mean inmates didn't know what you were in for," Patrick suggested.

"I know," Dwayne agreed. "I just can't see any of those guys texting me. And how would they get my number? I got a new phone after I got out."

"Why a new number?" Ryaan asked, curious.

"'Cause I wanted a clean slate. I got myself together now. I'm in school. I'm working. It's not the best job, but it's a start."

Ryaan watched the frustration on Dwayne Henderson's face. Man, if he was really some sort of weapons dealer, he had the best poker face she'd ever seen. Which meant he was no dealer. She'd been in the business long enough to recognize the tells. Even the kids who kept up their appearances couldn't help but show off another way. They drove cars that were a little too rich for their blood, or they wore expensive clothes. Dwayne's polo shirt wasn't even label. His car was an '86 Camry and even his reading glasses looked sturdy but inexpensive.

Patrick took down the originating phone number off Dwayne's screenshot. "You willing to sign a waiver to let us pull your phone records?"

"You mean to see who I've called?"

"And texted. Right."

"And then you'll let me go?"

Ryaan nodded. She didn't want to tell him that they might be by to pick him up later in the day.

"Yeah. I'll sign it."

Patrick stood up. "Let me get the paperwork. I'll be right back."

Dwayne looked at his phone. "Can you hurry? I've got a stats recitation class in forty-five minutes."

The anger Ryaan had drummed up earlier was gone. Dwayne Henderson was no mastermind criminal. Hell, he didn't even seem like a criminal.

When Patrick walked back through the door, something had shifted.

Dwayne sat up straighter as Patrick crossed to him.

Patrick set his phone on the table in front of Dwayne and pointed to the screen. "You want to tell me what that is?"

Dwayne stared a moment and looked back up, baffled. "I have no idea."

"Really?" Patrick said as Ryaan looked at the image of a silencer. "They found that in the back of your car. My guys are searching the rest of the car now. They going to find anything else?"

"I have no idea how that got there," Dwayne said.

The phone on the table buzzed. Patrick snatched it up. "Yeah."

Dwayne pressed his hands into the table. The beds of his fingernails were rimmed in white.

Patrick's gaze drilled him. Something had happened. He lowered the phone and looked at Ryaan, nodding. To Dwayne, he said, "Looks like you're going to be missing class."

"I don't understand." Dwayne pushed away from the table.

"What was it again? Statistics?"

"Yeah," Dwayne uttered.

"I'd say your probability of going to jail has just gone up."

Dwayne stood, but Patrick pushed him back into the chair with a single solid shove. "Why don't you tell Inspector Ryaan about that gun we found under the seat of your car?"

Ryaan watched Dwayne. His expression was utter shock.

"How about Karl Penn?" Patrick asked. He pulled the file open again, splaying the pictures out until he found the one of Penn.

"I told you I don't know him. I've never seen him before," Dwayne insisted.

"Then you want to explain how he was killed this morning? Because the caliber of the bullets matches the ones we found in your car."

Dwayne's face went slack. His shoulders slumped. Beyond his glasses, his eyes began to water. He shook his head. For a moment, he said nothing. Then he looked up at Ryaan. "I swear, I didn't do that. I've never seen that gun or that man. This is all a huge mistake."

She listened for a hitch in his voice or a flatness in his eyes. His face would surely show some tiny glimmer of deccit. There was nothing.

Patrick crossed his arms. "Evidence doesn't lie, Dwayne."

As Dwayne began to cry, Ryaan wondered if she was losing her edge. Patrick dragged him out of the chair and read him his rights. Ryaan almost felt sorry for the guy.

CHAPTER 36

J.T. WALKED THE hallways in the department, feeling especially light. Everything was falling into place. Really, there was so little left to do. Still a few days to wait with no work. Such a rarity, J.T. could hardly imagine how to enjoy it. For so long, every day was calculated, planned. Behind schedule, on schedule. With so many other moving parts, it was always a challenge. But now, with no one else to worry over, with the damage done and the short-selling profits amassing, there was nothing but time.

Before that moment, J.T. hadn't stopped to imagine leaving the department. So many years in this little space, working with the same clueless people day after day. And then to be done. Not just with the department but with working. Because there would be no reason to work.

As the computer coughed and hiccuped through its booting, J.T. pulled out the morning's paper and flipped it back to the business section to read the article for the fifth—no sixth—time that morning.

Results of Mendelcom's ten-year trial of a drug that the company had announced increases the remission rate in prostate cancer patients by more than 40 percent have been declared invalid. Claiming a data loss, Mendelcom spokesperson John Anderson tells the Chronicle that the company is working on the data issue and is confident that the success of the drug will be proven.

In the meantime, an independent audit performed this week of the company's results show no consistent linkage between Mendelcom's billion-dollar Prostura and a reduction in the cancer. As recently as last week, the drug was being touted as the biggest gain in cancer research since the turn of the millennium. Shares of the company (MCOM listed on the NASDAQ) are down more than 92 percent since Friday's announcement.

According to J.T.'s math, they had made something approximating five and a half million dollars by shorting shares of Mendelcom across sixteen different accounts. J.T. had repurchased the last of the shares at the current price of $14.27 that very morning.

With the computer up, J.T. logged into the department's records system and searched Dwayne Henderson. There it was. Right in the center of the screen. Dwayne Henderson was arrested on suspicion of first-degree murder. The victim: Karl Penn.

J.T. had to smile. The door opened and people began to file in.

"You're in a good mood," a colleague said, passing

by with a bag lunch and a dented travel mug of cheap home-brewed coffee.

"Why not? It's going to be a great day." J.T. exited out of the records screen and slid the folded newspaper into the desk. It was going to be a great day. They all were. These last few in the department and all the ones after.

Finally.

CHAPTER 37

MEI AND JAMIE parked outside Blue. The club didn't open to customers for another hour, but the bartenders were there well in advance to ready the bar. Monday night was ladies night, which meant half-off well drinks. The bar reported it was one of their biggest nights—often bigger than Saturday. Mei wondered who went out and got drunk on a Monday, but she wasn't there to find out.

"You have a picture?" Jamie asked.

Mei pulled out the picture of Amy from her personnel file.

Jamie nodded. "Perfect. Let's go see what we can find out."

Mei followed Jamie into the club. The flashing, circling lights were off, and now Mei could see why the club was called Blue. The bar was solid cement, tinted blue, as was the floor. The walls were textured in various blue fabrics. One appeared to be thick blue corduroy, another blue velvet. Everything, in fact, was blue, including the bartenders' shirts, which Mei had thought were black on Saturday.

Jamie approached the bar where a woman was stacking glasses. "Can I help you?"

"I'm Jamie Vail. I'm an inspector with the SFPD, hoping to talk to someone who was here Saturday night."

"I was here."

Mei pulled out the picture of Amy and set it on the bar. If possible, Amy looked even younger in the picture. It was impossible to imagine the doe-eyed girl as a nefarious character.

"Something happen to her?" the bartender asked, leaning over the picture.

"No. She's fine," Jamie said without explanation.

She shook her head. "I didn't notice her, but that doesn't mean anything. I don't notice this type. Too fresh-faced for me. You'd want to ask Barney."

"Barney?"

"Yeah. He's our bouncer. Works the front door. Has a thing for faces."

"A thing?" Mei asked.

"He remembers them. He can tell you who was here which night, who was kicked out, went home and changed her clothes, and came back an hour later." The bartender smiled. "It happens more than you'd think. If she was here, Barney would probably remember her."

Mei looked around. "Where's Barney now?"

She checked her watch face on the inside of her wrist. The gesture reminded Mei of the bartender who had the tree tattoo. "Should be in the back by now, but he might be late. He's good with faces, but he's bad with a watch. I've got to finish this up, but go on back there and knock on the blue door. Tell him Joan said it was okay."

"Thanks, Joan."

"No problem."

"One more question. I believe you have a bartender with a tree tattoo," Mei said.

"That's Carina. She's not in until Wednesday night."

"Okay. Thanks." Mei tried to hide her disappointment. The bartender had been moving fast Saturday night. The chance that she'd noticed something in all the commotion was slim. But that was how they were going to break this thing. One of these slim chances was going to have to pan out. Maybe they would have to come back and talk to Carina.

Joan reached for more glasses. "You mind if I ask what happened?"

"Someone slipped one of your patrons Rohypnol," Jamie told her.

Joan nodded. "I figured it was something like that. It's pretty rare in here, but it's happened."

"Recently?" Mei asked, trying not to cling to the idea that this could be some random coincidence rather than a plot against her specifically. That part of it, the intimacy of someone's hatred, was so difficult to imagine.

"Last time I heard about it was last fall, I think. We watch the bar pretty carefully, but you can't see everything." Joan stacked her glasses and turned back to them. "You'd think women would be different, but we're all basically animals, I guess."

Mei tried to picture Amy Warner as the animal Joan described.

"Thanks for your help," Jamie said and led Mei across through the bar toward the blue door.

"I always felt safe, surrounded by women. It seems so naive now."

"A female rapist is uncommon," said Jamie. "But rape isn't the only reason people use Rohypnol. The drug makes the victim a very compliant partner."

Mei pictured the white van she couldn't even remember seeing. Had she gone willingly to a random car without a fight? Was it all just dumb luck that Sophie had seen her when she did?

Barney wasn't in the bar yet, so Jamie and Mei walked into the alley. Through the back door was a small cement porch. Three steps led down to the alley, which was paved but worn. Large potholes and loose gravel covered the surface. At the base of the stairs was a concrete pad with a sewer grate. She'd seen a thousand like it. Maybe that was why it looked familiar. Or maybe she really did remember something about coming out here that night. She had the vague sense that someone had been behind her. Mei walked slowly, scanning the ground for some sign that she'd been there. The alley was maybe fifty feet long. Two dumpsters lined the backside of the building. She thought about what might be inside them. What would they even begin to search for? When she reached the street, she turned back.

Jamie stood halfway down the alley, looking back at the building.

Mei scanned the upper floors. "You think maybe someone saw something?"

"It's a possibility," Jamie said. "But unlikely."

Most of the windows were small and high up. "They look like bathrooms."

Jamie nodded. "I think so, too. Not a lot of people staring out the window in the shower."

"You guys looking for me?" came a voice from the back door.

Barney was not what Mei expected from a bouncer. He was Chinese and only a little taller than Mei, but from the tight fit of his blue polo shirt, he was clearly someone who spent a lot of time in the gym. Mei tried to imagine him bouncing the women she'd seen Saturday night. Some of them were twice his size. Maybe he had help. She'd never seen a woman bounced out of a bar.

She also didn't remember seeing him. Maybe that was another sign that she wasn't in her right mind.

Jamie handed Amy's photo to Barney.

"Yeah. She was here Saturday." He glanced at Mei. "Same night as you and your friends. She came in a little before 9:00."

"Was she with a group?" Jamie asked, ignoring his reference to Mei.

Barney shook his head and passed the photo back. "Alone. Looked like a first-timer for sure."

"How long was she here?"

"Not very long. Maybe half-hour. Left out the front. In kind of a hurry."

"With someone?"

"Nope. She was alone when she left."

Jamie processed that a moment, making a note. "You remember anything else about her?"

Barney frowned. "Like what she was wearing? She wasn't dressed up. Not how most people come in," he said, meeting Mei's gaze.

Jamie thanked him for his time. The club looked so little like it had Saturday night, but Mei started to feel sick being there. She took gulps of air when she reached the street. Beside her, Jamie squinted in the sunlight.

"I was right about Amy," Mei said.

"You sound surprised," Jamie said.

"I guess I am," Mei admitted. "The way it was triggered was so strange."

"How do you mean?"

Mei thought about it again. "I had no memory of seeing Amy on Saturday night until I walked into the lab Monday. I saw her, then it hit me. I thought, she was at the club, but I still don't remember seeing her that night. Not exactly." Mei shook her head. "It's hard to explain."

"I've talked to a lot of women who have been roofied—and a few men—and what you're describing isn't uncommon. Other things like that might surface. Pay attention to them. You might stumble on something that links directly to our suspect. We need to talk to Amy Warner, too. She obviously knows a lot she's not saying."

Mei looked over at Jamie. The hard-edged exterior was so obvious, it was easy to miss the fact that Jamie was an incredibly good listener. Mei nodded. "Thanks for coming."

"It's my job, and I'd have done it anyway."

The logical step was to talk to Captain Finlay and Sergeant Lanier. Mei called and managed to get them a small slot on Finlay's calendar. Then she called and left a message on Lanier's voicemail. Jamie and Mei arrived back at the station parking lot almost a half-hour before their appointment with Finlay. Even as Mei walked through the lot with Jamie, she felt the momentum driving her toward the building. This was the first piece of evidence that linked to a live suspect. It felt concrete, irrefutable. Mei couldn't force herself to slow down.

She was almost jogging as she came through the department's back door, and Jamie Vail was keeping perfect pace. Amy Warner. Nothing about it made sense, but the evidence led right to her. Mei checked her phone for the tenth time.

"We've got lots of time," Jamie said.

"I'm nervous."

"Completely normal. I'd be surprised if you weren't," Jamie said.

They rode the elevator in silence. When the doors opened on the third floor, Mei almost walked right past Hailey Wyatt and Ryaan Berry, who were standing in front of them.

"We were just coming to see you," Hailey said.

"We've got news," Ryaan added.

Mei had to force herself to stop moving.

"We do too," Jamie told them. "You first."

Ryaan looked to Hailey, who nodded. "We got the phone records from AT&T for Karl Penn and Sam Gibson," Ryaan said. "We found one number they both called consistently over the past three weeks. Patrick got AT&T to triangulate all the calls coming to and from that number and guess where the triangulation leads us?"

Mei just shook her head.

"I give up," Jamie said.

"850 Bryant."

For a moment, Mei couldn't think of where that was.

"The department?" Jamie said.

"Here?" Mei whispered.

"Yep," Ryaan said. "Whoever is behind these attacks is making a lot of calls from right inside this building."

"There's more," Hailey said. "Hal called St. James Church and talked to the minister there. Turns out Justin Sawicki was a member there; he taught in the Bible school. Daniel Witter was one of his students."

"Daniel Witter?" Jamie asked.

"The one with the infected tooth?" Mei asked.

"Right," Hailey confirmed. "The one who died."

"Whose mother shot herself?" Mei was stunned. "Our link to these guys is a church?"

"The church and the department," Hailey confirmed. "The minister knew most of our shooters. Albert Jackson didn't recognize the name of St. James Church, but that doesn't mean he hasn't been there. The minister said they offer quite a few community nights to help the homeless, so it's possible Jackson has been there. Hal's trying to get in touch with the church administrator about talking to the director of the community outreach programs."

"And the others?" Mei asked. "What about Jacob Monaghan?"

"Monaghan's grandmother, Pearl Lasser, was a long-time member of St. James."

"Who does that leave out?"

"If we can link Albert Jackson, that's everyone except Dwayne Henderson," Hailey said.

"Who is Henderson?" Mei asked.

"The guy we arrested for the murder of Karl Penn."

"Karl Penn is dead too?" Mei asked.

Ryaan nodded. "Killed early this morning."

Mei shook her head. "So, our killer might be a member of this church and the department."

"Seems possible," Hailey said.

"Seems bloody likely," Jamie agreed.

Mei and Jamie exchanged a look.

"What's your news?" Ryaan asked.

Mei told them about seeing Amy Warner at the club, Amy's denial, and the bouncer's confirmation.

"Who the hell is Amy Warner?" Hailey asked.

"Exactly," Ryaan echoed.

"She's a twenty-three-year-old assistant tech in the computer lab. No way is she in charge of this thing," Mei said.

"But she's inside the department," Hailey said.

"Right, and she's definitely a lead in the right direction," Jamie agreed. "Mei and I are going to talk to Captain Finlay and Sergeant Lanier now."

"Text me after the meeting," Hailey said. "And I'll let you know if I hear anything else on the church connection."

"I think we're getting close," Ryaan said. Mei felt a chill off her words. It seemed like they all did. The four of them stood silently for a moment before Hailey spoke.

"We should keep this quiet," she said. "If we're talking about the department, we don't know who…"

"Looks like a pretty intense gathering," came a male voice from behind Mei.

Mei turned to see a man standing behind them. In his fifties, he was dressed in a gray suit and tie.

"Captain Marshall," Hailey said. "Good to see you, sir."

The captain stopped at the group and clasped his hands in front of him, rocking on his heels. "Hello, ladies. You having an interdepartmental gathering here in the lobby?"

"We're working a joint case, sir," Hailey said.

"Carry on, then," Marshall said with a tight smile before heading for the stairwell. The four women remained silent until the stairwell door closed behind him.

"Keeping it quiet makes sense," Jamie said softly.

"Just in case," Hailey added.

"Just in case," Ryaan repeated.

Mei said nothing, feeling very much at the center of the warning.

CHAPTER 38

MEI WAS ONLY in Captain Finlay's office for six minutes. Seven on the outside. She told Captain Finlay and Sergeant Lanier about seeing Amy Warner in the club and confronting her, but before Jamie could mention the conversation with the bouncer, Sergeant Lanier interrupted.

"What Ms. Warner does in her free time—within the bounds of the law—isn't our business," she said.

Mei felt like she'd been punched.

"Of course," Jamie said before Mei could protest. "But we're talking about the night on which Inspector Ling was drugged, and we've just learned from Inspector Ryaan Berry of Triggerlock that this Oyster Point robbery/cyber case has been triangulated to this building."

"Triangulated to this building?" Captain Finlay spoke up. "What does that mean?"

"It means whoever orchestrated the weapons robbery and set up devices in that warehouse to access the computer servers of one or more of those four companies is working from inside the department."

A frown settled deep into Captain Finlay's mouth.

"After the shooting at her home and the incident in

the club on Saturday, Inspector Ling has every right to be involved. This is her case," Jamie said.

Finlay frowned at Jamie. "I'm not sure about that."

"I agree with Captain Finlay," Lanier was quick to butt in. "This is clearly an issue for Internal Affairs now. I'm afraid it's a conflict of interest for us to discuss it with Inspector Ling."

Until now, Mei had thought of Sergeant Grace Lanier as prompt, thorough, professional. She was a transfer from the Sacramento department. There was murmuring that Lanier stayed clear of The Rookie Club for fear that assimilating with only women would be bad for her career. Mei had thought the comment was unfair. Until now. "If you feel conflicted, Inspector Vail, you should feel free to go as well," Lanier added.

Mei was shocked. She stared at Lanier who, at least, had the decency not to meet her gaze.

The sound Jamie made was a little like a chuckle. Mei watched Lanier flinch at the noise as though Jamie had said something sharp and vulgar. "I do have a conflict, Sergeant," Jamie said. "You have access to the one person who is clearly at the heart of this. If I may say so, Mei is not a likely candidate for these kinds of attacks. I do have some experience with personal vendettas against women. If it were up to me, I'd focus on Inspector Ling, not exclude her." With that, Jamie stood. "Thank you both for your time."

Mei stood, too, but when Jamie went for the door without awaiting a response, Mei remained. "As Detective Vail said, I am your best source. That you are not using me seems severely negligent on your part."

"Inspector Ling," Finlay interrupted, warning in his tone.

"With all due respect, of course," Mei added and joined Jamie at the door. Neither Finlay nor Lanier said anything as they left, but when Mei glanced back, Captain Finlay had turned his frown on Lanier.

*

Amy was not in the lab when Mei arrived. By the end of the day, it was rumored that she was on leave. Mei's team received an email from Lanier, informing them that they were to have no communications with Amy Warner, as she was part of an internal investigation. Mei got another email from Lanier with Finlay cc'd, letting her know they would be posting an officer at her house at night. She forwarded it to Jamie, who responded with one line: *"Bureaucracy at its best."*

Teddy and Blake asked her if she knew anything about what was going on, to which she replied she had limited information and wasn't in a position to talk about it. The two exchanged a few words of surprise. Amy, after all, seemed as harmless to them as she had to Mei.

Aaron, on the other hand, took the news by packing up early and leaving. He took his laptop with him. Mei replied to Lanier's email with a cool one of her own, letting her sergeant know that Aaron had left. She certainly hoped Lanier was looking into Aaron as well as Amy. She'd hinted as much in her email, but she wasn't surprised that Lanier's reply gave her zero information.

Everything made Mei jumpy. The little steam sounds that came from the coffeemaker while she was filling the copier with paper; the way the printer clicked on and sounded like it was going to print for no reason; the creak in the bottom drawer of her file cabinet.

There was no news on the Oyster Point case and nothing from Ballistics on the ammo search. By 5:00, Mei was jumping out of her skin, making herself crazy. She had to get out of the office. As Mei was packing up, Sabrina called. Her name on the screen of Mei's phone made her smile. A bright spot in all the craziness. "Hi," Mei answered.

"Hi. I'm so glad you answered."

"Thanks for calling."

"I wanted to hear how you are," Sabrina said. "But first I wanted to tell you that you got the apartment. The one on Bronte."

Mei froze at her desk. "I did?"

"Yes."

Looking at apartments felt like something from a different life. Three days ago. In a month, Mei could be in her own apartment. She tried to imagine having that conversation with Andy. She was staying in San Francisco and he should stay in Chicago. What if they hadn't caught Mei's attacker by then? Wouldn't Ayi be safer if Mei was living on her own?

"Mei? If you don't want it, you don't have to take it."

"No, I do," Mei said. "That is really great news."

"Okay," Sabrina said uncertainly. "They need to do some work on it, but you'll be able to move in on the first. I've got the paperwork. I thought I'd drop it off at your house."

"That would be great." Mei wished she could

remember the details of the apartment. "Any chance I could look at it again—maybe tomorrow?"

"Tomorrow is crazy."

"No hurry. Maybe over the weekend."

"Since there's no one living there," Sabrina said, "how about if I leave you my realtor key. It will open the lockbox."

"Won't you need your key?" Mei asked.

"I've got an extra," Sabrina assured her. "We can get together over the weekend and I'll get it back then."

"Perfect. Thanks, Sabrina."

"No problem. Let's talk tomorrow night or Saturday."

Sophie called a few minutes later, and Mei caught her up on the events of the day. "Amy?"

"Did you see her that night?" Mei asked.

"I barely know what she looks like, but I don't think so. I didn't see anyone who looked familiar other than our group. And Lanier cut you out of it?"

"Completely."

"I've heard she's a bitch," Sophie said.

"Well, she was today."

Sophie offered her a ride home. "We could grab a drink on the way?"

"Can't tonight," she said vaguely, unsure how much Sophie knew about The Rookie Club. "But I was thinking about going to take a look at my new apartment tomorrow."

Sophie let out a whoop. "You got it!"

Mei laughed. "Yeah."

"I can't wait to see it," Sophie said. "Are you excited?"

The answer to that question should have been so complex. Renting a place of her own without consulting Andy said in no uncertain terms that their marriage was ending. He would hear that clearly. That she didn't consult even her parents or Ayi spoke volumes as well. And yet, staking a claim on her own space, the independence of the decision, that felt distinctly right.

"Mei?" Sophie asked.

"I am," Mei said honestly. "Really excited."

Mei hung up with Sophie and hailed a cab to Ayi's. Waiting for the bus would merely have drawn out the process of the inevitable. If she told Ayi tonight, it was one less person to deal with tomorrow. She was due to fly to Chicago in three weeks, but it couldn't wait. She would see if she could find a reasonable flight to go next weekend. Moving forward felt really good.

At the house, Ayi was on the living room floor, using a little pair of scissors to trim a house plant. She wore her little brocade slippers and black jersey pants that she often wore around the house. On top, she wore a gray sweater, hanging long on her small frame. She looked like a teenager from the back.

"Did you stay home from work?"

Ayi started at the sound of her voice. "Mei Ling," she said, calling her by her full name. "Why are you here?"

"I'm home from work. What's wrong?"

Just then, Hui emerged from the kitchen, carrying a spoon. "You have to try this," she said, heading for Ayi. Two steps in, she realized something was wrong. Her gaze shifted from Ayi to Mei. Her spoon tipped and some of the liquid slid onto the floor. It was as though Mei had caught them naked.

The two shared a look, and Mei noticed that Hui

wore a pink sweatshirt. A cable car was stitched onto its front, just like the one Ayi had. Mei stared at it. On the right sleeve, just above the cuff was a black stain. Ayi's sweatshirt. Hui also wore the striped jersey pants Mei had seen Ayi in countless times. Hui in Ayi's clothes, cooking in Ayi's kitchen. Mei dropped her bag on the floor. How had she missed it? Ayi's willingness to stay with Hui after the shooting. Her reluctance, in fact, to come home. Mei had been so consumed with how she would approach her parents and Andy, with the job and then the attacks that she hadn't even seen the obvious signs.

"Hi," Hui said in her accented English, her free hand beneath the spoon, though most of the liquid had run off. Hui glanced between Mei and Ayi before returning to the kitchen.

Mei looked at Ayi. "You two—"

Ayi carried the pruned leaves into the kitchen along with the scissors. Mei followed. Her aunt threw away the leaves, wiped the scissors and replaced them in the knife block on the counter.

Mei stood in the doorway and watched the two women. Ayi took a spoon and tasted the soup, nodded to Hui, and spoke a few words too soft for Mei to hear. Not that she would have understood, as the two women spoke Mandarin to one another.

Hui nodded without looking at Mei.

"Come. It's time we talked," said Ayi and walked to the living room.

Ayi seemed to take a moment to decide where she wanted to have this particular conversation and opted for the living room sofa. Stepping out of her slippers, she sat with her legs beneath her and crossed her hands in her lap.

Mei sat opposite her. She was both surprised and so relieved. Looking back, there was a moment when it had occurred to her that Hui and Ayi were a couple, but Ayi's strong ties to Chinese tradition and Hui's marriage had thrown her off. It was only now that Mei saw the irony.

Ayi nodded. "Go on. Ask your questions."

"I don't have questions."

Ayi dismissed the notion with a wave of her hand. "Of course you do."

Mei paused. "I just never realized with all your Chinese traditions…"

Ayi smiled. "Being traditional is not at odds with being gay."

Mei watched her aunt. "I guess that's the part I can't always see."

"It's not always clear," Ayi agreed. "Your A Poh knew," she said, referring to Mei's grandmother, mother to Ayi and Mei's mother. Her A Poh had died when Mei was only twelve or thirteen. What Mei remembered of her was the way her eyes followed Mei's movements without any motion in her head. That and the smells of rubber and fish. "She knew before I knew," Ayi continued. "When I finally told her—and I was in my thirties then—she said, 'Men in the game are blind to what those looking on see clearly.'"

"You and my dad and the Chinese proverbs."

"Not your father's," Ayi corrected. "Those were A Poh's. Your father learned them from her."

"Do my parents know?"

Ayi shrugged. "I think they must."

Mei was shocked. "You've never talked about it?"

Ayi looked up. Hui stood in the doorway. She crossed the room quietly, with purpose, and sat beside Ayi. The two exchanged a look.

"These aren't things our parents would discuss," Hui said. "Living in China, there was little focus on such trivialities as falling in love. Honor, respect, legacy. Those were the things our fathers preached. And not to us, dear Mei. We are women."

Mei nodded. "I understand. It was very different. But your siblings," she said to Ayi. "Your sons," to Hui.

Hui nodded. "My sons have heard the truth. After their father's death, I chose not to remarry but to live my life as I wanted. My first son chooses to ignore what he has heard. He still speaks of suitable men for me. He occasionally invites them to dinner at my home in an attempt to find me a husband for my last years."

"And he knows you're gay?"

Hui smiles softly. "Hearing and knowing are not the same."

"But your younger son accepts you?"

"He does." Hui touched Ayi's leg. "He knows Ayi well, has dinners with us. He does not ask questions about our relationship, but he accepts us. Much as I think your parents do."

"They've met you?"

"Many times," Hui said. "Ayi and I have traveled to Chicago. We've seen them, and they've been here."

"But you've never told them that you are a couple?" Mei asked.

Ayi sat patiently. With only the slightest bit of body

language, so subtle Mei had missed it for months now, Hui understood Ayi's message that she continue. "In our generation, things weren't said explicitly," Hui said. "I imagine that's still true for a lot of people."

Mei nodded, thinking of her own parents.

"So we learned to read much more than we're told. My boys are more like you. They wait to be told. It is just a difference in our ages." She smiled softly. "I strongly suspect your parents know about Ayi and me. Just as I'm sure they know about you," she added softly.

Mei felt her face heat up, but neither Ayi nor Hui betrayed any emotion in their faces. Instead, they sat side by side, not touching but so clearly a unit. Mei felt like an idiot for missing it, but her mind was pulled instead to what Hui had said. Her parents knew she was gay. It seemed impossible. "If they knew, why were they so against me coming out here?"

Ayi glanced at Hui then back to Mei. "Knowing isn't always the same as accepting."

"So they don't approve."

Ayi shook her head. "It's not that simple, Mei. Parents want things for their children to be easy. Secure and happy. It's why your parents weren't thrilled when you wanted to be in the FBI. They thought it could get you hurt."

"And they think being gay could get me hurt?"

"Maybe not in the same way," Ayi began. "But not everyone in the world is accepting. Being straight is easier, Mei. We all know that. Easier to have a normal life, to be married, to have a family and children."

"You make it sound like it's a choice," Mei said.

Ayi smiled. "Of course it's not a choice. Your parents

know that, too. They also know that when you chose to marry Andy, it seemed like you would have it easier."

Mei stared at her feet. "I'm not happy with Andy."

Ayi nodded. "And you need to change that."

After a moment's silence, Hui stood. "I should get back to my soup. You can stay for dinner if you'd like, Mei. I made enough for all of us."

With that, Hui disappeared into the kitchen. As she walked away, Mei realized how much Hui and Ayi looked alike. Ayi's hair was less gray and cut a little shorter, but the way they walked, the small energetic steps. It made Mei think they'd been together a long time. Mei turned back to her aunt. "She's lovely, Ayi."

Ayi nodded. "She really is."

"I'm so sorry about everything that has happened here. I don't want you to be uncomfortable in your home."

Ayi glanced up at the gongbi print that Mei had finally picked up from the repair shop after work. "I will be okay. It has been nice to stay with Hui." She smiled. "We did it more often before you moved in."

Mei crossed to sit beside her aunt. "I found an apartment, Ayi. I'm going to move out in a few weeks."

"You don't have to move out because of us," Ayi assured her.

"It's not just that," Mei confessed.

Ayi seemed to understand. "I'm happy you found a place if that's what you want."

Mei nodded. "It is."

"But you haven't told Andy?"

Mei shook her head. "Or my parents. I don't know how to do that."

"It won't be easy, but it isn't your job to make your parents happy."

Mei had so many questions about how her parents would react, but Hui came in, carrying a serving bowl to the table. "Will you join us, Mei?"

Mei hesitated. She'd put enough on Ayi and Hui tonight. Mei needed time to clear her head, too. Was it really possible that her mother knew Ayi was gay? And that in sixty-plus years they had never talked about it?

"I'm afraid I have to go," Mei said, rising from the couch. "I've got a dinner with some people from the department tonight."

Ayi nodded.

"Yes," Hui said. "Your aunt mentioned your monthly rookie dinner. It sounds like fun."

"It is." Mei stood. "Thank you, Ayi." She hugged her aunt, something she rarely did. Ayi held her for an extra moment as though sending her off with an extra dose of reassurance. It felt like her blessing. Mei heard Hui's words. *In our generation, things weren't said so explicitly. We learned to read much more than we're told.*

You can do this, Ayi was telling her. I did it a generation ago. I have lived a happy life with a wonderful partner. "Thank you," Mei whispered again, and with that, Ayi let go. Mei grabbed her coat and headed out to her dinner.

Outside, the cool air filled Mei with a sense of renewed energy. No, it wasn't just the air. She had Ayi's blessing. And a role model. She paused to fill her lungs with all of it then started for the car.

CHAPTER 39

MEI DROVE AYI'S car toward Golden Gate Park. Although Ayi lived only two blocks from the park, Mei was rarely there and even less often at night. The traffic was sparse and the stars bright. Maybe The Rookie Club dinner was what she needed. She didn't know these women that well, but she had heard enough to know some of them had been through periods as hard as this one was for Mei, or harder. Everyone had surely heard about the shooting and the club, so it would be out there already. That in itself was a relief.

All the talk also meant that she was effectively out to the whole department. Not how she'd intended to do it, but again, it meant no more secrets. How long had it been since she'd been with a group of people who knew who and what she was? Hailey, Jamie, and Ryaan, they might have been the first ones ever. Now Ayi knew, too. Mei was slowly building her reality, surrounding herself with it and embracing it. That was a powerful feeling.

As she crossed through the far side of the park, her phone rang. An unfamiliar departmental number. "Ling," she answered.

"Mei, it's Grace. I'm sorry to call so late. Are you at home?"

Mei said nothing for several seconds. Was Grace someone she'd met at the club? "I'm sorry?" she said as though she hadn't heard the caller.

"It's Grace. Grace Lanier."

"Oh, Sergeant Lanier. I didn't recognize your voice," Mei said quickly. Or the fact that she'd used her first name. It probably meant she had bad news. Mei pulled to the curb in front of a house only slightly older and larger than Ayi's. "Is this about Amy Warner?"

Sergeant Lanier cleared her voice. "It is."

Mei waited.

"Is there any chance you might be able to come into the station?" Lanier asked.

"Sergeant, I'm due somewhere in ten minutes. I assume you're calling with important news. Can you tell me what it is?"

There were voices in the background. Mei heard a man's voice. At first, she assumed it was Captain Finlay, but the voice was wrong. Younger. More casual. One she heard all the time. "Is that Teddy?"

A moment of silence.

"Uh, hi, Mei."

"What's going on, Teddy?" Mei insisted.

"I'd really rather do this in person," Lanier said before Teddy could answer.

First, they didn't want her involved. In fact, she wasn't allowed to be involved. Now they wanted her to come down to the station at 7:00 on a Thursday. She had already been jerked around enough. "I don't mean any disrespect, Sergeant, but I believe I deserve to be informed of any new information immediately."

There was a beat then Lanier spoke. "Amy Warner came forward and informed us that she has been trailing you."

"Trailing me," Mei repeated, glancing out at the street around her. A car passed, a dad with his teenage daughter in the front seat, and disappeared around the bend. "Like following me?"

"Keeping track of your meetings—where you were, who you were with."

"Why?"

A moment of silence before the sergeant spoke. "She was receiving correspondence—via departmental email—instructing her to follow you."

Mei shifted the car into park and shut the engine off. "What? Who in the department?"

More whispering.

"Teddy, what's going on?"

"Ted—Teddy—has been helping me track the emails," Lanier said.

There was a moment of silence before Teddy said, "Someone spoofed Sergeant Lanier's email."

Amy thought Sergeant Lanier had asked her to follow Mei. No wonder she'd been so skittish. Someone accessed Lanier's account. "They do it with a virus?"

Teddy seemed hesitant. "Uh, no."

"Through the department's server or her actual account?" Mei pressed.

"Her account," Teddy said.

Mei was silent. Getting access to an individual email

319

account was the hardest route for spoofing. It meant someone had access to Lanier. To her computer or to her login credentials, which meant access to the department.

"Amy assumed the messages were from me, but I never knew anything about it," Lanier said, sounding a little desperate. "Teddy's been searching my computer for the last hour and a half, and he can't find anything."

"Whoever did this wouldn't have done it through your computer," Mei said out loud, her mind spinning. "Do you access email through the secure server from home?"

"Um…"

"She does," Teddy confirmed.

"That's the most likely breach point," Mei said. "Run a report on any remote logins to Lanier's account over the past thirty days. Check for both locations and IP addresses. Maybe we can identify the machine used to access the email server."

"Okay. I'll do it right now," Teddy told her.

"Call and let me know what you find." Mei glanced at the clock on the dash. It was 6:55. She was tempted to turn around and head home. Or go to the station. She glanced at the quiet street. "Do we have any idea if I'm being followed now?"

"We don't think so," Lanier said. A beat passed. "But we really don't know."

"Was Amy given a reason to follow me?" Mei asked.

"No," Lanier confessed.

"But she did it anyway."

Lanier didn't respond to that. Instead, she said, "An officer will be stationed at your home twenty-four seven."

Ayi and Hui would be protected. That was something.

"Until we can locate this person—the hacker," Lanier added. "What would help us is a list of everyone outside the department that you've been working with since—"

"Inside, Sergeant," Mei said, cutting her off. She took a breath and let it out. "This thing is happening inside the department. Jamie Vail and I tried to explain that to you in the meeting today. Ryaan Berry from Triggerlock and Hailey Wyatt in Homicide triangulated the calls from the cell phones we found strapped to those computers. They were able to track down three or four other cell phones involved. The calls coming from the one person they haven't located are coming from inside the Bryant Street building."

There was a long silence.

"Who has these reports?" Lanier asked.

"Ryaan Berry and Hailey Wyatt. Jamie Vail may as well." Mei thought if it weren't for Lanier, she'd have access to them, too. She changed her mind about going home. She was going to dinner. At the very least, she'd get a chance to talk through this latest development with Ryaan or Hailey or Jamie. In person, not on the phone. The phone. She all but dropped it. Surely they were bugging that, too.

"I have to go," Mei said, suddenly aware of every word. "I'll be in touch." She hung up as though it was her meeting to adjourn. And maybe it was.

She shut the phone off completely, a knee-jerk reaction from an older age of technology. With the right equipment, it wouldn't matter if her phone was off. Mei started the engine of the car and cranked the heat. Then, she checked that the doors were locked and pushed her seat back as far as it would go.

What would it take to bug an iPhone? These days, bugs were mostly software. In that case, turning it off had been smart. Mei tried to shake the chills, but even as the hot air filled the car, she was cold.

She tried to talk herself down. A bug in the form of an app seemed unlikely. She still ran an app from the FBI that scanned for spyware and programs running unauthorized code. It hadn't reported anything unusual. Mei was also very cautious about what apps went on her phone. At the moment, she had only nine. Not much of a place to hide a bug. Still. She should have checked it after her tablet had gone missing.

Mei popped off the hard, outer navy-striped case. Removed the thin rubber layer beneath it. Using the overhead light, she studied the phone's edges. No evidence that it had been pried open. She turned it over in her hands. Nothing. It was pristine. No scratch marks, no excess glue. It didn't mean someone hadn't accessed the battery. She'd have to pull it apart to be certain. She looked around the car. No flat surface. No good light. No magnifying glass. She couldn't do that here. She tried to reassure herself. There were no outward signs of a bug at work. Bugs drained a phone's battery. Her battery life was in line with the programs she ran. Bugs also created random screen flashes. She'd had none of those, either.

Mei pulled the rubber inner case over the white phone. The headphone jack caught her eye. A strange shadow. Something in there. Mei grabbed her purse off the floor and dumped the contents onto the passenger's seat. She scanned the contents for something sharp, a pen or a bobby pin, but there was nothing like that. Ayi's ashtray was filled with loose change. Only paperwork in the glove box. Desperate, Mei dug deeper. At the bottom of the glove box was a single safety pin. Perfect.

Using the sharp point, Mei dug gently along the inside edge of the headphone jack, applying pressure until she could go no deeper. Slowly, she pulled the pin back out. With it came a thin, curved device. Similar in appearance to a microprocessor, it was maybe half the size of the fingernail on her pinky finger.

Mei picked it up between her nails and dropped it into her palm. Bringing it close to her face, she studied it. Her expertise was on technology that ran processors and code. Nothing like this. Even still, looking at it she was sure that she was being tracked and monitored, recorded. She thought about the conversation she'd had with Ayi and Hui, her talks with Sabrina, her date with Sophie. Those were just her personal ones. What about Jamie and Hailey and Ryaan? Could the phone have picked up that conversation in the hallway? Did the killer know that they'd homed in on the department?

Mei had the momentary urge to throw the thing out the window, but instead she opened her wallet and dropped the bug into her coin purse. With the interior lights shut off, she pulled back into the street and headed toward Tommy's. Whoever was tracking her could see where she was going, but she had no choice but to take him—whoever he was—with her to dinner. The good news was that she was going to dinner with a roomful of cops.

CHAPTER 40

MEI PARKED ON a side street and walked down Geary to Tommy's. She held her purse tight against her, feeling overly conspicuous, like the tiny piece of equipment was broadcasting a siren down the street. As always, Tommy's was crowded. Mei pushed her way through the throng to the back. A couple of guys tried to stop her to chat, but Mei didn't even pause as she shook her head and passed.

The Rookie Club dinner was supposed to be a time to talk about work without talking shop. Tonight, Mei wanted straight shop talk. Ryaan and Sydney were already at the table. Jamie wasn't coming, but she hoped Hailey would arrive soon. She needed to hear every last theory about what the hell was going on. Across from them were two women Mei had met, though she couldn't remember their names. Mei took a seat next to Sydney who reintroduced her to Jess Campbell of the INS and Cindy Wang, a bomb expert. Mei opted for water when the waiter came for her order. Sydney raised her water glass and clinked it against Mei's.

Across the table, Jess and Cindy were talking, so Mei opened her wallet and emptied her coin purse onto the table top. Cindy Wang glanced over at the clinking of coins.

"I can loan you money, Mei, if you need it," Ryaan told her.

Mei didn't smile, but put the small square device in the palm of her hand and showed it to Ryaan and Sydney.

Sydney pushed Mei's hand lower, trying to focus on her palm. "I can't see without my readers. What is it?"

Ryaan looked at Mei who raised her eyebrows but said nothing. Sydney pulled a pair of reading glasses from her purse. After studying it herself, Sydney snapped her fingers at Jess and Cindy then pointed to the thing in Mei's hand. Ryaan pressed her finger to her lips. Mei held her palm out across the table so the others could see.

"Where?" Cindy Wang asked her and then mouthed, "Where did you find it?"

Mei lifted her iPhone with her free hand.

"Inside?"

Mei shook her head and pointed to the headphone jack.

Sydney took the device from Mei's hand. She turned it over in her palm then passed it across to Cindy. "She's seen enough of these," Sydney whispered to Mei.

Cindy handed the device to Jess and circled the table. Squatting beside Mei, she said, "It's a passive listening device, for sure. It might be pulling a little juice from the jack, just enough to keep it running."

While Cindy returned to her seat, Mei unrolled her silverware and laid her napkin flat on the table. Jess slid the device onto the napkin then Mei wrapped it carefully. She pulled the car keys from her purse.

"Where are you going?" Jess asked her.

"Going to put this thing in my car where it can listen to the traffic on Geary," Mei said.

Sydney took it from her. "Better yet, let it listen to traffic from my car." She met Mei's gaze. "Just in case it's doing more than listening. I'll get it to the lab tonight and have the third shift work on it." She paused. "I could go now."

Mei shook her head. "It can wait until after dinner. I'd prefer to have your brain power here."

"Okay," Sydney agreed. "I'll put it in the car and be right back."

Ryaan slid into the chair next to Mei while Cindy and Jess leaned in.

"What are you working on?" Cindy asked her.

"I wish I knew," Mei admitted.

Ryaan filled Jess and Cindy in on a few of the details of the case. Mei was grateful for the expertise at the table. When Hailey arrived, she took the chair on the other side of Mei. She pulled her purse strap off her shoulder and shrugged out of her coat before leaning into Mei. "I just saw Sydney. Jesus Christ. What the hell is going on?"

Mei had no answer for that.

Hailey ordered a lemonade. Mei was tempted to get a glass of wine, but she didn't want anything dulling her senses. Jess and Cindy ordered another round of margaritas though their first ones weren't quite half done.

Sydney returned a couple minutes later. Ryaan moved to sit across from Hailey so they could talk more easily.

"If there was one in your phone," Sydney said. "There might be others."

Hailey nodded. "Right."

"At least you know your phone is clean," Ryaan said.

Mei looked around the group.

Sydney put a hand on her shoulder. "You look exhausted."

"I heard our pharmaceutical company was in the paper this week," Ryaan said.

"Really? What paper?"

"*The Chronicle*," Ryaan said.

Mei wondered why her team hadn't flagged the article. "For what?"

"Some wonder drug that wasn't really a wonder," she said.

"I wonder if it has anything to do with the breach," Sydney said.

"I'll follow up with them. See if they'll talk to us now," Mei said and turned to Hailey. "Did you hear anything from the church?"

Hailey shook her head. "Not much. The director of the outreach programs wasn't there. Hal talked to a guy who works in the kitchen. He didn't recognize the name Albert Jackson."

Dinner arrived and a few minutes passed in silence before Ryaan spoke up. "A lot of soup kitchens have no way to track the names of their visitors. We may never link Jackson to St. James."

"If we can get in touch with the director, we could show a picture of Jackson," Mei suggested, picking at her green chili enchiladas. She wasn't particularly hungry.

"Someone must know how to reach the community director," Sydney said.

"The church administrator would, but she had gallbladder surgery yesterday," Hailey said.

"And the guy in the kitchen didn't even know the director's name?" Cindy asked.

"He said her first name is Jo," Hailey said. "Maybe short for Joann or Jolene."

"But no last name?"

"No. He wasn't sure about that. He thought it was something like Pollack or Bullock."

Mei froze, fork in the air. "Pollack?"

"What it is, Mei?" Ryaan asked.

The hair at the base of Mei's ponytail stood on end. "There's a guy in my lab named Aaron Pollack."

Mei thought again about Aaron. How strange and reclusive he'd been since her arrival. Why hadn't she considered him more seriously before? He had wanted her job. He was threatened by her presence. Disrespectful. Stubborn. Arrogant. Vengeful. That last one wasn't as clear. And violent? "Amy Warner has been tracking me for someone else," she said.

"What?"

"Somebody hacked into Lanier's email and sent Amy instructions to follow me. Amy thought the emails were coming from Lanier."

"So maybe it was Aaron giving Amy orders," Ryaan said.

"Maybe," Hailey said. Mei could tell her tone was shifting. "But the guy was guessing at a name. I'll call it in and get someone to look into it. But it's not Aaron working at the church… unless he's dressing as a woman twice a week." Hailey smiled, but Mei couldn't find her humor.

"I'm just tired," she said.

"I know. It's all-consuming when it's your life." Hailey took a long drink of her lemonade as though it were something stronger. Maybe she was speaking from experience.

Mei waited until the others had finished dinner. When the waiter came back for another drink order, she asked for her check. "I'm not much company tonight," she said. "I think I'll head home and get some sleep."

Sydney promised to call her as soon as she had information on the bug, and Hailey assured her she'd be in touch when she heard back from the church. As Mei walked out of Tommy's, the only thing on her mind was Aaron Pollack. If Amy was following her on someone's instructions, Aaron was the perfect suspect. It wasn't as though someone had spoofed Sergeant Lanier's email with a virus. No, this person had hacked into her account. Lanier loved Aaron. She still met with him on cases that had been in progress before Mei started. It wouldn't be that hard for Aaron to have accessed her office and her computer. People were stupid with their email passwords. Hell, she might have even told him. If he wanted to verify her email on his own computer, he could easily have sent a text to her phone and seen it on her screen. That was if Lanier even locked her phone.

Instead of driving back across the park toward home, Mei drove to the station. There would still be people working, but the station was a different place at night. She came in through the back doors and descended the stairs to their basement lair. At the FBI, she'd had an office with a window. Spending ten hours a day in the basement was another thing that took getting used to. The hallway was quiet but well lit. Sometimes when she came in early, the hallway was dark. It made her wonder who shut the lights down late at night. The only sound in the lab was the hum of the main server. Mei tucked her purse under her desk and looked around. Aaron's laptop was on his desk, attached to the docking station. She was sure she'd seen him pack it up when he left.

She scanned the room again. Jumped at the shadows from the equipment. Peered behind the large consoles until she was certain she was alone. Her heart pounding, she hurried to Aaron's desk. Shook the mouse until the screen on the large free-standing monitor came to life. Aaron was logged into the department's case system. He was uploading something to a Dropbox account. According to the pop-up screen, the process would be completed in another twelve minutes. Aaron was here somewhere.

She retreated from his desk to check the supply closet they used for a breakroom. Back in the hall, she listened at the door of the bathroom. She could take the entire laptop home and work on it there, but that meant tipping him off. She wasn't ready to do that.

Mei grabbed a flash drive from her top drawer and slid it into the USB port on Aaron's laptop. She took a screen shot of his desktop, moved the pop-up that showed nine minutes remaining out of the way and took another shot. She scanned the case details. The initial case was opened by the SFPD, but it was no longer one of theirs. It had been handed off to the DOJ. She hit page down and took screen shots as she went. What was Aaron doing?

Moving quickly, she dragged the images onto the USB and deleted the originals. The images were still on his computer, but he'd have to be looking for them. A door closed in the hall. Mei froze and counted to ten. When no one entered the lab, she kept working. She opened Aaron's email and scanned through the inbox. Nothing stood out. She didn't think he was stupid enough to keep evidence on his department computer. Mei checked for erased cookies and Internet history. Nothing. His browser history was empty. He must have been running a program that deleted his history.

She found his browser minimized. She touched it once and Aaron's private email server opened. The inbox appeared, and Mei took a screenshot. Every email subject was a sequence of numbers. At first, she thought they might be case file numbers, but there were too many numbers and no alpha characters. She clicked on one. The clock came up on the screen. "Don't bump me out," she whispered. "Come on. Come on." The list of emails disappeared, and she was bumped back to the logon screen. "Damn it."

She checked recent activity in his office email account, then his other programs. It wasn't enough. She tested Aaron's desk drawer. Locked. She paused to listen. All quiet. She retrieved the silverware she had stashed in her bottom drawer. Using the cafeteria knife on Aaron's desk, she pried open the lock and pulled the top drawer open.

The drawer fell open. There would be no hiding that she'd been through his desk now. She peered into the top drawer. Sticky notes, pens, most of it was the normal stuff. In the second drawer were old disks and an external drive. No way he'd leave anything on a drive at the station.

In the bottom drawer, she spotted his bag. She stared

at it. Going through his computer and his desk was one thing; those were department property. His bag wasn't. She checked the process update again. She'd been there four minutes. If he was in the building, he'd be back any minute.

She pulled his bag out of the drawer. In the main pocket was a case folder for one of his ongoing cases. She found car keys, a small umbrella, mints, his wallet with driver's license, credit cards. The billfold contained forty-odd dollars. Nothing unusual there. In the small pockets, she found a card for a personal shopper at Nordstrom. Behind that was an American Express Platinum card. In the name of Aaron Alexander Pollack. The card had a $350 annual fee or something. Designed for high-income executives, not lab techs.

Mei slid the card back and checked his bag for anything else she might have missed. One pocket had several pens, a pass for a swanky gym with a membership fee only someone earning six figures could afford, and a card for the Four Season's Half Moon Bay. Maybe Aaron had family money. Not a crime.

She put his wallet back and checked the hall again. Surely, he would be back soon. Rushing, she pulled out the case file. Pushed his bag back into the drawer. A white envelope slid out onto the ground. Mei flipped it over. Blank. She tore it open, pulled out a stack of folded pages. Case summary pages. She flipped through them, the cases unfamiliar. Then one caught her eye. She scanned the case number QF17643294AL. The same one she was not authorized to view. The shooting at Ayi's. Aaron had a printout of her case.

"What the hell are you doing?"

Mei jammed the pages under her arm and spun around. Aaron stood there, holding a cup of coffee and his phone.

She rose slowly. "I thought I heard your phone ringing in your desk. I was trying to find it."

Aaron looked at his computer screen which mercifully had gone black again. "I have my phone right here."

Mei backed slowly against his desk. She glanced at Aaron's coffee cup.

His gaze followed hers and he set the coffee on the far corner of his desk, out of reach. "What were you really doing?"

Mei reached back for the flash drive, but Aaron pushed her aside.

He pulled the drive out and held it up. "What are you looking for?"

"We know what you're doing."

Aaron grabbed her arm, digging his fingers into her biceps. "Give me those papers."

Mei jerked herself free and ran. Her phone was in her purse with her keys. She didn't stop. *Just get out of the lab.*

Aaron yanked her ponytail and brought her down hard on her back. She lost her breath. The linoleum vibrated through her pelvis and up her spine. The pages fluttered to the floor. Mei rolled over and dove for them. Swept them into her hand, scrambled back to her feet.

She saw the gun in his hand and froze.

"Guess you missed this when you went through my stuff."

Mei gripped the pages and remained completely still.

The pistol was a 9mm or maybe a .45. A bullet that would do damage. "Give me those pages," Aaron demanded, taking a step forward.

Mei stepped away. "You're not going to shoot me in the middle of the lab, Aaron. You'll go to jail."

"You don't have anything on me," Aaron said. His voice caught on the word "me," like he was choking.

"We do." She inched backward ever so slowly. "We know, Aaron. But we can help you if tell us who else is involved."

Aaron stepped forward again. A lumbering step like a drunk. Sweat shone on his face. "Why are you in my stuff? How did you know?"

"Everyone knows, Aaron."

The gun trembled in his hand. "They can't."

"The case files."

"How could they have tracked that?"

"Hailey Wyatt gave me your name," Mei said. "How do you think I ended up looking through your stuff?"

Aaron licked his lips. His eyes darted to his laptop and back. "Wyatt? Who the hell is Wyatt?"

"Homicide."

Aaron shook his head. "No."

Mei felt him shift. "Berry knows, too. And Blanchard."

Aaron seemed to flinch as she recited the names.

"O'Hanlan and Harris, too."

He wiped his face with his sleeve.

Mei took another step backward. Too far from the door. She glanced around. She needed a weapon. There was nothing.

"You're lying," he charged, extending his hand with

the gun toward her. But the motion was halfhearted. His hand shook.

Mei pushed. "I'm not, Aaron. They're pulling together an independent forensics team right now."

Aaron's gaze flickered across the room. He didn't seem to notice the sweat coming down his face. He braced the gun with his other hand as though struggling to hold it up. His finger shifted toward the trigger, he took a shaky aim at her.

Mei froze.

The lab door slammed open. Lanier barreled in. "Drop it," she shouted.

Mei dove from the line of fire.

Aaron hid the gun behind his back.

"Drop the gun," Lanier said.

"It's not what you think. It's just—I—It was a misunderstanding."

"Drop it now," Lanier commanded.

Aaron opened his hands and the gun clattered to the floor. Lanier stepped on it and slid it out of his reach. "Turn around and put your hands on top of your head."

"I—" Aaron started.

"Now," she demanded.

Aaron moved in a slow circle and brought his hands to his head. Lanier wasted no time cuffing his hands behind his back. She pushed him down. "On your knees."

He lowered himself slowly. She gripped his arms and pressed him to the floor. "Down on your stomach. All the way down." When Aaron lay flat, Lanier radioed for backup. Finally, she turned to Mei. "Are you okay?"

Mei gripped the edge of the chair and pulled herself

slowly into it. Her heart was pounding. "How did you know I'd be here?"

"Hailey Wyatt called me. She thought something might have sent you on a wild goose chase here in the lab." She glanced at Aaron. "I guess maybe Wyatt was wrong about it being a wild goose chase."

Mei nodded, holding up the crumpled papers in her hand. She stared at Aaron on the floor. The back of his dress shirt was soaked through with sweat. He was silent. Only the movement of his back indicated that he was crying. Arrogant and conceited, yes. Capable of something illegal, certainly. But killing two men and lighting the place on fire? Mei still couldn't see that.

Something would turn up on his computer. Some evidence to erase all doubt. It had to. She pressed her hand to the sprinting beat of her heart and willed it to slow down.

CHAPTER 41

RYAAN PUT HER hands around the mug of black coffee and looked around. The diner Hal had chosen for their coffee date was only three blocks from the station. Although Ryaan had driven by it dozens of times, she'd never been inside. It was mostly empty at this hour. The Friday lunch rush—if there was a lunch rush—had passed and what remained was a collage of San Francisco characters. A homeless man sat eating beside a window, keeping a close eye on his shopping cart of worldly belongings parked on the sidewalk out front. Two big black women talked to each other across a table in voices as large as they were, punctuated by outbursts like, "You know it, girl," and, "He deserves an ass kicking for that. An ass kicking." Ryaan had aunts who talked like that. Maybe her mother had been boisterous once upon a time, too, but not that Ryaan could remember. An older man was hunched in the booth beside them, wearing a set of old-style headphones and eating what looked like apple pie. Beside his plate was a Walkman.

Across the table, Hal added a third creamer to his

coffee and stirred it. "Hope it's okay. I'm not really a Starbucks guy."

Ryaan leaned back against the red vinyl, shifting to move off a sharp crack on the seat. "It's perfect." Mostly it was just nice to get away from the station where she'd spent the morning on the case against Aaron Pollack.

Hal laughed and leaned across the table. "You obviously haven't tried the coffee yet."

"I haven't, but I probably don't need any more coffee anyway. Not after this week."

Hal nodded. "I hear you. About time for a drink to celebrate."

It was hard to believe it was over. Case resolutions were often less than satisfying, but she couldn't remember one as disappointing as this. "Doesn't feel over. I guess I should be happy."

"What's the name of the guy they arrested?"

"Aaron Pollack."

"I've never even heard of him," Hal said.

"Me neither. Guy's a crime scene guy."

"Computers, right?"

Ryaan nodded.

"Kind of anticlimactic."

"It really is."

"Maybe we should have gone out for a drink instead," Hal suggested.

Ryaan looked up. "You mean this is anticlimactic?"

"No," Hal said quickly. "Did you?"

"No. I meant the case. I guess it hasn't sunk in yet." Ryaan thought about the Internal Affairs guys who swept in. "It's like that when it's internal."

"They kind of cut you out," Hal said.

"Makes me feel like it's not over."

"But it is?"

Ryaan looked up as the realization set in. "Actually, I don't honestly know. The paperwork Mei found locked in Aaron's desk included details about the Oyster Point case and the shooting at her house, so he's obviously involved. We know he was using his police access to feed information to a company in Silicon Valley."

"Feed them what?"

"Security information, from what I heard," Ryaan explained.

"Like weapons security?" Hal asked.

"No, like where data has been accessed, where cases uncover valuable resources."

"Resources?"

"Like the guns at Oyster Point as well as ongoing case information. Leverage to help them sell security packages. I don't understand all of it."

Hal's eyes narrowed. "Can Mei see him killing those two guys and lighting the place on fire?"

Ryaan shrugged. "I don't know if she feels like she sees anything clearly right now. It's been a rough couple of weeks."

"Well, I guess it will all come out eventually," Hal said. "Just have to wait, right? It's the same thing with the double murder. Internal has taken that over, too."

"You think those guys will solve it?"

Hal shrugged. "Usually they come to us eventually. They can't solve it themselves. Homicide—like Trigger-lock—isn't about sorting through a bunch of paperwork.

You've got to get out on the streets and get dirty. Internal Affairs isn't really good at that, you know?"

"So basically they're stalling the whole thing?" Ryaan asked. "They are cutting us out until they can prove we're not involved and then they'll pass it back?"

Hal sighed. "That's usually how it works."

Ryaan felt herself grow angry. "That's bullshit. And what about Mei? If Aaron has a partner out there, then she's still in danger."

"Hailey said the same thing," Hal told her. "She made Captain Marshall promise to keep a patrol car on Mei until they wrap up all the loose ends."

The waitress came back to top off their coffees but both mugs were still full. "Can I get you a piece of pie or anything?"

"Not for me, thanks," Hal told her. "Ryaan?"

"No thanks."

With a smile, the waitress left their ticket on the table and walked away.

"I feel like I need to do something," Ryaan said.

"What can you do?"

"I've followed up on every lead. We've got phone records from all of them. All burner phones, and we've traced all the numbers. I got a call from the city records to trace the owner of the building where the fire happened. There's been no claim for insurance, which is odd, so we assume it's being leased by the owner."

"Who owns it?"

"MCOMEND is the name. It's an LLC. The general manager of the LLC is a guy named Joseph Bullock, but that got me nowhere. I ran his record. He's clean. He hasn't renewed his driver's license since '96. No credit. It's like he fell off the earth."

Hal was staring at her, frowning.

"What?"

He pulled a small black notebook from his jacket pocket and opened it on the table.

"Hal?"

Flipping pages, he seemed not to hear her. "I got a message from the office at St. James Church yesterday," he said finally without looking up.

Ryaan nodded. "Yes. Hailey told us at The Rookie Club dinner last night."

"Did she mention the woman who heads up the soup kitchen for the homeless there?"

"Yeah, Pollack. That's how Mei made the connection to Aaron Pollack."

"But the guy said her name was either Pollack or Bullock." Hal found what he was looking for. He spun his notebook so it was facing Ryaan. His finger was pressed into the center of one page. Under it, she could clearly see two names: Pollack? Bullock?

Ryaan stared at the names. "So maybe it wasn't Pollack. Maybe the name was Bullock."

Hal raised his eyebrows.

"But I searched the system for Bullock. I couldn't find any current records on a Joseph Bullock," Ryaan said.

"You Google him?" Hal asked.

Ryaan looked up. "What?"

"Did you Google the guy?"

Ryaan started to laugh but Hal shook his head. With a straight face, he said, "I use Google all the time."

"Hal, there are not a lot of gun dealers on Google."

"You'd be surprised," Hal said. "Anyone with a Facebook page or a Tweet account or whatever it's called, they're all on Google. I Google everyone."

Ryaan smiled.

"Seriously. Ev-ry-one," he said again.

Ryaan raised an eyebrow at Hal. "Did you Google me?"

"Of course," he said, staring at his hands. "Most of the hits on your name are about the department."

Ryaan reached across the table and hit his hand. "I can't believe you did that."

Hal's face sobered. "I read about your brothers."

Ryaan sank into the booth. "That's on there, huh?"

"It's not like Ryaan is a very common name spelled with two A's."

Ryaan pushed her coffee cup aside. "Right."

"Shoot, Ryaan. I'm sorry. I didn't expect something like that," Hal told her. "I was kind of hoping to see a picture of you with a prom date or something."

Ryaan imagined Hal looking for old pictures of her. Who else had Googled her and learned about Darryl and Antoine? The Internet was a scary place. "It's actually easier than having to tell you myself," she said.

"Is that why you chose Triggerlock?"

"I guess." To have something to do with her hands, Ryaan drank a sip of her coffee. She grimaced. "This is awful!"

"Told you," Hal said.

Ryaan used a napkin to wipe off her tongue and took a sip of water. "You didn't say it with enough conviction."

Hal pulled his iPhone out of his coat pocket. "So, what's the guy's name?"

"Joseph Bullock."

Hal stood and came around to her side of the booth. Ryaan moved over to give him room. He sat so their arms were touching. She felt a little flush of heat.

"Okay, searching for Joseph Bullock." A moment later he scanned the results. "Here's a Joseph Bullock CPA in Lincoln, Nebraska."

"Probably not our guy."

Hal nodded and started to type again. His fingers were so big he kept hitting the wrong letter and having to back up.

"You need some help?" she asked.

"Nah. I'm used to it now. This is actually fast for me. How about we search for Joseph Bullock California?" After a few more errors, he managed to type it in and hit search.

Hal had a response in two or three seconds. He handed Ryaan the phone. "You scroll through. It'll go faster." With that, he put his arm around the back of the booth so they could both see the screen.

"An attorney in Burbank, California."

"Try it."

Ryaan hit the link and they landed on Joe Bullock's page. An attorney for Creative Artists. "What's an enter tainment attorney?"

"Movie stars, I think," Ryaan said. She pulled up the picture of a young blond Tom Cruise-looking guy. "Doesn't look like he'd own a building in Bernal Heights."

"Try searching under the news option instead of

the regular search," Hal said. "It's under that little drop-down arrow."

"You're good at this."

"I was serious when I said I Google everyone."

Ryaan hit the news button. The first article that came up was dated October 4, 1996. *Bay Area Geneticist Paralyzed in Life-Threatening Stroke.* Hal whistled as Ryaan hit the link to a San Francisco Chronicle article.

Ryaan read it aloud, "Dr. Joseph Bullock, head researcher at Mendelcom," Ryaan halted.

"Mendelcom," Hal repeated.

"That's one of the companies that was broken into." Ryaan skimmed the article. "Bullock was in the midst of filing a suit against his company when he suffered a massive stroke." She read to the end of the article. "There's no mention of what happened to him. October 4, 1996. This was almost twenty years ago."

"I wonder where he is now." Hal pointed to the phone. "Google Joseph Bullock Mendelcom wife. Sometimes another article will mention the wife."

Ryaan typed almost as badly as Hal had and her fingers were half the size.

"It's not easy, is it?" he teased, nudging her shoulder.

"Shut up," she said.

A followup article was published two months after the original. "Barbara Bullock," Ryaan said. "Looks like they placed him at the South Bay Stroke Center. The name makes it sound sort of spa-ish."

"I doubt it is." Hal reached over to zoom in on the article. "There's a daughter, too. Josephine. The woman at St. James was Jo. Short for Josephine?"

Ryaan felt a little buzz. It was some combination of a new lead in the case and Hal's proximity. "Brilliant, Hal," she said, leaning into him.

Hal chuckled and she felt the vibration in her own chest. "Now, let's find out where that center is."

Ryaan searched the center. "They're in Menlo Park, but that was twenty years ago. He's probably dead by now."

"Not necessarily," Hal said. "I've got nothing better to do. Go on and call them. I'll text Hailey and let her know we might have a lead. She can contact Mei."

Ryaan pulled out her own phone and dialed the number.

"Good afternoon. Thank you for calling the South Bay Stroke Center," came a man's voice. "How may I direct your call?"

"This is Inspector Ryaan Berry of the San Francisco Police Department. I'm trying to locate a patient of yours named Joseph Bullock."

"Hold on one minute, Officer, and I'll get you over to Records."

Beside her, Hal was talking to the station. "Can you run a search on Barbara and Josephine Bullock? Barbara would be roughly sixty and Josephine maybe in her thirties." Hal looked at her for confirmation. She nodded.

"Records."

Ryaan introduced herself again and asked about Bullock.

"If he was admitted in 1996, he'll be in the computerized records. But I can't release any information on a patient without a warrant."

Ryaan recognized the line. "Listen, I've got two

unsolved murders and twenty high-capacity weapons loose in the city. Somehow, it's leading me to Bullock and I don't know if that means someone's trying to kill Bullock or if he's trying to kill someone."

"Well, I can guarantee Bullock isn't trying to kill anyone. He suffered a massive stroke and he can't even feed himself. Now, that's all I can say."

"No," Ryaan pressed. "You can tell me whether Bullock is at your facility because I don't have time to jump through a bunch of bureaucratic hoops or drag this over to the DA's office for a warrant. I need to find this man before someone kills him."

"I really can't," the woman said.

"You have to," Ryaan said. "Listen to me. Take down this badge number and phone number. You have a pen?"

"Uh, yes."

Ryaan rattled off her badge number and the non-emergency phone number for Dispatch. "You call that number and confirm that the badge number I gave you is for Ryaan Berry of Triggerlock. That's me. I will call you back in two minutes because there are lives at risk here. Understand?"

"Um…"

"Do it now."

"Okay," the woman agreed, and Ryaan hung up.

Hal was grinning when she looked over. He pulled his arm off the back of the booth and clapped his hands. "Nicely handled, Inspector Berry."

"Nothing like putting the fear of a crazy gunman in someone's head."

"Ain't that the truth."

Ryaan glanced at her watch. "Ninety seconds to wait. What did you find out?"

"Not much," Hal admitted. "Tracy is going to text over what she can find on Barbara and Josephine."

Ryaan glanced at her watch twice more, took a sip of awful cold coffee, then redialed the stroke center and asked for Records. The phone rang twice and Ryaan thought maybe the woman was avoiding her. Finally, she answered. "Records."

"It's Inspector Berry."

There was a moment's hesitation before the woman said, "Bullock was transferred to a long-term care facility in 2009. Hang on—okay, here it is. He is at the Greensview Senior Center in Palo Alto."

"I appreciate your help," Ryaan said and hung up.

"Bullock's at Greensview Senior Center in Palo Alto."

Hal took out his wallet and set a five on the table. He leaned into Ryaan's shoulder and pointed to the door. "How about taking a drive, then?"

CHAPTER 42

MEI UNLOCKED THE lockbox on the apartment using the electronic key Sabrina had given her. The apartment key was inside, but the lock was old and stubborn and it took a few tries to make the key turn. Finally it gave, and Mei pushed open the door and slid the key into her back pocket with her phone.

She led Sophie into the living room and stood back to look out the window. The sky was brilliant blue, nothing like the gray at Ayi's. Already, her chest felt lighter, more open. She took a long breath. It was better than she'd remembered. Across the room, she peered down at the freeway. "Isn't it fabulous?"

Sophie joined her and laughed. "Not many people would rave about a view of the 101."

"Are you kidding? It's perfect."

"Well, you'll be safe up here," Sophie joked. "No one's climbing all those stairs."

"Right," Mei agreed. "And taking aim at the window will be tougher, too." The attempt at humor sounded flat in her own ear. The confrontation with Aaron left her terrified. She slept maybe a couple hours last night. Even the shooting at Ayi's didn't compare to the feeling she'd had watching Aaron with that gun. Like it was over. If Lanier hadn't arrived, she was sure he would have pulled the trigger. Aaron Pollack.

"You okay?" Sophie asked.

Mei took a deep breath. "I can't stop thinking about it."

"It's understandable. What's the news on Aaron?"

Mei took a deep breath. "Teddy was at the lab all night, processing Aaron's computer. He's been selling case information to a data security firm for almost three years."

Sophie whistled.

"Basically, the company collected clients by using Aaron's information to scare them into buying tens of thousands of dollars of unnecessary security." No wonder he had an American Express Platinum card, Mei thought. As a one-third partner, he probably grossed something like a million dollars a year. All right under her nose. And Lanier's nose, too. There was something so unnerving about the proximity of it all. Mei crossed her arms over her chest. "They're still digging," Mei added, "but there's already plenty there to put him away."

"But?"

Mei turned to her friend. "The business explains his expensive clothes and high-society girlfriend, but there still isn't anything to link Aaron to the weapons missing from Oyster Point." Mei shivered. "Or all the shootings." And the drugging, she thought but didn't say. She also couldn't figure out his motive. Aaron was making a lot of money from selling case information. That made sense. But what did he have to gain from the shootings?

Aaron had been frustrating and obstinate and rude, but a killer? Mei couldn't help feeling they were missing something. It left her even more skittish than before. If that were possible.

"I'm sure they'll make the connection to the rest of it," Sophie said.

Hailey had agreed. "So far he's been smart," Hailey told Mei earlier that morning. "Confessed to the white-collar stuff. We've caught him at that already. But he'll run out of luck soon and we'll get him for all of it."

Mei tried to feel the confidence that Sophie had, that she'd heard in Hailey's voice, but she didn't. Or maybe this was how these things felt when they hit so close to home. Maybe it would just take her time before she felt safe again.

"And you've got Amy in the hot seat, too," Sophie added. "Seems like she'd crack pretty easily with a little pressure."

"Yeah…" Mei began, but shut her mouth. A fire of adrenaline flared in her chest. "Hopefully," she said without looking over. Mei had told Sophie about Amy being at the club. But she hadn't mentioned that Lanier's email had been spoofed or the instructions Amy was getting to follow her. That had only happened last night. Had Sophie made that leap?

She felt Sophie watching her. When she turned, Sophie had moved away from the window.

Mei felt a shift as Sophie backed away from the glass. Her knees bent, she was like an animal ready to pounce.

Mei smiled and turned back to the window like nothing had happened. Stalled. Spun for an idea. She had not told a single person that she was coming to the apartment. Not Sabrina. Not Ayi.

A distraction. Something light to ease the tension. Get out of this building. She stretched her arms over her head and tried to fake a yawn. Failed. "I'm starving," she said. Her phone buzzed from her pocket. "Should we go grab some food?" she asked, reaching.

Sophie shook her head. "No." Tilting her head toward the hall, Sophie didn't take her eyes off Mei. "Let's see the rest of the place."

"Sure." Mei forced a smile. Her lips felt dry and stuck to her teeth. "The bedroom is like a shoe box," she said, trying to laugh. "It's right through there if you want to go ahead. I prefer the view out here."

Sophie didn't move.

Trying to act casual, Mei pulled her phone out. No one knew where she was. She'd left for lunch. She would just dial Ryaan, check in. As she looked down, the phone buzzed again. The screen was lined with activity. A call from Hailey. A text from Ayi.

The most recent was a text from Blake. *Mendelcom had a breach. Drug trial data erased. Heading there now.*

CHAPTER 43

GREENSVIEW SENIOR CENTER wasn't far from Ryaan's mother's house although she'd never had an occasion to notice it. Located on a relatively busy street, the complex looked more like an elementary school than a senior center. Only now did Ryaan notice it would be an elementary school without a playground. Ryaan and Hal pulled into the front lot and parked in the third and last row, the only row not reserved for handicapped parking. The front of the building was old brick. It may, in fact, have been a school. A set of black wrought iron doors closed off the front porch. Hal pressed the buzzer. Ryaan peered through the bars, which were an uncomfortable reminder of Karl Penn's house from Saturday night. She still had pains in the small of her back and a crick on the right side of her neck, but she had a lot to be thankful for.

Forcing the thoughts away, she focused on the building's tall double doors. They appeared original to the building, oak and well-worn with large plate glass centers. Ridged columns were carved on the outside edges of the door and what looked like ornate tapestries along the top edges which ended in what Ryaan could only think to call curlicues.

"How may I help you?" came a voice.

"I am Inspector Hal Harris. I'm from the San Francisco Police Department. I'm here to see a patient, Joseph Bullock."

Almost before Hal was done speaking, the door buzzed open. They entered the foyer where fresh flowers sat in large arrangements on either side of the door. White lilies and white roses and white Gerber daisies with the tiniest hint of red at their centers. Hardly the colors she would have chosen to brighten up the place. Then, Ryaan saw that they sat on large metal tripods that reminded her of the flowers at funeral homes. Hal gave the flowers a sideways look as he passed.

"Hello," someone called out to them. Two women sat behind a curved enclosure in the middle of the foyer. Both were gray-haired, but only one had the sunken cheeks and protruding eyes, the frail white-blue hands of the very old. One step away from being a resident. Or perhaps a volunteer from amongst them.

The younger of the two was talking on a headset while the other turned to Hal and Ryaan and smiled thinly. "You're here to see Mr. Bullock, is that correct?"

"It is."

She stood from her chair. "May I see your IDs please?"

Ryaan pulled her badge from its place on her holster and handed it down. Hal did the same. With a shaky hand, the woman—Marilyn, her name tag read—took down their names on a guest register, then lifted the book toward them. The way her hands shook, it looked like she might drop it on herself. Hal reached down to take it from her.

"Just sign by your names. I'll get Alison to come up to meet you. She's our senior nurse on call."

A few minutes later, a door along the hall opened and a woman came out to meet them. "I'm Alison Donnelly," she said, shaking each of their hands. She pulled a clipboard to her chest and rocked back onto the heels of her white Crocs. "You're looking to talk to Joe?"

"Yes," Hal said.

"Can I ask why?"

"It relates to a police investigation. I'm not at liberty to say more," Hal said diplomatically. "I'm sorry. I wish I could."

Alison nodded. "I understand. Are you familiar with Joe's case, then?"

"We're not," Hal answered.

"I've been here as long as Joe has," Alison told them. "In fact, we arrived the same month. In that time, he's never said a word to me."

"He doesn't speak?" Hal asked.

Alison shook her head. "But he can be very communicative. It depends on who's asking."

"How do you mean?" Ryaan asked.

Alison smiled. "Joe has his favorites and for them, he'll often answer questions by tapping. For the nurse he works with most often, Sherrie, he also has some limited signs that he can use. A few other nurses have worked out ways to communicate with Joe, but many—in fact, I'd say most—have not."

"How about other patients?"

Alison shook her head. "He doesn't socialize with any of the patients. Never has."

"He's an angry guy, I take it?" Hal asked her.

Alison started down the corridor, motioning for them to follow. "Yes and no. Stubborn is more like it, but bullheaded like I've never seen. Joe doesn't express anger—he's extremely controlled—but it's hard not to imagine that he's pretty angry at the world. He is highly intelligent, was a prodigy from an early age, completed Stanford at nineteen. He could have gone earlier, but his mother insisted he not start college until he was old enough to drive. From what I've heard, he was a brilliant geneticist before the stroke."

The hallway smelled of old people, the way Ryaan's mother's bedroom now did. She wondered what it was that made them all smell the same. How long before she smelled like that?

"We read that he was involved in a lawsuit with his employer," Hal said.

Alison nodded. "I read that, too, but I don't know any of the details. That was all over before he arrived at Greensview."

"Does Mr. Bullock have funds to support himself?"

Alison glanced over her shoulder as though talking out of turn. "Actually, I don't know about Mr. Bullock's financial health. His stay here is paid for by Mendelcom."

"Really?" Ryaan asked. "Are people in the company still in touch with him?"

Alison shook her head. "The only visitor he's ever had is his daughter."

"Daughter?" Ryaan asked.

Alison motioned to the door. "This is Joe's room."

Hal turned the knob and pushed the door open. The room was small but surprisingly bright and clean. Unlike the other rooms they'd passed, Joe's walls had been painted a light green. His bedsheets were green checks. The quilt was patchwork done in bright blues and greens. His pillows were yellow, though a little faded.

On the walls were a series of photographs. A tall sand dune with the ocean behind; the wind blew so hard that the grasses were bent almost to the ground and sand sprayed through the air like a light mist. Ryaan thought it might have been taken somewhere down by Carmel. Another was of the Golden Gate Bridge. A young man and a girl held hands, their arms in the V of migrating birds. Both were smiling widely. Ryaan thought it was likely Joe and his daughter, an image from before the stroke. Ryaan bent in to get a closer look, but the faces were too small and pixelated to identify. She wondered if Barbara had taken the picture. Several other photographs hung around the room. They all looked like amateur shots. All had been blown up a little too much, giving them a grainy appearance. On the last wall was a painting of steep cliffs and the ocean below. A tower of water sprayed up into dark, clear air and a lone bird flew high above the rocks, perhaps searching for dinner.

The decor distracted from the emergency call button beside the bed and the control panel on the wall where a hospital bed could be wheeled in and attached to replace Joe's regular one. The same generic off-white linoleum floor that was in every hospital room across the state was softened by a plush throw rug. The details in Joe Bullock's room made it feel like he had someone who cared a lot about him.

"Joe," Alison said to no response. Then, "These officers were hoping to ask you a few questions."

Joe didn't even look at them. Ryaan found it hard to imagine this man as an engaged participant in any conversation. Though his eyes were open, Joe's lips fell as though he were asleep. His focus appeared soft and was directed somewhere out the window. Ryaan stepped closer and looked out with him. She had imagined he might have a view there. While he did get natural light, the window faced an alley and a two-story parking lot. Not even a spot of green.

"Joe?" Alison tried again.

Hal walked over and pulled the chair from the desk, parking it opposite Joe. It was hard to ignore Hal. At six-four and somewhere north of two hundred twenty, it was like ignoring a truck parked on your front porch. Joe blinked once, but made no other indication that he'd noticed Hal.

"His daughter did all this?" Ryaan asked Alison.

She nodded. "She's here quite a lot."

Ryaan looked around. "Is there a picture of her somewhere?"

Alison scanned the dresser and table. "Joe, where's the picture of your daughter?"

Joe continued to stare out the window.

Alison shrugged. "I thought he had pictures of his daughter here, but I don't see them now."

They tried in vain to get Joe to talk to them for another ten minutes before giving up.

"Do you have contact information for his daughter?" Hal asked. "Maybe we could locate her."

"I'm sure we do up front. Here, let's cut through here." Alison opened a door across from Joe's room and led Hal and Ryaan through a large room with a piano and bookshelves, some sort of common room for the residents.

Ryaan slowed down to look around and noticed a series of photographs along the walls. "What are these?"

Alison turned back from the far side of the room. "Oh, pictures from our annual holiday party. Ah, I'll bet Joe's daughter is in one of these. Her name keeps slipping my mind."

"Josephine," Hal said.

Alison frowned.

"We got her name from the papers after his stroke."

Alison scanned the photos and homed in on one. "Here we go. Here's Joe and his daughter. This was in 2011, so it's a few years old."

Ryaan leaned in over Alison's shoulder and followed her finger to a slightly younger Joe. Sitting beside him with an arm over his shoulders, was a woman Ryaan knew.

"Holy shit," Hal said.

"What is it? What's wrong?" Alison asked.

Ryaan stared at the image. "We know her."

"Sophie Turner," Hal said.

"Sophie!" Alison exclaimed. "That's it. She goes by Sophie. The Josephine thing was throwing me."

Ryaan thought about the LLC that owned the apartment. "The name of that LLC is MCOMEND. The stock ticker for the company is MCOM."

Hal was staring at her. "There has to be something to that lawsuit."

Ryaan nodded.

"What are you guys talking about?" Alison asked.

Ryaan pulled out her phone and snapped a picture of Joe and Sophie. Hal pressed a business card into Alison's palm. "If anyone calls or shows up for Joe, you call 9-1-1 and then me. In that order, you understand?"

Alison nodded. "Is Joe dangerous?"

"I doubt it, but his daughter is," Hal told her.

Hal and Ryaan hurried through the recreation room and out to the main corridor. "I'll call Dispatch. You try to reach Mei."

Ryaan pulled out her phone. Hal was jogging by then, and Ryaan had to run to keep up. She called Mei at the lab. Got voicemail. She sent the image of Joe and his daughter to Mei's cell phone. In the message, she wrote. *Call me now.*

Hal informed Dispatch about Sophie Turner and warned them to send someone to Mei Ling's residence immediately.

"Where do you think she is?" Hal asked when they reached the car.

"Not at the station. I called there first," Ryaan said.

"You don't think she's with Sophie now, do you?" Hal asked.

"I hope not," Ryaan told him. She started to duck into the car when Hal grabbed her hand. She turned back to him and before she could react, he kissed her. It was brief but firm. Before she could speak, Hal ran around the car and got into the driver's seat.

"Sorry," he said, pulling his seatbelt on quickly. "Been wanting to do that for weeks." With that, Hal revved the engine and flipped on the lights and siren as they hurried back to the city.

Hal's radio squawked from the dash. "All available units. We have a Code 3 at the corner of Geary and Mason. Multiple gunshots fired."

Gunshots. Emergency.

"Repeat, all available units report to Geary and Mason. Code 3."

"Geary and Mason," Hal repeated. "That's the Tenderloin."

"Multiple gunshots." Ryaan imagined the guns that had vanished from the trunk of that car. "There are still eighteen guns out there from the warehouse."

Hal looked over at her. "You think Sophie Turner is there?"

Ryaan stared out the windshield. "I hope so."

Hal turned on his siren and lights and drove like a bat out of hell.

CHAPTER 44

MEI KNEW SHE'D given herself away. She thumbed the screen and tried to push the phone icon. Dial a number. Any number.

"Hand it over."

Movement in the corner of her eye. Mei looked into the barrel of a gun. Sophie motioned to her phone. "Give it to me."

Mei didn't look down but gripped her phone tighter. She was dead without it.

Sophie hitched the gun higher. "Now."

Mei glanced at the screen. Saw a name. A call. She pressed the lock button on the top. Started to raise her hands. Then tossed her phone underhand across the floor. Like a bowling ball. The phone flipped and skidded to a stop against the wall.

Something cracked across her cheek. A sharp pop in her jaw as the gun struck her. She howled, dropped to her knees. Saw black, then blinding white arrows.

"You have a hard time with English?" Sophie asked. "I said give it to me. Not throw it across the room." She spoke through gritted teeth.

Mei pressed the back of her hand across her lip, felt the blood. Slowly, she looked up. The gun was inches away. "Why are you doing this, Sophie?"

Sophie raised the gun again. Mei flinched.

Sophie laughed. The bully with a weapon. Mei said nothing. No one knew where she was. She had no weapon. Her purse was in Sophie's car. Her phone across the room. The apartment was completely empty. Nothing that wasn't nailed down. And no backup.

"Stand up."

Trembling, Mei pushed herself up. Her right cheek throbbed, her pulse pumping in her jaw. Blood was sour in her mouth. "You drugged me."

Sophie said nothing. Like she was waiting.

A game, Mei thought. Play the game. Back to the night at the club. When could Sophie have drugged her? Mei pictured their drinks. The wine bar was too quiet. The shots were too fast. Four of them on the first round of beers. Mei never put hers down. She was careful like that. It had to be that second bottle of beer, the one Mei ordered. Sophie had lifted them off the bar, handed her one. No. Sophie had waved to someone first then handed her one. "You dropped something in my beer when you pretended to wave. After you came back from the bathroom."

"Not bad, Mei." Sophie smiled. It made her sick. "Slow but not bad."

Mei glanced at the gun. The Sig 9mm held around ten rounds. Maybe she could get Sophie to burn through some of them, but ten…? That was a lot of chances.

She needed to buy time to think. "The bug on my phone." Mei's mind raced. When had Sophie planted that?

"In the elevator during the shooting? No. It had to be before that." *Play to her ego,* she thought. "How did you pull that off?"

"You left your phone in our office twice while you were filling out paperwork." Sophie was quick to answer. "It hardly took genius."

Mei remembered that. So careless, so unlike her. *Get her to talk,* she thought. "Why me?"

"You tell me," Sophie said.

Mei wanted Sophie to talk. "Because I am new in town," she guessed. "Unattached."

"Except that husband of yours in Chicago."

Mei felt sick. Andy. They hadn't spoken since Wednesday night. She'd asked for space. He gave it to her. And now…

Sophie grinned. Her upper gums were visible, pink and angry. She was suddenly ugly.

Mei shivered. Touched the tender skin on her face. "This can't be about guns. I can't believe you were really interested in that. Stealing them from the warehouse, spreading them out, that was all just an elaborate distraction."

Sophie shook her head. "I don't have time for this, Mei." She nodded toward the hall. "Let's go see that bedroom. There's so much glass in here."

Mei didn't move. She listened for sounds. No one was coming. Even if she could find a way to break the window and escape, she was four stories up. Stall. "Must be Mendelcom, then."

Sophie's head snapped up. Her eyes were too bright. The pupils were tiny black dots and the red vessels in the whites made her look demonic. "My father spent twenty years there."

"Working on that drug."

"Prostura was his baby," Sophie said. The gun dropped momentarily. Mei hesitated too long. Sophie aimed at her again.

"He must have worked on it for years," Mei said.

"Fifteen years," she snapped.

Mei spoke slowly to draw her out. "And he never got the credit."

"Mendelcom promised him a payout if his work led to this kind of breakthrough. They refused to pay, so Dad filed a lawsuit for breach of contract. A couple months into it, he had a stroke—at the office." Sophie's expression became small and pinched. "The stroke was genius for Mendelcom and easy. Spike his coffee one morning and he was out of the way."

"You think someone at Mendelcom caused his stroke?"

Her eyes were wild. "I know they did. All it would have taken was a healthy dose of one of their vasoconstrictors. It was perfect."

"What about the suit? And his attorney?" Mei asked.

"Retainer money ran out. The skunk walked."

"That had to be awful."

Sophie jabbed the barrel of the gun into Mei's chest. "Fuck you. I don't need your pity."

Mei shook her head. "Not pity, Sophie. I mean it."

Sophie stared at her, shook her head. Like she was having a dialogue with herself.

Mei shifted away from the gun. A tiny step at a time. "What happened?"

"I was in middle school," Sophie said. "Dad was in the hospital. Me against a giant like Mendelcom. They weren't going to pay a dime. They were happy to have him go. He'd already done the important work. Without him, there were just fewer expenses." Sophie seemed lost in thought. The gun was still close. Too close to make a move.

"Where is your dad now?" Mei asked.

"Living in a dingy senior home. That was the other genius move from Mendelcom. They paid up Dad's benefit package—made it look nice and generous—then they paid for a lifetime of care."

"That's—" Mei shifted onto her right foot.

"Nothing in comparison to what he was going to get," Sophie snapped. "He's been locked up since '96. He can't move. He can't speak. But he's still as sharp as ever. He could have gone on to do important things. He could have helped them develop another drug. But no. They just cut him off." She paused in her rant. Mei eased a few inches from the barrel. "So, I killed Prostura."

"By changing the results of the trial."

Sophie nodded. "Changed their results and wiped out the backups. Easy as that."

"You think Mendelcom doesn't have secure backups on a billion-dollar drug trial?"

Sophie smiled. A genuine smile. "Sam was able to create a virus in the backup. When Mendelcom realized the data was altered, they restored the corrupted backup. All of it, gone."

Mei knew it wasn't that simple. The data was still out there somewhere. It could be pieced together, but Sophie had certainly succeeded in making things difficult. The devastation to the share price alone would likely take years to recover. She thought about challenging her, but it seemed unwise. "What now?"

"Now, Dad and I retire. We spent every penny we had to short Mendelcom at its high. I have been buying it back since the news came out."

Mei's time was running out. Still no plan. "You can buy shares from anywhere," Mei said. "Why are you still here?" She touched her hand to her cheek, wiped the blood on her pants. Felt a hard shape in her pocket. The key.

"I needed a court order to get my dad out of that hell-hole. The bastards had medical power of attorney. Arranged by Mendelcom, of course."

Mei reached into her pocket. Gripped the key hard between her fingers.

"But it's all done now. Paperwork. Everything." Sophie looked at the gun and waved it at Mei. "If it weren't for having to deal with you, I'd be on my way to pick him up now."

Mei sprang.

She knocked the gun with her left hand and swung hard at Sophie's neck with her right. The key between her fingers cut clean through her skin.

Sophie screamed and grabbed her neck. "You bitch."

The key fell.

Sophie pulled her hand away from her neck to shove Mei. The wound was bleeding but not enough. Mei had missed the carotid.

Mei grabbed the gun barrel with her left hand, deflecting it as Sophie pressed it toward her. She grabbed Sophie's right wrist, fighting to aim the barrel away. Sophie howled in pain and Mei saw bruising around her wrist. She gripped harder, twisting, while Sophie struggled to lift the barrel to Mei's chest. Mei fought it down. Sophie was stronger. She had a better hold.

Dropping her hold momentarily, Mei drove her right across her body and into Sophie's face. The gun slipped. Sophie grabbed it back. A bullet discharged with a hollow pop. The glass window exploded beside them.

Mei put all her weight into twisting the gun away. Sophie screamed and drove the barrel against Mei's hand. The metal burned. The barrel dropped. The trigger went off.

Mei looked down at the barrel against her hip. Heat seared her side.

Sophie was laughing. Raising the gun to aim again. A stupid smile on her face, like she was winning.

A roar rose up from Mei's chest. Sophie flinched. Mei stomped hard on Sophie's instep. Sophie sank a few inches. Mei drove her weight into the outside of Sophie's left knee, hard and fast. Something cracked. Sophie moaned. Mei wrenched the gun toward the ceiling and drove Sophie backward with all her strength.

Both holding the gun, they stumbled a few feet toward the blown-out window. Sophie's left leg buckled and she fell. She let go of the gun. Her eyes went wide. Her mouth dropped open and she reached out. "No," she screamed. Mei felt the cold air. Sophie's arms windmilled as she tried to balance. She reached for Mei. "Help me!" Her fingers grazed Mei's jacket. Her scream pierced the open air and she was gone.

Mei froze and watched. Sophie's body fell in slow motion. And then not. Mei watched as it struck the pavement. As Sophie struck. Like a ragdoll on the pavement.

Mei backed slowly away from the window. A trail of blood followed. She touched her side. Thick and tacky, blood filled her hand and ran between her fingers. So much blood. She wanted to lie down. Her phone. She moved toward the door. So dizzy, it took forever. When she reached the wall, she lowered herself slowly onto her knees, every motion excruciating.

She took hold of her phone. The screen was cracked, but she swiped across the screen. Pressed the emergency button.

It didn't even ring. "911. What is your emergency?"

"This is Inspector Ling," she said. "I've been shot. Bronte Street."

"What's the street number on Bronte?"

Mei couldn't think. The room was spinning. *Don't close your eyes.* "Ma'am? Inspector Ling?"

"Don't know." She moved onto her side. Her phone dropped to the floor beside her face. "Don't know the number."

"Stay with me, Inspector. I'm tracking your location from your phone. We're sending police and paramedics now."

Mei nodded.

"Inspector?"

"Yeah," Mei whispered.

"You stay there."

"Yeah."

"Are you alone?"

"I am now," she said. Her eyes fluttered closed.

"I need you to keep talking, Inspector." The voice was urgent. "Keep talking to me, do you hear?"

"Okay," Mei said. Things were foggy. Confused. She'd

found her phone, called the police. "I used the emergency button."

"What emergency button, Inspector?"

"On my phone."

"Good," said Dispatch. "That was a good thing to do."

Mei licked her lips. "These phones are so clever."

"Good, Inspector. You keep talking."

"I love technology," Mei whispered, every word a fight. She took shallow breaths as the pain worsened. The effort was exhausting. The dispatcher kept talking. But her own words wouldn't come.

"Inspector, the ambulance is at your location. Are you in an apartment?"

"Top floor."

"Top floor," the woman repeated.

Mei nodded. She was trying to think of something else to tell the lady on the phone when she heard the merciful sound of pounding on the door.

CHAPTER 45

MEI WAS DREAMING in Cantonese. Her mother was speaking to her softly, the way she used to when Mei was young, before the ways in which Mei didn't fit in became a wedge between them that grew into a wall. Her mother used to whisper to Mei about what it was to be the middle child in China. There, birth order was significant. The middle child was known as the one accustomed to adapting, to compromise. Her A Mā was also the middle child, of three girls. Her older sister the controlling one and her younger sister, Ayi, the princess.

"We asked you to compromise too much," her mother whispered. She used the Cantonese *to-hip* with the characters for "prepare" or "ready" and "agree" or "unity."

"You were the united daughter. Never fighting like your sisters."

"We thought you were easy," her father said in a quiet voice.

"But we didn't know that we were asking you to be something you're not." Her mother was crying. "Ayi told us."

Mei smelled her mother's rose perfume and shifted in

her bed. Searching to hold onto her dream, she longed for the warmth of their voices. Her parents loved her. They accepted her. She felt like she was sliding off the bed. The mattress was angled and awkward, not like hers. She moved her hand and pressed up against a metal bar, like a railing. A jail, she thought, and then had the strange sense that maybe it was something else, some sort of tomb. She just wanted to go back to her dream.

"She's going to be okay, Mrs. Ling."

That sounded like Sabrina. Then she remembered Sophie, the apartment. It all flooded back. She had to fight to pull herself from sleep. As the voices quieted, the other sounds became more obvious. The low hum of machines, not like the quiet of computers but with similar parts. Louder, like the servers that ran in corporate offices. The whirring of heat sinks, fighting to cool whatever processors were at work in the room. An occasional beep. Lower pitched and longer than a computer's. She was in a hospital.

Mei tried to touch her face, but her hand was tethered. She opened her eyes. There was the sound of her mother gasping, her father's loud happy click. Their faces hovered above her.

"Zhu zhu," her father said. "You're awake."

Mei smiled. It hurt. It had been years since her father called her zhu zhu which translated to "small pig" and was not the kind of nickname an eight-year-old American girl wanted. "Hi, A Bàh."

Her mother rushed away from the bed and a moment later, she shouted into the hallway. "Get the doctor! She is awake. My daughter is awake."

In a flash, her mother was back, ducking under her father's arm to press herself against the bed's metal rail. "How is your pain? They had to pull a bullet out of you. Does it hurt?"

Mei nodded and licked her lips. "A little."

"Do you want some water?"

Mei nodded.

Sabrina appeared, handed her mother a pink cup with a straw, and gave Mei a little smile.

"Thank you so much, dear," her mother told Sabrina, taking the cup.

Mei had to close her eyes for a moment. Sabrina and her parents were in the same room.

"I'm going to go get some coffee," Sabrina said. "Can I get you some?" she asked Mei's father.

Mei opened her eyes as her mother pressed the straw to her lips. She watched her father with Sabrina and drank.

"Thank you," A Bàh told Sabrina. "Black would be great for me. Xue likes a little cream. Let me give you some money."

"I've got it, Mr. Ling. See you all in a little bit." She smiled at Mei and left.

Mei's parents stepped away from the bed as a nurse entered to take her blood pressure and temperature. "You're looking good. The doctor will be in shortly."

Mei's mother pressed her to drink more, then set the cup on the bedside table. "She seems very nice," her mother said, straightening the covers around her. "Sabrina, I mean."

Her father shifted on his feet.

"It's okay," Mei told them, trying to shift in the bed without pain. "This is a lot to get used to."

Mei looked at her father's pained face. "I'm sorry, A Bàh."

"For what are you sorry?"

"For this. For not telling you." Tears slid down her cheeks. "For not wanting to be married to Andy. For being what I am."

"No," her mother said. "You don't have to be sorry."

But it was her father Mei watched. He took her hand and clasped it between his own. "Zhu zhu, one happiness scatters a thousand sorrows."

Mei started to cry in earnest.

"Oh, A Bàh, enough," her mother scolded. "This is how your father talks—in riddles." Her mother touched her face. "Mei, please don't cry."

When she didn't stop, her mother took a tissue from the box beside the table and dabbed it across Mei's cheeks. Mei didn't try to stop the tears. Maybe it would be okay. They were here. "Your father is saying that your happiness matters most," her mother repeated.

Mei nodded. "Do you believe that, A Bàh? About happiness?"

"Of course, I do," he responded. "I am not a hypocrite. You are my daughter. If this is what makes you happy, I am happy, too." Her father leaned over and kissed her forehead.

"Thank you, A Bàh," Mei whispered. She might have slept a little, waking when Sabrina returned with coffee. "The nurse promised apple juice, Mei. Should be here any minute."

Her parents took the coffees from Sabrina. Mei's mother came back to the bed and whispered. "We will go and leave our things at Ayi's then come back."

"Okay, A Mā. I'll see you later."

Her mother started to walk away but paused a moment, watching her father talking with Sabrina. When she turned back, she spoke loud enough for all to hear her. "It's nice that she's Chinese," she said.

"A Mā," Mei said. "Go. Please, go."

Her mother laughed and her father made a guttural noise, his own version of amusement. Pausing at her side, A Mā touched her forehead to Mei's. "We are okay, Mei. You don't need to push us away now. We can understand."

Mei nodded.

Her mother kissed her, then joined her father in the hall.

When they were gone, Mei looked at Sabrina. "I'm so sorry."

"Don't be. Your parents are a lot like mine. Maybe they can tell my parents I'm gay."

"Oh, Sabrina. You haven't told them?"

She shook her head, horrified at the thought. "God, no. I'm an only child. They'll die."

Mei laughed and something stabbed in her side, melting the laugh into a painful cough. "Here I thought I was the only one."

"Seems like they took it pretty well."

"It does," Mei admitted. "We'll see."

Sabrina sat on the edge of the bed. Her expression softened. Gone was the brave face; she looked scared. Mei felt her own fear rise up.

"You called me from the apartment," Sabrina told her.

Mei pushed away the memory of her terror. "I was trying to call someone."

"It went to my voicemail," Sabrina said like an apology. "I didn't even hear it until you were already here."

"Sorry."

Sabrina took Mei's hand. "God, no. Don't be. I'm sorry." Her eyes welled up. "I was really scared." She blinked hard and swiped a hand across her eyes. "I heard Sophie's voice. She was so angry. I thought—"

Mei squeezed her hand. "I'm okay."

"I'm so glad. So, so glad."

Mei watched her.

"I don't want to lose you, Mei."

She tried to smile. "I'm here."

Sabrina let out a sigh. "I haven't dated someone in a really long time."

Mei smiled for real that time. "Me neither." She thought about Andy. That her parents hadn't mentioned him.

"But I'd really like to spend time with you."

Mei focused on Sabrina. "I'd really like that."

Sabrina leaned over and kissed Mei on the cheek, then softly on the lips. "Call me after your folks head home."

Mei laughed. "How about if I call you when I get out of here and you can come have dinner with Ayi and my parents?"

Sabrina smiled. "I'd love that."

They sat together for some time before the door opened and Hailey poked her head in. Sabrina squeezed Mei's hand. "I'll talk to you soon, then."

"Thanks," Mei said and watched her go. She tried to imagine them together, some day in the future. She couldn't. Not that it seemed like it wouldn't work out. There were just too many things to take care of first. The realization didn't make her sad or even uncomfortable. She had time. One thing she had now was time.

Hailey came in, followed by Ryaan. Hailey set a box of See's candy on the table. Ryaan carried a bouquet of irises. "Flowers or chocolate. Couldn't decide, so we brought both."

Mei tried to sit up in bed, taking shallow breaths as she adjusted herself upright.

"How are you feeling?" Hailey asked.

"Ready for a vacation," Mei said.

"Well, after Lanier and Finlay's grand screwup with Aaron Pollack, I'll bet you can get a nice long paid one," Hailey told her.

"So Aaron wasn't involved in Oyster Point at all?"

Ryaan shook her head. "We don't even know if Josephine—Sophie—knew what he was up to."

"Hard to imagine she just got lucky," Mei said. She wouldn't be surprised if Sophie had planned Aaron's part in it, too.

"We might never know," Hailey said.

Mei nodded. "I'm okay with that."

"You feel at peace about Sophie?" Hailey asked, pulling a chair up to the bed.

"You mean about going out with her or watching her fall out a window?"

Hailey smiled. "Thatta girl."

Mei sobered at the image of Sophie landing. "She didn't survive the fall."

"No," Hailey said.

"What about the guns?"

Hailey looked at Ryaan. "Actually, we found eleven in the Tenderloin. Bunch of kids shooting up a vacant bar. Got the AKs back and a couple other high-capacity."

"Was anyone hurt?"

Ryaan smiled. "Miraculously, no."

"So all the guns are accounted for."

Ryaan shook her head. "Still seven babies out there."

Mei didn't know what to say to that. Taking the flowers, Ryaan excused herself to get an extra water pitcher from the nurse's station to use as a vase. Hailey filled Mei's water glass and passed it over to her. "She's taking it pretty hard."

Mei nodded. "Is there anyone to hold accountable for the distribution of the guns? With Sophie gone, I mean?"

"Sophie pretty much disposed of everyone involved," Hailey said. "There was one other suspect—kid named Dwayne Henderson—but it looks like maybe Sophie tried to hook him and he didn't bite."

"Smart kid. Wish I'd seen through her bullshit."

"We all do," Hailey agreed.

Mei took a couple sips of water before the pain made it uncomfortable. She lay back and breathed through it.

"The pain bad?"

Mei nodded.

Hailey handed her a small white remote control. "Push this button. It'll deliver morphine through your IV."

"Every time I push?"

Hailey shook her head. "It's on a timer so you can't overdose."

Mei pressed the white button and closed her eyes until she heard the door open. Ryaan returned with the flowers in a pink plastic pitcher.

"Those are really gorgeous. Thanks again," Mei told her.

"Did Hailey ask about your plans?" Ryaan asked.

Hailey shook her head.

"What plans?"

"We weren't sure whether you're planning on heading back to Chicago."

"I don't know. Computer forensics was never this dangerous at the FBI," she said, trying to make a joke, but it wasn't funny. She had killed someone. Someone who was trying to kill her, but someone all the same. A woman she had trusted and thought of as a friend. A smart woman. Maybe even someone she could have helped. "I'm staying," she said finally.

"Good," Ryaan told her.

When had Sophie walled herself off and begun the race toward her own destruction? Mei couldn't reconcile the woman she'd come to know with the one who had tried to kill her.

"I still don't understand why she did it. Seems like there were better ways to help her father."

"We spoke to her father's sister this morning," Hailey said.

Ryaan brought a chair up to the bed and sat. "It's sad," Ryaan said. "Her aunt said Sophie was the only person Joe communicated with after his stroke. She was his translator, his counselor. She did everything for him. Sophie's mother, Barbara, left Joe about three months after it happened. She tried to take Sophie with her, but Sophie refused to leave her father. For a few months, Sophie tried to take care of him herself, but eventually Child Services put her back with her mother. The lawsuit took almost two years to resolve. It devastated the family's finances. Her mother had some issues of her own. Alcoholism, the aunt thought, and maybe substance abuse. The records are long gone now."

"We suspect some abusive boyfriends," Hailey added. "It's possible something happened with Sophie, but we'll never know for sure."

"She spent a lot of years waiting for the right time to destroy Mendelcom," Ryaan said.

"She did. And she found someone who could write code and hack into the system to overwrite those data files," Mei said. "Sophie said Sam had even figured out a way to corrupt Mendelcom's old backups. That's not everyday stuff."

"That, and she waited for Mendelcom to release the results on Prostura," Ryaan added.

Mei shivered and pulled the covers up around her arms. She stifled a yawn.

"You should get some rest," Ryaan told her.

"We'll have a drink when you get out of here," Hailey promised.

Mei nodded, knowing that it would be no time at all before they were swept into another case, some other crisis. "Thanks for coming by."

When the door clicked closed, Mei shut her eyes and

reveled in the silence. She could smell the floral scent of Sabrina's perfume, or maybe it was the flowers. When she was completely still, the pain under her ribs subsided. The fog of the painkillers was lowering. She would rest until her parents came back.

Ayi would show up, too. She expected to see Lanier and Finlay, Blake and Teddy. There would be face to save and blame to assign. Some of it might come her way, and she would be forced to fight. But for these few minutes, she was safe. She was alive.

Her parents knew who she was now. They accepted her. Eventually, her sisters would find out. They would either deal as her parents had or not, but it didn't matter to Mei. She knew who she was. A Bàh had quoted Sun Tzu, *The Art of War. If you know your enemies and know yourself, you will not be imperiled in a hundred battles.*

Mei did know herself, and her enemies were becoming clearer. A hundred battles? Maybe. Maybe not. Either way, she had survived the first.

There was still one person left. She lifted her phone off the bedside table, unlocked the cracked screen, and dialed her husband's cell phone number in Chicago.

For the first time in weeks, she hoped he'd answer.

"Mei," came his voice.

Her heart broke a little at the sound. "Hi."

"Are you all right?"

"Yes and no," she said honestly. "I'm in the hospital but I'm okay. It's a long story."

She remembered the times when he would have told her he had all the time in the world. They would have spent hours on the phone, talking. "I'm going to fly back to Chicago as soon as I can."

He took a quick breath. "But not to stay," he said after a beat.

"No," she told him. "Not to stay."

She reclined the bed and closed her eyes, focusing on the meditative sound of the processors and gave her husband the time he needed.

"Oh, Mei…" She could hear his tears.

Hers came, too. Silently. Her tears, the soft sounds of her husband. Saying goodbye to the greatest love of her life. So far. Around her, the sounds of the machines washed her with warmth. She was strong. Getting stronger.

When the next battle came, she would be ready.

AUTHOR'S NOTE

The first person I would like to thank is you—the reader. Thank you for reading this book and for following the Rookie Club stories. While we're at it, thank you for every book you've ever read. It is the greatest gift you can give an author like me. Without you, there would be no books, and what a terrible world that would be.

If you have enjoyed this book, please consider taking a moment to leave a review on Amazon or elsewhere. Reviews and recommendations are vital to authors. Every good review and every recommendation for one of my books helps me stay hunkered and warm in my basement, doing what I love best—writing dark, chilling stories.

To claim your free short story, to learn more about the Rookie Club or my writing, please visit me at www.dani-ellegirard.com.

Now, please turn the page for a preview of book five of the Rookie Club Series, Everything to Lose.

CHAPTER 1

IT WAS THE way he held her hand. His long fingers wrapped around her hand and held firm like he was saving her. His skin was warm and dry. Boys her age never had dry hands. He thought about what she'd said before answering, considered exactly what she was asking. He was calm, sometimes so serious. A grown-up. She studied him standing in the doorway.

It was the way he laughed. Not some hysterical cackle like guys at school, and not the I'm-too-cool-to-laugh that others put on. Though serious, he laughed softly, more with his eyes than his mouth.

Such a silly schoolgirl crush thing to say, but she swore his eyes changed colors. They might be the exact color of toffee, or they could deepen to the shade of black coffee. They could change in an instant. "On a dime," as her father liked to say when he was lecturing her about how lucky she was and how much she had been given, and how easily it might all go away if she made one wrong decision.

It was also that she knew he was the wrong decision, at least to everyone but her. He was not the one she was supposed to choose. Not one of the boys she'd always known, whose parents knew her parents, whose mothers were on the opera board with hers and only worked outside the home to raise money for the "underprivileged." Not one of the boys in designer jeans and shirts that were washed by someone who worked for them. In fact, not like most of the boys at City Academy.

He had lived on the street. He had been given nothing. His father had been in jail. Yet he was the one who asked the tough questions. What would she do? How would she be someone who counted? Challenging her to move beyond her comfort zone. And he talked about the chances of survival for someone like him, the slimmer chances of not repeating the patterns set by his father.

It was the way he stood at the door, giving her plenty of time to speak up, to say she didn't want to, that it was too much. They could go back to the way they'd been. To talking and holding hands if she wanted. But she didn't. As he closed the door, she scanned the mattress that lay on the floor. Covered in faded green sheets, a gray comforter. A single pillow lay at the top, propped against the bare white wall. One pillow, while her bed was a mountain of them. Why did anyone need all those pillows?

They had never come here before. This had been her request, but he'd tidied up for her. Although she didn't know if he'd moved things elsewhere, or if this was everything he had. The room was almost bare—no dresser and no closet. His clothes were stacked in three piles along one wall, two pairs of shoes lined neatly alongside. Books were stacked on the small table he used as a desk. Candles provided soft light, giving the room the smallest bit of ambience. The air smelled of ocean and coconut.

"We don't have to do this," he said again when they reached the mattress.

It was that he didn't apologize for the room or try to play off the way he lived. He was the first person she'd ever known who was truly real.

She took his hand, felt the tremor of energy as they touched. "I want to."

He waited a beat, watching her, scanning her face.

"Really."

Only then did he reach up to unzip her jacket, moving slowly, reassuring her that he would stop any time, for any reason. But she didn't. She wanted this. They both did. She was awkward. He was kind and careful.

It was that he didn't tell her he loved her just because they'd had sex. Afterward, he lay beside her, running his finger along the profile of her hip. She'd thought his naked form would make her uncomfortable; instead, she felt calm.

She wasn't a stupid high school girl at City Academy. She wasn't Gavin and Sondra Borden's daughter. She was just Charlotte. Charlotte naked in bed with a man.

It was how he was afterward. As he convinced her that she had to go home before her parents started worrying. She'd texted to say she was staying late to work on a school project. He wasn't into rebellion. He didn't need to make a point. Better to play by her parents' rules, he said, than to risk not being able to see her again. It was that he wanted to see her again.

He blew out the candles and reached for the door. He

grabbed his baseball mitt off the floor and tucked the ball deep into its pocket.

"You going to play some ball?"

"Thought I might toss it around a little. It'll distract me when you're gone." He took her hand and, together, they crossed through the darkened main room. The smell of burnt food lingered along with something like sour milk. He didn't live alone. Where were the others? The candles had been meant to mask the smell and the mixture was like something rotting on a beach. Anywhere else, she might have felt slightly sick.

Anywhere else, she might have walked out to the car by herself. As they crossed into the hallway, she was reminded of how different his world was. Along one wall were doors; on the other, a single dingy window that faced a patch of dirt in front of the building where, maybe once, there had been grass. The air was cold and the hallway dark but for a single bulb behind glass that was blackened with dust but miraculously unbroken. He led her down the corridor and into another hallway where the light hadn't been so lucky. Slowly, the light behind them faded away until the light pollution from the city's surrounding buildings and a few early stars cast shadows in the darkness. She stayed close to him as her eyes adjusted to the darkness. A door opened behind her and she turned back. Nothing there. She stumbled to catch up as they came around the corner. He gasped and shoved her forward.

She squinted in the darkness. His expression startled her. "What is it?"

Glass crashed. A grunt. Then he was no longer beside her. She screamed and reached out, but he wasn't there. She called his name. She huddled against the wall and fumbled in her purse for her phone. His hands were tight on her shoulders. No, not his hands. These hands gripped too tight. He twisted and she fought to break free. He launched her forward as she caught sight of dark brown, angry eyes. Familiar eyes. "What—"

The brown of his eyes flashed to black as he threw her from his grip. She reached out, hand caught in her purse strap. The stairs rushed toward her. Cement closed in. An explosion blackness.

CHAPTER 2

IT WAS ALMOST 9:00 p.m. when Sex Crimes Inspector Jamie Vail snatched the phone off her desk. She caught it before the Dr. Dre ringtone could play all the way through. Every time it rang, she reminded herself to ask her son to change it to "Brave" or maybe "Roar." Something empowering, and by a woman. Something that might make a victim feel a little stronger. Something more acceptable for a thirty-nine-year-old sex crimes inspector. "Vail," she said.

"It's Maxi."

Maxi Thomas was the trauma nurse Jamie worked with most often at San Francisco General Hospital. For almost fifteen years, the two of them had worked side by side on some of Jamie's worst rape cases. When Maxi called, it only meant one thing. "We've got another one." Jamie grabbed her blazer off the back of her chair. She glanced at the paperwork scattered across her desk that she'd promised herself she'd clear today. "Where?"

"Sixteen years old. Came into General about 7:40. Her parents just arrived. I've talked to them, but they haven't let me near her yet. Doctors are doing everything to protect the evidence. It should be intact."

Intact meant that no one had washed the girl's body yet. Probably because her condition wasn't stable enough. "Who brought her to the hospital?" Jamie asked.

"Don't know. Maybe a Good Samaritan who didn't want to stick around. Or maybe the perp dropped her off."

That would be a first. "I'm on my way."

"I should warn you," Maxi said, and Jamie recognized the tone.

Jamie forced herself to keep moving. "It's bad?"

"She's unconscious. Coma. They're not sure she'll make it."

"Drugged?" Jamie asked.

"Head injury."

"We looking for a beater?"

"Don't think so," Maxi said. "It might have been a fall. A little bruising on the wrists, so maybe a struggle."

"Are we sure it's a sex crime?" Jamie asked.

"The admitting doctor noted fluids. Tests came back positive for lycopodium."

Lycopodium was one of the powder-like substances used by condom manufacturers to keep the rolled up latex from sticking to itself. "Which indicates she had sex," Jamie said.

"Safe sex, no less," Maxi added.

There was obviously more to the story. "But—"

Maxi sighed. "But according to her parents, she's a virgin."

"And, of course, every sixteen-year-old tells her parents about her sex life. What did the doctor find?"

"There are signs of trauma," Maxi added. "Some tearing, bruises."

"Could indicate assault but could mean it was her first time," Jamie said.

"Right."

It was Jamie's turn to sigh. "But the parents want us to treat it as a possible assault."

"They do," Maxi confirmed. "And these are some particularly opinionated parents. With some serious pull."

Jamie pushed through the department's door and headed for the stairwell. Since she'd stopped smoking, the stairs were her best ally in the never-ending war with her size six pants. If she could afford a new wardrobe of size eights, it would be enough to surrender. "What kind of pull?" Jamie asked.

"The attending got a call from the mayor, requesting tightened security."

"The mayor's office called?"

"Not the office, Jamie. The mayor. No press, no outsiders. He also spoke to the head of security. All the video surveillance has been sent to you guys. They think they caught the guy on film."

"Well, that's good news." Jamie jogged down the stairs. "Who are the parents?"

"Gavin and Sondra Borden."

"I should know them?"

"If you read the society papers you would. Her grandfather was the first black attorney in San Francisco. Gavin Borden joined the family practice. They have two daughters. Charlotte, our victim, is a junior at City Academy."

Jamie's heart skipped a beat.

"That's where Zephenaya goes, right?" Maxi asked.

"Yeah." Her son was at City Academy on a scholarship. "I've never heard the name though. Z's a freshman, so junior girls are out of his league."

Maxi chuckled.

"I'm on my way."

Jamie reached the station's main floor, out of breath. Panting from the trip down the stairs. That was pathetic. She emerged into the hallway. Nodded to one of the crime scene techs she knew and a patrol officer who had helped her make an arrest a few weeks back. She caught the eye of an assistant district attorney she didn't want to talk to and ducked her head.

She was about to cross through the department's rear doors when her phone buzzed on her hip. She pulled it from the holster. "Vich," she said. "You get a call from the lab? SF General sent over some surveillance footage."

Vich was the nickname given to Alexander Kovalevich when he'd been in the police academy thirty years ago. A Boston transfer, Vich had joined SFPD sex crimes about four months ago. After the fallout from her divorce, Jamie had largely worked alone. Mostly because she was too surly for anyone to stand. At least until Vich.

"I got it all right," he confirmed.

"I'm heading over to the hospital to try to get the parents to agree to a rape kit."

"You need to see this first," he told her.

Jamie groaned, thinking about climbing the stairs again. Swearing off the elevator was plain stupid.

"We got the perp dropping her off," Vich said. "I'm

in the lab with Blanchard." With his Boston accent, he pronounced Sydney's last name "Blanchud."

At least the lab was only one flight away instead of three. She tried to do it without panting. Only partially successful, she found Vich leaning against a table. Behind him, the lab's fuming chamber was humming. It looked like they were trying to pull fingerprints off a broken wine glass. At the other end of the table sat the evidence drying cabinet, not currently in use.

Sydney Blanchard stood over the shoulder of a lab tech who was frantically typing on a keyboard. "There," she said, and the tech froze the image on the computer screen.

It was a grainy shot of a man holding a woman in his arms. The victim's feet were closest to the camera, making it hard to tell much about her. Jamie studied his face, the way his head was turned. Something about his stance was familiar. She scanned her memory for the suspects she'd interviewed over the years. Hundreds of them. Maybe a thousand by now. "We can't ID him from that," Jamie said.

"Can you enhance it?" Sydney asked the tech.

The tech was already running commands. Slowly, the image crystallized. The screen went black. "It will reload and hopefully be something we can use."

The image built one tiny layer of pixels every few seconds. Jamie resisted the urge to sit down. The ping of a text message.

DA wld b grt for Z. Not nearly as homogenous as CA. +C's a grt town. A frsh start.

Leave it to Tony to send a text in all sorts of outdated

shorthand and type out the word "homogenous." No way he was taking Zephenaya when he moved to Cincinnati for his new teaching job. She didn't care if the school in Ohio, Davidson Academy, was a better school or more diverse. Staying with her was best for her son. And best for her. She tried not to think too hard on whether she was confusing the two things.

On the computer screen, the top of the photo had appeared. In it was the dark sky in the background and the shape of cars in the parking lot. "We don't get a shot of his car?"

Sydney shook her head. "The camera only picks him up a few steps before this. Right here is the only time he looks in the direction of the camera."

Her phone buzzed again. *U know this = wht he needs.*

Tony wasn't wrong about that. Something was going on with Z. He'd been caught smoking, was suspended for cheating on a biology test. Not to mention that City Academy was determining whether he would receive a scholarship for his sophomore year.

Sending him off to Ohio was too extreme.

On the screen, the suspect was revealed in thin lines, top to bottom. First, the very top of his head formed. His hair was cut short. Next was a prominent forehead then the furrow in his brow. The screen froze, the clock icon spinning. "It's thinking," the tech said.

"Wish it would think a little faster," Vich said.

The phone buzzed again, reminding Jamie that she hadn't answered Tony's texts. Certainly, she couldn't afford to send Z to City Academy without the scholarship. But he was her child. She couldn't send him away. She hated the idea that Tony was moving to Ohio and breaking up their family, as untraditional as it was. Tony was like her brother. She hated the idea that he wouldn't be close. Losing her son was unthinkable.

The layers began building again. Slowly, the suspect's hooded eyes were unveiled followed by his wide nose. It was his full lips and the angular jaw line that gave it away. Jamie grabbed hold of the table.

Vich touched her arm, but she couldn't pull her gaze from the image.

"I'll put it through face recognition software to see if I can find a match against the database," the tech said.

Jamie cleared her throat to get the words to come out. "You don't need to do that."

The tech spun in his chair. "You know him?"

"His name is Michael Delman," she said.

"Delman," Vich repeated, putting it together.

"Right. The man who dropped off our victim is my son's biological father."

ABOUT THE AUTHOR

Danielle Girard is the bestselling author of *Chasing Darkness*, The Rookie Club series, and the Dr. Schwartzman Series—*Exhume*, *Excise*, *Expose*, and *Expire*, featuring San Francisco medical examiner Dr. Annabelle Schwartzman. Danielle's books have won the Barry Award and the RT Reviewers' Choice Award, and two of her titles have been optioned for movies.

A graduate of Cornell University, Danielle received her MFA at Queens University in Charlotte, North Carolina. She, her husband, and their two children split their time between San Francisco and the Northern Rockies. Visit her at www.daniellegirard.com.

Made in the USA
Monee, IL
11 December 2020

52107415R00236